PRAISE FOR
THE ANATOMY OF DECEPTION

"A lucky break for mystery lovers. Fans of historical fiction will also love this tale that evokes the evolving medical profession and the art world in late 19th-century America. . . . A cameo appearance by painter Thomas Eakins and an exploration of his artistic philosophy add to the novel's colorful and highly informative background." —*USA Today*

"Goldstone's research informs every page. He weaves history, atmosphere, medical procedures, and forensic details into a fascinating story. . . ." —*Boston Globe*

"Vivid period setting and amazing medical detail." —Marilyn Stasio, *New York Times Book Review*

"An increasingly complex tale of murder, body-snatching, and skullduggery . . . A clever and entertaining tale." —*Los Angeles Times*

"Packed with historical asides." —*Entertainment Weekly*

"If you enjoyed *The Interpretation of Murder,* you'll be gripped by this haunting and atmospheric thriller." —Tess Gerritsen

"An entertaining page-turner . . . Readers attracted to 19th-century medicine should find it especially appealing. . . . Grimly realistic." —*Richmond Times-Dispatch*

"Compelling . . . With this top-notch historical page-turner and his proven versatility in nonfiction, Goldstone can expect to win over many new fans." —*Publishers Weekly* (starred review)

Also by Lawrence Goldstone

Dark Bargain

with Nancy Goldstone
Deconstructing Penguins
The Friar and the Cipher
Out of the Flames
Warmly Inscribed
Slightly Chipped
Used and Rare

The Anatomy of Deception

Lawrence Goldstone

DELTA TRADE PAPERBACKS

THE ANATOMY OF DECEPTION
A Delta Book

PUBLISHING HISTORY
Delacorte Press hardcover edition published February 2008
Delta trade paperback edition / March 2009

Published by Bantam Dell
A Division of Random House, Inc.
New York, New York

Book design by Glen M. Edelstein

Library of Congress Catalog Card Number: 2007020465

Delta is a registered trademark of Random House, Inc., and the
colophon is a trademark of Random House, Inc.

ISBN 978-0-385-34135-6

Printed in the United States of America
Published simultaneously in Canada

www.bantamdell.com

BVG 10 9 8 7 6 5 4 3 2 1

To Nancy and Emily

March 14, 1889

———————— ❦ ————————

FOR DAYS, CLOUDS HAD HUNG *over the frigid city, promising snow, an ephemeral late winter veneer of white, but the temperature had suddenly risen and a cold, stinging drizzle had arrived instead. Jostled along in the derelict hansom, clad in her maid's blue worsted dress and plain wool cloak, her fingers and feet felt bloodless. The gloom that hung over the river penetrated the thin walls of the coach until it seemed as though she were breathing it.*

She tried to peer out but rain obscured the dirty window. The gas streetlamps were set so far apart that what little she could see came sporadically, in brief flashes. She had no idea where she was, and she wanted desperately to pound on the trap and tell the driver to turn around. She could hear the beating of her own heart.

As the last haze of daylight vanished, the carriage turned. When she was very young, she had hated the dark, but here there would be no sympathetic, whispering adult rushing to comfort her. The cab slowed, the driver making his way carefully on the rutted streets. An odor of filth and decrepitude befouled the air.

Finally, the driver reined the horse to a halt and she could hear his muffled voice telling her she had arrived. It was the first time in her life that she had ever been so alone.

It was also the first time that she had ever been truly afraid.

CHAPTER 1

AT CHRISTMAS 1887, FIFTEEN MONTHS before this story began, the world was introduced to a fictional character destined for such immeasurable acclaim that he would overwhelm his creator's efforts to be done with him. The essence of this character's appeal was not derring-do, as in the dime novels of Beadle & Adams, but rather in his uncanny ability to unravel a set of data that had stumped lesser men and proceed to a logical and incisive conclusion. He was so coldly rational that he was often compared to a machine, the Analytical Engine of Charles Babbage. His name, of course, was Sherlock Holmes.

To those of us engaged in medical research, however, the remarkable methods of Conan Doyle's consulting detective were not at all revolutionary—they were merely a popularization of the *modus operandi* we employed in our quotidian efforts to alleviate human misery. The connection of analytic detection to medicine was unmistakable. Doyle himself was a physician, as were both Joseph Bell, widely considered the model for the character, and Oliver Wendell Holmes, the man for whom the detective was named. And while Sherlock Holmes may have trod the back alleys of Victorian London to ply his trade, the scenes of our crimes were no less exotic and often even more grisly.

To make sense of nature's felonies against the human body, you see, physicians are compelled to study not only the living, but also those who have succumbed. Our clues lie in internal organs, blood vessels, skin, hair, and fluids, and we need as much access to these as Holmes needed to footprints, handwriting, or hotel records. It is only through painstaking examination of the data wrung from this evidence that deductions may be made as to what has caused illness and death, which, in turn, aids immeasurably in the care and treatment of those who might still be saved.

As Holmes' popularity soared, it thus became sport among physicians to match wits with the fictional detective, eager to demonstrate that if they applied themselves to murder, theft, and mayhem, they would achieve similarly sterling results. Although for most in the medical field, this exercise was nothing more than a diverting parlor amusement, for me, the game was to be all too real. It started early on a mid-March Thursday in 1889, when I strode through the gate in the high stone wall at the rear of University Hospital in West Philadelphia and entered the Blockley Dead House.

The Dead House, the morgue that served both University Hospital and Philadelphia General, was a squat, solitary brick building, a fetid vault filled with cadavers in various states of putrefaction. The air was thick and still, and heavy drapes were pulled shut day and night. It was a place of spirits, where the tortured souls of hundreds, perhaps thousands, who had died from abuse, disease, want, or ignorance would spend their last moments in the company of the living before they were removed for their solitary rest and placed in the ground forever. I have never been a believer in phantoms, but I could not walk through its door without feeling all of those abbreviated lives pressing down upon me.

But this grim way station was also a place of science. In this incongruous setting, Dr. William Osler, head of Clinical Medicine at the University of Pennsylvania Medical School, forced forward the boundaries of medical knowledge. Although not yet forty, Dr. Osler had transformed the Dead

House into perhaps the most exciting and advanced laboratory for the science of morbid anatomy in the entire world. I had given up private practice in Chicago and come East specifically for the chance to work and study with this astounding man. Apprenticing to Newton or Boyle or Leeuwenhoek could not have been more exciting. Others would call Dr. Osler the modern-day Hippocrates, but to me he was simply "the Professor."

I arrived at the hospital that morning poised for a journey into the unknown, no less than Stanley at the threshold of Zanzibar. In the changing room, I replaced my suit with the trousers, pants, and cap that were provided to the staff. The outfits were faded and blue, with a military air. A persistent rumor had them as leftovers from the late Civil War, and I often wondered if my father had once been dressed in just this way.

I was soon joined by those of my colleagues also invited to observe. There were nine of us that morning, a study in contrast. Some, like me, were experienced physicians; others had just begun internship. Most were products of Philadelphia or other large cities, although I myself had been raised on a small farm in southern Ohio. One of us was even a woman. Mary Simpson had been included at the Professor's insistence, despite the extreme disapproval of anonymous members of the board of trustees who had been scandalized by such an affront to nature. Two Georges epitomized our differences. Farnshaw, at twenty-one the youngest of our group, had been raised in great wealth and came to study with the Professor after graduation from Harvard; Turk, at twenty-eight the oldest, was the product of an orphanage, and had worked his way through the university unloading merchant vessels on the Philadelphia docks.

We assembled in the staff room and found the Professor already present and in a jaunty mood. William Osler was small, a sprightly man, scarcely five feet five inches, but he moved with such energy, such spring, that he appeared larger.

He was already significantly balding, the loss of hair provoking him to pay scrupulous attention to his mustache, which was full and walruslike, perfectly framing his mouth and reaching to the jawline on either side. The backs of both hands bore signs of a recent eruption of *verruca necrogenica*, anatomist's warts, a red and raised tubercular infection that gave the skin an appearance of dyed leather. It was a vile condition with which the Professor was regularly afflicted from contact with necrotized flesh, but he blithely treated each new outbreak with oleate of mercury until it receded.

"Well, well, well," he said, rubbing those reddened hands together, his speech, as whenever he was excited, lapsing into the flat Canadian cant that betrayed his origins, "this will be a fine day, a fine day indeed, eh? I believe there are five cadavers available. Let us not keep them waiting."

The Professor had every right to his enthusiasm. For all of his genius, it was rare he was given the opportunity to conduct a full day's study in the Dead House. Like most of those who toil to advance human understanding, he was also engaged in a constant battle against human ignorance. Until the Anatomy Act in 1883, just six years earlier, the use of cadavers for teaching purposes was actually a crime. The great anatomist William Smith Forbes of Jefferson Medical College had only narrowly escaped a term in the penitentiary for "despoiling graves." The liberalization of the law had done little to dispel the revulsion of many in society to the notion of cutting into a dead body, however, and resistance to the Professor's researches remained strong. Although the more enlightened could occasionally be persuaded to allow Dr. Osler to determine the cause of death of a loved one or friend, for the most part our material was drawn, as it had been for centuries, from society's most wretched classes.

Even here, however, there was opposition. A number of groups had recently been formed to attempt to end the "ghoulish practice" of dissecting the poor after death. The most prominent and vocal of these was Reverend Squires' Philadelphia League Against Human Vivisection. Either unaware or unconcerned that "vivisection" referred to the living, Reverend Squires blithely employed innuendo, humbuggery, and outright lies to entice society matrons to support his cause. He then used the money to thrust himself into the public eye, creating an outcry against the postmortem abuse of society's least fortunate. As a result, although we did not have to compete with wild dogs for the corpse of a convict, as had Vesalius centuries earlier, cadavers available for examination had become increasingly scarce.

Emboldened by the uproar, the official Blockley pathologist, Henri Formad, an eccentric, ill-tempered Russian, had taken to denying Dr. Osler use of the facilities. The Dead House attendant, a gaunt, lumbering creature whom the Professor had dubbed "Cadaverous Charlie," had soon followed suit. Whereas Formad acted merely out of professional jealousy and spite, Charlie, buoyed by the stipend he had received from the League, refused the Professor access to cadavers out of what he termed, in his broken English, "bazic human decency."

But Charlie was an enterprising sort, and he had also shown himself willing to accept a second stipend from the Professor to absent himself from the Dead House for hours at a time and leave us to our work. For an additional remuneration, Charlie, as he had done on this occasion, would actually inform the Professor when a promising supply of unclaimed cadavers became available. Dr. Osler seemed unfazed at the necessity of paying for what should have been provided by a grateful citizenry, but I was appalled that so brilliant a scientist was forced to skulk about like a criminal.

At seven-fifteen, when we exited University Hospital to begin our day, I strode quickly to overtake Turk. My colleague was not brilliant, but quick and clever, with an offhand wit I envied. I had made a number of overtures when he joined the staff, but Turk proved to be a man who resisted intimacy, and I had been unable to breach the wall of irony that he threw up around himself. The only member of the staff in whom he had shown any interest was the other George, Farnshaw, his complete opposite. But I continued to find myself drawn to Turk, even though my efforts at friendship were generally rebuffed.

"Five cadavers," I whispered softly, looking up at him as we crossed the path. Turk was over six feet and quite thin. He had the manner of those who are very tall of leaning down slightly, and it gave him a predatory appearance. "Dr. Osler must think he has unearthed treasure."

He nodded without turning to face me. "Yes. Treasure soon to go into the ground, instead of coming out of it. I hope he won't keep us here through the night." Turk was rumored to be well acquainted with the city's more disreputable elements, although he was silent as to where and with whom he passed his free evenings.

"It would be time well spent," I replied.

"You might think an evening elbow-deep in entrails is well spent," Turk observed grimly. "I prefer the theater."

At the Dead House, we paused just outside the heavy oak door that had seemingly been installed to prevent the dead from escaping. Pipes and cigarettes were lit. Even those who did not ordinarily take tobacco did so here in an effort to kill the stench. Still, as we entered the building, we were immediately overwhelmed by an ambiance so powerful that it seemed as if we had struck a wall. The first moments were always the most difficult, when eyes teared, breath came in gasps, and stomachs refluxed. These reactions soon passed, however. Human senses have a remarkable ability to adapt quickly to even the most objectionable stimuli.

The autopsy room was two stories high, with a gallery walkway on the second floor and a grimy skylight at the top. When the Professor attracted an especially large group of observers, the overflow stood upstairs, much as medical students in the 1530s had watched Sylvius perform his anatomies from the balcony of the operating theater at the University of Paris.

The room itself contained three large postmortem tables, the tops of which were soapstone, the legs iron. Shallow channels were cut into each tabletop, leading to a drain covered by a brass grating in the middle, which allowed the fluids released during the examinations to be discharged. The drain led to a ventilating shaft, which extended down into the floor and out of the building to a ditch in the rear that was regularly sprinkled with calcium oxide—quicklime.

A set of drawers with a zinc top was set against one wall, holding bottles of fixatives, sponges, basins, enameled dishes, empty bottles, and museum jars. Next to the drawers sat a capacious sink and, adjacent to the sink, a table held the scales used for the weighing of organs. A crude, high, red-painted desk stood on the other side of the room, upon which rested the book for recording autopsy findings. During each procedure, the Professor provided a steady stream of dictation and one of the students took down the information. Dr. Osler reviewed the notes at the conclusion of each postmortem to ensure that the record was complete and accurate. A coat rack abutted the desk and held aprons and gowns, next to a case on the wall housing autopsy instruments.

Beyond the sink, a doorway led into the mortuary, which contained a bank of cast-iron ice chests that could accommodate sixteen bodies. Charlie was responsible for maintaining the ice, which, even in early spring, required regular changing. A rear door led out to a gravel path where bodies and ice were received, and where wagons of undertakers took the remains away. Occasionally, simple services for the dead were conducted within the mortuary itself.

On the second floor, four rooms were set aside for study and research. It was here that we performed urine analysis, prepared culture media, and examined slides. One of the rooms was a small library and records storage area.

The Dead House held not only the deceased from the two hospitals, but also the bodies of paupers, criminals, and any unidentified, unclaimed corpse encountered within the city limits by the Philadelphia Police Department. Today's subjects represented a typically diverse assortment. The five chests holding cadavers available for autopsy had been marked by Charlie with white chalk; he had also left a scrawled note detailing the particulars of each case. The Professor could choose from a carpenter who had succumbed to a respiratory disorder in the hospital, a male Negro and a young woman found dead in the streets, an elderly woman who had probably died of stomach cancer, and a Chinaman with a gunshot wound.

"Quite a bounty, eh?" he exulted, a wide smile disappearing under the ends of his mustache. "Who shall be first?" He moved to the nearest chest. "Let's start with our carpenter." He opened the top to reveal a bald man of about forty, heavily muscled about the arms. Three of us lifted him out of the ice onto a wheeled table and rolled him into the autopsy room.

After the carpenter had been transferred to a postmortem table, the Professor assigned tasks. "Who'll take notes?" he asked. "Turk . . . no, you observe. Corrigan. You get the chore." Corrigan, a stocky, goggle-eyed, bandy-legged young man from South Philadelphia, was eerily reminiscent of a bulldog. He possessed the talent to be a first-rate physician but his dedication was suspect. He had taken notes just two weeks before, and assigning him the tedious chore again so soon was the Professor's way of chiding him to greater application.

As Corrigan sulked off toward the desk, Turk cast a grin his way. "Be sure to form your letters clearly," he called.

The Professor laughed and the rest of us chuckled as well. He rarely tolerated sarcasm in anyone else, but seemed to give Turk extra latitude. Perhaps he admired, as I did, Turk's rise from poverty. "Simpson," the Professor went on, "you will handle weights and measures, and Carroll will assist."

Simpson and I were almost always given the most responsible tasks. I was senior in experience, with almost five years in practice, and Simpson was without question the most devoted and hardworking young physician I had ever encountered. Fully cognizant of the risk the Professor had taken in including her on the staff, she seemed determined to leave not a scintilla of doubt that his decision had been the correct one. She was a square-faced, slightly thickset woman, three years my junior. Her speech, while lacking the lilt of the upper classes, was precise and well enunciated, indicating good schooling and, I assumed, an upbringing to match.

When we had all taken our places, the Professor doffed his coat, donned a heavy apron, removed the appropriate implements from the cabinet, and strode to the body. The jauntiness he had exhibited earlier had vanished, replaced by self-assured professionalism.

"We have here what you all can see is a large, powerfully built man, who the note says is German by extraction and was a carpenter by trade. He was admitted to the ward Wednesday last complaining of a cough and swelled feet. Chest measured eighty centimeters, with two-to-five centimeter expansion. Both sides functioned equally, percussion over lungs was normal, and there was nothing special on auscultation.

"After admission, he grew steadily worse, spending most of his time sitting up in bed to ease his breathing. Cough became hacking with expectoration of a bright red color and like currant jelly, dyspnea increasing. Feet became increasingly edematous, expectoration bloody, dyspnea exaggerated. Three nights ago, he became almost insensible with a highly weakened pulse. He was briefly roused with stimulants, but died late Tuesday."

The Professor grasped the anatomist's scalpel, larger and heavier than its surgical cousin. "We shall begin by opening the thorax." Starting at each armpit, the Professor made a deep incision diagonally downward, so that they met at the sternum. He worked smoothly and quickly, the lines straight and true like a draftsman's. There was a soft hiss as gases were released from the body, and the smell became almost overpowering. Each of us tried to remain stoic, but only the Professor seemed genuinely immune to the stench.

From this juncture, the Professor made a third incision down through the abdominal wall to just above the pubic bone, bypassing the umbilicus, leaving a Y-shaped cut. He then peeled back a fold of skin to either side of the rib cage and one over the face. The carpenter had been dead for thirty-six hours. That, combined with lying in the ice, kept the flow of blood minimal, although it was sufficient to cover the Professor's hands and wrists. What fluid did escape, I quickly sponged into the channels of the autopsy table.

While the Professor rinsed his hands after the skin had been cleared, I grasped a set of rib cutters, which resembled large garden pruning clippers. I cut through the ribs at the far side of both lungs, just under the skin fold, each snap of the cutters making the sound of a breaking twig. When the ribs were free, the Professor removed the anterior chest wall to ex-pose the organs underneath. From here, most anatomists used the Rokitansky method, extracting all the organs simul-taneously after cutting off their connections to the body, but the Professor, although he had studied with Rokitansky at the Allgemeine Krankenhaus in Vienna, preferred the Virchow technique, removing the organs one at a time. Of course, he had studied with Virchow as well.

"The body presents the appearance of a man dead of heart disease," he began, as Corrigan entered the data into a jour-nal. "There is a small amount of fluid in the abdomen." Using a siphon, I drew off additional fluid in the lining over the lungs and heart, placing each in a graduated cylinder, which Simpson measured and noted.

"In the right pleura, sixty ounces of clear serum, thirty ounces in the left, and eight ounces in the pericardium," she reported. The Professor then severed the coronary arteries, freeing the heart, which Simpson removed from the chest cavity and placed on the scale.

"Heart is large," she said. "Seven hundred ten grams." The heart was brought to an examining table and the Professor lanced it open. He spoke continuously as he cut, unmindful of the blood and other sera that once more drenched his bare hands, Corrigan scribbling furiously to get it all down.

"Right chamber distended with large, jellylike clots. Ventricle dilated, measuring twelve centimeters from pulmonary ring to apex. Tricuspid orifice dilated fifteen centimeters in circumference. Segments of heart healthy, pulmonary valves normal. Left auricle large and contains blood, with clots. Left ventricle dilated and contains gelatinous clots. Those about the trabecula"—he indicated the partition that separates auricle from ventricle—"are colorless."

The Professor instructed Simpson to measure each chamber and the connecting valves, with the measurements then recorded in the journal. He noted where muscles were fibroid or pale in color or valves thickened at the edges. When the examination of the heart was complete, it was left on the table and the Professor removed each lung, one hand at the top, the other at the bottom, and repeated the dissection process. He observed that in both were large spots of apoplexy—hemorrhaging—and the anterior borders were emphysematous. Tissue sections presented coarse appearance of brown atrophy. After the lungs, he examined the bowels, kidneys—on which there were several cysts—liver, and spleen.

The next step was to remove the brain, a delicate operation that only the most skilled anatomist could perform without mishap. Unfixed brain tissue has the consistency of gelatin and is notoriously difficult to handle. It had taken me months, but I finally mastered the technique and was now the only member of the staff to whom the Professor would delegate the task. After my first success, Turk had proclaimed me "Lord of the Runny Eggs."

I made a transverse incision at the back of the head from

ear to ear across the brain stem, then separated the scalp from the underlying skull and pulled it forward. After utilizing a bone saw to score the calvaria—the cap of bone at the top of the skull—I employed a skull chisel, known as a "Virchow skull-breaker," to remove it. I then moved with great care to gently lift the brain out of the cranial vault. My hands were soaked with perspiration and my clothes clung to me in the still air, making delicate movement laborious. I managed to remove the brain, which, as Turk had so aptly noted, felt like a mass of undercooked eggs, and placed it in a large jar of formalin fixative. After soaking for a moment, the brain tissue coagulated and was removed to a table and sliced for examination.

"The brain, as we would have expected," said the Professor after taking some cross sections, "presents nothing abnormal. The arteries at the base are opaque, but not rigid."

The remainder of the autopsy went quickly. The intestines were opened with an enterotome, a large specialized pair of shears. The major blood vessels were examined, but nothing further of interest was discovered.

When the examination was completed, ninety minutes after we began, the Professor washed his hands in the sink and then returned to the table. "Well, not too much question of what did this fellow in, eh?"

Those of us familiar with the Professor's teaching methods knew not to answer too hastily, but Farnshaw, four months removed from Harvard, rashly offered, "No, sir. Hypertrophy." Farnshaw was tall, like Turk, with a smooth, clean-shaven face, and the innocence that is the inevitable result of an upbringing in which wealth is utilized to insulate life's many pitfalls. So ingenuous was Farnshaw, however, that it was impossible not to feel affection for him. That he constantly stumbled in his barefaced attempts to prove himself worthy of our professional respect endeared him to us all the more. He was not, it must be said, a bad doctor, simply unseasoned, like newly hewn poplar.

"Indeed," replied the Professor. "An enlarged heart. Now, Farnshaw, this chap entered the hospital in relatively decent shape. Some coughing, but no evidence of advanced disease. What might have been done for him to prevent this unfortunate result?"

"Digitalis," replied Farnshaw triumphantly. My gaze met Simpson's for a moment and her eyes rolled upward. Digitalis, derived from the otherwise poisonous purple foxglove, was known to strengthen contraction of the heart muscle, slow the heart rate, and help eliminate fluid from body tissues. It had been popular for a century and was prescribed by almost every physician in the nation for almost every heart problem. Every physician except the Professor, that is.

"Simpson," said the Professor, "you do not seem to agree."

"No, sir," she answered, coughing slightly from being caught in the act. "I do not see how digitalis would have alleviated the symptoms or provided a cure."

"What then, Simpson?"

Simpson considered this for a moment but finally admitted that she could think of no treatment that would have been effective. Such a response might have been treated harshly by many who taught medicine—doctors were supposed to have a response for everything—but the Professor preferred no answer to an incorrect one, and so merely nodded and moved on.

"How about you, Turk?"

"Perhaps showing him Farnshaw's fee would have shocked him back to health," Turk replied.

"Ha! Quite right, Turk." The Professor chortled. "That is one aspect of medical education that Harvard does not ignore." He turned to the unfortunate Bostonian. Farnshaw's face had gone a deeper red than his hair. "Digitalis would no more have prolonged this man's life, Dr. Farnshaw, than would standing on his head. There was *nothing* we could have done for this man short of manufacturing him a new heart."

The Professor began to pace about the room, the fingers

of his right hand tapping into his left. "All we know here, Farnshaw, is that we *don't* know. We have permutated disparate pieces of data, but can come to no definitive conclusion. This patient died with all the symptoms of chronic coronary valve disease, but we find no affection of the valves and only moderate arterial degeneration. The kidneys are not especially fibroid and there was not sufficient pulmonary distress to account for the hypertrophy and dilation of the heart."

The Professor returned to his place at the center of the table and gestured at the cadaver, hand opened, palm up. "So what do we do, Farnshaw, when faced with a mystery?"

As so often occurs in youth, Farnshaw's reckless enthusiasm had been supplanted by abashed reticence.

"After we have recorded each bit of data, no matter how seemingly inconsequential or tangential to the case," expounded the Professor, now addressing all of us, "we form hypotheses and then pursue and test each one without prejudice or preconception until it is disproved. We distrust coincidence.

"In this case," the Professor continued, "there is evidence that circumstances that tend to produce and maintain a high degree of tension in the arterial system may lead to hypertrophy and dilation. Here, we have a subject whose occupation often involved intense exertion, and who had no history of syphilis, so it may be possible to connect his habits to the life of the disease. Still, as we cannot definitively account for the hypertrophy, we will simply chronicle the evidence so that we may compare it to similar instances in the future and seek correlations that may lead us to solve this riddle."

"Not a very satisfying conclusion," remarked Turk.

"On the contrary," replied the Professor. "We have discovered a case whose particulars do not correspond to accepted data, an illness or condition from which this man died that is not yet recorded in the literature. What I see here, Turk, is an opportunity, and hardly unsatisfying."

"Of course, Doctor," said Turk. "As you say."

"You are a good doctor, Turk, but I'm not sure that re-search is your *métier*," observed the Professor. "Perhaps you and Farnshaw should join in private practice. That way you may partake of those legendary Harvard fees."

Farnshaw again reddened, but Turk guffawed. "An excel-lent suggestion," he replied cheerily.

We all grinned, grateful for the break as the Professor strode over to check Corrigan's notes. As Simpson and I made to deposit tissue samples in specimen jars and return the re-moved organs to the body, I noticed her eyes on me, but her gaze flitted quickly away. For a time, Charlie had been respon-sible for putting things back in what order he could, and then stitching up the cadavers before burial. But Charlie, who had been known to tipple the alcohol in the specimen jars, was not always reliable. On one occasion, some months ago, a male cadaver ordered exhumed because of suspicion of foul play was found by Formad to have three livers. We now per-formed the chore ourselves.

After all was in order and the carpenter had been returned to the ice chest, the Professor moved to the next subject that Charlie had marked for him. This was the male Negro.

Following the same procedure, it soon became apparent from an extensively cirrhotic liver that the man had died of al-cohol poisoning. The case was undistinguished except the Professor declared that the condition of the left lung was ex-traordinary. "I have never seen an organ so infiltrated with bloody serum." The fluid had a uniform purplish red, viscous appearance. The Professor was at a loss to account for it, ex-cept to hypothesize that the subject, under the influence of drink, had gone to sleep coiled on his left side so that, while he was senseless, his gradually weakened heart propelled fee-ble charges into the pulmonary artery. By hypostasis, an in-creasing volume had reached the left lung until a state of extreme congestive edema was produced.

For our third specimen, the Professor chose the elderly

woman with stomach cancer. Her case was equally unremark-able and, when we had finished with her, it was only two o'clock. "Well," said the Professor eagerly, "it looks as if we'll have time for another."

As the rest of the group returned the dead woman to the ice, I remained in the dissecting room to wipe down the table more thoroughly. When I got to the mortuary door, the Professor was standing at the chest that held the girl found dead on the streets of unknown causes.

"A bit of a mystery here, eh?" he said, and swung open the lid.

Only because I was standing away did I notice Turk's reac-tion. For an instant, his body stiffened and his gaze froze on the cadaver. I stepped in hastily to see what had caused his re-action, and got a brief glimpse of a young, light-haired woman of perhaps twenty years of age. Although she had been dead for some days, she looked nothing like the street urchins we generally encountered. She had a beautiful figure and what seemed to have been clear, unblemished skin, marred only with distinct bruising to the upper left arm and milder trauma at the lower abdomen. As I leaned forward for a closer look, the Professor slammed the lid shut. The crack of metal on metal reverberated through the room.

"I've changed my mind," he said quickly. He took a deep breath and then smiled stiffly. "We've been at this for quite some time. No need to overdo, eh?"

Turk had recovered his equilibrium, but remained staring, his brow furrowed, at the closed cover of the chest.

CHAPTER 2

We returned to the dissecting room to clean up and put things in order for Charlie. When we were about to leave, we waited for the Professor to lead us back across to University Hospital. Instead he said somewhat brusquely, "I wish to remain here for a bit and check some notes. I'll see you all tomorrow. Thank you for your participation."

I lingered briefly, wondering if the Professor would wish to talk with me privately, as he often did. But he had busied himself poring through an old journal, so I made for the door.

Turk was waiting for me outside, hands in his pockets, his weight on his left leg, the very picture of ease. "Well, Carroll," he said, smiling affably to reveal a set of uneven teeth, "it seems that we're all free for the evening."

"Your wish granted," I replied. "Now you can go to the theater."

"What about you?" he asked. "You're not going to spend the night prowling the wards, are you?"

"I haven't decided," I told him, although that was probably my intention. There was always something more to do and, in truth, I lacked an alternative.

"Well, then, why don't you join me?"

"At the theater?" I wondered briefly at the coincidental timing of Turk's intriguing reaction to the young girl in the mortuary and his unexpected cordiality, but could not see how the two could be related. Perhaps it was simply that my overtures had borne fruit after all.

"Absolutely. I'll call for you at seven-thirty."

As Turk ambled back to the hospital, I turned to see Simpson standing next to me. A strand of hair had fallen out from underneath her cap, and she absently shoved it back into place. "So, you're spending the evening with the mysterious Turk?" She watched him recede down the path. "I suspect you will never be seen again in this hemisphere."

"I'm told white slavers generally prefer women," I replied.

"Fortunate, then, that he didn't ask me," said Simpson. "Although," she added, "I expect that I would not be to Dr. Turk's taste even in that capacity."

"Nonsense," I said quickly. "You're a very appealing woman."

"Appealing," Simpson repeated with a knowing smile. When she smiled, which was all too infrequently in the hospital, it altered her face utterly. "Now, there is an ambiguous word."

I began to babble a clarification, but she interrupted. "It's perfectly all right, Ephraim. I'm naturally cantankerous. Where are you going tonight, by the way?"

When I told her, she said, "The theater? What are you going to see?"

"I forgot to ask."

We started back along the path, not speaking for a few moments. I became increasingly uncomfortable in the silence, a symptom of my awkwardness in the presence of women, which I found odd, as I never thought of Simpson in those terms.

"We seem to have some time," I said, the words tumbling out by reflex rather than intention. "Would you like to join me in the doctors' lounge? I was going to have tea."

Simpson stopped, uncertain, her head cocked to one side. "All right," she replied with a mixture of curiosity and suspicion, her reaction to my invitation much the same as mine to Turk's. "I'll meet you there after I change."

When I had first gone on staff, "doctors' lounge" had conjured up the image of a commodious, collegial, high-ceilinged chamber, furnished with wing chairs and divans, similar to the illustrations of English men's clubs that I had seen in *The Saturday Evening Post*. In actuality, however, the room was small and uninviting, tucked into the southwest corner of the first floor, above the laundry. The only touch of gentility was Jefferson, the ancient, white-jacketed Negro attendant, on duty from eight in the morning until ten at night, serving tea or java, as well as surprisingly tasty biscuits.

I arrived first, obtained a cup of Earl Grey and two shortbreads, and then repaired to one of a pair of ocher club chairs in the far corner to wait. Only two others were in the room, Drs. Peters and Dodd. Both were elderly, from a generation of physicians that would soon pass into history. Each nodded to me perfunctorily.

Simpson arrived minutes later, wearing a dark blue wool dress with a high lace collar. While her garb was hardly *à la mode,* it was proper and not unfeminine. She had repinned her sorrel brown hair, which sparkled slightly in the afternoon sunlight that poured in through the west window. As she walked past, Peters leaned over to Dodd and whispered something. Both stared at her with undisguised distaste.

I stood and offered to fetch a beverage. I realized I probably would not have done so if we were both still on duty, but meeting Simpson thus, it would have been discourteous not to. She declined my offer, however, and got her own, not even glancing at the other two doctors as she walked across the room.

When she returned, she sat in the other chair and placed her cup on the table between us. After a few seconds, when she did not speak, I realized that it was I who would be forced to begin the conversation. I had too much respect for Simpson to open with platitudes, and so chose instead to say what had been on my mind.

"You puzzle me."

"Why?" she asked, looking me straight on. Her eyes were flecked with amber. I found it odd that I had not noticed previously. "I don't think of myself as an especially puzzling person."

"You are so diligent...as dedicated to medicine as any man, yet..."

"Yet?"

"Perhaps I am perplexed that you seem to believe that you can achieve personal fulfillment without those domestic qualities from which most women acquire satisfaction."

Simpson's lips curled slightly, as if I had committed some terribly amusing *faux pas* at a social occasion, but she did not wish to embarrass me.

"I am not sure how to respond, Ephraim. How do you know that I have not achieved domestic fulfillment?"

"I don't," I replied, stumbling over the words. "I just assumed that...well, with the hours you spend here...and you are not married...do not have children..."

Simpson suddenly flushed. "You know nothing of my private life," she snapped. "Nothing." She paused, regaining her poise. "I think, Dr. Carroll," she continued evenly, "that you shall be forced to accept that the nature of womanhood is changing. You can expect to find the Mary Simpsons of the world becoming more commonplace."

"Of course," I replied hastily. "I'm sorry. I had no intention of insulting you. I value you highly. I would rather work with you than anyone else on the staff."

"Thank you," she answered, seemingly assuaged but yet not prepared to grant full absolution. "I as well. And I am not insulted. I've become inured to the shortsightedness of men, although I did not expect such Paleolithic sentiments from you." She sighed and her expression softened. "I expect, however, Ephraim, that in your case, ignorance is vestigial."

"I suppose I should accept that as a compliment of sorts."

"It is."

"Surely you consider Dr. Osler an exception," I said.

"Of course," Simpson replied, taking a sip of tea. "I expect we both owe Dr. Osler more than we can ever repay. But what of your own domestic fulfillment? Do you expect to find it stepping out with Turk?"

"Not fulfillment, perhaps, but at least a relief from tedium."

"Is your life tedious, Ephraim? I would not have thought so."

"Each of us seems to have misjudged the other, then," I replied. "I've lived in Philadelphia for almost two years and have not succeeded in establishing any society outside of my profession, and not a good deal within it."

"But you are young and successful. There must be no shortage of opportunities."

"I prefer to live simply. I rent a small sitting room and bedchamber on Montrose Street from a widow named Mrs. Mooney. Most of my free evenings are spent in my rooms with a book or journal."

I looked carefully to see what sentiments my confession of dullness would engender, but Simpson seemed unperturbed. "Dedication to self-improvement is certainly admirable."

"Admirable perhaps, but hardly gratifying," I rejoined, encouraged by her response. "Except for those times when I am invited to dine with Dr. Osler or other members of the staff, or occasional visits to lecture halls or museums, my existence away from medicine is reminiscent of that of an aging widower or cloistered monk."

"So your monasticism is not altogether by choice?"

"Is your life so different?" I asked.

To my surprise, Simpson paused, considering her response. "Yes," she said after a moment. "It is. One is not required to seek self-improvement in isolation. But I daresay my ardor is no less than yours."

I began to ask her for elaboration, but she stood to leave before I could speak. "I have enjoyed this, Ephraim, but I must go now. I have other commitments."

"Are you sure?" I found myself not wanting our conversation to end.

"Another time perhaps. I really must go." Her expression turned serious. "Be careful tonight," she said. "With Turk, I mean."

I thanked Mary but assured her that there was no reason for concern.

As she left the lounge, I watched until the door had closed behind her.

CHAPTER 3

I PREFERRED THAT TURK NOT wait in Mrs. Mooney's drab parlor, so I was downstairs at the door as the hour for his arrival approached. I had been unsure of how to dress for the evening, but finally decided on a dark wool suit, coat, and silk Gibus topper. As the hansom pulled up, drawn by an aging bay and driven by a swarthy man in a shabby black coat, I realized I had blundered. The driver gestured from his high perch at the rear of the coach for me to step in. Turk sat on the far side, dressed in a worsted jacket of broad checks, brown trousers, brown overcoat, and a low derby.

"My, my," said Turk with a smirk, as I took the seat next to him, "aren't you the boulevardier? You best take care in that getup, Carroll. Every pickpocket and prostitute in Philadelphia will be after you."

"You said the theater," I replied coldly. "Shall I change?"

"No time," he replied, and signaled the driver to be under way.

"When does the show begin?" I asked.

"Starts at ten," he said. "We'll dine first."

"Ten? What show is it?"

Turk sighed. "Carroll, you are the most incurable prig. We are attending Bonhomme's Paris Revue. It is not *Hamlet*, Edwin Booth will not be in attendance, and no one will dust off your seat before you sit down. If someone offers to take your hat, don't give it to him unless you wish never to see it again."

The carriage headed north, eventually turning east on Market Street, toward downtown. The electric street lighting and macadam roads of Center City were in acute contrast to the gas lamps and worn cobblestones still in use in most of the city. Streetcar tracks branched off onto almost every cross street and, on Market Street itself, stanchions had been constructed for the imminent conversion of the streetcar line from horse to electric power. Carriage and foot traffic were heavy as we reached Center Square, with city officials, lawyers, businessmen, and younger, less well-dressed clerical and stenographic staff bustling about well after official closing time. As we rode around the square, the still unfinished City Hall, already seventeen years under construction, loomed over us. If ever completed, the monstrous granite edifice was destined to be the tallest and most expansive public building in the nation, larger than the United States Capitol. Mayor Fitler had recently moved in to great fanfare—perhaps to counter persistent allegations of massive graft in the granting of construction contracts—and the entire building was currently being wired for electric lighting.

We continued east on Market Street, passing Independence Hall. When we neared the waterfront, the cab once again turned north. Out of Old City, conditions fell off sharply. After more twists and turns, we were soon into a seamy area, the narrow streets closely lined with warehouses and small storefronts behind which questionable commerce and illicit activity were surely the norm.

Eventually, the carriage pulled up at a dimly lit establishment, with the words "Barker's Tavern" in chipped paint on each of two large, darkened windows framing a faded green wooden door. I was surprised to see a number of private carriages idling along the rutted street—broughams, even a landau or two.

"Ever been here before, Carroll?" my companion inquired.

I told him I had not.

Turk opened the trap and we alit, our carriage remaining with the others near the front of the restaurant. Once inside, however, I pulled up short. Rather than the den of iniquity I feared, filled with voluble drunks and questionable women, before me lay a bustling eating establishment. Not Society Hill, perhaps, but, with its large, open room, sawdust floors, checked tablecloths, boisterous young clientele, and aroma of broiled meat, Barker's environment was quite agreeable.

"Well, it doesn't look like much on the outside, but I'll warrant there isn't a better steak to be had in the entire city."

Turk was obviously well-known, because the man at the door, who wore a striped vest, arm garters, and boater, greeted him with enthusiasm and quickly led us to a table in the center of the room. While most of our fellow diners were male and, like Turk, casually but not inexpensively dressed, there was also a liberal sprinkling of women present. Most were young and attractive. They seemed to be enjoying the atmosphere without inhibition. As we walked through the room, an auburn-haired woman with startling blue eyes caught me staring and smiled back, causing me to avert my gaze, which seemed to amuse her all the more. Her companion, a tousle-haired man with his back to me, did not turn about.

Turk ordered two pints of Pabst. When our waiter left menus and departed, Turk leaned forward slightly in order to be heard and asked what I thought of the establishment.

"A good choice," I replied, "and a pleasant surprise."

"Thank you." He seemed genuinely pleased.

The beers arrived in iced mugs. Turk lifted his. "To the enjoyment of life," he said.

I nodded, then clicked his glass and drank. The beer was cold and went down smoothly.

Turk downed half his pint with the first quaff. "You don't get out much, do you?" he asked.

"I don't have the time," I replied. "Nor the means." I glanced down at the menu and saw the prices were extremely reasonable—only fifty cents for a porterhouse dinner, thirty-five cents for pigeon pie or grilled trout. Still, to dine at restaurants with the frequency that Turk seemed to would have placed an unbearable strain on my resources. "How do you manage?"

"I make the time," he answered. "And the means." He downed the remainder of his beer. "Go ahead, Carroll. Drink up. I'm paying for dinner."

"Not a bit of it," I replied.

"Nonsense," he said. "My invitation, my treat. You can make it up to me later."

Turk would not countenance further protest, so I thanked him for his generosity. When the waiter appeared, he ordered a porterhouse with potato and onions for us both, and also asked for another round of Pabsts, although mine was still half full.

We chatted idly for a while, until Turk abruptly asked, "So, what brought you to Philadelphia, Carroll? You're from out west, aren't you? Chicago, was it?"

"Ohio," I replied. "I went to medical school in Chicago and practiced there for more than three years."

"You must have made an excellent living in such a thriving city."

"Not really," I replied. "I worked with a doctor on the West Side. No one had much money."

"Healing the poor," said Turk. "Very commendable."

"Commendable or no," I said, "the experience was invaluable. I learned a great deal."

"Then you came here."

I was about to ask what he meant when our dinner arrived. The steaks were thick, large, buttered on both sides, and prepared to perfection. Turk was correct. I had not sampled a better piece of meat since I had arrived in Philadelphia.

"Where in Ohio?"

I looked over at him, attempting to gauge the source of his continued interest, but the questions seemed innocent enough. Perhaps he simply hated talking about himself.

"Near Marietta," I replied. "On the Ohio River. It is the only city in America named after Marie Antoinette."

Turk chuckled. "An interesting distinction. But you don't sound like someone from southern Ohio."

"I make an effort not to," I said.

"Very wise," Turk agreed. "And what made you choose medicine?"

"It was because of my father."

"He was a doctor?" he asked, taking a bite of his porter-house. Turk used his knife to slice his meat in the rapid back-and-forth manner of the lower classes. He chewed and swallowed quickly.

I shook my head. "No, but he was in the war, and was wounded in 1862 fighting with Grant at Fort Donelson."

"Wounded how?"

"His brigade was caught in a cross fire during a skirmish in the woods. My father and two other men snuck in behind the Confederates and attacked. They were terribly outnumbered. My father was struck by a minié ball above the right elbow. The two other men were killed but the brigade was saved."

"He was a hero then?"

"Yes," I said, taking another drink. "I suppose he was."

"Lucky," Turk muttered. "I would have settled for any father at all." He cut and ingested another piece of meat. "So what happened?"

"As they did back then, the wound was 'laid open,' . . . large areas of the surrounding flesh were exposed to the air . . . so barbaric . . . doctors believed it would promote healing. Just the opposite resulted, of course. Three days later the wound had suppurated and his arm had to be taken off. The field hospital was overwhelmed, so the amputation was performed by an assistant regimental surgeon . . . a Vermont baker with no formal medical training. They had exhausted their supply of laudanum, so my father lay in that hospital in agony for seven days and, when it was deemed he could travel, they gave him his papers and sent him home. He was determined that the loss of his arm would have no effect on his life, but farming less a right arm is not practicable. I have two older brothers who took up their share of the chores; I did what I could but I was very young. My father never stopped struggling to do his best until he died. It has been more than ten years now."

"Quite a story," said Turk.

"Yes."

"And so," Turk continued, "you became a doctor to provide better treatment to strangers than your father had received. You are an admirable fellow."

"Do you consider sarcasm obligatory?" Like the Professor, I was prepared to give Turk a certain latitude, but I would not be made the butt of offensive wit.

He sat back, looking hurt. "Not at all. I was being quite sincere. I think of you always as an admirable fellow."

"And a prig." But my irritation had passed. Turk had an uncanny facility to behave rudely without engendering lasting enmity.

"An admirable prig then."

I shrugged. "As you wish. What about you?"

Turk's smile vanished. "Me? Carroll, there is no me. I am a creation."

"A creation?"

"Yes. Just that." Turk's eyes went cold. "I am a creation of the base instincts of two people I never knew, and of the guilt and cruelty of others."

"I'm sorry for asking," I said. "It must be painful to speak about."

"Painful? Not painful at all," Turk replied casually, regaining his demeanor as if the previous moment had not occurred. "Merely facts. Someone like Osler might consider it scientific truth. But it turned out not to be truth, because, in the end, I've become a creation only of myself."

I thought of my reading, my practiced speech and dress,

my deportment . . . were we not all creations of ourselves?" "I suppose that's the best way to be," I agreed.

"The only way." He drained his glass and signaled for another. "And my creation fully intends to enjoy his life in wealth and comfort."

"Wealth and comfort have their place, certainly," I said. "But so does excellence. You could be a fine doctor."

"Are you implying that I am not a fine doctor now?"

"Not at all. You are obviously highly intelligent with excellent medical instincts. . . ."

"Better than yours?"

"I don't know." I considered the question. "Perhaps. You certainly have many qualities that I admire."

"Thank you."

"But I have something that you don't seem to," I persisted.

"And what might that be?"

"A love of the profession . . . a desire to heal. Perhaps that is what makes me such a prig in your eyes. We can do things in medicine today that would merely have been dreams even fifty years ago. I want to take the best advantage possible of every innovation, master every new technique."

"Bravo," Turk replied. "A fine speech worthy of an admirable fellow. So, what you are saying, Carroll, is that being a doctor is *important*. For *special* people in society. A higher calling. With a higher morality."

"I feel privileged to be a physician, not superior. Morality has little to do with it."

"In that I agree. Osler is your model, I presume."

"One could do far worse. Dr. Osler is committed to medicine and the good it can do."

"For its own sake?"

"For the sake of his patients."

"His patients?" Turk leaned back. His face had flushed from the beer. "You really think Osler doesn't care about making money? Then why did he come here in the first place? Weren't there enough patients in Canada?"

"He came for the opportunity," I said heatedly. "It was an honor to be asked to come to Philadelphia."

"A very lucrative honor," he retorted. "And if he gets a more lucrative honor somewhere else, he'll go there."

"No, Turk. You're wrong."

"Anything you say."

I decided to change the subject, to try to determine whether Turk's invitation had anything to do with his odd behavior in the Dead House, but I was clumsy in execution. "No, I apologize," I said. "Perhaps you're correct. Who can know the mind of another? To that very point, I certainly hadn't expected Dr. Osler to send us all home so early this afternoon. I wonder why he did that."

Turk shrugged, but our eyes met and for an instant I had a disquieting glimpse of the anger, of the smoldering intensity behind his mask of nonchalance. It was not the beer—this was not a man who would easily be rendered stupid by drink—but I had touched something and for a moment he could hide neither his malignity nor his curiosity.

"Perhaps he had theater tickets, too," he said, recovering again almost instantly. "He might be sitting next to us tonight, in fact."

"No," I pressed. "There was something decidedly odd in his manner with the final cadaver. You must have seen it."

"Not really," Turk replied, his eyes sweeping the crowded room. "I expect that he just didn't want to cut up someone so young and pretty." He removed his watch from his vest pocket. "It's time to be going," he announced.

I thanked Turk again for paying the bill and followed him back through the restaurant. We repaired to the hansom and journeyed south and farther east until, after about ten minutes, we reached our destination, the Front Street Theatre. I again was surprised by the plethora of carriages in the street.

There was a good deal of milling about on the sidewalk under the marquee—no one who could help it ventured into a street where so many horses were idling. The atmosphere was gay and boisterous, quite unlike, say, the Arch Street Theater downtown, where Mrs. Drew demanded decorum even if one had come to witness a comedic revival of Augustin Daly or a Dion Boucicault melodrama.

Turk jumped out of the hansom, gesturing for me to follow. We barged into the lobby, forcing our way past any number of our fellow theatergoers, each of whom, in turn, was endeavoring to force his way past those in front of him. The crowd was a remarkable polyglot—everything from common louts to finely dressed swells, and even a few couples in evening clothes. I'd heard that many otherwise fashionable members of society came to theaters such as this to mix with the more common elements of society, but I'd thought the tales apocryphal. I no longer felt so ridiculous in my suit and hat although, taking Turk at his word, I suspected those in better dress—like me—were at some risk of their possessions from pickpockets who had undoubtedly intermixed themselves in the throng.

Turk pulled me off to the side, where a sallow-faced man with slicked hair in a dilapidated cutaway coat was standing in front of a doorway.

"Ah, Mr. George," said the man with a small obsequious bow and a distinct burr to his speech. "So nice to see you again."

Turk produced two tickets, which the man examined. "Box number three," he said. "Up the stairs on the right."

"Mr. George?" I asked Turk as we climbed to the mezzanine floor.

"No one knows anything more about me than they need to," he replied absently. He stopped and took me by the elbow. "To people down here, I'm just 'George.' I would appreciate it, if we happen on any of my acquaintances tonight, that you remember that."

"Of course," I agreed.

Turk found our box and we took the two front seats. As he had predicted, the cushions were worn and lumpy. The once-burgundy velvet coverings had weathered into a dull brown and the floor had clearly not been swept in some weeks. Over the railing, I could see the crowd below, mostly those of lesser means, shuffling in their seats with anticipation, more like a bacchanal mob than theatergoers awaiting the evening's entertainment. The orchestra was a squalid bunch whose instruments appeared to have been rescued from the ravages of some great flood or earthquake.

Soon the house lights went down, the arc lights at the foot of the stage went up, and the musicians began to play. The sense of expectation in the air was distinctly primal. The curtain rose to reveal two lines of female dancers, one at either side of the stage, and at their appearance the audience broke into a cheer that sounded to me like a lascivious whoop. The dancers wore short, bodicelike dresses, purplish red stockings that ran in a crisscross pattern up to the middle of their thighs, and shiny black shoes. They danced with frozen smiles, and all were heavily rouged. Holding the front of their dresses up to reveal their legs to the bottom frill of the bodice, the women ran at each other, passing in the middle of the stage.

The audience encouraged every move with a cheer. Although the dancers exhibited scant artistry in their gyrations, there was an odd allure in the way these women flew about the stage; leaping and prancing, robust and ungainly. Finally, they formed a line, each dancer draping an arm over the woman to either side of her, and then kicked their legs in unison to the rhythmic clapping of the crowd below. The scene was at once repellent and fascinating.

The show lasted little more than an hour. The dancers were superseded by a female singer, and then a number of brief scenarios, each featuring a woman and sometimes a man in abbreviated garb, and each with a prurient theme. When the dancers returned to the stage, my eyes were drawn immediately to a tall woman with red hair and long, lean legs, who moved with a lithe grace absent in her peers. I was surprised that someone of such beauty and distinction was forced to work in Bonhomme's Paris Revue. Once or twice, she glanced up at our box and flashed a small smile.

"Well, Carroll," said Turk, after the show had ended and the gaslights had come up. He was forced to lean close to me and raise his voice to be heard over the raucous applause and wild yells for "encore" from the crowd. "What did you think?"

"It was very . . . lively."

"Tell me," he asked, "did you like the dancers?"

"Quite talented, I thought," I said. There was no harm in being polite.

"They are talented, to be sure," Turk replied. "Do you remember the tall one with red hair? We're having drinks with her. You are, I mean. She's best friends with my date."

I tried to stifle a grin. My experience with women might be woefully inadequate, but it was certainly serendipity to be thrown together by circumstance with the very woman one had been admiring in secret.

When we arrived at the stage door, ten or fifteen men were already waiting. A few appeared disreputable, but most seemed reasonably well-off. Many were older, in their fifties at least.

After about ten minutes, the cast began to emerge. The one with red hair was named Monique, Turk informed me, while he awaited Suzette. I spotted Monique immediately, walking with a dark-haired woman at least six inches shorter than she. Both waved excitedly when they spotted Turk and hurried in our direction.

"Hi, Georgie," cooed Suzette, who could only have been French if Ireland had been shifted to the continent. She took Turk by the arm. "Let's go. I'm parched." She squinted up at me. "Ooh. This must be your good-looking friend. Lucky Monique."

Monique sidled up and took my arm. She had full lips, a small, turned-up nose, and emerald eyes, an odd assortment of parts that went together well as a whole. "I am a lucky

Monique," she confirmed. "And what might your name be, good-looking friend?" Her voice was husky and sensual. She was apparently from the same part of France as Suzette.

"Ephraim," I said, taking a hint from Turk and giving as little information as possible.

"Well, Ephie," trilled Monique, "let's be going then."

Turk led us to the ever-faithful liveryman and gave him directions to someplace called "The Fatted Calf." The ride was brief, but we were four in a seat meant to accommodate three. To the giggles of the women, we squeezed together, Monique's arm thrown over my shoulder. She was uncorseted and I could feel the supple line of her breast against my chest.

Even from the street, The Fatted Calf emitted a din. The man at the entrance, an enormous, pink-faced ruffian with thick muttonchops, smiled at Turk convivially and swung open the door. As soon as we stepped inside, what had been a muddled roar became more distinct as loud conversation and hoarse laughter.

There was another man at the entrance to the large room, similar in look and bearing to the giant outside, only half his size. He yelled hello to "George" and led him through the packed tables. A film of dust hung in the air, diffusing the light and giving the room a translucent, netherworld haze.

As we negotiated our way forward, we were unable to avoid jostling those seated at the tables on either side of us, but no one protested. Many of the patrons appeared to be seamen, most of the lowest stripe, although I was sure that rogues of all occupations were amply represented. A goodly number of cheap and heavily made-up women were interspersed throughout the bar, and caused the room to reek of an odd mixture of sweat, stale beer, cigar smoke, and flowery perfume.

Suzette kept both of her arms grasped around Turk, pressing against him, and Monique took the same attitude with me. The soft flesh of her breasts and thighs now fully rubbed against me and I felt the beginnings of arousal, which, even in these circumstances, was highly embarrassing. Monique noticed it as well, and pressed even closer. As much as I wanted her to continue, I hardly wanted to announce my condition to the other patrons. I kept looking forward, following the other two, hoping it would pass before it became more obvious.

Finally, we reached an empty table at the far corner of the room, one which ordinarily would have been barely comfortable for two. Monique released my arm, and, mercifully, the fullness receded. Turk slipped a coin into the small man's hand and I thought it ironic that someone would pay to get a table in this establishment.

A thickly rouged young woman in a plunging white blouse and black bodice appeared immediately to take our order.

"Let's have champagne," decreed Turk gaily. "Ephraim here has generously offered to pay."

I hadn't, of course, and I suspected it would be costly, but it seemed only fair after the expense Turk had gone to for the tickets and dinner.

"Indeed," I said, "champagne it shall be."

Monique reached out and clasped my hand. "Oh, Ephie, I knew you'd be nice."

The bottle seemed to be at our table the next second. We toasted to life, and drank. The "champagne" had a tart, acrid taste, but none of my companions seemed to care. The first glasses were downed almost instantly, even mine, and then seconds. Soon, the bottle was empty. Another swiftly replaced it.

Monique, who admitted she was not French, claimed to be nineteen. Like Turk, she had been raised in an orphanage, where she had danced so avidly that the administrators had actually engaged an instructor to teach her the rudiments of ballet. She had shown promise and, two years ago, had gone into the world to seek employment with a dance company.

"I tried everywhere," she said, shaking her head in dismay.

I realized that she was far more attractive than I had first thought. "It's just too hard for a girl like me . . . who doesn't know anyone . . ."

"One more?" I looked up; the waitress was holding up an empty bottle.

There are two types of inebriation. With the first, one knows one is drunk and attempts to be on guard, albeit with varying degrees of success. With the second, far more dangerous, one has no idea that one's decisions and behavior have been slurred and thus proceeds as if nothing at all were amiss. At that moment, as I peered at the blurred bottle in the waitress's hand, I passed from one type to the other.

"Certainly," I agreed. "Let us have another."

The more Monique confided her travails in the world of dance, the closer she moved to me. She leaned forward, offering me her breasts. I could feel the heat come off her and she smelled of roses, yet slightly musky. Her lips shone and when they parted, I was aware of nothing else. I felt I would reach for her on the spot, when suddenly she leaned back with a smile.

"Suzette and I are going to the powder room for a moment, Ephie."

I was watching them move through the tables toward the rear, Monique's hips moving back and forth liquidly, when Turk interrupted my reverie in speech that seemed to slur. "I've been thinking, old boy, perhaps you were right about Osler. Why do you think he refused to autopsy that girl?"

I still retained just enough of my wits to remember that he was asking the same question I had put to him earlier. "You were probably right," I said, with a wave of my hand. "He probably thought she was too pretty to cut up."

"Yes," agreed Turk. "That must have been it. Still, you must have seen him jump . . . say, you did see . . . you told me."

"Did I?" I replied. "I don't remember."

"You did," Turk said, and then he paused. "We're friends now, right?"

"Absolutely." I nodded for emphasis.

"You like Monique?"

"Absolutely," I repeated. "She's beautiful."

"She likes you. I'm glad I got you two together."

"Absolutely."

"What did you see of her?"

"Who?"

"The girl in the morgue."

"Oh." I put a finger to my lip. "Roughly handled. Big bruise on her left arm. Didn' *you* see?"

Turk shrugged. "Does he ever talk about me?"

"Who?"

"Osler."

"Talk about you how?"

"C'mon, Carroll. Friends don' lie to each other. Did he say anything about me?"

"Nope."

"You sure? I know he talks to you."

"Absolutely."

Turk's eyebrows turned down, as pondering some question, but then he shrugged as if to dismiss the question entirely.

The girls returned a few moments later. They seemed to glance at Turk before resuming their seats. Monique had renewed her scent and I started to lean toward her, when the man from the door, shorter muttonchops, appeared at our table and put his hand on Turk's shoulder. "Someone to see you," he said gravely.

"Can't see anyone now, Haggens. Having far too good a time." Turk waved in mock gaiety.

But Haggens did not leave. "Better see this one," he said.

Instantly, Turk seemed to sober. He looked up at Haggens, their eyes held for a moment, and then Turk pushed back his chair. "Only take a minute, Carroll," he told me. "Entertain the ladies for me."

"I wonder what that could be about?" I asked, addressing

the question to the table after Turk had moved across the room.

"Oh, his fixing, no doubt," replied Suzette hazily.

"His fixing?"

"Oh yes. Georgie's a great fixer. If you need something you don't have, he'll get it for you . . ." She giggled. "And if you have something you don't want, he'll get rid of it."

Before I could inquire further, I heard the sound of shouting, loud enough to pierce the din. I turned and saw a highly agitated man with a turned-up mustache and beard arguing with Turk. I could not tell what the squabble was about, but the older man grabbed Turk by the coat. Turk pushed him and then moved forward, wagging a finger under his chin. Haggens appeared, seized the older man by the arm, and said something in his ear. The older man drew back, still furious, but reluctantly turned for the door, Haggens close behind to make sure he arrived there.

As they reached the exit, another man was waiting, a small man wearing a bowler hat, but otherwise obscured by a post. He moved forward for just an instant to take the older man's arm.

I bolted upright, the effects of the drink gone. Although it could not possibly be true, it appeared that the man in the bowler was Dr. Osler. I started to push out of my seat to get a better look, but the crowd had swallowed him up. No, I decided, after I was sure they were gone, I had been mistaken. Surely, this was a datum I had misread—Philadelphia is filled with small men in bowler hats.

My head swiveled back to Turk, who had remained at the other side of the crowded room, waiting for Haggens to return. They spoke, leaning close to each other. Haggens nodded, as if in grudging acceptance. Then he made his way across the room, vanishing somewhere against the far wall.

Turk returned to the table in a dark humor. His eyebrows were knotted together so acutely that he looked raptorish.

"Come, Carroll," he said brusquely, without sitting. "We're leaving. Sorry, ladies."

"But it's so early," moaned Suzette.

"Stay," said Monique, looking languorously at me. "Let's have another drink."

"It's not that late, Turk," I heard myself say. "Why must we leave?"

Turk grasped me under the arm and pulled me to my feet. His grip was extremely strong. "Carroll, when I say it's time to leave, it's time to leave. If you wish to get home with your health intact, I suggest you listen. Pay the bill and come with me."

The bill was somehow already on the table, and my stomach roiled when I saw that it was ten dollars, as much as I made in a week. I barely had enough to cover the cost and as I fumbled for the coins, Monique grasped my wrist. Her hand was warm and slightly moist. "Don't listen to him, Ephie. Stay. Have some fun."

I wanted very much to do as she suggested but Turk still had me under the arm. "I'm very sorry, Monique. You are lovely, but I must go. Perhaps another time."

Before she could respond, Turk had dragged me from the table. "Get a move on, Carroll. We have to leave now."

All the way across the floor, Turk looked around, as if waiting for someone to appear. He did not relax until the carriage had put some considerable distance between us and The Fatted Calf.

CHAPTER 4

I DID NOT ARRIVE AT the hospital until nine the next morning, at least one hour later than was customary. If not for my landlady, I might not have made it at all. It had taken her ten minutes of knocking on my door to rouse me and, after she had, it seemed as if the pounding had merely transferred itself to the inside of my skull. After I moaned that I was awake, Mrs. Mooney left me to struggle out of bed. When I finally made my appearance in the parlor, she peered at me over her spectacles in sympathetic reproach, as one would treat a favored pet that had uncharacteristically soiled the carpet. She insisted that I take coffee and a light breakfast, which I did only with Spartan will.

My memory of the previous night had taken on a preternatural aura. Although I was certain of the basic time line and some of the events remained clear, there were any number of particulars, especially in The Fatted Calf, that I could not be sure were actual occurrences or partially imagined. While I remembered with utter clarity the press of Monique's breasts and thighs, my brief glimpse of the man in the bowler hat had evolved into phantasm. The notion that it had been Dr. Osler seemed preposterous, but I somehow could not expunge the vision of him from my mind.

The ride home remained a blur. Turk had spoken little, but rather had seemed weighed upon by a great burden. I had assured him that since we were now friends, he could confide in me, but he had merely glared and may have even called me a moron. After he dropped me at my rooms, I had no memory of how I made my way upstairs and into bed. I vowed never to drink to excess again, a vow I had made a number of times in the past, but never since I had arrived in Philadelphia.

My disquiet, however, went deeper than memories clouded by cheap champagne. Had Turk not forced me to leave, there was no doubt that I would have committed an indiscretion with Monique. I had wanted to desperately and, had I succumbed, I would have engaged in a monumentally foolhardy act. Men of my generation could not take such risks. When desperation overcame reason, those who resorted to prostitutes—or dancers in Bonhomme's Paris Revue—did so at great peril. Disease was rampant and the protection that did exist, disgusting devices called condoms—thick, galvanized rubber monstrosities with a seam running down one side—were so unpleasant and unwieldy that few employed them. My one sexual experience had come during my tenure in Chicago and I had been lucky to escape unscathed.

Her name was Wanda. She was a Polish girl of eighteen, with blond braids and woeful eyes, the daughter of a patient. Our association began innocently enough—we visited the local arcade or took a streetcar to the lakefront and strolled under the stars. After about a month, she suggested that we return to my rooms. I was twenty-three years old; I allowed desire to overwhelm reason. Afterward, as we lay in bed together, I felt both an enormous feeling of well-being and a crippling rush of guilt.

I continued to see her, our time together consisting almost entirely of lovemaking. When I was with her, I could not restrain myself and as much as the release was ecstatic, it always left me wanting more. I didn't love her, however, and when I was not with her, I was inflamed with remorse.

Then, one night, she said that we should be married.

Wanda had every right to expect that our love affair would culminate in a proposal and it was the honorable action to take. But at the mere consideration of such a prospect, I was seized with dread. Marriage to her meant that I would pass my remaining days on the West Side of Chicago, growing old and beaten down by the poverty and despair around me. I realized too that Wanda had all of this planned. For her, marriage to a physician, regardless of circumstances, was a great step up, as it had been a great step up for me to have become a physician.

I told her I could not marry her.

I expected tears but, instead, Wanda flew into a rage. She shrilly inquired whether or not I intended to abandon her now that I had rendered her unfit for other men. I retorted that I was not a fool and was therefore well aware that I had hardly been the first man who had ruined her for others. At that, she softened her tone. She informed me that she was with child. I replied that I did not believe her, that I was, after all, a doctor, and if she wished, she could accompany me to the hospital where we could find out whether she was expecting or not. She leapt out of bed, gathered up her clothes, dressed, and departed, informing me on her way out that if I ever encountered her father, uncles, brothers, or myriad other relatives, I would be the worse for it. I left Chicago not a month later.

The episode caused me to realize what a complete fool I had been. How close I had come to precipitating my own downfall. Since then, when I could stand the strain no longer, I resorted, like most, to self-abuse. Yet, with all of that, the one feeling from last night that had not passed with the coming of the new day was an immense lust to be coupled with Monique, feeling her body thrusting against mine.

Once at the hospital, my headache still murderous, I called on the Professor in his office. I was reassured to find that he could not have been more open or in better spirits.

"My word, Carroll," he said, taking immediate note of my condition, "if I did not know you better, I would say that you had been gallivanting. Since I do know you, however, I assume that you simply stretched out in the middle of Broad Street last night and allowed the traffic to run over you."

I tried miserably to manage a small smile in reply, which the Professor laughed off as he bade me accompany him on rounds. He was so buoyant and lighthearted that the memory of the previous day and night began to seem more and more illusory. It was, after all, completely possible that what Turk had put forward as a gibe was actually true—that in the Dead House, the Professor had simply been shocked by the unfortunate woman's youth and beauty and found himself unable to cut into her flesh. As we headed for the wards, I felt foolish for my suspicions.

Going on rounds with the Professor was an opportunity to experience medicine at its apex. He had introduced an entirely new manner of training even first-year medical students to deal not only more effectively with illness but more humanely with the afflicted. He began, as was his wont, in the children's ward. The Professor adored children, and the sentiments were heartily reciprocated. (Years later, long after he had fled America for Great Britain, upon hearing that he was to be knighted, one of his young patients exclaimed, "Too bad. They should have made him *king*.") This day, we had been joined by, among others, Corrigan, Farnshaw, and Simpson—in fact, everyone who had been at yesterday's session in the Dead House, save one.

"Dr. Turk will not be joining us this morning," the Professor informed us. "He sent word that he has been laid low with a gastrointestinal ailment. I know how much we will all miss him, but we have no choice but to soldier on, eh?"

I took brief comfort in the thought that Turk had weathered the evening even less well than I until Simpson sidled up next to me. "You look positively dreadful," she observed quietly, with what I could not be sure was reproach or amusement.

"Thank you," I mumbled. "I was hoping someone would notice."

"Raw egg and Worcestershire sauce," she whispered. "Best thing."

"I believe I'd rather be sick," I replied, wondering how she had come by the information.

"At least you did better than poor Farnshaw," she continued.

"Farnshaw?" Had Farnshaw been there last night? I was confused, but then remembered that Turk had befriended Farnshaw for a time.

"Turk took him out to some dive near the waterfront, just after he arrived here. It had some odd biblical name. . . ."

"The Fatted Calf?" When Simpson confirmed my conjecture, I excused myself and sidled over to Farnshaw.

The young Bostonian had a compulsion to reveal everything that he knew to anyone who would listen, so it was not necessary to ask a direct question. I merely noted that Turk's illness might have been due to other than a microbe.

"I couldn't agree more, Carroll," my young colleague replied eagerly. "From the evidence I've seen, it's remarkable he can stand upright. I don't think you know this, but he asked me to join him out one evening just after I came on the staff."

"Really?"

"Yes," Farnshaw said. "He told me that it must be difficult coming to a new city and working with strangers. I thought it was quite decent of him. We went first to dinner at a very lively restaurant. . . ."

"Barker's?"

"Yes. How did you know?"

"I've been there myself."

"Ah. In any event, Turk could not have been more affable. He even insisted on paying, though by rights, the check should have been mine."

"Why is that?"

Farnshaw grew uncomfortable. "It's obvious . . . Turk . . . as we all know . . . must scrape by on a staff physician's remuneration, whereas I am . . . uh . . ."

"Rich?"

"It is not my fault that I come from means," he replied haughtily. "In any event," he continued, "after we had finished dinner, Turk invited me to see some of the city and suggested a drinking establishment he knew. It was down in the waterfront district, but he assured me that I was quite safe with him and that we should have great fun."

"And you went."

"I'm sorry to say that I did. Don't get me wrong, Carroll, it *was* great fun . . . for a time at least. But I'm afraid that I'm not as accustomed to revelry as I believed, and certainly not as much as is Turk. We drank prodigiously and I became somewhat intoxicated, although Turk, as I remember, was largely unaffected."

"Was it just the two of you, or were you joined by Turk's friends?"

"Just us. He did introduce me to a number of people, denizens of the place it seemed, including some most appealing ladies. He was quite familiar . . . he made sure everyone knew my name. 'Here's George,' he said or, 'Everyone, meet George.' I believe that by the time we left, half of the men and women in the establishment knew who I was."

"That was very generous of him," I said. "Did he ever take you there again?"

"No," said Farnshaw, demonstrating genuine puzzlement. "It was quite odd. When I told him on the way home how much I had enjoyed myself, he refused to even acknowledge me. Perhaps I embarrassed him by becoming intoxicated. I was quite ill, I'm afraid. It took three days to recover. But ever since, he has either ignored or made sport of me. Harvard fees, indeed."

"Turk makes sport of everyone," I reassured him.

"I know that," replied Farnshaw, "but I thought he liked me."

I felt more than a bit foolish to have been taken in by the same ploy used on my naïve colleague. I wondered why someone as calculating as Turk would waste his time on Farnshaw—or me, for that matter. Before I could inquire further, however, the Professor had moved to the entrance of the children's ward and swung open the door.

We entered a large and airy room with tall windows that admitted bountiful light. At his insistence, beds had been moved to be at least three feet apart and screens made readily available so that a young patient might enjoy a modicum of privacy during treatment.

In the first bed lay a boy of nine with dark eyes and a mop of black hair, who had been admitted the previous day suffering from dizziness and extreme fatigue. Blood had been taken and examined under the microscope.

"Hello, Giuseppe," the Professor said with a smile. "How are you feeling today?" Another of the improvements in the care of children was an identification card at the foot of each bed, so that a physician or nurse might address the patient by name. The Professor never needed to look at a card more than once.

"Johnny," the boy replied weakly. "Not too swell."

The Professor pulled up a chair. "Okay, then, Johnny, I was wondering if you could help me with something."

The boy looked suspicious.

"These are my students," the Professor went on, "and, well, some of them aren't very good." Two or three of my colleagues around the bed pretended to look aghast, which elicited a faint smile from Johnny. "I was wondering if you could help me teach them to be better doctors."

"What do I have to do?"

"I'm trying to teach them to remember four words—just four—but they can't seem to get it."

"I could do it," said the boy.

"They're kind of tricky."

"Ah, four words won't be no trouble."

The Professor stroked his mustache, then nodded. "All

right. Let's try. Each of these words stands for something that every doctor should do each time he sees a patient. Ready?"

"Yeah."

"The first word is 'inspect.' Do you know what that means?"

Johnny's smile broadened. Most of us attending stood blank-faced. Farnshaw had succeeded in appearing positively stupid. "To check something out," said the boy.

"Perfect!" said the Professor. He turned to us. "A natural, this lad is. That's right, the first thing a doctor should do is check out the patient, see how the patient looks and feels. So, Johnny, how do you feel today? What bothers you?"

"I'm real tired," the lad answered. "Every time I stand up, I feel like I'm gonna fall."

"Do your ears ring?"

"Nah."

"Are you eating all right? Do you get sick after you eat?"

"Nah."

"Does it hurt when you breathe?"

"Nah."

"Fine," said the Professor. "Now, on to the second word. This one is harder. Do you know what 'percussion' means?"

Johnny shook his head.

"It means to knock two things together and see what kind of sound it makes." The Professor stood. "Watch." Without warning, he rapped his knuckles against my head. Rounds had distracted me from my postalcoholic malaise but, although it was a physiologic impossibility, I felt as if my brain had shifted inside my skull.

"I just percussed Dr. Carroll here," he informed the boy with a grin, and I wondered if he had chosen me on purpose. "From the sound, I can tell you what's inside his head. Sounded kind of hollow, eh?"

Johnny was not the only one who agreed.

"Now, I'm going to percuss your stomach and chest." The Professor pulled back the sheet and the boy watched with curiosity as the Professor examined his abdomen and thorax. "Perfect," the Professor declared when he had finished. "Nothing bad going on there. On to number three, another tricky one. It's 'palpate.' "

"Don't know that one," Johnny said.

"It means to press on something, to see how it feels, if it's too hard or too soft. I'm going to palpate your stomach and your liver."

When he was finished, the Professor said, "The last word is the hardest, Johnny. It's 'auscultate.' It means to listen. For this one, we have something special." Dr. Osler removed the familiar device from the pocket of his coat. "This is called a Cammann binaural stethoscope. A lot of big words, but it just makes sound louder. Want to hear your heart?"

"Sure," said the boy.

The Professor put the earpieces in Johnny's ears and placed the diaphragm against his chest wall. The boy's eyes went wide. The Professor then listened himself. When he had completed the examination and tucked the stethoscope back into his coat, he asked, "Well, Johnny, my friend, can you re-peat the four words for my doctors here?"

Other than leaving the first "t" out of auscultate, the lad got all four.

"Congratulations," Dr. Osler exulted. "You now know the four points of the medical student's compass." "The four compass points"—inspect, percuss, palpate, auscultate—was to become one of the Professor's trademark teaching tools. "Johnny," he went on, "I want you to promise that when you decide to go to medical school, you'll come here and work for me."

Johnny, now feeling very good about himself, pursed his lips, looked up at the group clustered around his narrow bed, then nodded. "Sure," he said. "Why not?"

"And I'm going to make you a promise. You'll be out of here by early next week and you're going to be feeling a lot better."

This was, in fact, a routine diagnosis. Examination of a blood sample had confirmed a red cell deficiency—anemia—which, given the boy's slum address, was almost certainly due to iron deficiency in his diet. Simple anemia could be treated with an elixir rich in that element, although the boy's diet once he returned home was unlikely to prevent a relapse.

"Johnny, the nurses will be coming around with medicine. It isn't going to taste very good, but it's going to help you get better very quickly. The nurses are very nice women and I don't want you to give them any trouble about taking it. Then, they are going to give you a nice meal and I expect you to eat it without a fuss. All right?"

The boy agreed quite willingly and we moved on to the next bed, which was occupied by a scrawny girl with sunken eyes and stringy blond hair, no more than twelve. She had been here for over a week with a nontubercular pulmonary illness. "Well, Annie." The Professor smiled, pulling up a chair next to the bed while the rest of us gathered around. He took her hand and patted it softly. "How are you feeling today?"

"A little better today, Doctor." The rasp from her lungs was audible with each breath.

"Doctor?" he scolded gently. "Didn't I tell you to call me Willie?"

A strained smile played across the girl's pallid face. Her teeth, even at such a young age, were stained and rotting. "Willie," she whispered.

The Professor nodded. "That's better." Again he removed his stethoscope. "Now I'm going to auscultate . . . you remember . . . it means I'm going to listen to your breathing." The Professor listened to her lungs.

"Well, that certainly sounds better," he said to her after he was done. "In fact, I'd like some of these other doctors to listen also. Would that be all right?"

Annie smiled and nodded. The Professor had made her feel proud, part of the process instead of the subject of it. We took turns listening, the grate in her lungs roaring like surf in our ears. She was not in the least improved. As Simpson placed the stethoscope's diaphragm against the girl's protruding ribs, I saw moistness in her eyes and realized that my colleague was fighting for control. I then remembered that she was always stiffer and quieter in the children's ward. I surmised that despite her protestations, not having children of her own had not left her inured to maternal instincts.

When the examination was complete, the Professor reached down and smoothed the girl's hair. "Well, Annie," he said, "we have to move along and examine some other children who are *really* sick. I'll be back tomorrow. Will you wait for me?"

"Oh, yes, Willie." Her eyes had brightened and she seemed genuinely happy. But her tomorrows were not to be many.

As we moved away, one of the students, a boy of about twenty named Naughton, began to ask a question while we were still in earshot of the girl's bed. The Professor spun and faced him with a glare that closed Naughton's mouth like a bear trap. Particulars of a case were never discussed when a patient could overhear. In this case, particularly, there was little that needed to be said.

After rounds, the Professor asked me to join him for a moment. As we walked down the corridor, unexpectedly he asked, "Do you have any notion of where Turk is this morning?"

I said I did not, although I did not look him in the eye.

"Excuse me for embarrassing you," he said, "but when a physician who has not made a misstep in two years arrives at work appearing as you do, it is not difficult to diagnose the cause . . . or the means of transmission."

I admitted that I had been out with Turk, but added that he had dropped me at my rooms and I knew nothing of his whereabouts since then.

"What sort of fellow is Turk?" he asked.

"He is of extremely high ability," I replied, assuming that the Professor was reassessing Turk's fitness to be on staff.

"But?"

It was difficult to know where disloyalty to Turk ended and disloyalty to the Professor began. "His upbringing has left him angry and embittered," I answered. "I hope it does not cause him to squander his talent."

"Yes, I agree," the Professor replied. "Do you like him . . . personally, I mean?"

"Whenever I begin to like him, he does something to bring me up short. But he is difficult to dislike as well."

"Yes," mused the Professor. "Quite so." Then he brightened and placed his hand on my shoulder. "There's something else, Ephraim. If you are free tomorrow evening, I would like you to accompany me to a dinner. It is at the Benedicts' on Rittenhouse Square. Formal, I'm afraid. Starched collar, tight vest, and all. Are you up for it?"

"I would be glad to," I said.

"It is not strictly a social affair," the Professor noted. "Carroll, how abreast are you with the doings in Baltimore?"

He was speaking, of course, of the new hospital and plans for a medical school funded by an extraordinary endowment by the Quaker Johns Hopkins. Hopkins had amassed a fortune in dry goods and railroads and died childless in 1873, leaving seven million dollars to create the most modern medical facility in the world.

"I know," I replied, "that the hospital will finally open after years of delays but the medical school is still not as yet complete. There are those who doubt it ever will be."

"Oh, it will be, it will be. And when it is, it will be the envy of the nation. During that weekend I was absent last month, I traveled to Baltimore. Briefly put, I was solicited by the Hopkins board to accept the position of Physician in Chief at the hospital. It would, I was not displeased to learn, pay five times what I earn here. I was also offered the Professorship of Theory and Practice of Medicine when the medical school opens."

"That's wonderful," I exulted. For a moment, an echo of Turk's cynical prediction that the Professor would leave

Philadelphia for money alone rang in my ears. I quickly dismissed it. Advancement in any profession was remunerated, and the acceptance of higher pay was not necessarily evidence of greed. "Congratulations," I said. "There is no one who deserves it more."

"Thank you." The Professor seemed genuinely touched at my enthusiasm. "The offer was supposed to have remained private, but, doctors, I fear, are more uncontrollable gossips than spinsters. News of my visit has reached the board at the hospital here."

"Has your position in Philadelphia been compromised?"

"I suppose not," he replied, "although it did result in this dinner. Old Benedict—he's head of the trustees—has asked for an opportunity to persuade me to remain in Philadelphia." The Professor reached up and tugged at the dip of flesh under his chin. "It is all quite flattering, actually." Then he smiled and clapped his hands together. "But that brings us to you. If I accept the offer, I would like you to come with me to Baltimore as Assistant Head of Clinical Medicine. The position would apply not just to the hospital, but eventually to the medical school as well. Initially, you will receive two thousand dollars per annum, although I'm certain that you can at least double that with private patients."

I stared at the Professor, feeling my lower jaw moving but with no sound emerging. Finally, I managed, "Dr. Osler...I...am..." No more words came.

The Professor laughed, one loud cannon shot. "Well, Carroll, I believe I have for once struck you dumb. You look quite exceptional. Well, you've earned it. I knew you were a special sort the first day I saw you at rounds two years ago, and nothing has since persuaded me otherwise. You are professional, thorough, curious, and a fine doctor. As to your age, I suppose you know that for my first teaching assignment, I was younger than you are now."

I did know. At McGill University in Canada, Dr. Osler had

been granted a teaching position at twenty-three. His students dubbed him "The Baby Professor."

"And besides," he went on, "children of the backwoods such as ourselves need to stick together, eh?"

Although the Professor enjoyed stressing the bond of our rural upbringings, he was hardly a rustic. The Osler family had eventually settled in a wilderness town in northern Canada, it was true, but the Professor's father, Featherstone Lake Osler, had been the original choice to sail on the *Beagle* as ship's naturalist, a post that went to Charles Darwin only when the elder Osler declined. Though the Professor's father had then entered the ministry and been posted to Bond Head, Ontario, William Osler had been surrounded by books and learning during his entire childhood.

My boyhood, by contrast, had been dominated by a decidedly different set of stimuli. The fetid smell of our farmhouse still lingered in my nostrils, unwashed bodies mixed with the waft of cheap stew and even cheaper liquor. Yelling, tears, and the soft moans of my mother were never far away. I would continue to send money home so long as I was able, but I had not and would not return to Marietta. With four thousand dollars per year, I could finally make certain that no one in my family could have further cause to accuse me of ingratitude.

"Still," he continued somberly, "it will be difficult to leave . . . I have made so many friends." Then he brightened once more. "But as much as I prize my colleagues here, the Hopkins staff will be truly extraordinary. Welch, as you may know, will be running the show . . . brilliant pathologist. Lafleur, whom I taught in Canada, will arrive shortly. Halsted is already there."

"Halsted?" I asked.

The Professor's face turned dark, an instantaneous eclipse. "And why not Halsted?" he bristled. "He is the finest surgeon in America, probably the world."

I was stunned by the Professor's change in demeanor at

my query. "Why, yes, Dr. Osler," I sputtered, "I'm sure you are correct, but I thought that he . . ."

"Yes, I know what you thought," the Professor replied. " 'Drug addict.' You and everyone else."

"I didn't mean—"

"Of course you didn't," he snapped, though his irritation seemed directed no longer at me, but to an audience not present. "Halsted has been unfairly maligned for the better part of a decade. To think that a man of his genius has been reduced to . . . Well, it's not important now. Do you know that at this moment, he is perfecting a new surgical suture that will be largely subcutaneous and cause almost no tissue trauma and minimal scarring?"

Before I could respond, the Professor continued, more willing to expound on the prejudices foisted on a colleague than those foisted on him. "Halsted has pioneered one brilliant surgical advance after another. Just months ago, he had aseptic gloves fabricated by the Goodyear Company. Rubberized gloves are a huge step, Carroll. They promise to all but eliminate surgical infection."

"I had heard that surgeons in New York were beginning to use gloves," I said, "but I didn't know Halsted had pioneered them."

"It was typical," the Professor fulminated. "One of his nurses was experiencing sensitivity to the carbolic soap with which everyone—or at least almost everyone—now washes before surgery to try to achieve some level of asepsis. To eliminate the need for caustic material to touch the skin, he had the gloves fabricated. They can be rendered truly aseptic. Thousands of lives will be saved each year."

Dr. Osler took a step forward and actually placed an index finger on my chest. I was stunned. I had never known him to make physical contact in anger.

"Doctor, I would protect William Halsted as I would protect a treasure," he told me, almost in a growl. "The good he will do over what I hope will be a long life, the lives he will save, the suffering he will prevent . . . do you really desire that medical science deny itself a man such as this?"

"No," I replied, still not daring in my astonishment to move. "I suppose not."

"No supposing about it," he grunted. Then, like a kettle removed from a flame, he stepped back and emitted a deep sigh. "This is a simple issue that pits the prejudice of ignorance against the enlightenment of knowledge. Nothing could be clearer. I confess, Carroll, I cannot understand the way some people think." Dr. Osler withdrew his watch. "We'll just have time. Come with me, Doctor."

The Professor turned on his heel and headed back the way we had come. He took the far staircase to the first floor and emerged across the hall from the operating theater. He opened the door and bade me to enter.

"Burleigh will be clearing an abscessed bowel," he said with disgust. "You've never seen Burleigh at work before, have you? I believe you will find it enlightening."

Wilberforce Burleigh was perhaps the Professor's most impassioned critic on the staff. He was in his sixties, had been a surgeon for forty years, and thought that medicine was just fine as it was. Burleigh's eyes narrowed at our arrival and he glared at us as we strode up to the gallery, muttering to himself. I could distinctly make out the words "spying on me."

A moment after we had been seated, the patient was wheeled in, and Burleigh turned to the task at hand. An emaciated, sandy-haired man of about forty lay on the table, covered up to his chin with a sheet, his terrified eyes flitting about and his lower jaw quivering. The surgeon took no notice.

Burleigh was from the "flashing hands" school of surgery— everything the man did was based on speed. Quick work was not mere affectation. In traditional surgery, bleeding was only minimally controlled, usually with pads and pressure, and as a result more surgical patients died from shock than from their primary illness. What hemostasis did exist was achieved by other flashing hands, often eight or nine sets of them, belonging to the army of assistants that most surgeons employed in the effort to have every task attended to immediately. I'd heard that a wag at Yale called this process "nine women trying to have a baby in one month."

Recently, the development of mosquito clamps—small, scissor-shaped hemostats—allowed for more effective clamping of blood vessels. With bleeding controlled, the surgeon could work more slowly and carefully, but not every surgeon cared to slow his pace. Burleigh was notorious for continuing to place a premium on speed. He never tired of recounting that in 1846, during the first successful use of ether in surgery, Robert Liston had amputated a leg in mid-thigh in twenty-six seconds, or of bragging that he, Burleigh, had once performed eighteen operations in a single day. Fewer and fewer of that ilk were left, however, as almost every surgeon entering the field now followed the lead of the man who had invented mosquito clamps specifically to staunch blood flow during surgery—William Stewart Halsted.

Ten assistants stood at the table dressed in hospital uniform instead of gowns, while Burleigh remained in street clothes. Corrigan, the bulldog, who was not trusted to do more than take notes in the Dead House, was to the surgeon's immediate left, meaning that he was chief assistant. The Professor rolled his eyes at the sight.

Burleigh signaled another assistant and the ether cone was placed over the patient's face. As the drug was poured, Burleigh faced the gallery, which contained about twenty students in addition to ourselves, and announced, "Today, I will be treating a patient with acute diverticulitis, removing a suspected abscess from the sigmoid colon and then resecting the bowel." He smiled, parting an extremely full beard. "Please watch carefully. I don't wait for stragglers."

After the patient had been poked with a long needle to ensure that the ether had rendered him senseless, Burleigh removed a case in fine Turkish leather from his coat. I recognized it at once as the deluxe Tiemann & Company Patent Catch Pocket surgical set, advertised in their catalog at thirty-three dollars, the most expensive kit on the market. At eighteen surgeries per day, I surmised, Burleigh could well afford it. He opened the case, set it on a table behind him, and removed the large scalpel. Standing over the patient with what seemed almost malevolence, Burleigh lowered the scalpel to just above the abdomen, nodded to an assistant to note the time, and then cut.

Flashing hands was no understatement. Burleigh made a swift paramedian incision on the left abdominal wall, about two inches from midline, beginning just under the rib cage and ending five inches below the umbilicus, cutting in one motion through the skin, subcutaneous fat—minimal due to the patient's physique—and the anterior rectus sheath. As he spread these aside, four of his assistants dove in with pads. Burleigh then called for a retractor, cut the rectus muscle itself, and placed the retractor laterally, instructing a fifth assistant to hold it still. The entire process was completed in seconds.

I glanced at the Professor, but he gave no sign anything was amiss. A paramedian incision was the correct choice—the rectus muscle is not divided, the incisions in the anterior and posterior rectus sheath are separated by muscle, and incisional hernia is less likely—but the length of Burleigh's cut was far too long. It would be much harder to close, chance of secondary infection greatly increased, and control of the organs inside the peritoneum would be difficult.

By the time I returned my gaze to the table, two assistants were frantically applying pressure to the larger vessels, while another sponged away fluids. Burleigh should here have switched to the small scalpel for a finer cut, but instead, in the interest of speed, he used the same large instrument to incise the posterior rectus sheath, *transversalis fascia*, and peritoneum. When he encountered the epigastric vessels, a geyser of blood shot out of the patient, spattering everyone on the right side of the table. Corrigan grabbed a hemostat and tried to clamp the artery, but with blood obscuring the cut end, it took him at least ten seconds to achieve the result. All the while, Burleigh was snarling, "Get that *closed*, damn you!"

The rule in surgery, with so many crowded around the table, was "no talking except the big man." Burleigh was particularly loud and abusive. As soon as Corrigan had placed the clamp, Burleigh screamed for another. The disorganization in the efforts of the team was palpable.

When finally the bleeding was sufficiently controlled so that Burleigh could see, he began to incise the peritoneum to access the colon itself. Suddenly, the patient began to squirm on the table. Burleigh screamed once more, this time to increase the ether. If the patient's diaphragm began to move, the bowel could bubble and, especially with this huge an incision, it might force sections of intestine out through the opening and into Burleigh's face.

The patient once more lay still as the additional ether began to take. Burleigh proceeded to the target. Still furious, he yelled, "Hold that still, you fool!" The eyes on the assistant holding the right angle retractor went wide, and he struggled to remain perfectly motionless. Burleigh began his inspection of the colon, performing the task as rapidly as possible. He found the diverticular abscess that he expected almost immediately, but there was no way of knowing what, if anything, he missed.

He clamped the colon on either side of the abscess and then, still using the scalpel with which he had cut through the outer skin, he excised the section. After reaching into his case for a length of silk suture and a needle, he stitched up the anastomosis. From there, Burleigh closed the incision in layers, sealing the giant opening with stitches far too large, in each case using the same needle and suture.

When he was near the end, Burleigh asked for the time.

The entire operation had taken under forty minutes. He seemed disappointed and glared at Corrigan and the other assistants. When he had tied off the last external suture and the ether cone was removed, Burleigh nodded at the assistant keeping time and stepped back. Blood was everywhere, on the table, the floor, and soaking everyone's clothing.

Burleigh turned and faced the gallery. "As you can see," he exclaimed proudly, "the operation was a success."

Even before the last syllable was out, the Professor was on his feet. "We can go now," he said to me softly. As we left, I could feel Burleigh's eyes on my back.

Once we were out in the hall, the Professor asked, "So, Doctor, what did you think?"

"Ghastly. The entire process was highly septic, he used the wrong instruments, tissue trauma was severe, he did not examine the affected area for additional damage, and the stitching was worse than could have been achieved by an inebriated seamstress." I might have added that my indignation at watching Burleigh at work had shocked the last aftereffects of drink right out of my system.

"And the result?" The Professor was attempting to speak evenly, but he was so angry that his face had gone pale and his mustache quivered.

"The patient will be disfigured for life."

"No. The patient will die. I would say, Ephraim, that it was the most appalling piece of surgery I have ever seen, but unfortunately I have been forced to witness all too many other examples." He pounded a fist into his hand. "Damn!"

"How can Burleigh be allowed to continue here?" I asked.

"Because he's been here for four decades, that's why," the Professor fumed. "There is a ridiculous reluctance among some in authority to toss out someone with whom they regularly share dinner and a sherry, even if he kills or mutilates his patients. Agnew tried to have him dismissed in '85, but Burleigh's friends on the board shrieked blasphemy."

"They should be forced to sample his methods," I said.

"Doctor, there is nothing more important than to obtain the best men in our profession, not just to treat patients but also to train the next generation. Do you understand? Nothing! That human beings are forced to endure the horrors of inept surgery is criminal. I would move mountains not to have to see the results of such butchery in the wards. And we would not in any surgical department with Halsted in charge." He cocked his head toward the operating theater we had just left. "This answers your questions about Halsted's fitness, I presume?"

It did. There would be no Wilberforce Burleighs at Johns Hopkins—but there would be an Ephraim Carroll. As the Professor walked down the corridor and disappeared around the corner, the words *assistant head of clinical medicine* played in my ears.

CHAPTER 5

AN ASSISTANT HEAD OF CLINICAL medicine cannot allow his energies to flag. I decided to busy myself with patients through the afternoon, head for the doctors' dining room at about six—where my choice, as always, would be overcooked pork chops or dried roasted chicken—and then spend the evening at the library or the forensic laboratory. I had also resolved to satisfy my curiosity on another matter, but needed to wait until well into the night to do it.

Planning cannot stand up to circumstance, however. My odd and tumultuous day took an additional twist when, just after Dr. Osler's departure, Simpson appeared at the other end of the hall. She beckoned me to join her.

"I've been hoping to speak to you," she began. Simpson, even in her uniform, now appeared to me as she had the previous day at tea—amber-flecked eyes and sorrel hair. "I thought I might reciprocate your offer. Are you free this evening? Or do you intend to repeat last night's bacchanalia?"

"I do not expect to repeat that for some considerable time," I observed, "but I was planning on reading case histories and studying tissue samples."

"Reluctant though I am to draw you away from scholarly pursuits," she replied, "I believe that I can offer you an alternative equally illuminating."

I pressed to find out what she meant, but Simpson demurred, so I assured her that I would be pleased to accept her invitation and asked when and where I should come with a carriage.

"That won't be necessary," she replied. "I'll come for you. Be out front at five forty-five." She dismissed my protests with a wave of her hand. "Consider it a step into a new world," she said.

Although there was much to do, I confess that curiosity as to what Simpson had in store kept intruding into my concentration and I found myself awaiting our rendezvous with mounting anticipation. At five-thirty, just before I went to change my clothes, I checked in on Burleigh's patient. The nurse on duty told me that Mr. Whitbread was running a fever of 101 and that his blood pressure was low. I considered sending a messenger to Burleigh's home, but what good would it do? Burleigh wouldn't come and the poor wretch had already gone septic. Dr. Osler had been correct. Nothing could save Mr. Whitbread now. I ordered Antifebrin to control the fever, and then silently said a prayer over him before leaving the ward.

Promptly at the appointed hour, Simpson pulled up in front of the hospital in what seemed to be a private carriage driven by an aging man with gray whiskers and a disinterested air. Carriage, driver, and horse, while not exuding prosperity, seemed well-kept and functional—much, I realized, like Simpson herself. I stepped in and the carriage took off, the driver heading south for a destination that Simpson refused to divulge.

When I asked Simpson who owned the carriage, she replied tersely, "Friends of mine."

We crossed the Schuylkill at the South Street bridge and continued south and west along Mifflin Street until just before South Twenty-second Street, where the carriage made a turn and pulled up in front of a three-story, brown clapboard building. Two women and three small children stood on the sidewalk outside. The women waved hello when they saw my companion.

"Where are we?" I asked her.

"You seemed confused as to the parameters of domestic fulfillment," Simpson replied. "I thought a visit here might help clarify the question."

Simpson alighted first and, before she went up the steps to the door, the children ran to her. She said hello to each of them by name. I followed her and my suspicion that this was no rooming house was confirmed the instant we entered.

The front hall led down the center of the building, with a staircase to the right. I saw at least six more children on the stairs or popping into or out of one of the rooms to either side of the hall. Two women moved between the rooms, occupied with some chore or other. The décor, I noticed, while not costly, was cheery and feminine—light colors, with a good deal of frill. The wallpaper in the halls was pale yellow festooned with cherubs.

"This is an orphanage," I offered, as Simpson led me into a parlor on the left of the hall.

She did not reply. Instead, she bade me sit in a chair near the fireplace and asked if I cared for a cup of tea. I thanked her, hung my coat and hat on a tree near the door, and took a seat.

"I'll be right back," she said, and ducked back into the hall. I was left waiting for a minute or two, during which time a boy and girl, each about seven or eight, peered in the doorway at me, then withdrew.

When Simpson returned, she was holding two cups of tea. "This is the Croskey Street Settlement House," she informed me as she placed the cups on the table and sat across from me. "It is not an orphanage. The children you see here live with their mothers. This building is part residence, part clinic, and part school."

"And the fathers?"

"The fathers are not present."

"This is reminiscent of a similar establishment for fallen women that I knew on the West Side of Chicago."

" 'Fallen women,' " Simpson repeated with a shake of the head. "Ephraim, could you please define a 'fallen woman' for me?"

"It is merely a phrase," I answered, trying to sound casual but knowing I had misspoken again. "To describe a woman who has a child out of wedlock. I presume that is who lives here."

"A phrase indeed," Simpson replied coldly. "A particularly insulting phrase." She shook her head slightly, as if trying to comprehend my stupidity. I realized suddenly that, in these matters, I knew nothing at all. "Do you consider the men who cause these women to have children out of wedlock to be fallen as well?" she asked.

Did I? What if fortune had played against me in Chicago? What if Wanda had been telling the truth about her pregnancy? Would I have married her then? "Not fallen, no," I replied, "but certainly beneath contempt and utterly without honor."

"But less culpable than the women . . ."

"No," I said, the vitriol in my response containing a measure of self-reproach. "More."

"A noble sentiment, Ephraim, but you are nonetheless misguided," Simpson said patiently, but with frustration, sounding like Dr. Osler lecturing the callow Farnshaw. "The correct answer is neither more nor less. Women are neither inherently the precipitants of sin nor too weak and fragile to resist it. That is the purpose of this settlement—to show women who have been forced to endure the scorn of society that they are worthy and may take a place with honor. That they have not 'fallen,' regardless of who might say or think otherwise." She placed her tea on the table and rose from her chair. "Would you like to see the evidence?"

Simpson guided me up the stairs and, for the next thirty minutes, I received a tour of the remarkable institution. The top floor contained sleeping quarters for eight women and their children. The bedrooms were small, but allowed for privacy and self-respect. The second floor contained two rooms set aside for learning and a large common room where the children could play together. The rear of the first floor contained a kitchen and dining area and, set in the corner, a surprisingly modern medical facility. Simpson was greeted by everyone we encountered with a mixture of warmth and deference.

When I expressed my admiration for whoever had begun such a progressive establishment, Simpson surprised me by reacting with venom.

"But eight women, Ephraim. Only *eight*. There are thousands who should be able to avail themselves of our services. Do you have any idea of what it is like for a woman who finds herself in such a predicament? A woman without means? What choices has she? She may remain at her home and live with disgrace, never marrying because she is considered tainted by other men. In many cases, her baby will be torn from her by her own family, given to an orphanage in an effort to expunge the shame. She can attempt to hide her disgrace by leaving home to have her baby and giving it to an orphanage herself, then return to live a lie and wonder for the rest of her life what has happened to her child. She can move to a new town, have her baby, and try to pass herself off as a widow. For the rich or the truly disreputable, there is abortion, the most loathsome option of all. Each option is ghastly. Each option is a lie. We try and provide an alternative that is not . . . for just eight."

"But surely your eight can be a start," I said. "A model on which other like institutions may be established."

"That is our hope. Otherwise . . ."

"You are the physician here?"

"Yes," she replied. "I provide medical services."

"Does Dr. Osler know?"

"Oh, yes. In fact he has contributed to our cause, most generously, I might add. In addition, he has come here often to help with medical problems that are beyond my capability."

"How did you come to be involved?"

"A patient," she said tersely.

I opened my mouth to inquire further, but she asked instead, "But please tell me. Do our residents remind you of the fallen women in Chicago?"

"I swear before the Almighty that I will never use that term again."

"The Almighty will be grateful," she replied. "I would like to hear about your time there, though. Did you enjoy private practice?"

Now that Simpson had revealed something of herself, she was asking me to do likewise. I wanted to, wanted to more strongly than I would have thought, but, as always, feared the consequences of revelation. Nonetheless, I resolved to try.

"There was little to enjoy, I'm afraid. I practiced on the West Side for three years, apprenticed to a doctor named Jorgensen. Jorgie, everyone called him. He was about sixty, drank quite a bit, and was in need of someone to help out and eventually take over his practice. Our patients consisted entirely of working people and immigrants. Sometimes we were paid, sometimes not. Often, we accepted whatever could be offered. I was able to barter rent in return for tending to my landlady's rheumatism, and was always sure of a supply of Italian sausage as payment for treating the scabies infection of the local butcher's wife.

"I came to understand that Jorgie's cynical demeanor, and even his drinking, helped him to cope with the tragedies that we seemed to encounter almost every day—a Lithuanian whose hand had been mangled in a grinding machine, a woman whose three sons had either died or been killed in three successive years, a series of children born with horrible deformities, untreated wounds that festered into infection, and endless victims of crime, violence, or neglect. There were rewards, certainly, in trying to provide some basic medical care to a segment of the population who could get it no other way, but mostly we simply flailed about."

"How did you ward off despair?" she asked, as would one who has been forced to fight despair herself.

"I'm not sure," I admitted. "Perhaps I didn't. I was constantly frustrated by the extreme limitations of medical knowledge. Finally, I realized that, despite whatever comfort I might be giving to these poor wretches, this was not the medicine I wished to practice. Perhaps that was despair and I didn't recognize it."

"Is that when you left Chicago to come here?"

How to respond? "Soon after. I decided that what I wanted was to help develop improvements in the science of medicine so that my work might help not just a few patients, but thousands."

"Do you ever regret the decision?"

"There is guilt sometimes . . . for abandoning Jorgie's practice and leaving his patients with even less hope than before."

We spoke easily for another hour, talking mostly of science and the even greater advances in medical care and technique that would be manifest in the coming years. The enthusiasm and energy she exhibited were in contrast to the extreme discipline that always dominated her behavior at the hospital. Unlike Turk, who thought medicine merely a means to wealth, here was someone who shared my vision and my hopes. Mary Simpson, I decided, was even more formidable—and more interesting—than I had previously been aware.

Soon afterward, I thanked her for an evening as illuminating as she had promised, and offered to see her home. She declined, saying she lived only a few streets away, and offered me use of the carriage. Instead of giving the driver directions to Mrs. Mooney's, I told him to return to the hospital. I had two unfinished chores to complete.

I arrived just after nine P.M. I waited for the carriage to pull away and then, rather than walking to the front door, headed down the street to the side of the building. Soon I was at a gate in the Blockley wall and, minutes later, I stood at the entrance to the Dead House. Low clouds were draped across the sky and a March chill had settled over the city. My breath formed plumes in the night air. I waited for a moment, my ears attuned to the sound of anyone else who might be wandering the grounds.

Charlie kept a spare key in one of the flowerpots that had been incongruously placed on either side of the door in a miserable attempt to provide a dose of cheer. When I was completely sure that no one else was about, I quickly retrieved the key and slipped inside.

When the door was shut, I was alone in the dark, in the silence, alone with the dead. Science deserted me and I felt as if I had ventured without leave into forbidden terrain, perhaps even to purgatory itself. At any moment, I feared cold fingers on my cheek or a grasp at my ankle. I tried to be furious with myself for fearing the dark like a child, but my palms remained moist and my breath shallow and labored. Forcing myself inside, I felt my way to the drawers where the matches were kept. With some difficulty, I located the box and, although even through the thick curtain the illumination might be visible to a passerby, lit one quickly all the same.

As soon as the match was struck, I felt an enormous wave of relief. In the light, even from one match, the Dead House was again simply a set of rooms in which I sometimes worked. I removed the smallest candle from the shelf and placed the match to the wick. When the flame had taken, I shielded the light with my hand and moved quickly to the morgue. I intended to discover why Turk and the Professor had reacted so strangely yesterday to the corpse of the young woman.

The morgue was windowless so, as soon as I shut the door, I could move about with impunity. I walked to the receptacle that held the young girl and swung open the lid.

It was empty. I checked the other four chests that held yesterday's subjects. Two were empty as well. Two held cadavers that had obviously been brought in since.

I was puzzled. Generally, three or four days at least were required to make arrangements with the city authorities for public burial, and Charlie had assured the Professor that each of the cadavers had arrived just the day before. Why had these cadavers been removed so rapidly? Charlie could have been mistaken, of course. Still, he had never made such an error in the past.

I remembered that Dr. Osler had remained behind when the rest of us had left the autopsy session to return to the hospital. Could the Professor have been responsible for the disappearance of the bodies? Unlikely, I decided. He was hardly intimate enough with Charlie to join with him in a conspiracy. The mystery of the young girl in the ice chest, it seemed, would remain, at least for the moment, just that.

Disappointed that I had risked this nocturnal visit for naught, I blew out the candle, replaced the matches, and was on my way, my departure not nearly so eerie as my arrival. I crossed back to University Hospital to discharge my second errand.

As I reached the third floor, I hoped that this visit would be for naught as well, that Annie, the sad girl with the pulmonary infection, would be asleep, since rest came so sporadically to her because of the inability to take in sufficient oxygen. But if she was not, I intended to sit with her at her bedside.

As I got to the door of the children's ward, I heard the sound of low conversation inside, odd at such an hour. I pushed open the door only a crack and peeked in. There was the Professor, sitting at Annie's bedside, reading to her.

March 7, 1889

SOMETIMES IN LIFE, SHE REALIZED, no choice is a good one. Still, it was surely better to take action, to make your own decision, than to have your life ruled by others. Now that she had elected a course of action, as distasteful and fraught with danger as it was, she felt stronger.

She had astonished herself just to get this far. Who would have imagined that she, who never so much as purchased her own eggs and bacon for breakfast, had planned and executed an elaborate conspiracy, and then arranged through an intermediary to meet a complete stranger in a waterfront saloon? Her heart had been in her throat since she slipped into the carriage that she had hired surreptitiously earlier in the day. What if she was observed? No matter, though. This had to be done.

Within seconds of meeting him, she knew he could not be

trusted but, again, she had no alternative. She had planned to offer only half the agreed amount until the job was finished, but he had insisted on the entire sum in advance. She prayed it was sufficient to ensure, if not his loyalty, at least his competence. And his silence.

CHAPTER 6

BOTH THE PROFESSOR AND I left the hospital at four the following day in order to prepare for our dinner engagement at the Benedict home. On rounds, Simpson and I, in unspoken agreement, had conducted ourselves as before, neither of us acknowledging that we had met away from the hospital. We had, however, passed a look between us when Turk for a second day failed to appear for rounds.

At six-thirty, Dr. Osler's carriage came for me at Mrs. Mooney's. The Professor's consulting practice, which he ran out of a small office on South Fifteenth Street, had begun to thrive, and with the supplement to his university salary, he had been able to acquire clothing suitable for a man whose future greatness was an accepted fact to all in his field. Fees from private patients, mostly hospital cases who needed care after discharge, had allowed me to acquire at least the rudiments of proper dress, although I had yet to replace my cutaway frock coat with the new, tailless "tuxedo," and my low formal boots were stiff as iron.

The hesitancy I felt about that evening's dinner was not limited to fears of sartorial inadequacy. I would be attending as the Professor's assistant, my first assignment in that role, and I did not want to bring even the slightest obloquy upon him as a result of my woeful lack of experience in better society. How would I fare at the home of Hiram Benedict, who, in addition to heading the board of trustees of the university, was chairman of the Pennsylvania Merchant Bank? My only

knowledge of the manners of the rich had come from books—
The Rise of Silas Lapham by William Dean Howells, or *The Europeans* by Henry James, Jr. ...

The Professor's hansom was a proper affair, crisply lacquered and pulled by an elegant black horse. He looked me up and down as I climbed on board. "Very well turned out," he said.

I was grateful to the Professor for the sentiment, but I nonetheless continued to feel as though those serving the soup were certain to be more fashionably attired than I. When I noted that I did not feel as if I belonged at a gathering of such eminence, he laughed.

"Eyewash," he declared. "They are just people, Carroll. You will do wonderfully. Best get used to the rich—this is hardly the last time that you will attend an affair of this sort. Hospitals don't build themselves, eh? In modern medicine, the ability to chat amiably over dinner is almost as important as recognizing scarlet fever."

I was relieved to hear that among the guests would be Weir Mitchell and Hayes Agnew, the Professor's closest friends in Philadelphia. I had met each man previously; perhaps their presence might lend at least a semblance of familiarity to the occasion.

Mitchell, in addition to being one of the world's leading authorities on nervous diseases, was also a noted novelist and had recently taken to writing poetry, but his manner with patients could be eccentric in the extreme. Once he had been asked to see a woman whose condition was sufficient to convince her attending physician that she was dying. After a cursory examination, Mitchell dismissed everyone from her room, and then walked out himself a few minutes later. Asked whether the patient would live, he replied, "Oh yes, she will be coming out in a moment. I have set her sheets on fire." When the terrified but obviously robust woman burst out of her room and ran down the hall, Mitchell nodded and said, "There! A clear-cut case of hysteria."

Agnew, the man who had tried unsuccessfully to oust Burleigh, was an eminent surgeon and esteemed professor of anatomy at the university. Eight years earlier, he had attended James Garfield in a doomed attempt to save the President's life after the latter had been shot. Just turned seventy, Agnew had recently announced his retirement.

"And then, of course, there will be the women," the Professor added, mischief playing at the corners of his eyes. "The presence of a couple of bachelors like us will require the balance of two attractive and charming ladies."

"I'm always happy to share a table with attractive and charming ladies," I replied without enthusiasm. On Rittenhouse Square, among the millionaires, chatting amiably at dinner might prove daunting. I was certain to be paired with someone who knew less about rural Ohio than I knew about Patagonia.

"As am I," Dr. Osler agreed, unable to mask his eagerness. "When I arrived in Philadelphia after accepting my chair, everyone seemed quite astonished when I stepped off the train alone. They had somehow gotten the notion that I was a married man. Agnew later told me that he had come to the station more to meet Mrs. Osler than me, because he had been told that she was a Buddhist. I have never quite deduced how that rumor got started. My colleagues quickly overcame their disappointment, however, and replaced it with what seems to be a competition to see which one of them will succeed in introducing me to my future wife. Tonight, Mitchell tells me that my dinner companion is to be young Gross' widow, Grace."

Dr. Samuel W. Gross had recently died of sepsis at age fifty-two. Although a noted physician and surgeon in his own right, he had toiled in the shadow of his father, Samuel D. Gross, who himself had died at age seventy-nine only five years before. The elder Gross had been the dominant figure in American surgery and medical education for four decades.

"Mrs. Gross is a direct descendant of Paul Revere, you

know," the Professor observed, "although that is not as significant in the wilds of Ontario as here."

"Perhaps you should carry a single lantern, since you come by land," I offered. "Do you know who has been invited as my companion?"

"I believe you will be seated next to Abigail Benedict, the old boy's daughter. Do you know of her?"

I admitted I did not.

"Well, Carroll," he said, reveling in my ignorance, "it might have been best to wear armor."

All too soon, we pulled up to the Benedict home, a wide-fronted, granite Greek revival with a small second-floor balcony over the entrance on Walnut Street, facing south on Rittenhouse Square. The carriage came to a halt and we were met by a liveried Negro coachman who helped us down and ushered us into the house.

I had on occasion strolled across Rittenhouse Square and seen the mansions, a line of monuments to rewards of class, but had never before been inside one of them. However exalted my expectations for what I would find, they nonetheless proved inadequate. The second I stepped across the threshold, I was overpowered by opulence. The foyer was a huge oval, two stories high, with a promenade ringing the second floor, and topped by a stained-glass skylight, a celestial incarnation of the layout in the Dead House. The entire building appeared to be illuminated by electric lighting. Directly opposite the front door, a staircase of gleaming white marble snaked up to the second floor, lined with oil portraits of gloomy colonials or musty dowagers. Thick, ornately patterned Oriental rugs lay on either side of the mouth of the staircase. As I perused art and furnishings worthy of a museum, the four thousand dollars I was to receive at Johns Hopkins did not seem at all like a great deal of money.

Mr. and Mrs. Hiram Benedict waited to greet us. Benedict was in his late fifties and immense, well over six feet, with a large gray mustache and an even larger stomach. He wore what seemed to be an embedded glower, and there were tufts of white hair growing from each ear, giving him the mien of an angry Etruscan god. Mrs. Benedict was portly as well, white-haired, and handsome, wearing a gown of green lace, buff lace gloves, and a diamond tiara. Four long strands of fat pearls draped over her more than ample bosom.

"Thank you for coming, Dr. Osler," said Benedict, stepping forward. "We are honored that you have joined us this evening." He turned to me. His eyes were sapphire and, although a bit rheumy, his gaze was nonetheless penetrating. "And this must be your young protégé. It is good to meet you, Dr. Carroll." Benedict's voice was deep and seemed to roll out from within him. He spoke with the casual ease of a man comfortable in his supremacy. "May I present my daughter, Abigail."

I had not seen Abigail Benedict as we entered but, from the moment she appeared at her father's side, I knew she was remarkable. She was not pretty in the way that women were typically thought to be pretty—her nose was a trifle long and her lips a bit full—but I was transfixed all the same. She wore a high-necked gown of black velvet and no jewelry whatever. She was tall, like her parents, auburn-haired and lean, with her father's extraordinary blue eyes.

I knew those eyes. I had seen them at Barker's restaurant two days before. A fleeting smile played across Miss Benedict's face and I knew that she remembered as well.

"Dr. Carroll," she said, stepping forward and extending her hand assertively, as would a man. She was not wearing gloves, revealing long and graceful fingers. "I have been looking forward to meeting you. I expect you to regale me over dinner with exotic tales of modern medicine."

I took her hand and bowed, unsure if I was being mocked. How could anyone be sure of anything, standing amid the wealth of the pharaohs in a room the size of an operating theater, opposite a rich and beautiful woman who expected me to be witty and entertaining?

"I believe I warned you to wear armor, Ephraim," said the Professor.

"Oh, I hope I am not as frightening as all that," Miss Benedict said.

"Perhaps you would like to escort Dr. Carroll into the drawing room to join the other guests?" suggested Mrs. Benedict.

"I would be happy to, Mother," Miss Benedict replied. She took my arm properly, not like Monique, but I found the very propriety somehow more discomfiting. The drawing room was cavernous and created the illusion of seeing those inside as at a distance, in the manner one would observe an acquaintance walking on the other side of a boulevard. The ceiling was at least twelve feet high, ringed with dentil molding. A chair rail divided the walls between the buff-painted bottom third and the deep green brushed silk wallpaper that covered the rest. Another immense crystal chandelier hung from the ceiling, again lit by electricity rather than gas or candle.

What must it be like, I wondered, to live in such luxury?

The guests had divided themselves into two groups, split according to profession. Drs. Mitchell and Agnew stood in a small knot near the door, chatting and sipping champagne with their wives. Mitchell was invariably the first person to be noticed in any gathering. Tall and gaunt, he wore an imposing full gray beard and had more than once been compared to Uncle Sam or President Lincoln. I'd once overheard a student exclaim that to sit in Weir Mitchell's class was "like being taught neurology by Jehovah himself." Agnew, short, bald, and jovial, with a full white mustache, was a perfect match for his short, jovial, white-haired wife.

The Mitchells and the Agnews apparently knew Miss Benedict well, and everyone spoke quite cordially. There was an ease to their manner, a nonchalance that I knew I must perfect if I was ever to fit into this society. I did not say a great deal, preferring to observe, but nor did I embarrass myself.

"Excuse me, please," said Miss Benedict after a few minutes, "but I must introduce Dr. Carroll to our plutocrats." She nudged me gently from the physicians and escorted me toward a group of six people across the room.

The three couples varied greatly in age. Abigail Benedict led me first to a wizened, sallow man named Elias Schoonmaker, who, from the tone of his skin, appeared to be suffering from a liver disorder. His head bent slightly forward when he spoke, eyes rolled upward, as if he were a stern clergyman passing judgment on a sinner. His wife was a squirrel-like woman whose dress and demeanor seemed more suited to the Puritan era.

The second couple was much younger, in their early thirties. The man was tall, full but not fat, clean-shaven, with dark hair parted on the side. He wore spectacles, but they did not obscure a pair of powerful Benedict blue eyes. "It's a pleasure to meet you, Dr. Carroll." He thrust his hand forward. "I'm Albert Benedict." His smile held charm and distance. "I'm a great admirer of your profession. How thrilling it must be to save a life."

I acknowledged the compliment, but there was a serrated edge to Albert Benedict's casual manner that was unsettling, as I assumed it was meant to be.

"The excitement of science," he continued, too enthusiastically, "so much more vital than the idle pursuits."

Miss Benedict's jaw tightened. "My brother is a banker, Dr. Carroll, which is hardly an idle pursuit," she responded immediately. "Of course, it becomes a bit more idle when one works for one's father."

"It is true," her brother agreed amiably. "My father's dynastic aspirations have eased my path to glory, Dr. Carroll. Everyone, I suppose, tries to hitch their wagon to some star or other. Success comes simply in choosing the right star."

I felt a momentary flush as the Professor flashed in my mind. Miss Benedict opened her mouth to respond, but before she could get the words out, her older brother, ever smiling, shot her a brief but frozen glance and broke off the exchange. Albert then introduced me to his small and fragile-looking wife, Margaret, whose elaborate pearl choker served only to make her appear more birdlike. Margaret Benedict was extremely polite, with the perfect diction and practiced gestures that bespoke a finishing school education. They stood together but, instead of appearing as a unit, she and her husband seemed to occupy separate space.

The third man was the most striking of the three. He was no more than fifty, but with a bearing so severe that the upper half of his face appeared not to move when he spoke. Miss Benedict introduced him as Jonas Lachtmann.

"A pleasure to meet you," Lachtmann said to me, managing to sound disagreeable while attempting to be cordial. "And this is my wife, Eunice," he added, gesturing to an attractive but lifeless woman with graying strawberry blond hair.

"Jonas is one of our leading citizens," interjected Abigail Benedict. Whereas she and her brother had carped at each other in sibling irritation, her hostility for this man was conspicuous and profound.

Lachtmann did not reply. Provoked or not, it was obvious that no one outside the family took liberties with Hiram Benedict's daughter.

"And how is Rebecca?" Miss Benedict continued, and then turned to me in explanation. "Jonas' daughter is on holiday in Italy. She is one of my best friends." She exhibited no outward change in demeanor, but I sensed this subject was disturbing to her, although she herself had raised it.

"She is quite well," Lachtmann replied, refusing to warm even to the subject of his child.

"I believe she has gone into the countryside on her way to Rome, my dear," added Mrs. Lachtmann stiffly. "That, at least, is what she intended in her last letter from Florence. I think the mails are probably even less reliable there than in the rest of Italy, which means they are not reliable at all."

"I hope that the travel has not been too oppressive," Albert

Benedict remarked. "Europe can be quite difficult for the uninitiated."

Mrs. Lachtmann smiled, although it fixed on her face as a pinched line. "Our daughter seems to be enjoying herself."

"Please convey my best regards when you next write to her," Benedict said.

"Yes. Philadelphia is not the same without Rebecca. Everyone says so, don't they, Albert?" added Margaret Benedict.

Before he could answer, Miss Benedict interrupted. "As much as I know how much you'd all like to chat with Dr. Carroll," she said, her unease now a bit more apparent, "I'm going to tear him away."

She led me, seemingly with relief, across the room to a table at which a retainer was pouring champagne. It was a thrill to be alone with Miss Benedict. She seemed content to be in my company and I had never met a woman as beautiful or sophisticated—or so desirable.

We each took a glass and, before we drank, she held hers up and said, "To new acquaintances." At the first sip, I recognized that what had just crossed my palate was related to what I had imbibed with Turk two nights earlier in name only.

As we stood off to the side, observing the scene, Miss Benedict informed me that Elias Schoonmaker was a Quaker from Malvern, one of the newly fashionable towns on the Main Line. Schoonmaker had amassed a sizable fortune in supplying lumber to fuel the building boom. He was considering an additional endowment to the university because he was envious of the other Quaker in Baltimore, even though the other Quaker had been dead for almost two decades.

"And Jonas Lachtmann?"

"Jonas is an extremely unappealing man. He is a speculator . . . quite pedestrian. He will make money in anything . . . land, grain, railroads . . . he has no interest in producing something tangible, only in making money from those who do. If there is a new hospital facility, Jonas is sure to find a way to profit by it." Before I could ask, she added, "He disapproves of his daughter's friendship with me. He thinks Rebecca is being inappropriately influenced."

"I am sure he is misguided in that sentiment."

She laughed. It was deep, throaty, and enticing. "My brother and I do like each other, you know," she said, in a quick pivot. "He can be horribly bossy though. Albert thinks he's Father."

"And it is your role to prevent his delusions from progressing."

She placed her hand on my shoulder, a remarkably forward gesture, but one that sent a charge through me. "Why, thank you, Doctor. Your description is perfectly apt."

At that moment, Hiram Benedict and Mrs. Benedict entered with the Professor and another woman, obviously the aforementioned descendant of Paul Revere. Although I learned that she had been considered a "Boston beauty" in her youth, Grace Revere Gross was, in fact, a plain woman, thickset with a broad, square face. Her deep maroon gown was of a hue dark enough to suggest mourning, but not so much so as to render her unapproachable. She had taken the Professor's arm, and seemed enthralled with him in a manner quite transparent in one so recently widowed. At the sight of her father, Miss Benedict removed her hand to her side.

"I'm sure your doctor will like her," she whispered, gesturing toward Mrs. Gross. "She's extremely rich." Before I could protest, she asked abruptly, "Do you dine at Barker's often?"

That this beautiful heiress had frequented the same establishment as I had with George Turk defied belief. "No, it was my first time," I replied, unwilling to expose my lack of sophistication by elaborating further.

Miss Benedict tilted her head for a moment and stood perusing me as if I were a curious tissue sample. Finally, she asked "Are you an art lover, Dr. Carroll?"

"I think I can appreciate a fine painting, but I am scarcely a connoisseur."

"Let me show you something then," she offered, leading

me once more across the vast drawing room out into a hall. I stopped when I noticed a photograph on the wall of three soldiers, one of whom was instantly familiar.

"That is General Grant," I said, and then noticed the tall thin officer next to him in the picture. "Your father?"

"Yes." Miss Benedict nodded. "Father was a colonel. That picture was taken in Virginia just before General Lee's surrender."

"Your father was present at the surrender?" I felt as if someone were squeezing me about the chest. The privileged in peace seemed to be privileged in war as well.

"Father had distinguished himself at Petersburg, so he was promoted to General Grant's staff and served in the honor guard at Appomattox," Miss Benedict replied with obvious pride. Then she grinned, gesturing to the trim officer in the photograph. "As you can see, he did not always appear as he does today."

"My father served with General Grant as well," I blurted before I could stop myself, "although earlier in the war."

Miss Benedict insisted on hearing particulars, so I was compelled to recount the tale of my father's service—although I did so in far less detail than with Turk—his return home, and my birth on July 2, 1863, the first day of the bloody struggle at Gettysburg. When she pressed for more, I explained how the Reverend Audette had noticed my promise in school and had sponsored me, even providing the funds for me to journey to Chicago to study at Rush Medical College.

"Your life could have sprung from Horatio Alger," Miss Benedict remarked, and once again I was uncertain if I was being praised or mocked.

We continued on to a sitting room that opened onto the hall, and Miss Benedict directed my attention to two paintings hanging next to one another on the near wall. The first was a richly detailed depiction of two men in a racing scull, resting over their oars after obvious exertion, drifting down a river that ran through a public park. Looking closely, I could detect the exhaustion in their faces, and it gave them a nobility that was emotive. A broad oak tree grew on the far bank, its rippled reflection perfectly reproduced on the water's surface. Small, flat clouds peppered the sky and, from the golden hues, it must have been late in the day, early autumn perhaps.

The second painting was a portrait of a young woman with fair hair, head and shoulders only, set against a darkened background. Whereas the first work was remarkable for its realism, this canvas used broader swatches of color and was therefore more suggestive. The subject of the portrait was obviously quite beautiful, although the artist seemed to be attempting to capture a resolute mood, a combativeness that I found both jarring and arresting. There was something else, however, something...

"Does the painting shock you, Doctor?" Miss Benedict asked, breaking into my thoughts.

"Who sat for this portrait?" I asked.

"It's Rebecca Lachtmann," she replied. "Jonas' daughter." The disquiet she had exhibited in speaking with her brother and Jonas Lachtmann had returned.

"Rebecca Lachtmann?" I repeated. "Your friend who's on holiday in Italy? Are you sure?" I cursed that the cadavers in the Dead House had been removed before I could get a close look at the young girl.

"Am I sure she's my friend or am I sure she's in Italy?"

"Italy," I said.

"Yes," she replied evenly. "I am quite sure. Do you know her?"

"No," I said, drawing back from the portrait, relieved. "I thought for a moment I might, but I couldn't."

"All right then, Dr. Carroll," said Miss Benedict, "if you are sufficiently recovered, which of these paintings do you prefer?"

"Well, they're quite different," I began, looking at each more carefully, "both excellent in their own way... but I believe I would choose the first."

"Bravo, Dr. Carroll. You have chosen the work of one of America's foremost artists. That was painted by Thomas Eakins."

I knew of Eakins, not for scenes of rowers, but for his infamous medical painting, "The Portrait of Professor Gross," which depicted an actual bone resection performed by Samuel Gross, late father-in-law of the Professor's dinner companion this evening. It was a huge canvas, over six feet wide and eight feet high, and had been completed thirteen years earlier to be exhibited at the national centennial. At the time, the painting had so scandalized Philadelphia for its excessively realistic portrayal of gore and suffering that the overseers of the exposition had refused to display it. The patient in the image was etherized, with a long retracted incision in his left leg, Gross, his hand wet with blood, standing over him holding a scalpel. The patient's mother could be seen cringing pathetically in the shadows. Scandal or no, for its realism and unflinching portrayal of a surgeon at work, "The Portrait of Professor Gross" was now the most well-known painting of its kind in the nation. The artist himself had attended the surgery and had included himself in the composition. Mrs. Gross' late husband was visible in the gallery as well.

I also knew that Thomas Eakins and scandal were easy companions. He had been forced to resign three years ago as director of the Philadelphia Academy of the Fine Arts after he produced a fully nude male model for his female students to draw. After the outcry and his dismissal, the artist had been so distraught that he was sent to the Dakotas for a rest cure by Weir Mitchell himself. Upon his return, he had retired to the seclusion of his studio. His reputation had never fully recovered, although I had heard at the hospital that he had recently been commissioned by some of Agnew's students to create a portrait of their beloved professor.

Eakins' notoriety notwithstanding, I found myself turning from the rowers and once again examining the portrait of the young woman. The eyes on the canvas seemed to be staring directly at me. The overall effect of the subject's unwavering gaze was of slight incongruence, an imbalance that was almost certainly intentional. It made the face at once familiar and distant.

"Who painted this one?" I asked.

"I did," replied Abigail Benedict.

"You? I didn't mean to . . ."

"Not at all." She spoke without a trace of annoyance. "Thomas is one of our great painters. I studied with him, as a matter of fact. As an additional matter of fact, it was he with whom I was dining at Barker's two nights ago . . . when our paths crossed the first time."

I wanted to respond, but could not turn my attention from the painting. I moved closer and then farther away, but the power emanating from the canvas did not diminish with distance. "The portrait is . . ." I searched for the right word.

"Thank you, Dr. Carroll, but I already know it's good."

Suddenly, I realized why I was having a difficult time turning away.

"Eakins replicates reality. You distort it," I offered, "but in doing so, you create an effect more commanding."

"Reality is unimportant." There was an urgency in her voice that I had been unused to in women, but now reminded me of Simpson. "*Truth* is what an artist seeks. This is a wondrous age, Doctor. For the first time in centuries, we are not merely painting differently, but instead introducing an entirely new way to *see*." As she spoke she moved her hands in broad strokes, as if holding a paintbrush to a spectral canvas. "Art, although Thomas is slow to appreciate it, is no longer merely an effort to reflect life, but to interpret it, to find truth under the skin. Even more exciting is that, in doing so, painters have demanded that their audiences no longer be merely passive observers but, through their imaginations, participants in the process."

"Anyone who can exhibit such ardor can hardly be engaged in an idle pursuit," I noted.

Abigail Benedict reached out and her fingertips touched my cheek. The breath went out of me. "That is very sweet of you," she said softly. "Albert doesn't really mean what he says, you know. My brother is actually quite proud of my painting, but is intensely jealous of the freedom."

"The freedom to create?"

"Yes, that. But also the freedom to live. He is the older. He feels his life was preordained. I do much as I please. It is sometimes . . . hard for him."

A bell rang and I heard a servant announce dinner. As we returned to the drawing room, Hiram Benedict appeared at our side. He glanced at me as if I were a flea. Miss Benedict took his arm, much as she had taken mine. They made an unusual pair, the outsized, imperious banker and his bohemian daughter, but, whatever their differences, he obviously adored her and did not think me a suitable escort, even to fill a chair at a dinner for sixteen.

We made our way through a glass-roofed vestibule, which contained an enclosed goldfish pool, into a palatial dining room, even more opulent than the drawing room. Members of the seemingly limitless staff stood along the wall as we entered.

We took our places behind our chairs and I peered down at an array of silver as varied and extensive as instruments in a surgical tray, polished to an even higher sheen. I held out the chair for Miss Benedict. She and I were seated at the far end of the massive mahogany table, near her mother, her brother, and his wife. The Professor sat diagonally across at the other end, next to Hiram Benedict, with Mrs. Gross next to him. Jonas Lachtmann was seated opposite the Professor.

Dinner was a nearly three-hour affair. I believe I witnessed more food at the Benedict home that evening than I would have seen in a month in Marietta. The meal began with fried smelts with tartar sauce, turtle soup, another fish course, and then a meat course, a poultry course, vegetables, and salads, followed by a variety of desserts. There were at least six wines served. Conversation was light and social, as befitted mixed company. Notwithstanding her remark when we had been introduced, Miss Benedict did not ask me about modern medicine, but rather joined in the general banter.

When the desserts were done, Mr. Benedict suggested we adjourn to the drawing room for brandy and cigars, and that the ladies retire to the parlor. Everyone made for their respective destinations, although Miss Benedict made little secret of her distaste for the convention.

Once we had been served our brandies, it did not take the elder Benedict ten minutes to come to the point. "So, Osler," he said, "have you decided for certain to leave us? Or might we be permitted to use our powers of persuasion to keep you in our wonderful city?"

This degree of bluntness would disconcert most, but the Professor was at home with direct conversation.

"I am flattered that you think enough of my abilities to want me to remain," Dr. Osler said. "Whatever decision I make will not be easy or without regret. My associations here have been the most rewarding of my life. But the Johns Hopkins Hospital and eventually the medical school will be unique. The position offered me might easily be described as once in a lifetime."

"We intend extensive improvements and expansion of the facilities here," said Albert Benedict with a nod toward Schoonmaker. "If you remain, your degree of authority will be every bit as great as in Baltimore, perhaps even more so."

"And in a city with far greater resources," added Jonas Lachtmann.

"Will there be women in the student body in Baltimore?" interjected Elias Schoonmaker, and the room fell silent.

"Definitely so," the Professor replied easily. "There will soon be any number of women doctors in America, Mr. Schoonmaker. We must give them the best training available."

Schoonmaker was about to retort, "Not here," when Mr. Benedict spoke over him. "A progressive notion, Dr. Osler. Quite in tune with the times."

"Is it equally progressive to employ drug addicts?" Schoonmaker asked sourly. "It sounds to me that the Baltimore hospital will have no moral standards whatever, Dr. Osler."

It was Agnew who responded. "Dr. Halsted has been cured, Mr. Schoonmaker. He is no longer dependent on drugs and will not be in the future. And let us not forget that he became addicted only because he insisted on experimenting on himself rather than on a patient. Local anesthesia will be a great boon to doctors and patients alike. Halsted was experimenting with a new drug called cocaine, an extract of the coca plant, to find the proper dosage."

"He had no way of anticipating the effect," the Professor added. "Coca leaves have been used for centuries as a medicinal agent, but it has only been in the last decade that we have succeeded in extracting the active agent. The drug continues to exhibit enormous promise. When Dr. Halsted discovered he had become addicted, he immediately checked himself into a hospital. As to his current condition, he has been living with Welch in Baltimore, and Welch has assured me that he has remained in perfect health."

"That's curious," said Mitchell, frowning. "I saw him here in Philadelphia not two weeks ago."

"Impossible," replied the Professor.

"No. Not impossible at all. He was right on Market Street. We spoke briefly, and he told me that he had been doing some private consultations."

"Ah, that explains it then, eh?" The Professor smiled. "I

was under the impression that he had already joined the Hopkins staff full-time."

"Drug addicts are never cured," Schoonmaker insisted. "We don't need men like that. We have many fine surgeons on staff already."

"Like Wilberforce Burleigh?" The words were out of my mouth before I knew it.

"Dr. Burleigh is an exemplary surgeon, young man," Schoonmaker shot back. "He once performed eighteen successful operations in a single day. He also happens to be one of my closest friends."

The Lord must truly be merciful because, at that moment, there was a knock at the door, which then instantly flew open to reveal Abigail Benedict in the doorway. She was wearing a wrap, bright red with long tassels, a blaze of color against the black dress. "If you don't mind, gentlemen, I'd like a walk in the garden. I'm going to borrow Dr. Carroll."

No one objected, least of all me.

Miss Benedict led me through the halls out into a garden at the back of the house. It was thickly set with shrubbery and ornamental trees, pathways meandering through, all surrounded by a high brick wall. The air smelled of pine. A strong late-winter chill was about, but walking in the garden with Abigail Benedict had rendered me insensible to the elements.

She waited until we could neither be seen nor heard by those inside. Flickers of light from the house played across her face. "Fascinating, wasn't it? Welcome to polite Philadelphia society."

"You heard?"

"Elias would have been audible in New Jersey. He loathes modernity, an unfortunate point of view for a man seeking posterity by endowing a hospital. He's never had to be polite to anyone, so he isn't. Dr. Osler is hardly the first person he has repulsed with his behavior."

"An odd choice to persuade Dr. Osler to remain here," I offered, daring to show nothing of the attraction I felt for her.

"My father had little option. Elias insisted on being present. After all, it is his money."

"Lachtmann too seems an ill-considered choice."

Miss Benedict moved to the far side of an elm, even deeper into the shadows. "Jonas can actually be quite effective and even charming when he chooses to be."

"He did not choose to be this evening."

Miss Benedict smiled. Her lips seemed luminescent. "I believe I am in large part to blame. I infuriate him, but he is afraid to cross my father."

"The portrait?"

"No, no. He detests the portrait, of course, but his is a far more powerful dislike." Her bitterness was palpable. "Jonas holds me responsible for the moral dissolution of his daughter. Rebecca does not comport herself to the standards of a proper Philadelphia young lady, at least as defined by her father. That is why she is currently in Italy."

"*Are* you responsible?"

"For her moral dissolution?" Miss Benedict laughed, as if at the absurdity of the term. "Actually, I am not, although it is not outlandish of Jonas to think so. The only difference between me and Rebecca is that I am open about my behavior and she is surreptitious."

I was bewildered. "You mean that Miss Lachtmann was sent to Italy to paint?"

"To paint?" she asked incredulously. "Is that what you think?" She sighed. "No, Dr. Carroll, I do not mean to paint. I mean this." With that, Abigail Benedict put a hand to my cheek, pulled me to her, and kissed me, deeply and rapturously.

She pulled back, studied my face. "You are an interesting man."

"I want to see you again," I said, the words coming out more as a gasp.

"Aren't you moving to Baltimore?" she countered lightly.

"Baltimore is not far," I replied.

"I suppose we shall find out just how far," she said. "But if you wish to see me again, why don't you call on me tomorrow? I'll take you on an outing. Shall we say, about eleven?"

"Yes," I replied eagerly. "By all means. But might I come by at one instead?"

"One? Ah, of course. It's Sunday. You go to church."

"Yes, I do. Perhaps you would care to join me?"

"One will be perfect," she said.

CHAPTER 7

THE FOLLOWING MORNING, I ATTENDED services at the Third Congregational Church. I had chosen this particular flock because of Reverend Powers. Rare among theologians, he mirrored the spirit of impassioned inquiry that I so admired in the Professor. His choice of subjects for sermons would have shocked Reverend Audette, who took a literal view of Scriptural commands, whereas Reverend Powers preferred that his parishioners consider the meaning of any passage they encountered. This enlightened approach to God's teachings seemed more suited to my majority and present surroundings, just as Reverend Audette's had been to my childhood in provincial Marietta.

This morning's sermon was entitled "The Role of Conscience in Christianity." Reverend Powers began by recalling the recent conflagration over slavery and noted that both those who held slaves and those who demanded abolition had cited Scripture to justify their views. After reading passages favored by each side of the question, Reverend Powers closed the Bible and leaned forward on the pulpit.

"They could not both be correct," he observed, "for as Aristotle demonstrated, two opposites cannot exist simultaneously without one giving way. If that is true, then how is the Christian to choose the proper alternative? Does Scripture, which seems to support opposites, become irrelevant in our search?"

He had paused to allow this question to sit with the congregation. Then he intoned firmly, "No! Scripture is never irrelevant to moral questions, not if we employ it correctly. The word of God does not exist merely to allow us to browse until we discover a passage that we may extract to support a conclusion upon which we have already arrived. God's word exists to inspire us to seek the truth within ourselves, to probe our *Christian consciences* in order to determine what is *right*. Human slavery, as every person in this room of God's house knows, *was not right*. It is not then possible that Scripture could justify the enslavement of human beings."

Reverend Powers concluded by instructing each of us to seek God's truth, not just in Scripture, but in our daily lives. "God has embedded within each of us a power for good, knowledge of what is right and what is wrong. And it is only by allowing that which God has granted to flower, to be with us as we make our life decisions, that we may live as true Christians."

I thanked Reverend Powers profusely as I left the church. He could not have known it but his sermon was of particular moment to me. The two aspects of my life that had the most meaning—the spiritual and scientific—were often seen to be in conflict in the modern world, and how the two could be reconciled had become an even greater controversy since the publication of Charles Darwin's stunning work thirty years ago. (That the world owed the work to the decision by the Professor's father to opt for Canada rather than the sea is one of history's ironies.) I was as drawn to empiricism as to God but ever since I had become involved with the science of medicine, I had encountered a surprising degree of prejudice. A shocking number of otherwise intelligent people viewed the pursuit of natural science as an un-Godly act. The misguided Reverend Squires, who had founded the League Against Human Vivisection in his determination to prevent autopsy, was hardly the only example of blind rejection of knowledge in the name of spirituality. There were even some who claimed that disease should not be treated and suffering not relieved, since each represented an expression of God's will, which should not be interfered with by Man.

Reverend Powers' sermon, however, had put a fresh perspective on the problem. When one introduced conscience into the question, it became a simple matter to determine whether or not any human pursuit was consistent with God's dictates. Certainly, one needed look no further than Dr. Osler to find a man of science who lived God's grace by seeking goodness and truth within him.

When I arrived at Rittenhouse Square, one of the large oak double doors was opened by a tall, pale-skinned, funereal servant who evoked a formally dressed Cadaverous Charlie, the Dead House attendant. When I identified myself, he stood aside, allowing for me to enter.

No one else acknowledged my arrival, nor was I ushered into a sitting room to pass the time. Instead, the servant slid away, leaving me to wait, hat in hand, for Miss Benedict to descend the stairs. This she did five minutes after my arrival, bounding down like a young boy. The energy with which she obviously embraced life was intoxicating. Instead of a dress, she wore green trousers, a pale blue man's shirt, and a small cap common to the working classes, a mode of attire only possible if one were wealthy enough to avoid identification to the rank one evoked. I might have been scandalized if not for the knowledge that it was I who was the rustic, and she the cosmopolite.

At the bottom of the stairs, she leaned toward me and kissed me on the cheek. It was in no way a match for the passion of her kiss in the garden, but when she touched me, I felt a dizzy surge from the memory of it.

"Do you have a carriage?" she asked.

I told her a brougham was waiting outside. I had thought

of engaging a hansom, but could not chance appearing unaware of the proper etiquette.

"Why was I left alone in the vestibule?" I asked. "Did your
parents dislike me that much?" The feel of her lips had lingered, as the Cheshire cat's grin.

"Mother actually liked you quite a lot."

"That leaves 'Father,' " I reminded her.

"Father doesn't like anyone," Miss Benedict said as we exited. "You're in excellent company."

When we had mounted the carriage, Miss Benedict gave
the driver an address on Mount Vernon Street, which was almost due north and, I estimated, about twenty minutes ride
from Rittenhouse Square.

"What is on Mount Vernon Street?" I asked.

"Since you expressed such an appreciation for Thomas'
work, I thought you should meet him."

"Thomas? You mean Eakins?"

"I do," she replied. "I thought it would be enjoyable for
you. Doctors likely do not have much opportunity to see the
inside of an artist's studio. Think of this, then, as an operating
room of a different sort. Consider it my contribution to your
education."

"Thank you," I replied. "Perhaps one day I can reciprocate
and allow you to sit in on an autopsy."

"Perhaps," she agreed, not seeming to appreciate that I
had been joking. "Thomas has, you know. Sat in on autopsies,
I mean. He is obsessed with the study of the human form.

"It is a great honor to be invited to the studio," she continued. "But Thomas has been through some extremely trying
times. The dismissal from his position at the Academy affected him quite deeply. . . ."

"It was not entirely without cause," I offered, and then
immediately wished I could have the comment back. But instead of the irritation I expected, Abigail reacted with aplomb.

"I will grant you that Thomas is as naïve as to the sensi-
bilities of polite society as you are," she said. Point taken, I

thought, stung. "He could not believe that removing the loincloth from a male model in the presence of female art students would cause such a fuss."

I decided quickly that even I would not have been that naïve.

"Before you pass judgment," she added, anticipating my reaction, "you should know that after Thomas was dismissed, thirty-eight students resigned in protest. They established the Art Students' League so that they could continue to study with him."

"I'm sure he is a fine teacher," I said.

"He is a brilliant teacher," she replied. "In any event, he was so distressed that your friend Weir Mitchell sent him west for a 'rest cure.' " Miss Benedict frowned. "The quack."

"Mitchell is an excellent physician," I countered, reflexively defending my profession. "There is no man more knowledgeable of nervous disorders."

Miss Benedict sniffed. "He's a quack. He thinks the brain functions like a kidney."

We continued north, passing through an industrial area, then crossing railroad tracks into a residential neighborhood. Overnight, the weather had turned warmer, and the streets were bustling, men, women, couples, and families out for a Sunday stroll on a lovely, early spring afternoon. I could determine from their clothing that the area was prosperous but hardly rich. When we reached Mount Vernon Street, the brougham pulled up at a narrow and slightly shambling redbrick, four-story house that matched the address Miss Benedict had given the driver. As I perused the scene, I noted a solitary man at the end of the street who seemed to be simply enjoying a sunny day. He was hatless, with a handlebar mustache, and wore a short jacket and checked vest, and was made conspicuous by being the only person on the street not in motion.

I descended the carriage first and then extended my hand to help Miss Benedict down, but she ignored it and brushed past me, skipping up the steps. A woman of about forty opened the door. She had a long but pleasant face, a trim figure, and was dressed in a paint-stained gingham dress. I was drawn to her large, quite expressive eyes, which were deeply brown. Her hair was disheveled and she wore no rouge or lip paint.

"Susan!" exclaimed Miss Benedict happily and the two women embraced.

"It's so nice to see you, Abigail," the woman replied, holding Miss Benedict at arm's length and taking her in. "It's been weeks. You look wonderful."

"As do you, Susan," said Miss Benedict. She gestured toward me. "This is Dr. Carroll." I extended my hand as Miss Benedict added, "Ephraim Carroll, I'd like to introduce Susan Macdowell Eakins, Thomas' wife and one of the finest painters in the United States."

Susan Eakins ushered us into the foyer. The hall was long, narrow, and dark, and the entranceway minimally appointed. A parlor was to the left, with walls painted brown and wide-board floor planking rather than tiles, décor more common to farmhouses in Ohio than four-story homes in Philadelphia. The scent of gas mixed with a mustiness that I associated with aging.

On the walls hung five large paintings. Each was in the carefully detailed style of the rowers I'd seen at Miss Benedict's, but only the first four seemed certain to have been rendered by the same hand: a western scene—cowboys, obviously painted during the trip to the Dakotas; two portraits; and finally, over the mantel, a provocative rendering of a group of nude men standing on a large rock ledge that extended over a pond. His dismissal from the Academy of the Fine Arts apparently had not cured Eakins' need to shock.

The last painting, on the far wall, was of two seated women. Its background was darker, yet the faces and hands of both women seemed to have been illuminated by an unseen light from the left. It was similar to others, but at the same time different.

"That is Susan's," remarked Miss Benedict, as I walked forward to examine it. "It's called 'Two Sisters.' Brilliant, is it not?"

Although I agreed heartily that it was certainly an arresting portrait, it did not, I thought, have the power of Abigail Benedict's rendering of Rebecca Lachtmann.

Susan Eakins led us to the stairs, informing us that Eakins was in the studio. As we ascended, Mrs. Eakins told me that her husband had been raised in this house and, upon his return from studies in Europe, had actually engaged with his father in a written contract to lease the studio and receive room and board for twenty dollars per month. His mother had died some years earlier, but Benjamin Eakins still lived here, although the old man spent most his time in his rooms on the second floor.

The studio occupied the entire top floor. Huge windows set on a slant under high ceilings faced north and let in a profusion of light. The lower panels were attached to long push-rods so that they might be opened for ventilation. Although a breeze wafted through the studio, a smell of paint, mildly acrid but agreeable, permeated the large room. Unlike the downstairs hall where paintings were hung for individual effect, here virtually every inch of wall space was covered with paintings, works in progress, and a surprising number of photographs, the vast majority of which were of unclothed men and women. The artist's obsession with the human form had certainly not been understated.

In the center of the room, coming forward to greet us, was Thomas Eakins himself. He was about my height, slim, with chestnut eyes, hair flecked with gray on top, close-cropped without a part, showing more gray at the temples. I guessed him to be in his mid-forties. A thin wisp of beard framed his face and an untrimmed mustache adorned his upper lip. Eakins' features were, in fact, not dissimilar to those of his wife; they might be siblings as easily as spouses. Even upon first glance, there was a kinetic quality about the man that

made him seem to be vibrating even when he was standing
still.

After Miss Benedict made the introductions, he extended
his hand, which was stained with a variety of colors of paint.
"It's a pleasure, Dr. Carroll," he said, his voice incongruously
high-pitched. He glanced down at his fingers. "Don't mind
the paint. It's dry."

I told him how flattered I was to be asked to his studio and
that I had admired "The Portrait of Professor Gross" on my
visits to Jefferson Medical College.

"Thank you," said the painter. "You are more discerning in
that regard than the general public."

"I am sure that the picture will eventually be recognized
for its greatness," I replied.

A thin smile darted across his face. "Perhaps you would be
interested in one of my current projects."

He directed me to a giant canvas in the center of the
room—taller than I and almost twelve feet wide—held in
place by block and tackle strung from the ceiling and supported by framing set about two feet off the floor. A number of
smaller drawings were placed in front, as was a ladder to allow Eakins to reach the top. The painting was of Hayes
Agnew in an operating theater, the portrait that had been
commissioned by his students. The drawings were all preliminary sketches.

"It is not quite finished," said Eakins, "but I think you may
find it instructive."

"Instructive" was hardly adequate—the painting was as-
tonishing. If it was not finished, I could not tell where more
work was needed. The detail was so remarkable that I felt as if
I were present at the surgery. The composition depicted
Agnew, a surgical knife held with thumb and first fingers of
his left hand, supervising a mastectomy. Agnew himself had
stepped back from the operating table and was lecturing to a
packed gallery of students whilst an assistant did the actual
cutting. Another assistant had just lifted an ether cone off the

face of the patient, an attractive young woman with dark hair whose healthy right breast was entirely exposed. Although the realism was remarkable, perhaps even more so than in "The Portrait of Professor Gross," the visible breast, full and shapely, gave the work an undeniable prurience.

"They asked for a standard portrait," said Eakins, "but I thought for seven hundred fifty dollars, they deserved something more elaborate. I only received two hundred dollars for the Gross painting, you know. Each of the students who commissioned this work is recognizable in the gallery."

"We hung it just recently," Susan Eakins said. "Because the canvas is so large, Thomas painted most of it on the floor, either sitting in a chair or cross-legged. I was astounded that he could attain proper proportion at such an angle to the work but, as you see . . ."

"Susie flatters me," said Eakins, clearly pleased to be so flattered.

"More than once, I found him here in the morning, asleep at the foot of the canvas," she informed us.

"It is a remarkable work," I said.

"Thank you," he replied. "It is real. That is what is most important. A photograph would provide no more accurate a rendering. Tell me, Dr. Carroll, can you detect any significance more to your area of endeavor?"

"A comparison with your previous medical painting, you mean . . . of Gross?"

"Precisely correct, Doctor," he said. "So then, what do you see?"

"In the Gross painting," I offered, "both the surgeon and his fellows are wearing street clothes, while here Agnew and his assistants are wearing gowns." It was a lucky thing he hadn't painted Burleigh.

"That is the easy one," said Eakins. "Go on."

"There are only medical personnel near the operating table, which is set off from the gallery by a barrier."

"Yes."

"A nurse is assisting."

"Yes, yes," agreed Eakins with impatience, "but you are missing the most significant difference."

I didn't particularly enjoy being quizzed like a student, but with Abigail standing attentively, waiting to hear my response, I forced myself to think on the point. Then I had it.

"The aseptic instrument tray," I said.

"Indeed," he said. Eakins' intensity was so great that it was fatiguing simply to be in his presence. "Since I painted Gross, immense advances have been achieved in surgical technique, and I wished to portray them. Lister's teachings on asepsis have finally penetrated American medicine. But there is one recent development that I have not included because Agnew has not."

"Surgical gloves," I said, now fully up on the game.

"Exactly. Gloves were introduced earlier this year, but are still experimental. But they will be in common use shortly, I am certain. Halsted is a brilliant man."

"Yes."

"I'd like to paint him one day," mused Eakins.

My notice turned to the hangings on the walls. Nudes in art were quite traditional, but I had been unaware that the practice had been transferred to photography. As I looked a bit closer, I could not help but to observe the identity of one of the models.

"Yes, Dr. Carroll," said Eakins, motioning to a series of photographs of a frontally nude male holding a nude female in his arms, "those are of me. I hope that a man of your learning and sophistication is not repelled by the human form."

I was too busy staring at the photographs and realizing that they were, in fact, of my host, to remark on my sophistication.

"Photography is the future, Doctor," he continued, leading me by the elbow, "although with Eastman's invention I expect a proliferation of amateurish profanities." George Eastman had introduced the box camera the previous year and photography had instantly become a wildly popular avocation.

"Look at this series. I took them about eight years ago." He had stopped at a group of seven photographs of a young woman, completely unclothed, standing either facing the camera, with her back to it, or in left profile. In the frontal poses, she wore a black mask that totally obscured her face. The mask created the sense that the woman had been forced to pose, that her clothes had been removed against her will. To my embarrassment, I found the series arousing, forbidden. But Eakins himself seemed oblivious to the sexual content.

"Look at the musculature," he declared, "how the entire physique changes depending on whether the model stands evenly, favors one leg, has her hands at her sides or on her hips." He spun me toward him. "Anatomical accuracy—that is what we get from photography!"

He continued to prowl along the walls, past array after array. One was of a group of unclothed men on a rock ledge at a pond. I found this photograph disturbing as well, and wanted to look away but, not wanting to appear a prude, I instead commented how precisely he had recreated the scene in his painting.

"Painting life *is* life," Eakins said. "We explore the human condition through truth, not romanticized images. My God, I *despise* the Pre-Raphaelites!"

I did not know what a Pre-Raphaelite was but did not say so. I was aware, however, that while both Miss Benedict and Eakins saw painting as a quest for truth, each saw its realization in opposing artistic styles. Finally, we came to one group of photographs, those of a nude woman from the back and in profile, and I involuntarily stopped.

"Quite correct, Doctor," said Eakins, "it is Susan."

It was indeed—eight photographs of the bared breasts, buttocks, and pubis of my hostess. Her figure was quite magnificent and it was all I could do to hold myself from spinning around and comparing the photographs to Susan Eakins herself. Would nudes of Abigail Benedict be here as well?

Eakins took my stupefaction for awe. "Yes, these are wonderful, are they not?" he said.

"That's enough, Thomas," interposed Susan Eakins, unexpectedly at my side with Miss Benedict. "Allow Dr. Carroll to breathe for a moment." Standing next to a stranger who was looking at nude photographs of her did not seem to bother her in the least. "Have you eaten?" she inquired of me.

Rather than repair downstairs, she offered refreshments at a small table in the studio. We partook of sandwiches, fruit, and lemonade amidst the smell of oil paints, as Susan Eakins recounted how she had first met her husband. She had, it seemed, come to the 1876 exposition expressly to see "The Portrait of Professor Gross." Although the painting was ultimately consigned to an army hospital, she had seen it in a gallery, and decided she would study with whoever had been brilliant enough to create it. She enrolled at the Academy the following week, and eight years later, she and Eakins were married.

"I'm told you found my behavior with female students at the Academy somewhat questionable," Eakins said abruptly. Miss Benedict had obviously mentioned the remark I had made in the coach. "It's quite all right, you know. I would feel the same in your place. . . . What a harebrained thing to do. That Eakins must live in the ether. Well, Doctor, I studied with Jean-Léon Gérôme in Paris, one of the most renowned painters in France. Do you know what he is most famous for? Slave auctions—painting nude women surrounded by leering men before being taken to what I believe is referred to as 'the fate worse than death.'

"The real issue, of course, is not my judgment, but this country's commitment to Puritanism. It stifles creativity everywhere. Can you really tell me that the Neanderthals surrounding medicine are any less backward than those surrounding art? I simply choose to ignore them. I hope for the sake of the sick that you do as well."

He was correct, of course. The Professor would never allow Revered Squires or Elias Schoonmaker to suppress his researches, so why should Eakins allow the trustees of the Academy of the Fine Arts to dictate to him? Still, the pursuit of science was intrinsically moral—art was more questionable.

Eakins' argument also made me more curious about the true nature of the relationship of these three people. Their mutual ease and understanding might merely be friendship—how easily wealth mixed with art—but might also be something more. There was little reason to believe that they would hold more inhibitions in their sexual behavior than they had exhibited anywhere else in their lives. I tried to feel disapproving, but their mode of living was magnetic. What must it be like to live in almost total freedom? Unfettered by society's conventions, where the very definition of morality is of one's own making? I had always been taught that such a way of life would lead inexorably to wickedness, yet I felt a draw to this group that could easily overpower reason. Part of that draw, a terrifying large part, was the longing I was developing, deep and desperate, for Abigail Benedict.

"I'd like to show you another canvas," Eakins said, urging me out of my seat and directing me to the far end of the studio. "I painted this one seven years ago, but I am sending it to Paris to be submitted to the Salon. I'd like your opinion."

Before me was a painting of an elderly man wearing glasses, seated at a table, leaning over a large sheet of writing paper, completely absorbed in forming characters on the page. The subject was at once intense and serene.

"It is arresting," I offered.

"Yes," agreed the painter. "It is called 'The Writing Master.' The model is my father. As you can see, I am capable of painting clothed figures." He gestured back to the table. "But come, Doctor. We must talk."

After we were again seated, the painter, now quite calm, asked softly, "I wonder, Dr. Carroll, if we might ask your assistance in a matter of some importance?"

"Of course," I replied. "I am at your service."

"Thank you, Ephraim," said Miss Benedict. She reached out and squeezed my hand. "I knew you would help."

Excited as I was to feel Miss Benedict's hand on mine, the gesture left me wondering just what I was about to be asked to do. Eakins noticed my expression and laughed easily. "Don't worry, Doctor, it is nothing nefarious, although there is some delicacy involved. We would ask your discretion."

"I believe I may be trusted with a confidence," I replied. This explained the invitation to the studio. There was undoubtedly a professional question in the offing—drug addiction or venereal disease, most likely—but I waited for Eakins to tell me what his predicament might be. I was stung a bit at Miss Benedict's lack of candor, but nonetheless pleased with the prospect of demonstrating professional sophistication in a room where I lacked sophistication in every other way.

But instead of the painter, it was Miss Benedict who spoke. "It concerns Rebecca Lachtmann . . . the subject of the portrait I showed you last evening."

"Is Miss Lachtmann having a medical problem in Italy?" I asked, taken aback.

"Not exactly," Miss Benedict replied. Her face, which had reflected only unease the night before, now showed grave concern, fear. "Rebecca does have a . . . situation . . . but she is not, I fear to say, in Italy. She has not, as far as I know, ever been to Italy."

"Where is she then?"

"She is here in Philadelphia."

"Her parents believe her to be overseas, however?"

"Yes," said Eakins.

"Why, then, are you seeking my assistance?" I asked, bewildered.

"Rebecca's problem is of a very personal nature," Eakins offered. "She did not want her parents to know . . . her father can be an extremely difficult man. . . ."

"Ephraim has met Jonas," Miss Benedict interjected somberly.

"So, Dr. Carroll, you know what we mean," Eakins continued. "Rebecca made elaborate plans to deceive her parents into believing that she was touring Italy when, in fact, she was in the city seeking assistance. But now we have lost touch with her."

So I was not being asked for medical expertise at all. This was a far more pedestrian errand. "You wish me to make inquiries to see if she is a patient somewhere under another name?"

"That certainly," replied Eakins. "But also if she has sought treatment through less traditional channels."

"I am not aware of less traditional channels," I replied coldly.

"You must help us, Ephraim. Help me," said Miss Benedict, her voice just above a whisper. "But please do not ask for more information. There are issues of personal intimacy involved."

I had not come here to be enlisted in an intrigue, especially one initiated by moral weakness. Moreover, I would not know where to begin. Rebecca Lachtmann might be anywhere. She was, in actuality, unlikely to be a patient in any hospital, at least in Philadelphia. Anyone of her description would attract attention no matter what name she used. Yet if I refused to offer assistance, I was certain that I would not see Abigail Benedict again.

"I am not sure how much I can be of help," I replied, "but I will be pleased to do all that I can. Do you have a sketch?" I glanced about at the walls. "Or a photograph?"

"I have a photograph," said Eakins. "You will use it discreetly, of course."

"I understand the nature of your request," I replied evenly.

Eakins nodded, stood up, and walked across the studio to a large case with many drawers. He pulled open one of the drawers, riffled through the material inside, and extracted a plate. I wondered of what nature the photograph he returned with might be, but Eakins was no fool. The print, although slightly grainy, was of only the head and shoulders of a beautiful young woman with light hair. She was recognizable as the woman in the painting I had viewed at Miss Benedict's, but only because I had been aware of that fact in advance. More disturbing, however, was another resemblance, one that I had discounted when I had been assured that the subject of the portrait was alive and well in Italy.

I studied the photograph carefully and, though the similitude was strong, there was no way to be positive that this was the woman I had seen in the Dead House. *Distrust coincidence,* the Professor always said. It would have been foolish to conclude that a cadaver I had glimpsed for a second or two in an ice chest and a photograph or a portrait that had intentionally distorted reality were all of the same person. But neither could I definitively conclude that the three pieces of data were unrelated. *Distrust coincidence, perhaps, but do not discount it.* I must approach this problem as any other—accept coincidence only as a working hypothesis, and then test that hypothesis until it is disproved. Or not disproved. "Less traditional channels." Perhaps. It seemed that I might be able to be of some assistance after all.

As Miss Benedict and I reemerged on Mount Vernon Street, the sun was lower in the sky and a coolness had once again set in. The streets remained busy, although most of the families had disappeared, replaced by couples. As we were about to enter the brougham, I observed a mustachioed man in a derby. He was, I was certain, the same man who had been loitering about on our arrival, but he now wore an overcoat and was at the opposite end of the street from where he had been taking the air previously. What's more, he had been joined by a second man, similarly attired, and they seemed engaged in conversation. When we were seated in the coach, I looked out the window, but the corner at which the two men had been standing was now deserted.

"I'm very grateful to you, Ephraim," Miss Benedict said.

"Thank you," I replied, but did not turn to face her.

She once more placed her hand on top of mine. "Is there something the matter?" she asked.

"You did not need to pretend an attraction in order to enlist my aid. I would have been happy to help in any case."

Miss Benedict did not withdraw her hand. "Is that what you think?"

"Would you think differently in my case?"

"Perhaps not," she admitted. "But you are mistaken all the same."

"Are you saying that your need for someone in the medical profession to help you find your friend has no relevance?"

"I can understand your suspicions," she said simply. "But they are without foundation."

"And what about Eakins? Do you deny that you have feelings for him as well?"

"You are asking if I am involved with Thomas. The answer to that question is no. I was at one time, however. I will not deny it. I have been involved with a number of men. It is not uncommon in my circles, Ephraim. Does that make you care for me less?"

Now she had asked it. I felt my training, everything that I had learned about propriety, the contrivance of her behavior, pushing at me, but after only a moment's uncertainty, I pushed back. "Nothing could make me care for you less," I answered.

CHAPTER 8

INSTEAD OF PROCEEDING DIRECTLY TO the wards, I waited for Turk in the changing room the next morning. That he had evaded discussing the cadaver in the ice chest during our evening out together simply added to my resolve not to be put off again. Dr. Osler's reaction must certainly have a rational explanation, but the same might not be true of Turk. I must discern whether a link existed between him and Rebecca Lachtmann. It had been three days since Turk had last been present at the hospital; his illness should have run its course. My determination to be firmer in my inquiries turned out to be moot, however, when again Turk did not appear.

I immediately informed the Professor, and he was concerned as well. He had also expected Turk to arrive, weakened perhaps, but on the road to recovery.

"Perhaps I should visit his lodgings," I suggested, "and see if he needs our assistance."

"I'm sure that it won't be necessary to disturb him. He knows well enough to seek assistance if he needs it. . . . No, by God, you're right, Carroll. We can't take the chance."

I was relieved that the Professor agreed. "Do you happen to know where Turk resides?" I asked.

The Professor looked at me blankly. "I thought you did."

"No," I said. "On the one occasion I met him socially, he came to call for me, but I'm sure I can obtain his address in the records office."

The records office was located, appropriately it seemed, in the basement. After explaining the circumstances, I inquired of the chief clerk, a Mr. McCann, as to what information he possessed on Dr. Turk. McCann informed me the records were confidential, and I informed him that I was acting for Dr. Osler. He glowered, but then retired to a cavernous file room in the rear, emerging about five minutes later carrying a large folder.

"Turk, you say?" he asked, slapping the folder on the countertop and beginning to leaf through its contents. "George Turk?"

I assured him that was the proper name.

"No Turk here," he insisted, as he riffled through the last of the sheets of paper.

"There must be," I said. "George Turk has been on the staff of this hospital for at least six months."

McCann leaned on one elbow. He was a robust man of about fifty, with a full beard and a large, bulbous nose. "This here"—he gestured at the file—"is a record of everyone who works at this hospital. And there's no George Turk."

How could Turk have worked here and not . . . Then I had an idea. "Mr. McCann," I asked politely, "are pay records kept in a separate file?"

He shook his head. "Not kept in a file at all. We keep pay records in a *ledger*." He emphasized the final word as if he were talking to a child.

"Might I trouble you to check the *ledger* then?"

McCann sniffed. "No need to be smart about it, Doctor." He gathered up the file and once again disappeared into the back room, reemerging eventually with a large ledger book. This he placed on the countertop and swung open, all with great affectation.

"Now, we're looking to see if we paid a Turk, George Turk, who doesn't work here," he said, leafing through the pages, quite amused with himself. "Turk." Then he stopped and a look of amazement crossed his face. "Why, I'll . . . here it is."

For McCann, an inconsistency in the records caused him as much consternation as the Professor would experience if he autopsied a cadaver and discovered no heart.

"Let me see," I said, and McCann swung the ledger around. Listed in the entries for each week was "George Turk, M.D.—$8," the last being the previous Wednesday. It pleased me, I confess, to learn that I received two dollars more per week, although I suspected the main sources of Turk's income were such that they would not be listed in the book.

"So, Mr. McCann," I asked, "how is it that Dr. Turk is being paid eight dollars per week if he does not work here?"

A deflated McCann ran his fingers through his beard, tugging as if in self-reproach. "I don't know. Someone must have removed his sheet from the file."

"And there are no duplicates?"

"Never had a need," he admitted.

"So that means, I take it, that there is no official record of Dr. Turk's particulars . . . where he resides, for example?"

McCann shook his head. "None." He was still perplexed. "I don't understand how this could have happened. We are so careful. Perhaps it has simply been mislaid."

"Perhaps," I replied. "Who adds or removes records?"

"Just me and two assistants," he replied, gesturing to two middle-aged men wearing eyeshades sitting at desks across the room. "Let me ask."

McCann engaged in an animated discussion with each of the two and then returned. "No one knows anything about it. They'd have signed for it if they'd taken a record out."

I thought for a moment. "Mr. McCann, is the office kept locked?"

McCann nodded. "Every night, after we close."

"Is the office ever empty during the day?"

"Never, except sometimes at lunch."

I assured McCann that the loss must certainly have been an oversight and the records would surely turn up, then I thanked him for his help, and left. There was nothing further to be gained in this office nor, I was confident, would Turk's records ever be seen again. Whoever had removed the document had obviously wanted to keep Turk's personal information from anyone in the hospital, and the most likely person to have that motivation was Turk himself.

At seven-fifteen that evening, I arrived at Barker's. The man in the striped vest and boater who had seated Turk and me the previous Thursday was once again at his post near the entrance. In my most affable tones, I wished him a good evening and asked if he remembered my visit with that excellent customer, the well-known bon vivant, Mr. George.

The man eyed me with equal parts cynicism, suspicion, and innocence. "We get lots of folks in here, friend. You think I remember everybody?"

"Come, my good man," I said cheerfully. "You and Mr. George clearly knew each other well. You called him by name."

"You're mistaken," the man said.

"Perhaps you are correct," I agreed, and then removed a dime from my vest pocket. I had seen from Turk what excellent service could be elicited from some well-placed expenditures.

"What do you want with him?" asked the man.

"I am a friend and coworker," I replied. "He has been absent from work and I fear he is ill."

The man held out his hand and I dropped the dime in it. "So," he asked, "what do you want from me?"

"I was wondering if you knew where his lodgings were."

The man in the boater emitted a sound very much like a snort. "I thought you said you was his friend. Don't you know where he lives?"

"If you wish me to be the one answering questions, I would ask for my coin back," I said.

The man deposited the ten cents in his trousers. "Don't know," he said tersely.

"No idea?" In truth, I suspected that for a man as reclusive as Turk, Barker's would be a dead end, but I was forced to make the attempt.

"None."

I then asked the man how often Turk patronized the establishment, who he generally dined with, and if he seemed to have any acquaintances among the staff. I learned only that Turk ate at Barker's at least once per week, either alone or in the company of women, and that he did not seem to have had any intercourse with employees beyond general banter.

Perhaps I might succeed in establishing a link between Turk and Rebecca Lachtmann without speaking to Turk at all. I removed the photograph that Eakins had given me from my jacket. "Is this one of the women he dined with?"

The man looked at the photograph carefully with what seemed to be surprise. "No," he said. "One this pretty, I'd remember. Mr. George went in for the . . . well, more obvious, if you know what I mean."

I did indeed. I thanked him, left, and made for the Front Street Theater. It was still early, so I had no doubts that if Monique and Suzette had arrived, I would find them unengaged.

I had little trouble gaining entrance backstage, this time paying only five cents and, for no additional cost, was told by the grizzled sentinel at the stage door that the dancers all shared a single dressing room. I walked down a darkened, musty corridor to the room he had indicated and knocked on the door.

"Who's that?" yelled a voice from inside. "Open the damn door and come in."

I continued to stand in the hall, certain that the woman who had called out assumed another woman was outside. After a few moments, when no one came to the door, I knocked once more, this time loudly announcing that a man was waiting.

"I don't care if you're a horse," a voice yelled back. "I'm not getting up."

Having no choice in the matter, I tentatively opened the door, although not sufficiently to allow me to see inside. "Is Monique or Suzette here?" I called.

I heard another voice, distinctly Monique's. "It's Ephie," she said happily.

A second later, the door swung upon. Standing before me was a tall woman with red hair, wearing a thin silken robe that hung open, revealing the undergarments beneath it. The woman I gazed upon bore almost no resemblance to the lithe, sexual dancer I remembered from the other evening save for her eyes, which shone the same striking green as before. Her skin was pocked and puffy, and there were lines visible around her eyes and mouth. Mostly, however, she wore an air of decrepitude, as if she were a ramshackle tenement that might collapse in a strong gust of wind.

Monique seemed oblivious to the distaste I felt looking upon her, and reached out and threw her arms about my neck, her breasts pressing against me. She began to kiss me, but I pushed her away with disgust, astounded that this woman had been the object of sexual fantasies just days before.

I required information, however, so I could not simply turn and leave. "I'm sorry," I said to her. "I'm not in the habit of behaving in such a fashion in public."

Monique turned about and addressed the others in the room. "Ephie here is a shy one," she trilled. "I think that just makes him cuter, don't you think so, girls?"

There were six of them, including Suzette, all in approximately the same stage of undress. One of the women, hard-looking with straw-colored hair, had her breasts exposed, but she made no move to cover herself. Instead, she stared intently in my direction in a kind of dare. The effect was more repugnant than arousing.

"I need to speak with you," I said to Monique, backing into the hall. "It is a matter of some urgency."

Monique had enough experience with men to sense lost ardor, and her expression instantly went cold. She pulled her robe shut and stepped into the hall. "What is it?" she demanded.

"I need to find George."

"Why ask me?"

"Because you know him well ... well enough to come along the other night."

"What do you want with Georgie?"

"I think he may be ill. Have you seen him?"

"Ill, is it? Sure it isn't about money?"

"Certainly not," I replied with umbrage.

Monique found my indignation amusing. "We're not usually in the habit of discussing our acquaintances, but just for you, I'll tell you that we ain't seen Georgie since last Thursday, when he was with you."

"I will need to see him at his lodgings then."

"What's this really about?" she asked.

I tried a different tack, injecting a note of bluff. "I think he is in some trouble of which he is not aware. I need to alert him as soon as possible."

"Alert him?" she said. "You mean you want to help Georgie and you want me to help you help him? You and me ... just a couple of Good Samaritans?"

Whatever else she was, this woman was in no way stupid. "No. Not Good Samaritans. But he surely may be in some trouble, and he needs to speak with me as much as I need to speak with him. Do you know where I might find him?"

Monique mulled this over. "What's in it for me?"

"Nothing," I said with finality. "But if I do not get in touch with him and he finds out that you withheld his whereabouts,

I believe he will be none too pleased. In that case, I think you will have the opportunity to ask the same question of him."

Monique nodded. "Well, well, you're sure a surprise . . . Ephraim."

"Why? Because I did not allow you to ruin me?"

"Ruin you?" she sneered. "Ha! That's a laugh. That's what you men always think. You got it backward. It ain't women like me who ruin you, it's men like you that ruined me."

"Whatever you say," I replied. "Are you going to tell me where George resides or not?"

"I don't know," she said sourly. "Suzette might." She ducked back into the dressing room and emerged a minute or two later. "She's never been to his place either, but she said one night she heard him tell a coachman to take him to the Barchester Hotel."

"One last thing," I asked. "George's 'getting rid of' services . . . were they well known around town?" Perhaps it was he who had disposed of the body.

"No more than they had to be, I expect, although anyone interested enough could find out. And lots of us girls were plenty interested."

Abortion! Not disposal. Not drugs or venereal disease. Detestable! If this was true, Turk was a more monstrous character than anyone had suspected. None of this was demonstrably connected to either the cadaver or to Rebecca Lachtmann, of course. If only we had performed that autopsy.

"Thank you," I said to her, endeavoring not to give anything away.

Monique and I stood for a moment, looking at one another. The woman before me had ceased to be either the object of desire of the previous Thursday or the object of contempt of a few minutes before. Instead, I saw her for what she truly was—a pitiful creature, forced to scratch out subsistence plying the scant resources Providence had granted her, and even they were fast becoming exhausted. Five years from now, perhaps a good deal sooner, they would have deserted her entirely and her life would turn increasingly bleak. I realized that one of my greatest achievements since leaving Ohio, the most important product of all my study and self-betterment, had been to procure the means to a comfortable, even prosperous, middle age.

Monique seemed to sense the honesty between us as well. She smiled ruefully and said, "It's all right, Ephie. You take care. Be careful of Georgie. He's a bad one to cross." She patted me on the cheek. "And remember, if you ever get tired of society women, pop on down here."

"I will," I promised, although we both knew that we would never see each other again.

I arrived at the Barchester Hotel at about nine-fifteen. It was on East Cumberland Street, about one half mile northeast of Temple University, in a neighborhood that was neither seedy nor prosperous, prominent nor notorious. The hotel's anonymity seemed ideally suited to a man who wished to keep even the most fundamental details of his life hidden.

I entered the small lobby and strode across an aging black and white tile floor. The clerk, an indifferent, scowling lout, awaited me, arms braced on the front desk, aware that I was not there to take a room. I asked for George Turk and described him, lest he used an alias even here, but the clerk claimed that no one of that name or description was registered. When I attempted to pursue my inquiries, he shrugged and turned away.

I had succeeded first with bribery, and then with bluff. This man, I thought, would be far more susceptible to the latter. "Before I go, sir," I said, "I will simply inform you that I am a doctor. I am attempting to locate Mr. Turk on an extremely grave matter involving a prominent family in this city. If death results from my inability to contact him, the police are certain to become involved and they may reasonably be expected to take a dim view of anyone who impeded my inquiries."

The clerk turned about. He stood gazing at me with

rodentlike eyes, his expression stolid. I feared my gambit had failed, but then he asked, "Prominent family? Which prominent family?"

"I am not at liberty to say, and you'd best hope that you do not have cause to find out."

The clerk's forehead wrinkled and I could see that the turn in the conversation was taxing his limited reason. "Turk's in trouble then?" he asked. Hearing him use the name told me that I was getting closer.

"Not as yet, but he will be if I cannot locate him quickly. I might add that I believe he will be none too pleased to learn that you prevented me from contacting him. As I suspect you know, he is a dangerous man."

I had no specific evidence, of course, that Turk was dangerous, short of Monique's assertion, but when the clerk began to nod involuntarily, I knew that she had not been speaking idly.

"He doesn't stay here," the clerk said, "but I take messages and deliver them to his rooms. Nothing out of sorts, mind you, but Mr. Turk is a man who likes his privacy."

"You are paid for this service, of course," I said.

"He ain't my kin," the clerk replied, by way of explanation.

"And where do you take the messages?" I asked. When the clerk hesitated, I slammed the flat of my hand upon the counter. "Hurry up, man, or no one will have any privacy to value, least of all you."

"All right," he grunted. "Mr. Turk has rooms on Bodine Street . . . that's three blocks east of here and two north, just this side of the railroad tracks. He rents from a Mrs. Fasanti. She's a widow. It's not a rooming house proper, but this way Turk figures no one will come looking there."

"Thank you." I nodded curtly. "I do not believe I need to tell you that if word of this gets out, it will go badly for you."

"Don't worry, Doc," said the man with a vinegary smile. "I'm not about to go bragging about talking to you."

I followed the clerk's directions and in ten minutes found myself in front of Mrs. Fasanti's, a brick-fronted row house that was scarcely more impressive than Mrs. Mooney's. I was surprised that Turk's lodgings, even in this part of town, were not more generously appointed.

I walked up the steps and knocked on an aging wooden door, upon which the varnish had raised up and begun to peel. It swung open almost instantly to reveal a haggard woman with graying hair, thick glasses, and an expression that showed both suspicion and fear. She did not offer a greeting or ask what was my purpose in calling, but stood silently, waiting for me to speak.

"I am looking for George Turk," I told her.

"Who are you?" the woman replied coldly.

"My name is Carroll. I am a doctor and a friend of Turk's and I need to see him. Is he in?"

"Friend?" she said, suddenly excited. "A doctor? Come on, then. Quick. He's up here." She beckoned me inside, gesturing with urgency, and then turned and led me to a flight of stairs. "He's in a mighty bad way, Doctor," she said over her shoulder, "but George didn't let me call no one."

We reached the second-floor landing and, as we turned left and walked down a narrow hall, I was hit by a distinctive acrid odor. "How long has he been ill?" I asked.

"Three days," she told me. "It's been hell."

The smell got stronger as we neared the end of the hall. She had placed a rolled towel on the floor in front of the door to Turk's rooms in an attempt to keep the odor from permeating the rest of the house. As soon as the woman opened the door, the stench hit me.

As accustomed as I was to dealing with the sick and the terminally ill, at the sight of Turk lying motionless on his bed, I recoiled. In four days, he had aged decades. His eyes were vacant; his skin hung on a shrunken body. His mouth drooped open, and he seemed insensible, with breathing extremely labored. His appearance, coupled with the overpowering odor of diarrhea, made diagnosis simple—here were the classic symptoms of cholera.

I spun on Mrs. Fasanti. "Why is this man not in a hospital?"

She shook her head quickly, looking terrified. "Do you think I wanted to keep him here . . . cleaning up and emptying chamber pots? He wouldn't let me call no doctors. He told me they was gonna kill him."

"Kill him? Who? The doctors? Whatever are you talking about?"

"I don't *know,*" she insisted. "But he wouldn't let me call no doctor. He wouldn't let me tell nobody."

"But he paid you well," I said harshly.

"Of course," she answered. "Do you think I was gonna do this for free? I was scared of catching it myself, but he told me as long as I got rid of everything and kept my hands clean, that I'd be all right."

"And you believed him?"

She stared at me hard. "Well, he is a doctor hisself, isn't he?"

At that, I heard a sound and turned to the bed. Turk was calling, "Carroll," but in a voice so soft and grating that I could hardly recognize my own name. I went to the bed and could see he was trying to speak, but his tongue was swollen and his lips cracked and peeling from advanced dehydration. Without warning, his arm flashed out and I felt a clawlike grip on my wrist. "Carroll," he groaned once, but as he tried to form another word, he stiffened and then fell back to the pillow. I knew at once that he was dead.

CHAPTER 9

EVERY SUSPECTED CASE OF CHOLERA had to be reported, so after confirming the lack of pulse or breathing and covering poor Turk's face, I had no choice but to inform the police.

Once a scourge that killed millions across the civilized world, cholera had largely been brought to heel by modern science. Although much of the public still blindly feared contagion, since Robert Koch identified the *Vibrio cholerae* bacillus in Egypt six years before, doctors had learned that the disease is transmitted only by consuming food or water contaminated with high concentrations of the bacteria. A high concentration is required since *Vibrio cholerae* is acid-sensitive and most of the organisms are destroyed in the stomach before reaching the intestines. Little are most people aware that they ingest small amounts of *Vibrio cholerae* almost every day. Transmission can be prevented through proper sanitation. Washing thoroughly with carbolic soap after handling contaminated material also eliminates any possibility of acquiring or transmitting the disease.

As such, I knew Mrs. Fasanti was no threat to others, so I instructed the woman to report Turk's death to the nearest precinct house personally. With respect to Turk's assertion to his landlady that someone had been out to do him in, I assured her that it was likely delirium brought on by his illness and, in any case, there was no reason to introduce the notion of foul play into the proceedings. She readily agreed, more than willing to keep the story as bald as possible.

Before I allowed Mrs. Fasanti to leave, however, I required some information. "How much did he pay you not to call the authorities?"

"I won't give it back," she sputtered indignantly. "Not with what I had to do these past three days."

"If you do as I say," I replied, "no one will ask for your money, and the police will leave you alone. Now, how much did he give you?"

Mrs. Fasanti looked to the floor. "Two hundred."

"Two hundred dollars?" A fortune. Any lingering doubt that Turk was involved in illicit activity was dispelled. "Did he ever have visitors here? Anyone at all?"

"Almost never," Mrs. Fasanti replied. "He didn't want nobody to know where he lived. I'm surprised he told you."

" 'Almost never'? Who came here?"

"There was an elderly gent who came once."

"Elderly?" I asked. "How elderly? What did he look like?"

"He wasn't *real* old. Had a mustache and a beard. Funny kind o' glasses." She gestured across her hair. "Kinda thin on top."

It occurred to me that the description, cursory as it was, corresponded to the man with whom I had seen Turk argue at The Fatted Calf.

"Anyone else come here?"

"A couple of girls," admitted Mrs. Fasanti.

I showed her the picture of Rebecca Lachtmann, but the woman shook her head. I tried one last question. "Tell me, Mrs. Fasanti, did Turk send word to the hospital last Friday that he was ill?" If he had not, how could the professor have known of his "gastrointestinal ailment"? Although it was likely delirium, Turk had, after all, told her that a doctor was out to kill him and, had Dr. Osler been in my place, he would certainly have asked the same question.

She thought for a moment and then nodded. "Yeah. He had me send a boy."

"When? What time of day? Was it early?"

"Real early," she confirmed to my relief, although I had not seriously suspected the answer would be otherwise. "He didn't get home until after three the night before," the woman went on, "and he was already sick. Woke me up comin' in. Told me to send someone first thing."

Three? Turk had dropped me at Mrs. Mooney's no later than one. I sent Mrs. Fasanti on her way to the local precinct house and, as soon as she had gone, I pulled back the sheet and conducted a cursory postmortem examination on my former colleague. Poor Turk had been ravaged, the agony of his last days etched on his face. The immediate cause of death certainly appeared to be extreme dehydration. For the condition to become sufficiently acute to kill in such short time, cholera was the most obvious culprit.

As far as I was aware, there had been few cases of the disease in recent months, and those that had occurred were largely confined to the waterfront district, where Turk, I knew, was no stranger. Still, with cholera now a far less prevalent threat, what if Turk's pronouncement to his landlady had *not* been delirium? It certainly no longer came as a surprise that Turk might have made enemies fierce enough to want him dead. But a doctor? It would be a simple matter to determine whether the death was as it seemed with an autopsy. Formad, pathologist or no, might be squeamish at dissecting a possible cholera case, but the Professor would leap at the opportunity. I completed my examination, scrubbed my hands in the basin with the bar of carbolic soap that Mrs. Fasanti had purchased at Turk's direction, and then turned my attention to his possessions.

I was not sure what I was looking for—a notebook, perhaps, or other material to indicate the source of his extensive funds, or perhaps some piece of trivia that would establish a link with Rebecca Lachtmann. I had never had cause to search anyone's rooms before, and I feared to be too obvious in my rummaging with the police on the way. I looked briefly through his desk and the large oak armoire that held an extensive and costly wardrobe, but could discover nothing untoward. In the sitting area was a bookcase filled with the works of Greek philosophers, particularly Plato. There were also an impressive number of medical books, as well as Bancroft's ten-volume history of the United States. Here, away from the fleshpots, Turk apparently engaged in intellectual pursuits. As with Monique, I felt a melancholy that came with intimate revelations, in this case the portrait of a talented, highly intelligent, and in many ways admirable man, done in by bitterness and greed.

Three grim, burly, uniformed police officers arrived soon after, with a wagon to transport Turk's body to the destination on the Blockley grounds with which he had been all too familiar in life. It was a small matter to avoid controversy with the authorities. I merely told the officers the truth about missing Turk at the hospital, seeking him out at the professor's suggestion, the mislaid records, and my subsequent conversations with his acquaintances. As I promised, I saved Mrs. Fasanti any unpleasantness by noting that Turk was a doctor and that she had acted under his direction, isolating the area where the illness was located and following sanitary procedures elsewhere in the house. They were none too pleased to have been called only after the fact, but they did not feel competent to challenge one physician discussing the behavior of another.

The policemen wrapped Turk in a clean sheet that they procured from the landlady, avoiding all but minimal contact with the body. Then they hefted the bundle and carried it out the door. Given what I had heard from Monique, I felt a far deeper wrenching watching Turk's corpse removed than I would have thought possible. I asked Mrs. Fasanti how she intended to dispose of his belongings. She reacted to the question with annoyance.

"I woulda sold them," she maintained, "but who's gonna want them now? I'll just have to pack the lot and leave it for the junk man."

"I would like the books," I said.

"Sure," she said, brightening. "I'll let you have them all . . . for just . . . ten dollars."

I glared at the repulsive woman. "I had a different price in mind."

"Yeah?" Her eyes narrowed at the prospect of haggling. "How much?"

"Nothing," I replied.

"Noth . . ."

"I think that my saving you the additional attention of the police ought to be payment enough. If you disagree, however—"

"Take them," she snapped. "They ain't worth nothing anyway."

"Yes," I said. "I'm sure that's true." I told her, if the police approved, I would send a boy to fetch them. Then, still quite shaken but feeling that, in taking the books, I would salvage something of the memory of their owner, I sadly left for home.

CHAPTER 10

AS SOON AS I ARRIVED at the hospital the following morning, I sought out the Professor and told him what had transpired at Turk's. As with the police, I related the events precisely as they had occurred, but omitted any mention of Turk's possible activities as an abortionist or of Rebecca Lachtmann. The Professor, after all, had reacted strangely at the sight of the cadaver in the ice chest as well.

"Kill him? You said he thought someone was trying to kill him?" the Professor asked incredulously. "That's why he didn't seek help? What could possibly have made him think that? Must have been off his head. But anything's possible, I suppose. Cholera is a bit out of the ordinary as well. Where would someone with Turk's knowledge of the disease have contracted cholera?"

I noted Turk's attraction to the underside of Philadelphia and his habit of frequenting establishments near the waterfront.

"That accounts for it, I'm sure," the Professor replied. "Have we had any other cases?"

"The police said that this is the first in some weeks, but isolated outbreaks are common near the docks."

"Hmm. Bad luck for Turk then, eh? Too bad. I'm going to miss him. He had a first-rate mind, Turk did, and I continued to hope that he would begin to apply himself more seriously. Frankly, Carroll, I was hoping that he would begin to emulate you."

I knew that the Professor meant his remarks in a compli-
mentary fashion, but I was not all that pleased in being described in effect as a humorless drudge.

"Well, no time to waste," said the Professor, moving for
the door. "Let's hurry across to the Dead House and see what
did poor Turk in, eh?" As Turk had died of a suspected com-
municable disease and without next of kin, no permission was
required for an autopsy.

For those unacquainted with scientific inquiry, it might
seem ghoulish to express anticipation at the prospect of cutting open one's coworker, but for us dissection was as natural
as conversation. The Professor had made it widely known that
not only would he instruct that an autopsy be conducted on
him after his death, but that he intended, as he was failing, to
predict what the anatomist would find and expected the eventual results to be matched against his prognostication. If I had
expired under circumstances of the least suspicion, it would be
my absolute wish that the Professor perform a postmortem.

The Professor was so impatient to race across the grounds
that I was able only to locate Simpson and Farnshaw to join
us. Farnshaw seemed stricken by the news that it would
be Turk on the table but Simpson was more circumspect.
"Cholera?" she asked, as Farnshaw walked ahead. "An odd af-
fliction, don't you think, for a man with Turk's training?"

I agreed, but mentioned Turk's predilection for the waterfront district. Simpson remained dubious.

"I don't see that it matters much where he spent his time.
For a doctor, cholera is a disease that one almost has to *want*
to contract."

"We will soon know," I said.

"Soon know?" Simpson repeated. "Then you suspect . . ."

"I don't have any reason to suspect anything," I protested,
none too convincingly.

Simpson moved closer and lowered her voice. "There's
more to this, Ephraim. I know there is. You must tell me
what's going on."

But I couldn't do that. I did not know for certain what was going on myself and, I confess, I did not want to mention Abigail Benedict to Mary Simpson.

Simpson took me by the arm. It was the first time she had ever touched me. "Ephraim, I told you to be careful before. That admonition is even more crucial now. Involvement in this can lead to no good. I'm certain of it."

It only seemed to occur to her as she finished speaking that she had her hand on me. She pulled it away as a blush crept up her cheeks.

"Thank you, Mary," I said. "I will do as you say."

When we arrived at the Dead House, Formad was upstairs and the Professor had already bounded up to speak with him. He reappeared a few moments later. As I had suspected, although Formad was entitled to conduct the autopsy, he was more than willing in this case to cede his authority to the Professor. Although Koch's work had made it possible to handle the dead in addition to treating the living, Formad had refused to purge himself of the common misconception that proximity to a cholera patient would put one at risk.

Our late colleague was in the first chest in the mortuary. The Professor swung it open, and there before us lay the gray, desiccated form of George Turk. His lean frame was emaciated as if by famine, his ribs and ilia protruding and prominent. His features seemed to have acquired a new placidity and I thought of his bookshelf filled with the classics.

The others had also paused. One's own mortality is reflected in the face of a dead friend, and even the Professor must have felt that one day it would be he lying in the ice. The moment quickly passed, however, and we removed Turk from the ice chest, wheeled him to the table, and set to work.

Farnshaw took notes while Simpson and I assisted. Once the Professor had made the usual cuts in the torso, creating the Y-shaped opening, my initial squeamishness ceased. The procedure went quickly and smoothly, and the results were completely consistent with death by dehydration. We focused on the digestive tract, from which a number of samples were taken. We took great care, of course, since direct contact with *Vibrio cholerae* in the intestinal tract was to be avoided. Turk's stomach contained only a small amount of brown fluid, and the duodenum and small intestine contained small amounts of yellow mucus. The large bowel contained yellowish brown mucus, and the area of the throat at the back of the mouth, the esophagus, and the trachea also contained brown mucus. A fatty infiltrate was detected in the liver. The kidneys contained yellow deposits. A cursory examination of the brain cavity showed evidence of increased cranial pressure. The immediate cause of death was cardiac failure, unremarkable since severe dehydration leads to a change in blood chemistry, which in turn often leads to a collapse of the circulatory system.

"I think that is about all we're going to learn," said the Professor, after all the material for slides had been secured. "If there are no objections, I believe we can return the organs and close up."

I never contradicted the Professor in front of others—and rarely in any case—but on this occasion I was forced to interject. "Are you not going to take hair follicle and toenail samples, Doctor?"

The Professor eyed me for a moment before replying. "Of course, Carroll. I was intending to do just that after we closed. I was unaware that hair follicles or toenails are found inside the thorax or abdomen, but perhaps my anatomy is not up-to-date." I began to stutter an apology, but before I could speak, the Professor said, "Farnshaw, why is Carroll insistent on follicle and toenail samples?"

Farnshaw put down his pen with a start. "Well," he began, "perhaps . . ."

"You have no idea, do you?"

"No, Dr. Osler," Farnshaw admitted.

"Simpson?"

A smile played at the corners of Simpson's mouth, which,

although she never took her eyes from the Professor, I knew was meant for me. But then, instead of responding with the correct answer, she said, "I don't know, either."

"Well, Carroll, why don't you tell them then?" the Professor said.

"Hair follicles and toenails are the most reliable places to test for residual arsenic trioxide. The chemical remains in those areas after it has been flushed from other parts of the body."

"And why test for arsenic trioxide?"

"The symptoms of arsenic poisoning can easily be confused with those for cholera. Those affected die of severe dehydration, often in the same time period as those with cholera."

"So, it is your theory, then, that Turk was poisoned."

"Not a theory, but it cannot be ruled out."

"Quite so. Quite so. Very good work. Would you be so kind as to take the samples?"

As I began to do so, the Professor asked, "How can we test for arsenic poisoning, Farnshaw? Or did they not cover unnatural death at Harvard?"

"Marsh's test," replied Farnshaw instantly. "Developed by James Marsh in England about . . . 1835, I believe."

" '36," noted Simpson.

"Quite right," said the Professor. "Go on, Farnshaw."

"Marsh was angered when a poisoner was acquitted of his crime because the test used for detecting arsenic, passing hydrogen sulfide through it in hydrochloric acid—"

"Hahnemann's test, yes?" prompted the Professor.

"Yes," agreed Farnshaw. "Hahnemann's test allowed the resulting arsenic sulfide to deteriorate before it could be used in evidence. Marsh decided to create a better test. He started with nitric acid, but eventually discovered that mixing the suspect substance with sulfuric acid, exposing the product to zinc, and igniting the resulting gas, would result in a silvery deposit on a cool surface if arsenic had been present."

"Bravo, Farnshaw," said the Professor. "My faith in Boston is restored." He turned to me. "Only one thing wrong with your approach, Carroll. Marsh's test does not always detect small amounts of arsenic in hair or toenails. In this case, however, there should be no problem. If arsenic was the cause, there should be plenty of it around. Well, let us finish with poor Turk here and go upstairs and see what we find, eh?"

Thirty minutes hence, we had prepared and were viewing slides taken from Turk's intestinal tract under a microscope in the chemistry room on the second floor. We checked six separate samples.

"Anyone detect *Vibrio cholerae*?" asked the Professor, but no one had. "It appears Carroll's notion has gained credibility."

We soon set up the apparatus for Marsh's test. The Professor warned us that arsine gas, the initial product of the sulfuric acid–zinc process, was quite deadly, and thus we had to take care to ignite the gas as it escaped the tube. As the experiment began, we waited to see if the distinctive silvery product would form on the cold ceramic plate that Simpson held near the stream of combusted gas. Within seconds, we all knew the truth. I had known it, I suppose, all along.

Turk, as he so correctly determined, had been poisoned.

CHAPTER 11

THE POLICE CAME TO THE hospital the following morning in the person of a diminutive, sandy-haired sergeant named Borst from the Fifth Street station, who tended to clench and unclench his fists as he spoke and in general conduct himself with bullying pugnacity. We later learned that his moniker on the force was "Brass Buttons." He specifically asked to see the Professor and me, and we convened in the Professor's office.

Brass Buttons Borst made little effort to hide the fact that he believed himself to be investigating a conspiracy rather than an isolated death and, further, that he was likely in the company of two of the conspirators. "Once we discovered that we weren't dealing with cholera," he said after some preliminary questioning, "we broke the quarantine on Mr. Turk's rooms. What do you think we found?" The smirk that accompanied the question left little doubt that it was meant to be rhetorical.

The Professor was quite capable of matching pugnacity when aroused. He turned his back on the sergeant and walked to the window. "Are you waiting for me to guess, Sergeant Borst?"

"Five thousand dollars. In cash."

"Five thou..." I exclaimed. "In his rooms?" My cursory survey of the premises had apparently been severely lacking.

"Yep. Under the rug in the bedroom. He cut the nails out of one of the floorboards...left the nail heads in so it would lift up without being noticed...and then stuck a package with five thousand dollars in the hollow underneath. Lucky for him the mice didn't get it."

"I would hardly describe Dr. Turk as lucky, Sergeant," said the Professor, still refusing to turn around.

Nor Mrs. Fasanti, I thought, for settling for two hundred dollars when she had walked across five thousand dollars every time she had to fetch Turk's soiled chamber pots.

"Perhaps not," acknowledged Sergeant Borst. "Still, where would a young doctor like Turk get that kind of money?"

The Professor finally deigned to face the policeman. "If you are asking me whether he could have come about it honestly through the practice of medicine, you know as well as I that the answer is no. If you are asking me if I had any idea of how he was obtaining it dishonestly, the answer is also no."

"How about you, Dr. Carroll?" Borst asked, sizing me up as the more easily intimidated. "You have any idea what Turk was into? You was the one who tracked him down, wasn't you?"

"I did not know him well," I replied. "Turk was a remarkably secretive man. Until last week, I had never seen him outside of work. As you know, it was only by speaking to those we encountered on our evening out that I discovered where he actually resided."

"Yes. One of those you encountered was Brigid O'Leary. You're lucky to still have your teeth."

"Brigid O'Leary?"

"I think she calls herself 'Monique'...at least this week."

"Yes," I admitted. "She helped."

"So, Doctors," said Borst, raising himself up on his toes, "let's see if I've got this right. One of you finds the body, even though nobody is supposed to know where this hospital doctor lives, getting help from a woman as handy with a knife as you are with a pillbox, then you decide to check to see if he was poisoned even though it looks like cholera, and when we look in his rooms, we turn up a small fortune, but nobody here knows anything about anything, is that what you're saying?"

The Professor placed his fingertips on the desk and leaned forward. "Sergeant Borst," he said with exaggerated patience, as if he were addressing someone who still believed in spontaneous generation, "you have done everything but accuse me and Carroll here of having some illicit involvement with Turk, either during his life or at the end of it. I will simply say to you that I am shocked that a member of the hospital staff has conducted himself in the manner that Turk apparently has. If, however, you do not find that statement satisfactory, I suggest you state your accusations plainly. If not, I have patients who are awaiting me."

Borst stood fast. "Don't be so sensitive, Doctor," he replied with a challenging grin. "If—or when—I'm ready to accuse you, you won't have to guess about it. There's two ways that I can think of where's a doctor can most easily make that much money on the side—drugs or illegal operations—and it's a pretty trick to do five thousand dollars worth of either the way that this fellow did without no one knowing about it."

"I cannot say that *someone* did not know about it," retorted the Professor, "only that *we* did not know about it."

Borst pursed his lips, then nodded. "All right, Doc. If that's the way you want it. But we have a killing here and, as you two were so helpful in showing us, the amount of arsenic that this fellow swallowed was just the right amount to make it look like cholera. That means that whoever slipped this fellow the poison knew what they were doing . . . follow my reasoning?"

He was correct in that the dose would have been required to be administered with some precision to mimic death by cholera. Too much would have killed Turk within minutes; too little might have allowed him to recover. In other words, whoever had poisoned Turk had knowledge of the substance that could come only with experience or education.

"I follow your reasoning precisely," the Professor replied. "Let me ask you this, then: If we were the someones, why would we be the ones to tell you that it was arsenic poisoning and not cholera?"

"I ain't got that part figured out yet," Borst admitted. The man was like a terrier, marking his boundaries. "And I didn't say you were the ones that done it. I don't think you are ... couple of respectable fellows. But that don't mean that you don't have some idea who did ... and why they did. I know you doctors think that what you do for a living gives you the right to play God, but we lowly police don't see it that way. So I'll say good day for now, but I expect we'll get to chat again."

"We are always at your service, Sergeant," said the Professor.

And in that mood of mutual dissatisfaction, Sergeant Borst turned to leave. Before he reached the door, however, I cleared my throat. "Sergeant," I said, "may I ask a question?"

"Why not?" he replied. "You sure ain't given me no answers."

"I was hoping to take Turk's books as a remembrance. Would it be acceptable if I had them sent to my rooms?"

"*Books?*" he replied, the smirk returning. "Sure." Sergeant Borst heaved an exaggerated sigh. "You people got the strangest ideas."

"A singularly unpleasant man," observed the Professor, after the sergeant had departed.

"Yes," I agreed, "but far from incompetent. And I believe he is correct in his assumption that drugs and illegal surgeries are the most likely to be so lucrative." With all that had passed, I still had difficulty believing that Turk had sunk to such depths as to mutilate women simply to line his pockets.

"That is assuming that Turk's funds were acquired through the use of his medical expertise. Let us not dismiss the possibility that his medical career was coincidental to whatever other activities he was engaged in."

"You think that likely?" I asked.

"As you said yesterday, I believe, 'not a theory, but it cannot be ruled out.' In any case, what I said to that disagreeable fellow is true. I am shocked to find out that a member of the staff has betrayed us so. I'm saddened too, Carroll. He was so bright . . . so very bright. It is a tragedy that it all ended like this."

"Yes," I agreed.

"I need to speak with you on a different topic," the Professor interjected. "This one, I hope, a good deal happier. As I'm sure you expected, I intend to accept the appointment in Baltimore. I will submit a letter of resignation today to the university and send a telegram to Johns Hopkins. This weekend, I will visit Baltimore and I would like you to accompany me. You can have a look at the facilities—which promise to be extraordinary—and you can also meet the men with whom you will be working."

"Thank you," I replied. "That will be excellent. And may I please express my gratitude once more for your consideration."

"Applesauce," replied the Professor, with a wave of the hand. "There is no gratitude necessary. I will say once again that no man need be grateful for that which he has earned."

"May I ask you something, Dr. Osler?"

"Of course."

"If the dinner had gone better . . . or at least not so poorly . . . would your decision have been the same?"

The Professor laughed. "The dinner had nothing at all to do with it," he replied. "Weir and Hayes both knew before we even set foot in old Benedict's palace that I was going to leave. In fact, they both pressed me to do so—quite adamantly, I might add."

"But . . ."

The Professor walked over and clapped me on the back. "You know nothing of politics, my boy," he said. "Just as well, actually, eh? When three plutocrats invite you to dinner, you go to dinner. I'm just lucky they handled it so poorly . . . made it easier. Besides, Weir had told me in advance that Schoonmaker had been opposed to retaining me. He evidently considers me something of a wild-eyed revolutionary. As it turns out, the major objections on the board to what I was trying to accomplish here came from him."

"You mean including women among the student body."

"That certainly, but also the curriculum changes, the requirements that students spend time in the wards...just about everything, really."

"So my comment about Dr. Burleigh made no difference."

"None. Benedict, I am told, had to use all his persuasive powers for Schoonmaker to go along with keeping me on, but I suppose once the old boy was forced to actually share a table with the evil Osler, he couldn't go through with it." The Professor smiled. "But the evening was far from unproductive. I found Mrs. Gross quite enchanting. A very handsome woman, don't you say?"

"Yes, quite handsome indeed," I replied instantly, thinking of the plain, squared-off woman with whom the Professor had shared dinner.

"I suppose you know that we attended the theater together and are dining tonight. And you, I am sure, have found a way to see Miss Benedict, eh? You were obviously quite taken with her."

"I suppose my behavior was excessively forward."

"Forward?" laughed the Professor. "Ephraim, it was hardly you who was forward. In fact, you gave every impression of a puppy dog trotting after his master."

"Miss Benedict is quite good friends with Lachtmann's daughter."

"The girl in Italy? So I was led to believe."

"What of Lachtmann?" I asked. "Had you known him before?"

The Professor eyed me strangely. "By reputation, certainly. We had never met previously."

"Dr. Osler," I began, "do you remember...?"

"Remember what, Ephraim?"

"Nothing. It isn't important."

CHAPTER 12

IF TURK KNEW HE HAD been poisoned, his refusal to be taken to a hospital was not delirium, but instead lent credibility to his insistence that a doctor was trying to take his life. But which doctor? And why?

There were a plethora of facts with no confirmation—the cause of the young girl's death, her identity, the medical problem for which Rebecca Lachtmann was seeking treatment, the identity of the man who had appeared at The Fatted Calf, and whether my hallucinatory sighting of the Professor had been hallucinatory after all. But the most pressing unknown, that which threatened not only my future but also everything that I had come to believe in, was what role, if any, the Professor might have had in the death of George Turk and possibly of Rebecca Lachtmann. Distrust coincidence indeed. I knew the instant that I withheld mention of Rebecca Lachtmann in Dr. Osler's office that I feared he was involved in some way.

I needed to unburden myself, to talk the questions through. There was only one person in Philadelphia in whose judgment and discretion I trusted sufficiently.

I knocked on the rectory door at about seven and Reverend Powers himself answered. I inquired whether or not I was interrupting his dinner, but he assured me my visit was welcome. He escorted me through the hall, allowed me to pay my respects to Mrs. Powers, and bade me join him in his study.

He poured us each a small glass of port and we sat in two red leather wing chairs set on diagonals to each other, with a small, low table in between.

"I am in need of guidance," I said.

"I'm happy to be of whatever help I can," the Reverend replied, leaning back, allowing me to tell the tale at my own pace.

I took a sip of excellent port and then began. I detailed the incident in the Dead House, stressing that my observations had come at the end of a grueling day and that I could not be precisely certain of what I had seen. I then described my evening with Turk, attempting to be as complete and as unsparing of my own behavior as possible. I told him of Eakins, Rebecca Lachtmann, and Abigail Benedict. I omitted nothing, not even my suspicions of the Professor and my hallucinatory vision of him at The Fatted Calf. I found myself speaking as well of my work at the hospital, the great respect with which I and everyone in medicine held the Professor, and how intensely flattered I was by his decision to offer me such an important post at Johns Hopkins. By the time I had finished recounting Sergeant Borst's visit, I had spoken for almost an hour.

"I am sorry, Reverend," I said, embarrassed. "I have been interminable."

"Not at all," he said with an easy and genuine smile. "As you were flattered by Dr. Osler's faith in you, I'm flattered by yours in me. In addition, it is an intriguing tale and does not strain concentration in the least."

I thanked him for his understanding and asked what course of action he would advise.

"I cannot advise a course of action, Dr. Carroll," he replied. "Every man's actions must come from his own Christian sense of what is right. Perhaps, however, I can help you plumb your conscience."

"I would be grateful."

"You are, I take it, aware of no specific behavior by anyone involved that would require you at this point to notify the authorities?"

"That is true," I replied. "The great dilemma in all of this is a lack of certainty on any front. The Professor may have known of Rebecca Lachtmann, or he may not have. He may have had some awareness of Turk's activities—whatever they were—or he may have been as surprised as I. Rebecca Lachtmann may have been the cadaver in the Dead House, or she may be alive and safely secreted somewhere in the city. Miss Benedict may have feelings for me, or she may be pretending simply to secure my assistance. There has been sufficient peculiarity of behavior to create irrepressible doubt on nearly every count, but not enough to suggest resolution. I can be sure of nothing. I am a man of science, Reverend. I am used to the unknown, but not to ambivalence. I feel an increasing desperation for answers."

"And you do not think Dr. Osler was the man to whom Dr. Turk referred in his comments to his landlady?"

"No."

"Well, then, why not inform the authorities of your suspicions and let them try to make sense of things? They are certainly more capable of settling these issues than you."

"I cannot, Reverend Powers. Sergeant Borst made little secret of his dislike of doctors and the man would certainly, at the very least, cause a scandal. One does not have to be guilty to be judged guilty. Even if he was completely without culpability, if Dr. Osler was seen by Johns Hopkins to have been involved in disreputable activities, even peripherally or simply by his association with Turk, the hospital might withdraw its offer. His career might be ruined."

"Your future would also be in doubt, would it not?" asked the Reverend.

"There is no denying it," I said. "But I ask you to believe that while I have no desire to risk all that I have worked for, in this I am guided by a different motivation."

"Loyalty to your superior?"

"He is not simply my superior. He is more like . . . There are two types of parenthood, Reverend Powers, one an accident of birth and the other an adoption by choice."

"And you feel toward Dr. Osler as you would feel toward a father?"

"Yes."

"But what of your own father?"

My own father? My mouth opened to once more begin the well-practiced legend, but I did not. "My own father was a drunk and a wife-beater. He was shot for desertion during the war."

Reverend Powers nodded without evidencing surprise. I might have just told him that the sun would rise the next morning.

I realized in that moment how desperately I wanted to tell him, to lance the abscess of my memory, and the entire squalid tale came flooding out. "My father enlisted soon after Fort Sumter. The farm was doing poorly . . . mostly because of his own laziness and penchant for drink . . . and he thought, as did most people in Marietta, that the war would be short, and so the army would be a good way to acquire some ready cash. Events played out quite differently, of course, and in February 1862, he found himself in Kentucky, at Fort Donelson with Colonel Grant.

"My father was part of a brigade ordered to mount a frontal charge at the rebel lines. Instead, he turned and ran, and was shot down by one of his own officers. The wound suppurated and it was determined that his arm had to be amputated. As a deserter, he did not rate the regimental surgeon. The assistant assigned the task completely botched the surgery. Afterward, my father lay in the field hospital, moaning, loathed, and ostracized. When it was deemed he could travel, he was thrown out of the army and sent home. It was only because the officers felt that the loss of the arm and the agony he was forced to endure from the butchery were punishment enough that he was not shot.

"When he returned, he told my mother and my brothers that he had lost his arm in a heroic action, in which he had charged an enemy position to save his comrades. He was lauded and we had more callers at the farm than my mother could remember. A collection was even taken up in the church. It was only when one of the neighbors from the same troop returned home two months later with the genuine version of events that my father's deceit was revealed. From that point on, our family was reviled.

"My father descended even deeper into bitterness, drink, and abuse. My brothers became responsible for almost all the chores, and my mother's main task seemed to be to try and deflect his rage. After he died in '76, I found out that I was the product of a night of whiskey and violence, which ended with him forcing himself on my mother."

There. It was out. I sat, waiting for the look of revulsion. Reverend Powers, however, seemed completely at ease. He merely took a sip of port, rolling the stem of his glass between his fingers. There was no sound in the room, except the muffled ticking of the clock.

"So you chose to become a physician yourself in retribution?" he asked.

"Perhaps," I admitted. "Of everyone, my father held the most antipathy to the doctors who had treated his wound. 'Robbers,' he called them, as if it were they who were responsible for the loss of his limb, rather than his own cowardice."

"But how could you make your ambition a reality with your family destitute?"

"I was always bookish. My mother decided that having a learner in the family was desirable, and sent scrawled notes to the schoolmaster, Reverend Audette, asking for help. He agreed to tutor me. I spent hour after hour in his study or on walks in the woods. He was the most educated man I'd ever met.

"After my father died, he encouraged me to join a

seminary, but once he realized that my calling was in science, offered to help find the right place to study. He said that the finest medical colleges were back East, but eastern schools were costly and attracted students who would look down on someone from an Ohio farm. A boy like me, from the West, he said, should look to the West. The country was opening up and every new town would need a doctor. He suggested Rush Medical College in Chicago and I agreed.

"There remained the question of cost, of course. One day, Reverend Audette asked me into his study and offered to endow my education. When I protested, he told me that I would be doing a service to him by accepting. He was childless and widowed and said that he had more money than he needed to last out his days. To aid me in pursuing such an honorable career would provide him with posterity."

"You must have been very grateful," said Reverend Powers.

"I have never ceased being grateful," I replied.

"So it seems you have done *him* a great service as well, then, by justifying his trust. What has he had to say of your great achievements?"

"He died just before I left Chicago."

"I'm sorry. And your mother and brothers . . . they must be extremely proud."

"Yes . . . well . . . I send them money."

"Ah." Reverend Powers thought for a moment. "Which do you think is the greater need, then," he asked, "to justify Reverend Audette's trust or to wipe away the sins of your family?"

I was stunned by the question. "I'm not sure," I replied. "Do you think of my family as sinful?"

"Do you?"

Did I? The immediate answer was yes, that I despised them all . . . my father for being a drunk and coward, my mother for allowing him to abuse her without protest, my brothers for being uneducated louts, and all of them for wanting nothing from me but pieces of silver. But was it true? Or was I merely ashamed?

"No," I said. "Not sinful."

"Perhaps it is Dr. Osler then. Do you feel a need to justify his trust as well?"

"Of course. It is only natural."

"Yes," said Reverend Powers. "Only natural. But do you feel that he has an equal need to justify your trust in him?"

"Dr. Osler owes me nothing," I said with finality.

"Of course." Reverend Powers replaced his glass and rose from his chair. "I hope I was of help, Dr. Carroll," he said, but with a note of distinct warmth.

"You gave me no answers," I said.

"That is not my role, Dr. Carroll," he replied. "I was hoping simply to allow you to see the questions." He placed his hand on my shoulder. "You must trust me when I tell you that you know all you need to know. The voice of Christ lives in all of us. Some simply listen better than others. You are one of those who listen quite carefully. I have no doubt that you will take the correct course."

I was flattered at his words, but nonetheless departed feeling less than satisfied. I had arrived with questions and was evidently supposed to leave with more questions. Still, I had too much faith in Reverend Powers to simply dismiss his remarks. Perhaps I was asking the wrong questions. And if that was true, what should I be asking?

When I returned home, I discovered that the boy I had hired earlier in the day to retrieve Turk's books had been efficient in the task, and two boxes awaited me in my rooms. One of the boxes contained the Greeks and the other the Bancrofts. They were, as I had instructed, packed carefully, and I found myself comforted as I removed one volume after another of Plato, Aristotle, and Thucydides, and placed them in my own bookshelves. I decided to read one of them before bed, and chose a volume of the *Dialogues*. After all, Socrates had imparted wisdom by means of the interrogative. Perhaps I might glean the Reverend's meaning from the pages of Turk's books.

I remained in my sitting room long into the night, the light from the gas lamp casting a warming glow, reading the wisdom of the ancients until at last I felt that I could rest.

CHAPTER 13

I AWOKE THE NEXT MORNING surprisingly refreshed after so little sleep. Finally, I understood what Reverend Powers had meant, and I understood myself. I was not seeking truth because of Abigail Benedict, nor to protect my career, so inexorably tied to the Professor's, nor to attain justice for Turk, nor even because my conscience told me that it was the moral and Christian thing to do. I was seeking truth so that I might at last live in peace.

My own father had been no father at all; Reverend Audette, for all his generosity, had underestimated my abilities and recommended me to second-tier medicine; Jorgie, while caring, was a fumbler. It was only in Dr. Osler that I had found a man in whom I could place my trust and affection.

But the glimmer of suspicion I now realized I had felt from the moment he had slammed closed the cover on the ice chest in the Dead House had ripened into full-fledged doubt. Pretending to deny doubt hadn't made it disappear, but merely left it to fester like an untreated wound. Soon, I would leave Philadelphia for Baltimore to work with Dr. Osler in a manner more intimate than ever before. I surely did not want to lose another father, but nor did I relish the prospect that every time I looked at Dr. Osler I would wonder if I had once again been betrayed. I had no choice but to pursue this matter wherever it led.

That evening, I remained at the hospital until about seven, and then returned home for a light dinner. At half past nine, I engaged a carriage and headed for The Fatted Calf. I did not know exactly what information I wished to elicit from the man Haggens, only that I wished to begin to fill in the picture, much, I expect, as Eakins would fill in detail on a canvas once he had settled on the basic sketch.

The hour was early for such an establishment, so, when I arrived, the giant outside the door was lolling about, without the guarded tension I had observed the previous week. He did not challenge me as I walked past him into the largely empty saloon. Few of the tables were occupied, and those by men with thick hands and dark expressions, sitting silently with their liquor.

I had not realized how vast an establishment it was. With the tables situated as close as they were, The Fatted Calf might easily accommodate two hundred revelers. Nor had I realized how downtrodden—everything in the room, from the floor to the walls to the tables to the glasses on the bar, appeared to be embossed with a layer of grime. If Turk actually had acquired a gastrointestinal ailment from drinking in this place, it would have been no surprise.

I strode across the room to the bar, my boot heels echoing softly on the pitted floorboards. A man behind the railing was polishing the glasses, using a dirty towel that left them looking no cleaner than when he had started. He ignored me until I asked for Mr. Haggens, at which point he looked up with a decidedly unfriendly expression. "What do you want with him?" Under the gruffness, however, he was a bit taken aback at my dress and demeanor, likely endeavoring to decide if I was someone to be feared or robbed.

"I have business with him. Please tell him that I was in last Thursday with George Turk."

"Tell him yourself," grunted the bartender, who directed me to a door at the far end of the room.

When I knocked, an indistinct voice responded from inside, so I opened the door and walked in. Haggens was seated at a dilapidated rolltop desk, piles of papers before him, with a surprisingly elegant Waterman fountain pen held in his hand. I was reminded that The Fatted Calf was, after all, a business like any other, with records to keep and accounts to pay.

"I'm here about George Turk," I said simply, assuming that Haggens was far too clever not to know Turk's identity.

Haggens did not look up. "I know who you come about," he said.

"I suppose you know that he is dead." I was confident Sergeant Borst's inquiries were now a matter of common knowledge in this part of town.

"I suppose I do," Haggens replied. He pushed himself away from the desk and leaned back in his chair. "And I know who you are, too. You know, Doc—it is Doc, right?—this is a pretty dangerous place for a gent like you to be wandering around in. Why, there's stabbings, and shootings, and all sorts of things that happen to those who come down here and don't know what they're doing."

Although I had come prepared to be threatened, now that I was actually facing a threat, I realized that no amount of preparation was enough. An immense effort at self-control was going to be required if I was to come through this.

"Yes," I replied, "I'm sure that's true. Nonetheless, Mr. Haggens, I think it would be best for you if I retained my health. I believe we can be of help to one another."

"Oh, yeah?" he replied, his eyebrows rising in mock surprise. "And please be so kind as to inform me how you can help me?"

"My inquiries are limited. Once I find what I'm looking for and relay my information to the appropriate authorities, it will end the matter. If, however, the police proceed on their own, their interest will assuredly be more open-ended. Sergeant Borst impressed me as a rather determined fellow."

Haggens considered this. "Borst is that," he conceded. He thought some more. "So you're telling me, Doc, that if I tell you what you want to know, you'll keep me out of it? You know that if you cross me, I'll kill you sure, even if I have to do it from the clink?"

"I have no reason to cross you," I said. "This is an honest proposition." "Honest" was an odd word to use with this fellow but it was, in fact, the case. "More than that," I added, "I was hoping that you might be persuaded to look out for me a little."

Haggens smiled, this time more genuinely. "Well, you're sure a surprise, Doc." He was the second person from the docks to tell me that. "Turk said you was a chump."

Although the sentiment hardly came as a revelation, it stung all the same. "But Turk is dead and I am here."

"True enough," Haggens admitted. He pulled out one of the drawers of the desk and reached inside. For an instant of panic, I feared he would withdraw a weapon, but his hand emerged instead with a bottle of whiskey. "Drink?" he asked.

"No, thank you," I replied. "The last time I drank here, I was much the worse for it."

Haggens laughed. "Oh, yeah. You had the 'champagne.' This is the real stuff, though."

"Thank you, no."

Haggens shrugged. "Suit yourself," he said, pouring one for himself. "Have a seat, then." He gestured toward a wooden chair against the wall. "Okay. What do you want to know?"

"First of all," I said, "do you have any idea who killed Turk or why?"

"Not a clue. Going to have to do better than that, Doc."

"Who was the man last Thursday night that Turk argued with, then? What was the argument about?"

Haggens rubbed his hand across his chin. Apparently, agreeing to speak with me about illicit activities was not the same as actually doing so. "All right," he said finally, more to himself than me. "Don't know the gent's name. Been in here once or twice before. Always for Turk. Must have money though . . . good clothes . . . expensive. What they was fighting about? Well, Turk was no stranger to artificial stimulation, if you know what I mean."

"You mean the man came here to ask Turk for drugs. What kind of drugs?"

"People down here don't mix in each other's business, Doc. Not good for the health. Turk was supposed to have something new . . . special. It ain't from here. Comes in by boat, I think." Haggens eyed me. "Understand, this is just guesswork. I don't know none of this personally."

"Of course," I replied.

Haggens regarded me skeptically, then went on. "Anyways, this gent come in last Thursday all in a lather. Said I was to get Turk right away or there'd be bedlam. So I went and got him away from you and the ladies. As soon as Turk got there, this fella starts screaming at him, wanting to know what was the big idea about something or another."

"The man wanted drugs?"

"Not sure. Looked more to me like a deal gone bad." Haggens downed his whiskey and poured himself another. "I seen a lotta fellas in need, so to speak, but this gent didn't have the right attitude for that. Talked more like an equal than a customer."

"What exactly did he say?"

"Nothing all that clear. The gent told Turk that he'd better do right by him. Turk warned the gent to watch who he talked nasty to, especially down here, 'cause folks end up dead on the docks all the time. That seemed to take the old boy's steam out."

"There was someone else, wasn't there? Someone who came for the other man."

"Yeah. Popped in just for a minute. Stayed by the front door. Never saw him before or since. Little fella with a big mustache in a bowler."

Since Haggens had proved so amenable to imparting information, I resolved to get all I could. "Turk had other businesses going, didn't he? Something more in the 'getting rid of' description?"

Haggens eyed me. "You sure know a lot about a lot. He helped women who got themselves in trouble."

"Helped?"

"Best help there is, Doc. Can make quite a bit of cash that way. Maybe you want to consider taking up where he left off?"

So it was true. Turk, you evil man, preying upon desperate women in crisis and amassing five thousand dollars doing it. You deserved to die. I felt for a moment that I would vomit. But I had learned enough of Haggens to maintain a composed demeanor at all cost.

"No, thank you," I replied, as casually as I could. "Where did he do all of this? Not here?"

"*Here?*" Haggens looked genuinely aghast. "You looked like a pretty smart fella until that, Doc. *Here?*"

"Where, then? He must have had some base of operations for all this commerce."

"He had a place, sure. Down on Wharf Lane somewhere, I think. Never knew exactly. Didn't want to know."

"I've never heard of Wharf Lane."

"No reason you should have. Only one block long and not a block you'd ever wanna be on."

"One last thing," I said. I withdrew the picture from my coat and asked Haggens if he had ever seen the woman in the photograph before. Although there were still substantial gaps in the hypothesis, I was now convinced that I would eventually find a link between Turk and Rebecca Lachtmann. I could only hope that the link did not stretch to Dr. Osler. Haggens stared at the picture for an extremely long time.

"I'm not sure. Maybe. Got a name?"

I told him that I did not. Haggens' brow furrowed as he continued to examine the photograph. "I'm really not sure. Could be though. She got a friend? Tall one with dark hair?"

"Possibly," I said, feeling my skin prickle. "She might."

"Maybe. One night. About a month ago. Two like that are unusual in here."

"Were they alone?"

"Don't remember no one with 'em, but I figure there must have been. Two like that alone . . ."

"Were they with Turk? Or was Turk here that night?"

"Don't remember. Truly."

"All right, Haggens," I said. "Thank you for your help."

"Why, you're very welcome." I rose and turned for the door. "Oh, Doc," Haggens said, "one more thing. Did you see Mike out front?"

I assured him I had.

"Looks like a pretty rough customer, huh?"

I agreed he did.

"Well," said Haggens, "he don't look half as mean as he is. Long as you keep to your deal, old Mike out there'll help keep a watch on you whenever you're down here. I get a whiff that you're going back on it, Mike won't be your friend no more. Get me?"

I got him. I was about to leave when one final thought occurred to me. "Tell me, Haggens, do you think Mike might remember either of the two women or the little fellow in the bowler?"

He snorted. "Mike don't know what day it is. He ain't out there for his memory."

I spent the carriage ride home pondering whether, when Reverend Powers spoke of Christian conscience, he had allowed for running afoul of the police, investigating abortion and murder, and making bargains with thugs along the way.

When I arrived, Mrs. Mooney had already gone to bed, but I found a small envelope addressed to me on a table in the vestibule. When I opened it, inside was a note written on fine, cream-colored stationery. *Dear Dr. Carroll*, it read, *I need to see you urgently about the matter we discussed. Please make arrangements to call on me tomorrow evening.* It was signed, *Affectionately, Abigail.*

CHAPTER 14

THE NEXT MORNING, WHEN I arrived at the hospital, I learned that little Annie had died during the night.

Death tears at a doctor. Although each of us knows that a certain percentage of our patients will not survive, no physician ever becomes inured. Inevitably, there are some patients who take on an almost symbolic quality, who epitomize the struggle in which we continually engage against fate and inevitability. It is often, as was the case with Annie, those very patients whose survival is least likely who engender the most personal reaction.

When I arrived at the Professor's office, I had never seen him so despairing.

"She had no hope, of course," he said as I entered. "Her lungs, I'm sure, were virtually destroyed." When he looked up, I saw that his eyes were red. "She was sent to work when she was five, did you know that? Running errands in a paint factory. Twelve hours a day. By the time she was eight, she was mixing paint. After she got sick, they threw her out. She lived on the street for more than a year before she was finally put into an orphanage. She had no memory of her parents. She wasn't even sure how old she was. What a sad, wasted life."

"It's a great tragedy," I agreed. "Her spirit was so light."

"Yes," said the Professor, seizing on the term. "It was light, wasn't it? If we could have saved her, Ephraim, we could have helped her salvage her remaining years. You could see that she was intelligent. She could have gone to school...." The Professor slumped in his chair. "What a terrible business this can be."

"I'm truly sorry, Dr. Osler," I said softly.

He dismissed the sentiment with a short wave of his hand.

"Do you know the actual cause of death?" I asked.

The Professor shook his head. "Not precisely, although I suspect toxicity in the environment in which she worked contributed greatly."

"When will you conduct the postmortem?"

The Professor looked up. "I won't. Couldn't bear it, Carroll. I've arranged for her to be buried in a private cemetery."

I nodded, relieved at the remarks despite the horrible circumstances. Dr. Osler's behavior with the female cadaver might have an innocent explanation after all. There were indeed, it seemed, cadavers that even he could not cut into.

When we met for rounds, it was clear that everyone had been as deeply affected as had been the Professor. Corrigan's face was ashen and Farnshaw appeared similarly. The death of one doomed little girl had pointed up to us the limits of our powers to heal and the fragility of our profession. Only Simpson preserved control, almost certainly because she had been forced to prove every day that she was not susceptible to female emotion.

I took her aside when rounds had been completed. "Perhaps you would be willing to step out with me for a moment," I said to her. "I need air."

Simpson's face was set, as if in stone. But at my request, a thin smile appeared briefly on her lips. "*You* need air, Ephraim? Of course. Thank you for asking."

We left the hospital and walked to the pathway along the river and turned south, away from the Blockley.

"I cannot bear cruelty to children," she remarked after we had gone a few paces.

"There is something particularly execrable about those who would abuse the helpless," I agreed.

"That girl . . . such extraordinary will . . ."

"She certainly brightened everyone who came near her. I will miss her as well."

"Do you like children, then?" she asked. "Many men do not."

"I liked Annie," I replied, but then considered the larger question. "Yes," I said finally. "I believe I do like children."

"It is the principal reason that I became a doctor," Simpson confided.

A nobler reason than mine, to be sure.

We walked a bit farther, watching the boats on the Schuylkill. A small private sailboat had caught the wind and was racing across the path of a steam packet boat heading upriver. As the sailboat came closer to view, it was possible to make out a young man at the tiller and a woman in the bow, both obviously of means, enjoying the maneuver, although an officer on the packet, leaning over the rail shaking his fist, did not share their amusement. Imagining the carefree woman to be Abigail Benedict was not difficult . . . but could I have been the man?

Simpson broke into my reverie. "If you're not busy this evening, Ephraim, perhaps you could come by the settlement house. There's something I want to show you."

"I'm sorry, Mary," I replied, not able to completely tear my eyes from the sailboat, "I cannot." In reply to Abigail's note, I had sent a boy to the Benedict home to leave word that I would arrive at eight. "Perhaps another evening."

"Of course," she answered, but her voice had gone distant. Her eyes were now on the sailboat as well. "We should be getting back now, I think."

⌁

When I knocked on the Benedicts' door at the appointed hour, opening it was not a servant but rather Albert Benedict.

"Dr. Carroll," he effused, shaking my hand warmly, dripping *noblesse oblige*, "it's a pleasure to see you again. Do come in."

Benedict ushered me into a parlor, where we sat on either side of a brilliantly polished tea table on which sat a crystal decanter.

"It's a Hennessey, 1825," he told me. "Privately bottled. The family owns a vineyard in Jarnac. Hennessey will blend and bottle every vintage for anyone who sells them grapes. This one is quite good."

The cognac was indeed superb; smooth, without any bite at all.

"You are here to see my sister?" Albert asked after a moment.

"At her request," I replied.

"So she mentioned. Tell me, Dr. Carroll, what are your intentions?"

"I am not sure that I know your sister well enough to have intentions, Mr. Benedict, although this seems a question more for your father to be asking."

Benedict sipped his cognac. "Well, Dr. Carroll, as my sister pointed out, I've been ordained to take his place and have therefore been delegated certain tasks with which I might gain experience."

"And I am one of your tasks?"

"Not you specifically. Abigail is one of my tasks."

"Abigail seems more than able to fend for herself."

Benedict removed his spectacles and polished them with a silk handkerchief that he took from his vest. "You might be surprised," he replied. "In any event, we take a dim view in our family of those who attempt to prey upon the weakness of women."

"I don't find women to be particularly weak," I rejoined, wondering how he could make such a statement with Abigail as a sister. "Certainly no more so than men."

"Women are gullible and naïve," insisted Benedict. "They

are easily swayed by flattery or pleasing prevarication. It is the natural order of things."

I was stunned. These were sentiments that I associated with Elias Schoonmaker's generation. "I'm not sure Darwin would agree," I replied simply.

"Darwin dealt with physical traits. I am speaking of essential character." Benedict leaned back in his chair in studied relaxation. "Dr. Carroll, I will be blunt. We have quite a bit of money, as you know, and as such my family is an appealing target for some who wish to improve their circumstances at our expense."

I was supposed to be insulted, of course, to rise to the bait, to point out that it was his sister who had pursued me and not the other way round, and that I was not even sure of her motives. Protestations of innocence, however, were what people as rich as the Benedicts doubtless heard every day. Instead, I remained silent and, after a moment, he continued.

"It is only because your professional reputation is so excellent and that you work with Dr. Osler that we will take no action at the moment and allow you to continue to call on my sister." Benedict spoke easily, casually, as if menacing potential suitors was a common event. Perhaps it was. "Abigail has, I might add, expressed an interest in you, but she always was susceptible to charm." Charm? This man thought I had made my way on charm? "If, however, we find that your attentions are motivated by a desire to improve your social or financial position or are in any other way insincere . . . well, Dr. Carroll, we can make things extremely difficult for you, and we can do so whether you are in Philadelphia, Baltimore, or Constantinople."

Ten days ago, I would have been overpowered—one of the most dominant families in the city, perhaps the entire nation, had promised to break me unless I behaved exactly as I was told. But I was not the same man as ten days ago. During that period, I had been threatened with prison by Borst and bodily injury by Haggens, uncovered a murder, and put the work of a decade at risk. While I certainly did not take the Benedicts lightly, the threat issued by Albert seemed rather benign compared to the others.

"Mr. Benedict," I replied, "I understand your position exactly. Although I can issue all the appropriate assurances of honorable behavior, you would still have every reason for skepticism. I am sure, after all, that the most convincing assurances come from the worst rogues. Your father . . . and you, of course . . . will, I know, judge me by my demeanor, not by anything I say."

I had not expressed the appropriate fealty, but nor had I challenged his authority. A stalemate, if he would allow it. For the moment, evidently, he would, as, without further conversation, he rose. "I will fetch my sister," he said evenly. "Wait in the sunroom."

I was escorted by a retainer through the labyrinthine house to a small room at the back whose ceiling and walls were glass. It was filled with greenery and flowers, and the moon was visible overhead. The air was as thick as I imagined the tropics to be. Five minutes later, Abigail walked in. She was once again dressed simply and looked all the more alluring for it. She closed the door behind her and took my hands in hers. We sat in large fan-back wicker chairs.

"Why did you want to see me?" I asked without preamble.

"Is that all you can say? Rather brusque, is it not?"

"I'm sorry," I replied. "It has been an extremely difficult day."

"Why, Ephraim?" she asked softly.

The use of my Christian name brought me up short, as I am sure it was intended to. "A patient died. Someone I had been attending."

"I don't understand how you endure all that death and suffering," she said. Her empathy seemed genuine.

"Sometimes we can prevent death and alleviate suffering,"

I replied. "Thanks to men like Dr. Osler, we are getting better at both with every passing year."

"Still . . ."

"Yes. One never gets used to the tragedies."

"Was there something special about this patient . . . the one today?"

"She was a child. Twelve or thirteen, although no one knows for sure. She was very brave."

"I'm so sorry," Miss Benedict whispered. "Of what did she die?"

The scene on the river flashed before my eyes. "She worked in a factory owned by the very type of person who has dinner here. Someone who made a great deal of money while girls like Annie were slowly suffocated."

She pulled back. "That isn't fair," she exclaimed. Her eyes began to fill with tears. "That really isn't fair."

I could not believe I had allowed such a hurtful remark to escape my lips. Yet the anger I felt was real. "I am sorry. Truly. It was not at all fair."

Miss Benedict regained her composure but sat up straight in her chair and folded her hands in her lap.

"You are angry, and not simply because of your patient. Are you going to tell me why?"

"Do you know George Turk?" I asked.

"No. Should I?"

"Are you sure? George . . . Turk." I repeated the name slowly for emphasis. I refused to be anyone's fool, not even hers.

"If I said that I don't know George Turk, I don't know George Turk. Who is he, anyway?" Abigail Benedict replied, the muscles in her jaw knotting. Her egalitarian sentiments notwithstanding, she was still Hiram Benedict's daughter and unaccustomed to being cross-questioned.

"He was the man that you went with Rebecca Lachtmann to The Fatted Calf to meet," I said. A guess, certainly, but one

that fit all the facts. And it was hard to imagine any other reason for them to be at Haggens' establishment.

Her face changed instantly. The bellicosity vanished, replaced by astonishment. "So that was his name. How did you
find out?"

"That isn't important," I said. "Why did you go to meet him?"

"I went so that Rebecca would not have to go alone.
Thomas accompanied us. None of us knew his name, only
that he had been recommended as someone who could help."

"Who recommended him?"

"I'm not sure. Someone Thomas knows."

"And did Turk help?"

"I don't know. He was supposed to come to us but he
never arrived. We waited at that revolting place for well over
an hour but no one approached us. I wasn't lying to you. I
don't know the man."

"Didn't know. George Turk is dead. He was poisoned."

"Poisoned? When? By whom?"

"The police are currently attempting to find out. If she did
not meet him that night, did Rebecca ever succeed in making
contact?"

"Not that I know of, but perhaps she did later."

"I think it is time that you gave me more of the details," I
said.

Abigail Benedict's expression hardened once more. "No,"
she replied. "I don't think it is."

"But why?" I asked. "How can I help if I don't know precisely what to look for?"

"I don't think I want your help. I thought I did, but apparently I was mistaken. I do not want the help of someone who
does not trust my motives, who sits back smugly passing
moral judgments on me, my family, and my friends, who eyes my
every action as if I were some bacterium under a microscope.
No, Ephraim, Thomas and I will have to muddle through without you. I do hope that you have sufficient honor not to trans-
mit any of what you were told in confidence to others."

The words hit like a slap. When she made to stand, I leapt up. "Please, Abigail. Sit down. Please." Her hands remained on the arms of the chair, but she made no further move to leave the room.

"You are completely correct," I went on. "I have behaved like a fool and a cad. I do trust you . . . I think I do . . . but . . . it is simply . . ." I felt my breath gush out. "It is simply that I am terribly attracted to you and I fear betrayal."

"Or perhaps my father and brother are correct. Perhaps you are attracted to our money," she said. She seemed on the verge of sneering at me and I became desperate to turn her anger.

"Why would you accuse me of that? What cause have I given you to believe such a thing?"

"What cause have I given you to believe that my motives are deceitful?" she retorted. "If you insist on thinking the worst of me, why should you protest when you are afforded the same treatment?"

"I deserve everything you have said," I agreed, in full surrender. "There is no reason that you should believe it, but circumstances would be so much easier for me if it *were* your money. The sad fact is that I think about you obsessively and constantly."

She smiled, a soft and beautiful smile. An actress onstage could not change mood so often or so quickly. "Is that how you think of it? As sad?"

"I fear that will be the upshot, at least for me. I can think of no reason why it should end any other way."

"Can't you?" she demanded.

"Are you still angry? You have every right to be."

"If people were held to every stupid thing said out of passion, the species would soon go extinct."

"Thank you," I said, feeling hauled back from the edge of a precipice. At that moment, I knew that I would do anything to help her, and spewed out those very sentiments.

"I find you very gallant, Dr. Carroll," she said, "when you

are not being churlish, of course. Perhaps we might try to begin anew."

"I would like that," I said.

"Please sit down, then, and let us go on. We must find Rebecca quickly. She may have simply secreted herself, but she may also be ill. It has been two weeks, and I feel certain she would have contacted us if she were able. It has been dreadful, sitting here helpless. I love her as I would a sister. Can you not understand that?"

"Yes, of course I can," I replied. I placed my hand on hers and she did not resist. "But I need more details." If my hypothesis for the overall chain of events was correct, the news, I feared, would not be good, but I owed Abigail the truth.

"I cannot provide them until I speak with Thomas," she said plaintively. "We made a pact and I will not break it. If Thomas agrees— and I'm sure he will—we will tell you everything we know. Until then, I would ask that you act on faith a bit longer."

"Of course," I said, trying to live up to the reputation for gallantry with which she had endowed me. "Why was it that you wanted to see me if not to give me information?"

"The situation has become more complicated. Jonas has grown suspicious of Rebecca's whereabouts. I'm not sure what aroused him but we must be more careful."

"What is he likely to do?"

"One can never tell. But Jonas is dangerous. He has already killed at least two men."

"Killed?"

"The first was in California when he was just starting out in business. Jonas did not come from means, you know. He shot a man who had cheated him in a business deal. It was called self-defense, but Father told me that Jonas had paid the local sheriff to give false testimony. Then, just after he arrived in Philadelphia, about ten years ago, a footpad accosted Jonas and Eunice as they were leaving a restaurant. The man had a knife and demanded money. Jonas disarmed the thief and then beat him to death, right there on the street. The police called that self-defense, as well."

"And you didn't feel the need to mention these incidents when you enlisted my assistance?"

"I had no idea that matters would become this complicated. I'm telling you now because I care about what happens to you. I would understand fully if you withdrew."

"No," I replied. "I'll continue on."

"Thank you, Ephraim."

We both stood. Abigail moved opposite me, very close. I could feel the heat from her skin and smell the aroma of her lavender bath salts. Her lips parted and we stood for a second looking into each other's eyes. Then, as if at a signal, we each leaned in toward the other and our lips met. Without breaking contact, she shifted and pressed against me. I'm not sure how long we kissed, but it was blissful and eternal.

I left the Benedict home drifting as if on a cushion of air. This had been a week of remarkable happenings, but none more so than this.

I had never been in love before.

February 1, 1889

SINCE SHE WAS SMALL, SLEIGH rides in
the country had been her favorite winter frolic.
Swathed in furs, the rush of the wind against her
cheek, the muffled clomp of hooves in the snow, the gaiety of
her companions—all pure joy. Pure freedom. Why, then, could
she not abandon herself, if only for a few moments? Why must
fear intrude, even here?

She had been resolute in her determination to forget. If she
willed it never to have happened, it would not have. And so,
she had said nothing and shown nothing, not to family, not to
friends. She had thrown herself into the season. No one had
sparkled more at balls, had shown more wit or enthusiasm for
the theater, museums, or exhibitions.

And then she was late.

At first, she would not think about it, could not confront it.
When she did, the horror overwhelmed her. Private shame
might be borne, but public disgrace was unthinkable. Her

position and that of her family would be forever sullied. For the remainder of her life, she would be unable to look anyone in the eye and not see her shame reflected back at her. But worst of all, by far worst of all, was that all this must be endured not for the one she loved but rather for the one she loathed.

As the sleigh emerged from the wood onto an open field, she looked up at the sun, dulled by a gray sky. Perhaps it would still come. Perhaps she might still bury the incident within her. Yes, certainly. It would all come out right in the end. It had to.

CHAPTER 15

I HAD BUILT MY LIFE on discipline, on gathering data and making decisions only after reflection and analysis. Even after circumstance had thrown me into a maelstrom of intrigue, I had tried to maintain the scientific principles that had brought me success in the past. But love is a glorious compulsion to behave against one's own best interests, and, if the risks were greater, so were the rewards. To be sure, without fulfillment of the heart, all other success is hollow.

The irony that my only chance at such fulfillment had been created by the murder of George Turk and the enigma of Rebecca Lachtmann did not escape me. What if, after the skullduggery had ended and the mysteries were resolved, I was left with the love of a woman to whom mere access would have been unthinkable before? What a strange and welcome turn of fate.

Thus, in my sorry state of hope and rapture, I met the Professor at the Broad Street Station at ten the next morning for our journey to Baltimore. Daniel Coit Gilman, president of the Johns Hopkins University and director of the hospital, had reserved a first-class compartment so that we would be allowed to pass the two hours in peace and comfort. How different this would be from my third-class journey from Marietta to Chicago a decade before.

We settled in opposite each other, and were soon under way. The locomotive gained speed and we headed west, crossing the Schuylkill in view of the hospital, the immense

Blockley complex standing like a leviathan just beyond. As Philadelphia slipped by, the Professor gazed out the window, as if it were a segment of his life receding rather than a spot on a map.

"It will be a great adventure, Carroll," he said softly, but did not turn from the window.

"Yes," I agreed. "To be a part of the finest medical facility in the nation . . ."

"And what will be the finest medical school. Think of it. We'll be able to help prepare the next generation of doctors . . . perhaps even to set the standards of medical education. Even if we each treated ten thousand patients in the course of our careers, it pales before the numbers that those whom we train will treat. We can bring knowledge and humanity into the wards everywhere.

"To be in the position to make a genuine difference, Carroll," he mused. "How few get that chance, no matter how brilliant or talented. What a stroke of luck, to be here, at this time."

"Whatever luck may be involved," I said, "it is no more than you have earned."

"Thank you for saying so," he said, and then heaved a sigh. "Still, it is an enormous privilege . . . and an enormous responsibility."

Two people who spend as much time together as the Professor and I can sense when conversation is no longer desired and, seconds later, seemingly at the same instant, we each reached into our respective valises and withdrew a book.

I had brought a second volume of Turk's Plato, this one containing *Republic*. I knew of the essay, of course, but had never delved into it. It seemed appropriate now to read of the philosopher-king while traveling with a man who might actually fit the role. I placed the volume in my lap, crossed my leg in order to rest it on my thigh, and then lifted the cover open with my thumb.

I felt myself start. Cut into the inside of the front board

was a latchkey. It was shiny and black and I knew instantly that its home was a door on Wharf Lane that led to the lair from which Turk had conducted his nefarious activities.

I quickly shut the book and saw the Professor eyeing me. "Is everything all right?" he asked.

"Oh, yes, Dr. Osler," I said. "Quite all right. I was just thinking of the enormity of my good fortune."

"All of it deserved," replied the Professor, accepting the explanation. "What are you reading?"

When I told him, he smiled and nodded. "Good man. Plato is indispensable."

"And you?" I asked, anxious to deflect focus from the volume in my hands.

"It's called *Servetus and Calvin*. Written by Robert Willis, a Scottish physician, about ten years ago." I was certain now that he did not think anything amiss. He closed the book gently and ran his fingertips lightly across the front. It had a black cloth cover, with imitation gold letters on the spine; an inexpensive volume but one, from the manner with which he handled it, that had substantial meaning for him. "Do you know of Servetus?"

I confessed that I did not.

"He was a remarkable man and a brilliant physician, responsible for one of the great discoveries in anatomy, one which altered the course of medicine for all time."

I was no medical historian to be sure, but nor was I a novice, and I could not imagine any great discovery in anatomy of whose attribution I was unaware. I had read, I was certain, of all the great anatomists—Galen, Vesalius, Harvey, even the Arabs, Avicenna and Averroës. The Professor sat across from me, amused at my perplexity, and eventually raised a cautionary finger.

"Ah, Carroll, I did not say Servetus received credit for his discovery."

"Who did?"

"Harvey."

"You mean that Servetus discovered blood circulation *before* Harvey?"

"Precisely. Seventy-five years before, to be exact. In 1553." The Professor tapped the cover of the book. "Servetus confined his theory largely to pulmonary circulation, but hypothesized about greater circulation and even the presence of capillaries. Until then, everyone had missed the role of the heart, even Vesalius."

"Why didn't Servetus receive credit if his discovery preceded Harvey's?"

"Servetus' discovery was contained in a theological text he called *Christianismi Restitutio*—the 'Restoration of Christianity'—which was judged heretical by both Catholics and Protestants. One thousand copies were printed and all were thought to have been destroyed, most on the order of John Calvin, who presided at the trial at which poor Servetus was condemned. He was burned at the stake in Geneva . . . a grisly death . . . they used green wood that burned slowly and Servetus was roasted for thirty minutes before he finally died. It was not until over a century later that the first surviving copy of *Christianismi Restitutio* surfaced, well after Harvey had published his great work in 1628. Three copies have been unearthed in all, the last of which, in fact, was not found until ten years ago, when it was discovered quite by chance on the shelves of the library at the University of Edinburgh. It turned out to be Calvin's own."

"Calvin ordered all the copies destroyed, but kept his own?"

"Apparently. Evidence that the Edinburgh copy was Calvin's is indisputable."

"How did it get to Edinburgh?"

The Professor shrugged. "No one is quite sure, although it seems to have come through the Marquess of Queensbury."

"As in the rules for pugilism?"

"The same family, although I am uncertain as to who specifically acquired the volume or under what circumstances."

"Quite a tale," I said.

"More than that, Carroll. I'm drawn to Servetus. He was a Spaniard by birth. Brilliant . . . a prodigy. He was a theologian, a geographer, and a linguist, in addition to his medical skills. He spent his life searching for truth and was guided strictly by the dictates of his own conscience. He cared nothing for the judgment of others. His great heresy, according to Calvin, was the belief that God exists in all men. No one in European or American history more epitomizes the struggle for freedom of thought."

"You feel kindred to Servetus?" I asked. "I have never thought of you as heterodox."

"We all fight ignorance with truth, Carroll," he replied, "and conscience is our only guide."

"Do you not believe in Scripture, then?"

"Of course I do. God's word must always be paramount. But all too often, I'm afraid, theologians interpret God's word based on their own prejudices . . . and sometimes with more sinister motives. Can there be any more telling example than the resistance to our work? Think of that dolt, Reverend Squires, trying to prohibit autopsy. And think of the reaction to the writings of Darwin. Evolution is evidence of God's wonder, not blasphemy . . . and where does it say in the Bible that Man should not attempt to learn about the workings of the body? No, Carroll, it is individual conscience that provides our most reliable guidepost."

"My pastor, Reverend Powers, agrees with you."

"An enlightened man."

"He is that. But why is Servetus not better known?"

"He is something of an underground figure in Europe," the Professor went on. "I came across some articles when I was in Germany and have been pursuing his story ever since. Servetus was terribly flawed, but deserved much better from society. Flaws of personality must be overlooked in those who could bring such benefit to the world."

With the Professor in such an expansive mood, I decided to explore his views of another rebel. "Dr. Osler," I asked, "what do you think of Thomas Eakins?"

" 'The Portrait of Professor Gross'? Very realistic rendition, as far as it goes. He is doing a similar depiction of Agnew, I believe."

"Do you know anything of the man?"

"Something of a rake, is he not?" replied the Professor. "I confess that I do not understand the art world, Carroll. It is all well to produce renderings of the world in which we live, but too many of these people seem to revel in immorality. Even in 'The Portrait of Professor Gross,' Eakins chose to sensationalize, to emphasize the horrors of surgery rather than its benefits. Old Gross is depicted more as a Jehovah figure passing judgment on the wretch on the table than as a man who was doing everything he could to save his patient's life."

"But there is value, is there not, in making us see the world through fresh eyes, even if the view disturbs us?"

"There is value in truth, Carroll, and truth is not found in sensationalism."

I decided not to press the point but the Professor had not finished. "I suggest you reconsider the time you spend with those people. You have a brilliant career ahead of you. It would be a great tragedy if, after all your efforts, you let it dissipate. Abigail Benedict would turn any man's head. But if you are not careful, Ephraim, she will move on and you will be ruined. You should put an end to your late-night meetings."

"How did you know?"

"Hiram Benedict told me. He asked if I thought you a suitable match for his daughter."

"What did you say?" I wondered how the Benedicts had communicated details of a visit that had taken place just the night before.

The Professor smiled. "I told him that you would make a superb addition to his family."

I was confused. "But I thought . . . you just said—"

"Just because I hope you will make a decision on your own does not mean that I will make it for you."

With that, we returned to our reading. I was careful to open my book in the center, keeping the inside front cover concealed. While the Professor seemed to become instantly immersed in his *Servetus*, I was unable to concentrate at all on Plato.

Destiny, I realized, is a combination of desire and timing, or luck as the Professor put it. A man can put any degree of effort into shaping his fortune—as I had—yet it will all be for naught if the opportunity to manifest that effort does not avail itself. I had purged my speech of the twang that marked me as a western rustic; worked tirelessly to become knowledgeable and proficient in my field; read philosophy, history, and literature in addition to anatomy and biology, so as not to be judged as narrow; learned to dress and carry myself like a gentleman; and, most of all, sought out the most exalted stage on which my profession was being played. The result had been an appointment to a high position at a prestigious institution, when I might have droned out my days only one step up the ladder from Jorgie, a respected but nondescript physician at a well-regarded but hardly noteworthy hospital.

But luck only reveals itself in retrospect. George Turk, Rebecca Lachtmann, and, most of all, Abigail Benedict had now entered the mix, and whether my encounter with her would seal my good fortune, as I hoped, or my doom, as the Professor feared, could only at this point be guessed at.

My musings were interrupted as the train slowed at the outskirts of Baltimore. The Professor glanced up, closed his book, replaced it in his valise, and stretched.

"Well," he said, "it begins."

When we alit from the train ten minutes later, two men

waited to greet us on the platform. One, whom I took to be Daniel Coit Gilman, was about sixty, white-haired but for dark eyebrows, with muttonchops that met at a full mustache over a shaved chin. He wore a frock coat, and was tall with a slightly shambling look. The other man was about the same age as the Professor, bald and of medium height with a carefully trimmed mustache and Vandyke. He stood extremely straight, almost military, but broke into a smile when he saw the Professor.

"Willie," he exulted, grabbing the Professor's hand and clapping him on the shoulder. "It's glorious to see you." I had never heard anyone except poor Annie call the Professor "Willie" before.

"Good to see you too, Willie," the Professor rejoined, pumping the other Willie's hand so hard that it seemed as if he were trying to draw water. The Professor gestured toward me. "And this is the man I told you about." He positioned himself between us. "Ephraim Carroll . . . William Welch."

So this was Welch, who was to head the entire faculty and be the Professor's superior. The Johns Hopkins staff, then, would not only be brilliant: It would have the energy of youth.

The older man, Gilman, had waited patiently—and happily—while the two Willies greeted each other, which I considered a remarkable show of diffidence and self-assurance. A man like Hiram Benedict would surely have taken umbrage at not being the first introduced. Now, however, Gilman stepped forward and extended his hand, not just to the Professor, but to me as well.

"Doctors," he said, "it is an honor to have you at Johns Hopkins."

The ride to the hospital was brief but memorable. As we crossed the downtown and emerged on the east side of the city, a remarkable sight came into view. On the top of a rise was a massive redbrick structure, topped by an enormous cupola and two towers. It seemed to stretch to the horizon. To

the east of the main structure were a plethora of other buildings, constructed of the same material, all of which were
clearly part of the hospital complex.

As we drew closer, I realized that the main building was
not a single structure, but rather a number of separate facilities placed in proximity to one another. I asked why the hospital had been constructed in compartments.

"We did that intentionally," said Gilman. His voice was
high-pitched and had a break that was incongruous in such a
legendary scholar. He'd been enticed ten years before to leave
his post as president of the University of California, and had
personally overseen the hospital's design and construction.

"Since, as we know, most contamination and contagion
are airborne, John Shaw Billings, who was our guiding spirit,
designed the hospital not only to separate the administrative
areas from the wards, but also to segregate other functional
sections...laundry, dispensary, commissary...to minimize
transmission. All the buildings, or 'pavilions' as we call them,
are extremely well ventilated so that noxious air does not set-
tle. It was a good deal more costly to design the hospital in
this fashion, but the trustees were quite serious in their intention to create the finest medical facility in the world."

The first item on the agenda was a luncheon to welcome
us to the hospital and introduce us to our fellow doctors
and the professors at the university. The interior of the new
building glistened. Double doors opened onto a long, well-
appointed, wood-paneled room, with large windows facing
west. There were at least fifty others already present and, as
we walked through the doorway, they began to applaud. The
Professor stopped short and I thought he might actually
blush.

Welch, who had been scrupulous in treating me with the
same respect as he showed the Professor, led us both into the
hall, and he and Gilman began to make introductions. We
moved from one small knot to another, and the names were
soon swimming in my head. Although the professors at the

university tended to be in their fifties and sixties, most of the medical staff was young, the oldest being in their early forties.

As we reached the far end of the dining hall, we came upon a man standing alone. He was not tall, but had a thick chest and gave the impression of great strength. He was serious-looking, like a stern schoolmaster, but impeccably dressed in a dark suit with a brilliantly white collar and dark blue silk tie. He appeared to be older than the Professor or Welch, and was light-haired and balding, with a carefully trimmed, turned-up mustache and a beard cut close to his cheeks. Behind his *pince-nez*, his eyes were an odd blue-green and arresting, as if they had been lit from the rear.

Even had his demeanor not been so haunting, there was little danger that my memory of this man would be lost among the others. I had seen him before—not at a medical facility, but at The Fatted Calf, where he had been taken away by a short, mustached man in a bowler hat.

The Professor extended his hand, smiling. "Doctor," he said, "I am so pleased to see you again."

The other nodded and accepted the Professor's hand, but there was little warmth in his demeanor. "And I you, Doctor," he replied evenly.

"Ephraim Carroll," the Professor said, "I would like you to meet the finest surgeon in America, Dr. William Stewart Halsted."

I took Halsted's hand. His fingers were short but his grip was firm and confident, his stub of a thumb pressing into the flesh of my hand. His eyes unflinchingly held mine. I could read nothing from his gaze and hoped that he read nothing from mine.

"It is an honor, Dr. Halsted," I said, after it was clear that he would not speak first. "Dr. Osler speaks of you in exalted terms."

Halsted nodded perfunctorily, but otherwise did not change expression. The effect was unnerving. I could not imagine that he recognized me from The Fatted Calf—I had been across the room. Might he have seen me somewhere else, perhaps with Turk earlier that evening, or outside Mrs. Fasanti's when I had come upon my dying colleague? I fervently hoped he had not. I was violating strict scientific method to think so, but the man before me was so startling... so chill and controlled... that at that moment I had not one scintilla of doubt that he was capable of visiting Turk at his home and, by either force or subterfuge, inducing the younger man to take poison.

At luncheon, conversation centered on the hospital, and through the first courses Billings explained the theory behind the planning and construction. The Johns Hopkins University was the first institution of higher learning in the United States constructed specifically to promote research. The hospital, although physically removed from the university campus, was to be an extension of that mission, as would be the medical school, which Billings said would be complete within three years.

Billings, a surgeon by training, but a man who had emerged as the nation's most forward-looking thinker in public health and hospital design, had been persuaded by Gilman to join Johns Hopkins after a brilliant career in the army. He had been the man who had convinced the trustees to make research and medical education integral to the hospital's mission.

Although the discourse was fascinating, for me the event was dominated by the man diagonally across from me. Dr. Halsted spoke very little, even when he was asked about the many improvements in both surgical technique and equipment upon which he was currently engaged. But laconic or not, Halsted's brilliance was inescapable. In ten words, he could express an insight that seemed a century ahead of its time. I understood very quickly why the Professor considered this man a treasure to be protected, as one would encase a rare gem in a museum. Belying his deportment, Halsted seemed to have a human side as well. During his discussion of surgical gloves, he mentioned that Caroline Hampton, the

nurse whose sensitivity to carbolic soap had spurred the innovation, was now his fiancée. As soon as the discussion moved
to other topics, however, Halsted once again retreated into silence. But, to me, his presence dominated the table.

After luncheon was done, we toured the hospital and the
facilities, which, as I had come to expect, were nothing short
of miraculous. Every possible innovation had been incorpo-
rated into the design of the wards and the operating theaters,
and the laboratories were more extensive than anything I
had ever seen. Even the Professor seemed awed. When we
had completed our tour, it was near dusk, so we repaired to
Gilman's home, where we would be staying, to relax until dinner. Gilman and his wife left us to ourselves, placing a bottle
of sherry and two glasses on a tray on the sideboard.

"Well, what do you think, Ephraim?" demanded the
Professor after each of us had poured a glass and settled into
an extremely commodious side chair. "Quite an establishment,
eh?"

"Indeed," I agreed enthusiastically. "With a staff to match.
I will feel like an interloper on Olympus."

"Ha! This may surprise you, Ephraim, but I find the atmosphere a bit intimidating myself."

"Intimidating indeed. And no one more than Halsted. Has
he always been such a presence?"

The Professor pulled at one end of his mustache. "In fact,
the frost in his demeanor is a recent phenomenon. He used to
be an extremely affable and outgoing chap. Did you know that
he was also a superb athlete? He rowed, played baseball, performed gymnastics . . . do you know what football is?"

"It's a sport that some colleges play, isn't it? Sort of tug-of-
war in reverse. A lot of fellows lined up in opposition, each
side trying to a push a ball over a line by shoving the other fellows backward?"

"That's pretty much it," agreed the Professor. "It takes
strength and a certain ferocity. The university has a team, although I've never seen the game. It has become quite popular,

I hear, at Yale. Halsted was one of the originators of the sport and named captain of his team at Yale."

"I was not aware that he was such a violent man," I said.

"I didn't say he was violent, only that he played a violent sport in college. He fancies dachshunds as well."

"Of course," I said quickly. "But you also said that he used to be affable. What changed him?"

The Professor sighed. "It was the cocaine."

"And you are sure he is no longer under its influence?" Both Monique and Haggens had indicated that Turk was in the drug trade. What other reason could there be for a man like Halsted to seek Turk out?

"Why would you think otherwise?"

"No reason at all," I ventured hastily. "But cocaine craving has proven to be so terribly difficult to overcome. . . ."

"You cannot imagine," sighed the Professor. "It's been torture for the poor fellow. And to think it was his own fearlessness that caused the problem in the first place."

"How do you mean?" I asked.

"He always proceeded according to what he thought best, regardless of personal consequences. Some years ago, when his sister suffered a postpartum hemorrhage, Halsted performed an emergency transfusion, using his own blood, and saved her life. When his mother became ill one year later, he diagnosed the ailment as gallstones. Her physicians insisted he was wrong and refused to operate, so Halsted performed the surgery himself, although he had never operated on a gallbladder before. He saved her life as well.

"When the opportunity came to experiment with cocaine as an agent to block sensation in individual nerves, he chose to use himself as the first subject. After he became addicted, he was shunned by those very colleagues who had lauded him. Only Welch, who had been the chief pathologist at New York Hospital, stood by him. Eventually, Welch brought him here to stay in his home. Is it any wonder that a man who has been through such an experience would undergo a change of personality?"

I agreed that it was understandable.

"Understandable?" exclaimed the Professor. "Inevitable, more likely." Then he paused, as he often did when a revelation overtook him. "But why all this interest in Halsted?"

"It is just that he is so riveting," I replied, attempting to keep my response casual. "A man of such ability who has been forced to overcome an immense obstacle cannot help but be an object of fascination."

"It's true. Excuse my shrill tone, Ephraim. It's simply that those of us who have witnessed his ordeal have become extremely protective of him."

"Yes," I agreed. "I understand."

CHAPTER 16

WE PASSED AN AGREEABLE EVENING with the Gilmans, and then retired early. The return trip to Philadelphia, late Sunday after another round with the Hopkins staff, was more subdued than our ride south, both the Professor and I retreating to our thoughts.

At the hospital on Monday, Simpson was curious about the visit to Baltimore, but I could not spare the time. She was matter-of-fact as I hurried off to discharge my duties, but she nonetheless seemed insulted at my avoidance. I did not want to cause her distress, but I was preoccupied by what I must do that evening.

After I had finished for the day, I once more made my way across the city. I arrived soon after six and Mike stepped aside to let me pass, even venturing a small smile. I was now, it seemed, an accepted member of the Fatted Calf family.

Haggens also seemed pleased to see me. "Well, Doc," he said with a grin, "welcome back. Didn't expect to have the pleasure again so soon." His affability, as always, was offset by the sly squint that he never seemed able or willing to suppress. "I'd like to think you came because of our classy décor," he went on, "but I figure it's because you want something."

"True enough, Haggens," I replied. I discovered I was becoming more comfortable in his company. There was a freedom in Haggens' world that was absent in mine: I was finding it held great appeal. I had also come to understand that, so long as I did not betray him, there was little threat of arbitrary violence. "The last time I was here, you offered me your associate's services if I ever needed to wander about alone down here. I was hoping the offer was sincere."

His brow furrowed slightly as he calculated the implications of my request. Haggens was as accomplished in the science of survival as was the Professor in the science of medicine. After a few seconds' consideration, he smiled once more and turned his hands palms up, the universal protest of innocence. "Why, of course I was sincere, Doc. Just where is it that you want Mike to escort you to?"

"Wharf Lane."

The grin vanished. "Turk's place? You found it?"

"Not exactly." I related the finding of the key. I made a point of mentioning where Turk had hidden it, deciding that Haggens would appreciate the irony.

"Plado?" he asked. "Some old Greek?" Haggens shook his head at the wonder of it all. "But how do you know what door the key fits?"

"I don't," I replied. "But I believe you said that Wharf Lane is only one block long. Turk certainly did not do his business out of a storefront, so I assume the key must fit a door that leads somewhere else. There can't be too many possibilities—upper floors or back rooms. I thought I would just try all the locks, until I found the correct one."

"Oh, you did, did you? Just kinda mosey down Wharf Lane tryin' locks. People down there don't take kindly to strangers sticking keys in their doors."

"And thus, Mike," I said. "If he is all you say he is, of course."

Haggens stroked his chin for a moment, then nodded. "And what if you find something?"

"I would have to see what the something is, but I could then inform the authorities according to the terms of our bargain. There would be no need to mention you at all. After all, I found the key in a book."

Haggens glowered. "You sayin' I can't read?"

"Of course not," I replied without apology. "But the circumstances under which I came across the key have nothing whatever to do with you, and there would be no reason for Borst to suspect that I had not found out about Wharf Lane through devices of my own . . . from Monique, for example."

Haggens' smile returned. "Okay, Doc. No offense taken."

"Can I have Mike, then?" I asked.

"Sure," Haggens replied. "I think I might toodle along with you as well."

"You? Why?" Haggens' presence had not been in my plans and definitely added a layer of menace. If what we found in Turk's den turned out to be a threat to him, Haggens could simply instruct Mike to make certain I was never seen again.

Haggens rose. His attendance, it seemed, was not to be negotiable. "What's the matter? Don't you trust me?"

"Frankly, no. Should I?"

"You wound me," he said. He took a step for the door and then stopped. "Oh, yeah. One other thing."

"Yes?"

"We're chums, right?"

"To the end," I replied.

"Thought so. Well, since I'm doing all this for you, I thought maybe you might do something for me?"

"And what might that be?"

Haggens heaved a sigh. I braced myself for whatever conspiracy he was about to try and involve me in. He glanced about and, even though we were alone in the room, lowered his voice and said, "I been having some trouble breathing, Doc. Especially lying down. Sometimes I wake up in the middle of the night and I can't breathe hardly at all. Then I get dizzy when I stand up. What do you think it is?"

A medical question! It should not have been a surprise. No doctor can go anywhere without fielding inquiries, often from complete strangers, whether on breathing, or itches, or pains, or bathroom habits.

"Did you ever have rheumatic fever?" I asked.

"Yeah," Haggens replied, "when I was a kid. Do you know what I got?"

"I can't be sure without an examination. At the least, I would have to listen to your heart."

Haggens started to unbutton his vest.

"No, no," I said. "I can't do it now. I need my stethoscope. Are you willing to come to the hospital?"

Haggens cocked his head as if I had suggested he turn himself in to the police.

"All right," I said, realizing that I had just bought myself insurance. "I'll come back later this week. No one will know. That is the way you want it, I assume."

Haggens nodded. "Just so, Doc." He rebuttoned his vest and reached for his coat. "Well, let's go see what Turk was into." He removed a kerosene lantern from a shelf and bade me to follow him out.

I had arrived at The Fatted Calf during last light. As we left, the streets were fully in the dark and, although it was still early enough to be the dinner hour, a sinister pall lay over the neighborhood. Wharf Lane, according to my host, was only about a five-minute walk, and so I set off, strolling along the Philadelphia docks with Haggens and Mike, whereas the previous day, I had walked the corridors of the Johns Hopkins Hospital with the Professor, William Welch, and Daniel Coit Gilman.

After a few minutes of winding down narrow thorough-fares, we turned off a derelict avenue into a street whose broken stone thoroughfare was scarcely wide enough to accommodate a wagon. Haggens nodded to indicate that we had reached our destination. I had expected a ramshackle series of storefronts, but was unprepared for the hovels and boarded-up windows that graced both sides of Wharf Lane. Not one of the gas lamps was lit, so the street was illuminated only by the indirect light that bounced its way into the narrow track from streetlamps on the larger roads. Turk could not have chosen a more repulsive spot.

Haggens lit his lantern and turned down the wick so that it gave off only sufficient light to allow us to make our way. There was no need to call any more attention to our presence than was necessary. As we began down the lane, Mike lagged a few steps behind, clearly ready to intercept anyone who attempted to surprise us from the rear. Haggens, I was certain, despite his lack of bulk, would be more than a match for anyone sufficiently foolhardy to try a frontal assault. And, although I saw no revolver, I assumed that both were armed. Still, each made it a point not to walk too close to the buildings on either side, a strategy that I immediately emulated.

Wharf Lane was as exhilarating as it was terrifying. More than that, I was, and there is no better word, *proud* to be accepted by these men. They lived by their wits and their courage, without artifice, making no apologies for their behavior, and conducted themselves, once one understood their rules, with an odd sort of integrity. I at last understood why the underworld held such allure for those forced constantly to endure the strictures of polite society.

The task of finding the proper match for Turk's key seemed at first as if it would be easier than I had thought. Many of the doors to the buildings were boarded up entirely, or had otherwise obviously been out of use for substantially longer than a week or two. By the time we had reached the end of the lane, however, there had been only three locks that were possible and none was the home to Turk's key. I turned to look back, wondering if we had missed something. Perhaps, I thought with despair, the key was for something different entirely.

"Come on," said Haggens, "we'll try the alleys."

I asked what he meant and he explained that there were alleys that backed the buildings on either side that also provided access. The alley was, if possible, even more sickening. The stench was as bad as in the Dead House and, as soon as we turned in, I heard a soft rumble and then scurrying. Through the haze, I detected movement about halfway down and, as my eyes adjusted to the scene, I realized with a start that it was human.

"They're like rats, Doc," said Haggens. "Don't worry none. They want less part of us than we do of them."

The form had disappeared, somehow blending into the architecture and piles of waste. To reach bottom in Haggens' world was to be reduced to bestiality. Was this what awaited a woman like Monique, I wondered, when her looks abandoned her entirely?

We made our way up the alley, looking for a door that might spell success. About three quarters of the way to the next street, I saw it. It was grimy and the wood was split, but the lock was in decent repair and the ground in front showed signs of recent traffic. I slipped the key into the lock; turned and clicked. Haggens nodded to Mike to remain downstairs, and we stepped inside.

A staircase just ahead looked swept or as if something had been dragged down, as did the rotting planks that passed for floorboards. I exchanged glances with Haggens and we began to climb to the second floor. He let me lead, no doubt in case there was some threat at the top. We came to another door on the landing, this one without a lock since the only access was from the street. Haggens turned up the light just a bit and we stepped through.

There could be no doubt as to the purpose of the room. Heavy drapes hung across the windows and, in the center, stood a long wooden table with a darkened oilcloth laid over it. A pile of clean sheets lay folded on a low table in the near corner. There was a sink on one side of the room, a burner on another table in the corner, and a cabinet mounted on one of the side walls. The doors of the cabinet were open, revealing a set of sounds—metal rods with rounded ends used to explore anatomical cavities—vaginal dilators, and curettes. Gynecology was not my specialty, but it was clear all the same: These were the tools of the abortionist.

A wave of disgust overwhelmed me. It was sin enough that

Turk padded his wallet performing illegal operations, but to require women to come to this disgusting and filthy room in order to have it done was ghastly. Even Haggens, hardened as he was, seemed dumbstruck at the enormity of the crime.

It took me a few moments to recover my wits, but when I did, I immediately undertook to search the room. I had come to this appalling place, after all, not simply to confirm that Turk had been an abortionist, but to try to confirm a link to Rebecca Lachtmann.

I began by a cursory inspection. The instrument case had evidently been a recent addition. The wood was clean with an unmarred finish, and the implements inside had been kept clean and polished. The locking clasp was in good repair, so it was a matter of conjecture why the door was open. It was possible, of course, that someone had been in here before us to search, but I could not imagine who. More likely, I thought, Turk had been forced to leave hurriedly on his last visit here and neglected to lock the cabinet properly.

The table and the oilcloth over it were grim indeed. There was ample staining to indicate that much fluid had passed over it. I could only assume that Turk had laid a clean sheet over this one whenever he performed his revolting procedures. The burner was used for sterilization; nearby, I found a pan in which he had placed the instruments. Other than that, except for some tumbledown chairs, there was nothing, no evidence whatever to lead me to a next step.

Haggens, who had been spooked from the second we entered the room, sensed my frustration and tried to use it as a means of ending the inquiry.

"Ain't nothing to find, Doc," he said, a strange warble in his voice. "Let's go before someone figures out somebody's up here."

"Not yet," I disagreed. "I'm sure there's something." I scanned the room once more, convinced that it was simply too bare. Abortion wasn't Turk's only illicit trade. Hadn't Monique said that he would get rid of what you didn't want, but also that he would get you what you needed? Haggens had spoken of some new drug. I was certain there should be some evidence of such activity here, but saw nothing. Then I remembered Borst and how I had bungled the search of Turk's rooms.

"Check the floor, Haggens. There will be a loose board somewhere." If Turk had used the trick at Mrs. Fasanti's, where no one knew of his presence, he would certainly secrete contraband here, where the threat of intruders was much more real.

Haggens placed the lantern on the table and we began to check the floorboards. The wood was old pine, with a good deal of rot. Some of the boards pulled up with almost no effort, but nothing was underneath except rodent excreta.

"Come on, Doc," Haggens cried when the search proved fruitless.

"No!" I said sharply. "Try the walls."

One wall was wood planking, the others plaster. We moved quickly, trying to find a false front. Finally, I came to the instrument cabinet and grasped the sides. It moved out from the bottom. The cabinet was not attached to the wall, but merely hung on it. I lifted it off, placed it on the floor, and saw what I was after.

A square was cut into the plaster. I jiggled the cutout and removed it easily. Once I had, Haggens' desire to beat a hasty retreat disappeared.

"Would you look at that," he exclaimed, and brought the lantern closer.

The opening, which was only about one foot square, masked an alcove at least twice that size. Turk had cut and then reinforced the joists to create a storage area. Inside were five packages of different sizes, each wrapped in oilcloth and tied with string. We removed them and brought them to the table.

Haggens reached to the largest of the five, but I held up my hand to stop him. Our positions had become reversed.

Haggens now deferred to me, a phenomenon attributable to the almost superstitious dread that had come over him at the sight of the stained cloth on the table. As inured to common violence as he was, I ventured that the sight of that oilcloth was the first time he had ever had occasion to imagine abortion in its grisly reality—fetus and placenta wrenched out, with sera gushing forth, as a helpless woman, her legs spread, lay moaning, debased, and miserable.

I was interested in the smallest of the packages and opened it first. Inside was what I had hoped to find: a small notebook, which, on cursory examination, appeared to hold records of Turk's transactions. I was beginning to know Turk and, from the moment I realized that there were no such documents in his rooms, I expected to find them here. He was far too opportunistic to leave no records at all. The entries were categorized by individual letters, or small combinations, and I would be quite shocked if some of them were not related to his associates or contacts, perhaps even to Halsted himself. And, if I could confirm that what I suspected about the entries was true, I would have proof of the motive for Turk's murder.

I slipped the notebook into my coat and we opened the other four packages. The first three each held a tin container bearing a stamp identifying it as the property of the Bayer Company of Wuppertal, Germany. There was other writing on the tins, but my knowledge of German was restricted to those terms that had entered medical terminology, so I could not decipher the meaning. One word I did understand was *verboten*—forbidden—and it appeared at the top of each of the tins.

The fifth package contained a revolver, a derringer, and a supply of ammunition for each.

We returned our attention to the tins and, when we opened them, discovered that each contained a white powder encased in two additional layers of oilcloth around a sheath of waxed paper. No moisture or foreign substance would penetrate such elaborate wrapping. I had taken the precaution of bringing with me a small specimen jar, which I removed from my pocket and filled with the powder.

I whispered to Haggens that we must return the room to precisely the state in which we had found it—so, when the police arrived, there would be no sign of our presence. I was surprised that he acceded so readily in repacking the white powder and returning it to the cutout, but he was so anxious to leave that room that he likely would have agreed to any request. It took only a few minutes to complete the task and, after a quick walk about with Haggens' lantern, we closed the door behind us. It was not until we had reached the street that Haggens began to regain his usual sinister demeanor.

Even Mike had been affected by the surroundings. "What took you so long?" he wanted to know, glancing up and down the alley with quick jerks of his head, his voice between a challenge and a wail. It was the longest speech I had ever heard from him. Seeing Mike afflicted with nerves caused me to experience a wave of nerves of my own, and I realized that this errand had been far more dangerous, even with my escort, than I had imagined. Without anyone saying another word, we made our way quickly but cautiously up the alley and back to The Fatted Calf.

When we arrived, Haggens told Mike to get a drink at the bar and then led me into his office. He poured us each a glass of "the real stuff," and this time I did not object. I had not lost my wits during our sojourn but, now that we were safe, I could not stop my hands from shaking. Haggens, once more in his element, grinned when he noticed and poured me a second drink after I quickly quaffed the first.

"So, Doc," he said. "What now?"

"Just as we agreed," I replied. "I give Borst the key. I tell him how I found it, inform him that when he was drunk Turk had mentioned Wharf Lane, and then let the good sergeant do the rest."

"Seems a shame," said Haggens.

"The powder? We had to leave it there, Haggens. You cannot expect me to involve myself in illicit activity."

"You kept the book, though," he pointed out.

"Only to protect the innocent," I rejoined.

"Yeah, Doc. I see. A public service." There was not much that got past Haggens.

"In any event," I said, "we both got what we wanted."

"Yeah," he said with a shrug. "I suppose." I stood to go and Haggens got out of his chair as well. "Ya won' forget what we talked about, will ya, Doc?" Haggens tapped his chest. "You were gonna..."

"Yes, of course," I replied. "I'll be back later in the week." It seemed I was not yet completely free of him.

"Thanks. Like you said . . . we're chums now."

As I left The Fatted Calf, I nodded at Mike, who was back on duty. He once again favored me with a nod and even said, "Night, Doc." It was comforting to be on Mike's good side, although I had little doubt that he would, without compunction, snap my neck like a carrot if Haggens so instructed him.

Although it seemed that it had been hours since I arrived, it was actually not yet eight-thirty. That gave me ample time to stop at the Fifth Street police station on my way home. When I arrived, I was told that Sergeant Borst had left for the day, which disappointed me not in the least. I wrote him a note detailing my discovery in one of Turk's books of a key that I had reason to believe was to his lair, which I had just remembered that he had mentioned was on Wharf Lane. I wished the sergeant good luck in his endeavors, and left both key and note in an envelope for him to open in the morning.

CHAPTER 17

I WAS QUICKLY DISABUSED OF any notion that the note-book would provide an epiphany. When I looked more closely, I saw that Turk had coded the entries, and though I did study them for a time, hoping that he had simply used abbreviations or some other transparent method of disguising the data, the cipher remained incomprehensible.

Remembering an admonition in an Edgar Allan Poe story that the best place to hide something is where everyone can see it, I placed the notebook on my bookshelves among some octavos. I left a note for Mrs. Mooney, asking that she order some material on cryptography from the lending library, but even if I could make nothing of the code, the journal might provide solid secondary evidence. The contents could prove illuminating if other information came to light that gave some indication of records that Turk had obviously thought so im-portant as to require coded entries.

I also needed to preempt Borst. The sergeant was sure to pay a return visit to the hospital, so I told the Professor first thing the next morning of my discovery of a key cut into the cover of one of Turk's book's—I neglected to say which one—and that I had turned it over to the police.

The Professor frowned deeply at the news. "The last thing we need at this moment is scandal," he grumbled, but added firmly, "but of course you did the right thing." He shook his head. "Turk seems to be more trouble dead than he was when alive. I was saddened at Turk's death, as you know, but now I am merely angry."

"Yes," I agreed. "It was easy up until now to see him as compelled by circumstance, but it seems that his malevolence was far more profound."

As we proceeded with rounds, the Professor was uncharacteristically tense and somber. He snapped at Simpson when she failed to check a patient's chart, did not make sport of Farnshaw, and was even subdued in the children's ward. His disquiet, I was certain, was not due merely to the general inconvenience that revelations of Turk's activities might cause, but to the more specific prospect that Halsted or even he himself would be sucked into the eddy.

Late morning, Sergeant Borst finally made his appearance. "Well, Dr. Carroll," he said, once we adjourned to the Professor's office, "you were quite a help."

I thanked him, although the remark contained obvious sarcasm.

"Yes, indeed. As a result of your lucky discovery, we now know that Dr. Turk was engaged in some very unpleasant activities."

I asked what he had found.

"Well," began the sergeant, "Wharf Lane is about the worst part of town there is . . . but you wouldn't know about that, would you?"

I assured him I would not, except by reputation.

"Your Dr. Turk had gotten himself a room on the second floor of one of the buildings. Not knowing which one, though, we had to go up and down the street and alleys to find the right building." He looked at me. "I suppose you had the same problem."

Did he know? I had to evade the question without specifically denying my visit. "Yes," I said, looking Borst in the eye, "but luckily Turk had given me a ball of string to make sure I didn't get lost."

"Very clever," sniffed Borst.

"So," said the Professor with irritation, "are you going to tell us what you found or simply continue wasting our time when we have work to do?"

Borst bounced on his toes, his lips pressed together. The sergeant was used to intimidating with his swagger and, like most bullies, did not take it well when one of his intended victims pushed back at him.

"All right, Doctor," he said, and then proceeded to recount in detail the primitive conditions under which Turk performed his abortions. As the policeman described the dirty, stained oilcloth, a look of revulsion passed across the Professor's face.

"Disgusting," he said. "I am ashamed to ever have been associated with such a man."

"As well you should be, Doctor," said Borst. He had said nothing about the cutout in the wall, however, and I wondered if he had found it. I was certainly in no position to ask, however.

"So," I inquired instead, "does this discovery help in your investigation?"

"A good question," Borst replied. "The answer is yes and no. Yes, because anything we can do to fill in the details of Turk's life helps, but no, because it doesn't move us along in figuring out who killed him, or even why."

"I'm sorry," I said. "I was hoping to help solve the riddle."

Borst eyed me for a moment. "Were you, now? Well, maybe you were." He continued to stand in the center of the room, rocking back and forth on his toes, but neither the Professor nor I continued the conversation.

"All right, then," Borst said finally. "I'll be back if I have any more questions." He spun on the balls of his feet and made for the door. He opened it, began to step into the hall, and then turned back. "Oh, yes. I almost forgot. We found a hidden compartment, just like in his rooms."

"More money in the floor?" I asked.

"No. Not in the floor. This time it was in the wall. Behind where he hung his tools."

"Instruments," corrected the Professor reflexively.

"Instruments," repeated Borst.

"How much?" I asked.

"Nothing. It was empty."

"Empty?"

"Yeah. Empty. Surprised me, too. Unless whoever killed Turk cleaned it out after he was dead." Borst waited for a reaction but, when neither of us provided one, added, "But I'll give you two this. I don't think it was either one of you. Can't imagine gentlemen like yourselves wandering down around on Wharf Lane." A playful sneer passed across his face. "Had to make sure though, didn't I?"

After Borst left, I could not suppress a small smile of my own. This would be the last time that I would romanticize Haggens.

The Professor misinterpreted my expression. "He is an amusing sort of ruffian, isn't he? All that bluster, bluff, and assumption. Would never do in our business, eh, Carroll?"

"No. But I do think we should tread softly in his presence, Dr. Osler. He wants very much to prove our involvement, whether true or not."

"Yes, quite correct. The mediocre always try to bring down the mighty. Perhaps now that he has come to an impasse, this incident might begin to fade, at least until we are safely in Baltimore."

"Perhaps," I acceded. "Although I suspect Sergeant Borst gets most of his results through tenacity rather than inspiration."

"Yes." The Professor nodded. "It might be well to move up the date of our departure."

After I took my leave, I made for the chemical laboratory. Although many analytic techniques—chromatography, crystal tests, and microscopic examination—would be perfected in the coming years, chemical analysis at this point remained in a formative stage, essentially little more than trial and error. In this case, however, I was able to compress the process and make an educated guess. Since I was dealing with what I assumed was a powerful new drug, I would first seek to determine if the substance was from either the morphia or cocaine families. The only reliable test for the former was Frohde's, published in 1866 in an article, "Zum Nachweis des Morphiums." Frohde had introduced molybdate in concentrated sulfuric acid into powdered morphine and observed a set of distinctive changes. The powder turned violet on contact, changed to a strong purplish red, which eventually faded to a weaker brown until finally turning green. Molybdate in concentrated sulfuric acid had since been dubbed "Frohde's reagent." As it contained a description of the only definitive test for morphia, the article had been translated from the German and was well known to physicians and chemists. I had first used Frohde's reagent while I was a student in Chicago.

The lab was empty but still I chose a station at the far end where I might only be casually observed if anyone else arrived. I placed a small amount of the powder that I had taken from Turk's lair in a test tube and introduced Frohde's reagent. As soon as the powder struck violet, I knew that I was dealing with a morphiate. The other color changes followed as expected. While a positive result narrowed the question, it did not fully solve the puzzle. There were not, to my knowledge, any morphia derivatives that would rate the praise heaped on this powder by Haggens and his associates, nor had anyone discovered an additive that would render morphia so much more potent.

My next stop was the medical library. I had never heard of the Bayer Company before, so I pored through available medical directories and journals to find out who they were, but at first could find no record of the company at all. Fortunately, with so many members of the staff having studied in

Germany, there was a section devoted to imported periodicals and reference materials. In a directory of German corporations, I found a listing for the Bayer Company of Wuppertal, a chemical firm. Checking some entries in a German-English dictionary, I discovered that Bayer was a dye maker. I couldn't be sure of the extent of Turk's depraved activities, but I felt certain that selling dye was not among them.

The Bayer Company having been identified, albeit perplexingly, I read through journals for any literature relating to a new, exceedingly powerful morphia derivative. For over an hour, I found nothing until, in an 1874 edition of an English publication, *Journal of the Chemical Society,* I came across an article by a researcher at St. Mary's Hospital in London named C. R. Alder Wright entitled "On the action of organic acids and their anhydrides on the natural alkaloids."

Wright was trying to determine the constitution of some natural and purified alkaloids and had boiled powdered morphine with acetic anhydride for several hours. The resulting liquid, which he called "tetra acetyl morphine," was an acetylized derivative that, given the change in our understanding of the morphia molecule, would now be referred to as "diacetylmorphine." Wright sent the compound to an associate, who tested it on animals and reported:

"Great prostration, fear, sleepiness speedily following
the administration, the eyes being sensitive and
pupils dilated, considerable salivation being produced
in dogs, and slight tendency to vomiting in some
cases, but no actual emesis. Respiration was at first
quickened, but subsequently reduced, and the
heart's action was diminished and rendered irregular.
Marked want of coordinating power over the
muscular movements and the loss of power in the
pelvis and hind limbs, together with a diminution
of temperature in the rectum of about 4°, were the
most noticeable effects."

After the extreme results of these animal tests, Wright decided that the drug was too powerful for practical medical use and no further experimentation was undertaken. Nor were there any recorded attempts to repeat Wright's experiment or synthesize the drug by other means.

While I could not, of course, be certain that the powder I had tested was diacetylmorphine, I felt confident that this article bore some relation to my discovery. How the German dye maker came to be involved, if in fact I was dealing with the same substance, remained a mystery. Still, there was every chance that when I discovered the explanation, I might also unravel the circumstances of George Turk's murder.

I remained at the table in the library for some moments, the journal open in front of me, trying to project where all of this might lead, deaf to the world. I did not hear the door open and close behind me, nor the sound of footsteps heading in my direction. I was, therefore, taken completely by surprise when I heard my name being called.

"Carroll, what are you doing in here? I have been looking all over for you."

My eyes darted about to see the Professor standing over me. "You missed afternoon rounds," he said.

Before I could make an explanation, he had placed his fingers on the open journal. "What are you looking at?" He leaned over to look. "Why are you interested in Wright's experiment?" he asked, a chill in his voice to which I was unaccustomed.

"You know it?"

"Certainly," the Professor replied curtly. "It was more accident than experiment. He boiled up some morphine in anhydrous acetic acid and came up with a morphia derivative that proved to be too potent for medical use. No one, as far as I know, has performed any further research."

"Yes," I said. "So it seems."

"So what is your interest?"

There was no lie that would not sound ridiculous, so I

resorted to a half-truth. "Turk had spoken of some intensely powerful morphia derivative."

"In what context?"

"He had simply stated that, with the predilection to use opiates at every stratum of society, it would only be a matter of time before the drugs were engineered to higher intensity. He said he expected that day to arrive sooner rather than later."

"Why didn't you mention it?"

"There seemed no point. Turk spoke of many things that evening and this seemed to be idle musing. But after listening to Sergeant Borst, I became curious. Turk had certainly created that compartment to hold something."

"And," asked the Professor, "what have you concluded?"

"This was all I could find." I gestured to the journal. "Turk must indeed have been merely speculating. He could hardly have based his evidence on a fifteen-year-old article about an obscure experiment that no one seems to have pursued further."

"Yes," the Professor agreed. "Hardly."

I closed the journal and replaced it on the appropriate shelf. I couldn't determine whether the Professor suspected me of duplicity or was merely unnerved by the prospect of a dogged policeman instigating a scandal on the eve of his greatest triumph. In either case, this was not a fortuitous moment to have him peering over my shoulder.

CHAPTER 18

EARLY IN THE AFTERNOON, I received a note from Abigail Benedict confirming our arrangements for the evening. She asked that I call for her at seven-thirty, as she had reserved us a table at Barker's.

When I arrived, she swept down the spiral staircase. Abigail was stunning, clad in a high-necked, deep maroon dress with a white lace collar, and, as always, without gloves or jewelry. Her hair was up, the first time I had seen it so, accentuating a neck that was long, thin, and graceful. She smiled as she reached the bottom step, and I moved toward her. I realized she had a scent all her own—almost flowery, but with a sensual hint as well. I had never noticed such things in the past. Abigail seemed to be the only thing in the room. She took my hands in hers and leaned in and kissed me. As I had hoped, seeing her was the perfect antidote to the intrigues that were weighing on me.

"You look quite dashing, Ephraim," she said, touching my cheek. "Shall we go?"

I led the way out to the carriage, floating rather than walking, and this time when I offered my hand to help her in, she accepted it. The skin on her wrist was soft, smooth, and very white. As soon as the carriage was off, she asked about my visit to Baltimore. I eagerly described the wondrous facilities at the new hospital, my conviction that Johns Hopkins would change the entire course of medicine in America. I feared I was being transparent about my own heightened prospects, but Abigail listened with great interest and enthusiasm. When I had completed my description, she asked a number of perceptive questions about the staff, potential professional jealousies, and the envy that such a place might cause in other elite institutions. I responded that I felt certain the competition would spur improvements and upgrades and that ultimately there would be benefit to all.

Abigail expressed how pleased she was at my good fortune but, as we neared Barker's, she abandoned talk of Johns Hopkins. Instead, she asked, "And what were your plans last night that you had to postpone our rendezvous?"

"I will tell you at dinner," I blurted, realizing only after the words were out that my findings all pointed to grim confirmation of Abigail's worst fears. I felt a rush of embarrassment that, in my zeal to solve the problem, I had forgotten the human stakes for her. I had been imprudent to agree to see her in a public place; I resolved to tread with extreme delicacy in my recitation of the facts.

"It has something to do with Rebecca, then," Abigail said, oblivious to the truth. "I'm excited to hear all that you have found. I'm so grateful for your assistance."

When we entered the restaurant, Abigail gave her name to the man in the striped vest. He gave a start upon seeing me, but I stared directly at him and he knew to keep silent. He simply nodded and led us across the room. Any hopes that I had for an intimate dinner *à deux* were dashed, however, when, as we reached our table, Thomas Eakins stood and offered his hand. "It is good to see you again, Dr. Carroll."

I nodded resentfully to Eakins but did not take his hand. Abigail could not help but notice my reaction to the painter's presence. As soon as we were seated and the man in the striped vest had left, she said evenly, "You said you wanted to know about Rebecca. I told you that Thomas had to be involved. He has agreed that you are a man to be trusted, and we want to tell you everything."

Whenever she and I were alone, we seemed unutterably

drawn to each other, but in the company of Eakins, our relationship became distant, fraught with suspicion, even adver-
sarial.

"It was my idea," said Eakins. "Abby didn't want to deceive
you as to my presence, but I thought that you might object and
we very much need to talk."

So it was "Abby," was it? I suddenly hated Eakins, but envied the power he exuded. Unlike the Professor, whose mag-
netism emanated from intellect and self-assurance, Eakins'
strength was feral. Women, I decided with some envy, claimed
to be attracted to the former but actually preferred the latter.

"It's true, Ephraim," Abigail said, placing her hand on
mine. "We are all in a terrible predicament. We may not be
doing everything correctly, but it is not because we wish to deceive you. Just the opposite. We want you to know the truth."

"All right," I agreed, speaking in measured tones. "Let me
know the truth."

"And then you will tell us what you have uncovered?" she
asked.

"Of course," I replied. The painter's presence had altered
the equation entirely. If they wanted the truth, they would
hear it.

Eakins began. "Very well. I assume you have surmised the
nature of Rebecca's medical problem."

"I have presumed that it was an unwanted pregnancy."

"Well," Eakins offered, "you are correct. Rebecca did find
herself pregnant."

"Are you the father?" I asked bluntly.

"The answer is that I am not sure," Eakins replied, but
without the guilt that such an immense admission should
have engendered. "There is the remotest possibility that I
might be, Dr. Carroll, but Rebecca was involved with someone else, a man whose identity she refused to reveal. He is
the more probable choice. But in any case, learning of her
predicament, I committed to help Rebecca in any way I could,
and it is a promise I intend to keep."

"We confided in each other about everything, but she would not tell me, either." A gloss of tears shone in Abigail's eyes. "I'm not even sure when the assignations occurred, although it must have been sometime in December. Looking back, I realize that I should have suspected that something was amiss. During the holiday season, Rebecca was so gay... *so gay*... if I had only paid more attention...." She reached up and quickly dabbed at her eyes. "Oh, God, what a fool I was."

"It's not your fault, Abby," Eakins interjected, reaching out to her before I could. "In any event, Dr. Carroll, even when Rebecca first realized that she was likely with child, she did not confide in anyone except her maid, Lucy. But she could not ignore her condition forever. In the first days of February, she finally told her mother. Eunice told Jonas, of course, although not even her father's fury could make Rebecca identify the man who had impregnated her. Jonas immediately made arrangements for a long family sojourn in Italy. Rebecca would have her child overseas, where it would be put up for adoption."

Eakins paused as our drinks arrived, and only the click of beer glasses being placed on the table punctuated the silence. "At first, she refused," the painter continued after the waiter had departed. "She told her parents that wondering for the rest of her life what had become of a human life that she had nurtured within her and then abandoned would be more than she could bear. She was insistent that any child that she did have, she intended to care for and raise herself."

Abigail had regained sufficient control to take up the tale. "Jonas would not hear of such an arrangement, of course, so finally Rebecca came to us. She had hatched a plan. She needed Thomas and me to help her carry it out."

"What was her plan?" I asked.

"She agreed to go abroad, but only if her parents remained behind," Abigail replied. "There was quite a scene, but what could they do? Allowing Rebecca to continue to be seen in Philadelphia was out of the question, and they could not simply pack her off somewhere against her will. So, Rebecca and Lucy the maid crossed on the first liner available, the *Alexandria*. When the ship docked in London, Rebecca and Lucy exchanged documents. They are almost the same age and physically quite similar. Rebecca sent Lucy on ahead with a pack of letters that she had written during the crossing and then turned around and immediately took the *Christina* back to New York City. Lucy, as Rebecca, undertook the predetermined itinerary, posting letters across France and into Italy. Everything seems to have gone according to plan, so I'm not sure what could have aroused Jonas' suspicions."

"I want to tell you that I stoutly advised Rebecca against this action," Eakins added. "I told her in the strongest terms I thought she should have the child in Italy and then defy her parents and insist on keeping it. But Rebecca would have none of it. 'You cannot imagine the lengths to which my father will go to keep up appearances,' she told me. After meeting him once or twice, I think she might well have been right."

"And so Rebecca, as Lucy, returned to Philadelphia to end her pregnancy," I said.

"Yes."

"What of raising the child herself?"

"She realized that was never really an option. She could not bring such disgrace on her family," said Eakins. "Termination was her only remaining choice."

I said nothing, but could not hide my feelings. Termination had not been the only remaining choice for the women at the Croskey Street Settlement. Of course, those women were not rich.

"You disapprove, Ephraim?" asked Abigail, her voice gone cold.

"I cannot countenance abortion," I said bluntly.

"Oh, can't you, now?" she snapped, her despair finding an outlet in anger. "How easily smug denunciations roll off your tongue! Do you think it is better to bring a child into the world who will be ripped from the arms of its mother and shoved into an orphanage to live a wretched and neglected life . . . to grow up not knowing its parents and likely die on the streets in misery?"

I thought of Annie. "No," I said, "it is not that . . . but . . ."

Eakins unexpectedly came to my rescue. "Wait, Abigail," he said. "You are being unfair. Dr. Carroll is quite right to be outraged. The concept of taking human life is repugnant. It must be all the more so to one who has dedicated himself to saving it. But, Dr. Carroll, I must ask you to try and look at this from a different perspective. Would you, as a doctor, save a patient who you know will simply live out life in agony? If Rebecca were to have this child, it would doom two lives, hers and the child's. Please understand, this is not a decision that anyone came to lightly."

"I love Rebecca," Abigail said, now as plaintive as she had just been furious. "If she was determined to go through with this, I wanted only to ensure that she was put into the hands of someone who would care for her safety."

"Like Turk?"

"I had nothing to do with that!"

"Rebecca refused to allow either Abigail or myself to be party to the specific arrangements," Eakins told me, "in case the facts should come out and the police—or her father—gained knowledge of the event. I am incensed with myself for agreeing."

"Why did she not simply have the abortion on the continent? And return at her leisure?" I asked. "Locating a disreputable physician to perform such a criminal act would be no more difficult in Europe than in Philadelphia."

"This was not something to be done in a strange city, with no friends to call upon in an emergency." Eakins then proceeded to recount the tale of Rebecca's return. He had journeyed to New York in late February to meet the *Christina* and thence returned to Philadelphia, having secured lodgings for "Lucy" in Chestnut Hill. The preparations for the operation

had been handled circuitously. Eakins had not known of anyone personally who might perform the procedure, and was
thus forced to make the most discreet of inquiries. Finally, an
actor who had at one time been a photographic subject—"a
thoroughly disreputable fellow," as Eakins described him—
had contacted an acquaintance who had once been in need
of a similar service and who had in turn contacted an acquaintance of his who had then made contact directly with
Rebecca.

"You never knew the identity of the abortionist?"

"Never," replied Abigail. "It was as I said. We were to be at
that horrible place at ten o'clock on an appointed night,
where Rebecca would be contacted by someone who would
make the final arrangements. She was to give him two hundred dollars. Rebecca didn't even know if the man contacting
us would be the one performing the operation or just a go-
between. But, as I told you, no one approached her. We remained for over an hour and then left."

"Clearly, Rebecca didn't stop there."

"Two days later, I met her at her rented rooms. She told
me that she had contacted the man who had given her the instructions and that the problem had been resolved. She refused details, saying only that she had made arrangements
both for the operation and for a convalescent facility afterward where she would be under a nurse's care. She promised
to be in touch when everything had been completed. She was
actually quite proud of herself for managing everything. That
was just over two weeks ago. The last I heard from her."

"How was she intending to deal with her father?" I asked.

"She intended to confront him with a *fait accompli*.
Don't be deceived by Rebecca's youth . . . she is a formidable
woman, every bit the match for her father. Jonas would have
no choice but to acquiesce. He adores Rebecca."

"Now that you have the details you requested, Dr.
Carroll," Eakins interjected suddenly, "perhaps you can tell us
what you have uncovered."

I was jarred. So caught up had I been in hearing their tale, that I had completely forgotten that I would now be forced to reveal that their friend was quite possibly dead. I had no shortage of experience in bearing bad news to patients and relatives, of course, and it was always with genuine pain that I did so, but nothing in my experience had prepared me for this. After hearing how much Abigail blamed herself, seeing her blot away tears, I desperately did not want to be the bearer of such news to her. But what else could I do?

Calling on my professional demeanor as best I could, and treading delicately on the particulars, I described the incident thirteen days before in the Dead House. I selectively recounted my evening with Turk, and concluded the rendition with a bowdlerized version of my investigation, locating his rooms, his death in my presence, and then my dealings with Haggens.

When I had completed the tale, no one spoke. Eakins turned to Abigail and began once more to reach for her, but stopped himself. I too wanted to comfort her, but could scarcely take a woman in my arms in a public place. Seeing her grief, I knew with utter conviction that I loved her deeply. My jealousy about Eakins was based only in my shortcomings, not hers.

"Poor Rebecca," Abigail said finally in a choked whisper, dropping her hands into her lap. Her face had become a blank, as if now even tears would have been inadequate. "I suppose I knew all the time, but refused to admit it."

In that second, I knew I could not let my revelations be the source of her desolation. I had to prove to her that all was not lost. "Wait," I interjected quickly. "I know this is dismaying news, but it is hardly the end. All I have said is conjecture. Conjecture, Abigail! I can be in no way certain that the corpse I saw for only a brief moment was Rebecca. Nor has any other evidence been brought forth to support that conclusion. It is certainly not impossible, in a city where so many die young, that the woman in the morgue merely bore a close resemblance to your friend."

At that, Abigail straightened in her chair, her eyes alert and hopeful. Encouraged, I continued. "I am a scientist, Abigail. I don't accept something as true simply because it is probably true, nor should you."

"He's right, Abby," said Eakins, grasping eagerly at my words as well. "There's no reason to give up now. Dr. Carroll will continue his inquiries, isn't that true, Dr. Carroll?"

"Certainly," I agreed.

"Is there no way to determine if Rebecca was the woman you saw?" Abigail asked me.

"At this juncture, there is no way to be certain without an exhumation."

"An exhumation?" she exclaimed, horrified. "That would be barbaric."

"I did not say that I would recommend such a course now," I said, "merely that if Rebecca is not found, it might be the only eventual alternative."

"Yes, Abby," Eakins enjoined. "Not now. For now, we will keep looking. Dr. Carroll will tell us how to proceed. After all, he's done a splendid job so far. I for one would not have believed that he could have found out as much as he has. And who knows that at any moment Rebecca won't appear at your door?"

Abigail was frantic to maintain hope. "Will you, Ephraim? Will you keep looking?"

"Of course," I assured her. She had not turned to Eakins in her moment of greatest anxiety; she had turned to me. I am embarrassed to confess that my spirit soared at the knowledge. Then, to complete my triumph, she said to the painter, "Thomas, I thank you for being here, but I would like to be alone with Ephraim."

To my surprise, Eakins was more than amenable to the notion. He rose immediately, made his farewells, and strode to the door. I followed him with my eyes as he moved across the room in that coiled way he had. I was about to turn back to Abigail when, just as Eakins reached the exit, the man with the handlebar mustache who had been waiting outside his house on Mount Vernon Street got up from the bar. Like a shadow, he followed the painter out.

Although there was no solid evidence, I felt certain that this unknown man was an agent of Jonas Lachtmann. I might fall under his gaze next, I knew, but before I could weigh on the perils of further involvement, Abigail leaned forward. "Ephraim, could you please take me home?"

She was silent on the ride to Rittenhouse Square, and I knew better than to intrude. I helped her down from the carriage and walked with her to her door. "I'm sorry the evening turned out so disastrously," I said.

She forced an ephemeral smile. "I'd like you to come in," she said softly. "There is something I want you to see."

She led me quietly through the foyer to a set of back stairs. Holding my hand, she led me to the second floor, then down a hall, past a number of closed doors to a narrow staircase at the far end.

She mounted the first step, still holding my hand, and then stopped and turned about. Smiling softly once more, she bent and kissed me lightly, her lips brushing fleetingly across mine. Our eyes held for a moment before she turned to lead me up the curving staircase.

At the top was a small hall, with three doors. Abigail reached into her bag, withdrew a key, and then walked to the far door and turned the lock. The door opened onto a dark room, and she beckoned for me to enter. Only after I had done so did she turn the switch on the wall to engage the electric light. She closed the door behind us.

This was her studio. Not as expansive as Eakins', perhaps, but still quite large. There were a number of canvases in the room in various states of completion, all in the same powerful, disturbing style as her portrait of Rebecca Lachtmann. An easel in the middle of the room evidently held the painting that she was working on, but a sheet was draped over it and I could not discern the subject.

Without speaking, Abigail gestured for me to stand in front of the easel. She stepped to the side, grasped the sheet, and pulled it off.

The portrait was of me.

It was unfinished, some of the borders still simple sketch lines, but she had done substantial work on the face. I stared at myself in utter fascination. As in her portrait of Rebecca, Abigail had bent reality just enough to project a subjective image while preserving instant identification of the subject, and once again utilized the bold, flat swatches of color that forced one's gaze to the eyes of the subject on the canvas.

Those eyes—my eyes—had been rendered a powerful chestnut—like Eakins'—more arresting, I thought, than in life, and gave off intelligence, strength, and resolve. The portrait had a kinetic quality, but with an overall impression of sensuality, the very combination of traits that I envied in Eakins.

Could this be the way she saw me? Or perhaps it was the way she wished to see me. I stared at the painting for some moments.

"Do you like it?" she whispered.

"It is the most remarkable thing that has ever happened to me," I replied honestly. "I want to be the man in the portrait rather than myself."

"You are the man in the portrait," she said. "Come with me." She led me to a door at the far end of the studio. "Sometimes when I'm painting, I don't leave here for days. My meals are left outside." We had reached the door. Abigail pushed down on the handle. "I had Father fix a place for me to sleep." She swung open the door to reveal a small bedroom. "It's completely removed from anyplace else in the house," she said, leading me inside.

Two hours later, we lay in her bed and I felt the deepest and most profound sense of well-being I had ever known. Love-making with Abigail had been a transcendent experience, not like the mere animal release with Wanda. I wanted to stroke her skin, smell her hair, feel the warmth of her against me, blend our bodies and our souls together for eternity. For the first time, I understood the true nature of addiction—I would risk anything not to lose these sensations.

She reached over and touched my cheek. "I miss Rebecca."

"Yes," I replied. "I know."

"You have given me hope, Ephraim, or perhaps only a respite. In either case, I am grateful. But I cannot continue to live with uncertainty. I must know the truth. You will find out the truth for me, won't you?"

I thought of her painting of me. *That* man would do anything necessary for the woman he loved.

"Of course," I said.

It was going to be dangerous, I realized, trying to live up to a portrait.

CHAPTER 19

I SKULKED OUT OF THE Benedict house before sunrise, leaving like a thief through a door at the back of the garden. I had not been the first to tread that same path, I knew, but I could not let that concern me. There was no point in going home, so I went directly to the hospital. I succeeded in gaining a few hours' sleep curled up on a settee in the doctors' lounge.

When I awoke, I made once more for the library and, using the German-English dictionary and phrase book, I laboriously drafted an inquiry to the Bayer Company. With apologies for my *grauenhaft Deutsch*—my atrocious German—I asked about their experiments with diacetylmorphine. As a physician, I added, I was extremely interested in the analgesic properties of the substance and would be most interested to learn of the results of any clinical tests. Then I went to the cable office and was informed by a young and eager clerk whose skin still bore marks of a recent eruption of *acne vulgaris* that a number of relays would be required after the message was sent by transatlantic cable, but should arrive in Germany within a day. Any response would be held for me on a will-call basis.

The clerk then not only insisted on explaining the many ways in which the miracle of modern telegraphy was changing the world, but also on favoring me with a rendition of the tribulations in establishing a worldwide system of communication. Did I know how many times the cable snapped when being lowered into the pitching waters of the ocean? Was I aware of the persistence of Cyrus Field and those other visionaries who refused to abandon the project even though most investors refused to continue their support?

Although I was impatient, lest I be missed at the hospital, the boy's enthusiasm was infectious. He had as much zeal for the future of electrical communication and magnetics as I did for diagnostics and surgery. A new century would be upon us in just over a decade and, with breathtaking advances in virtually every field of human endeavor, the world did unquestionably belong to the young.

I returned with about fifteen minutes to spare before afternoon rounds. I saw Simpson in the halls, but when I approached her to say hello, she nodded perfunctorily and turned to leave. I inquired if there was anything the matter, but she assured me quietly that there was not, so I joined the others and entered the main ward.

In the second bed, we encountered a newly admitted patient, a nearly comatose male in his twenties, with an exceptional set of symptoms. He had been found lying in the street, mumbling incoherently, and been brought to the hospital by the police. The man showed severe muscle spasticity, and there was a bluish tinge to his lips and fingernails. His breathing was slow, labored, and shallow, his pulse weak, his blood pressure low. The man's tongue was discolored and his pupils, when we could rouse him sufficiently to open his eyes, were mere dots. He appeared to be severely constipated with a spasmodic gastrointestinal tract.

"Morphia poisoning," said Corrigan immediately, "but I've never seen it so severe."

"Nor I," Simpson added. She seemed genuinely puzzled.

When the Professor finished his examination, he noted from the accompanying documents that the man was a denizen of the waterfront district. "Any ideas, Carroll?" he asked pointedly.

I looked at the Professor, trying to determine whether his

question was genuine or rhetorical, but he gave no indication of his thinking.

"None," I said.

⌐⌐⌐

"You're becoming quite a regular," Haggens grunted as he ushered me into the office later that evening. "Getting a little more attracted to the criminal element, Doc?"

"Do you want me to listen to your heart or not?" I asked, brandishing my stethoscope.

Haggens dropped his bravado, as he had done in the room on Wharf Lane. "Yeah. I do," he replied meekly. Swagger did not hold up well against the prospect of a medical examination.

I instructed him to remove his vest and shirt. Haggens seemed slight in clothes, but bare-chested, he was deceptively broad across the chest and his arms were thick cords of muscle.

"I was a prizefighter, Doc," he said, noticing me notice. "Gave it up, though. Much better ways of making a dollar."

"I'm sure you were quite adept," I said, breathing on the stethoscope's diaphragm to warm it.

"I can still go a round or two."

I was certain he could. I instructed Haggens to take deep breaths as I auscultated front and back. There was a soft rumble directly over the heart during the resting phase of the heartbeat, which became more distinct just before contraction. With Haggens' history of rheumatic fever, it was a simple matter to determine the problem. I told him to dress.

"Is it serious, Doc?" he said, a look of genuine fear passing across his face. What power physicians possess!

"Have you had a cough? Was there blood in it?"

"I had a cough a while back," Haggens answered softly. "No blood, though."

"That's good," I said. "Do you ever get a constriction . . . tightening in your chest?"

Haggens shook his head. "That good too, Doc?"

I nodded. "Are you ever tired?"

"All the time," he said.

"No, I mean *very* tired."

"Sometimes," he said. "Do you know what I got?"

"I think so," I said. "You have the symptoms of a condition called mitral stenosis, which is a narrowing of one of the valves in your heart. It prevents adequate blood flow between the chambers."

"That sounds bad," he said.

"Not necessarily. In many cases the condition doesn't progress. If you can tolerate the symptoms and they don't worsen, you should be fine."

"What if they do worsen?"

There was no point in lying. Haggens was far too savvy to be taken in by platitudes. "If your symptoms worsen, you could eventually develop either blood clots or an infection of the heart muscle called endocarditis."

"Bad?"

"Either can kill you."

Haggens digested the information, sizing up the alternatives as he had when I had asked to borrow Mike. Like many patients, now that he knew the facts, he was able to consider his condition coolly and rationally. "How long is eventually?"

"There is no way to know. But most of the time the condition will stay as it is."

"Anything I can do for it?"

"Well, you might want to drink less. Coffee won't help you, either. And you might want to try to avoid nervous stress."

Haggens guffawed. "Avoid stress? Down here?"

"Well," I said, "do your best. We have another matter to discuss, however."

Haggens dropped his eyes in mock shame, as he buttoned his shirt. "I know, Doc. I was a bad boy."

"Yes," I agreed. "How many people have tried it?"

"The stuff?"

"Of course, the stuff. I didn't mean the revolver."

"I heard rumors that some of it has gotten around."

"What did these rumors say as to the effects?"

"Rumors said that this is the best stuff anyone has ever tried."

"Not everyone thought so, I'll wager. I would venture to say that some who tried it received an unpleasant surprise." The patient I had seen earlier in the hospital, for one, I thought.

"Unpleasant surprises are everyday happenings down here, Doc."

"Yes," I agreed. "I'm sure. Has anyone died?"

Haggens turned his palms up. "Do I look like the town undertaker?"

I took a breath. I was about to take my association with Haggens into dangerous territory. "I need whoever is selling it to stop selling it. If they don't stop selling it, people are going to keep showing up at either the hospital or the morgue with symptoms of poisoning that will force me to tell the police what I know about this mysterious substance." Haggens began to speak, but I put up my hand. "And please don't tell me how dangerous it would be for me to do so, or that I would be in just as much trouble as this unnamed party to whom I refer. I already know that. But I cannot allow people to die, and remain a physician. I do hope, however, that I will not be forced into the position of having to make a choice."

Haggens cocked his head and lightly rubbed the first two fingers of his right hand across his lower lip, trying to choose how to respond. I decided to help him.

"You make a good living down here, Haggens. Why jeopardize it? It would not please me to make good my threat, but I cannot remain silent while poison is being sold, no matter who profits by it."

Haggens continued to size up the situation. "I could make it that you don't ever leave this room alive," he said. "Thought about that?"

"Yes."

We remained there in silence for some moments, my life suspended in the air between us. Finally, Haggens narrowed his eyes and gave a nod. "Okay, you win." He broke into a grin. "Can't kill my own doc after all, can I?" He raised a finger and wagged it in my direction. "But don't forget. You owe me one."

"I do indeed," I agreed. I smiled back at him. "I don't suppose you'd give it back to me?"

Haggens shook his head slowly. "That far I can't go, Doc, not even for you. Here's my deal: As long as a bunch of poor unfortunates don't show up sick or dead, you stay outta my business and I stay outta yours."

Now it was me who had to deduce what Haggens had in mind. The upshot was that the issue was moot. If Haggens found a means to deal with the drug in a manner that did not make users sick, I would not know that it was being sold. If I had no evidence that he was continuing the forbidden commerce, I could not act to stop him.

"All right, Haggens," I said, thrusting out my hand. "It's a bargain."

Haggens shook my hand and heaved a sigh. "I'm going to miss it if you stop coming down here, Doc. It's quite a nice change dealing with such a high-class chap."

I would miss him too, although I would never admit to it. "Well, Haggens, you never know. Maybe I'll come by from time to time just for a drink."

"You'll always be welcome, Doc."

"Thank you. One more thing before I go. If you won't give me back the, uh, stuff, would you mind giving me one of the tins that it came in?"

"Empty?" Haggens looked at me as if I had lost my wits.

"Have you changed your mind about giving it to me full?"

"No chance."

"Then empty will do."

Haggens considered for a moment. When he could not think of what underhanded ploy I might be attempting, he agreed.

He asked me to leave the office. When, a few moments later, he called me back in, one of the empty tins was sitting on his desk. He gestured with his head that I should take it.

"Thank you," I said, making to leave. I tapped my chest. "You will try to relax more."

Haggens chortled. "Sure. Anything you say. I always wanted to die of old age."

CHAPTER 20

IT WAS TIME TO KEEP my word to Abigail and determine
once and for all the fate of Rebecca Lachtmann.

As the city was responsible for providing funeral services
for the indigent, I assumed that the Department of Health
would have a record of a young woman recently buried in
Potter's Field. I sent word to the hospital that I was ill, then
journeyed downtown to check the records of recent interments. To my surprise, not only was there no record of anyone matching Rebecca Lachtmann's description receiving a
public burial during the previous month, but the number of
public burials—only twenty-five—seemed to be far fewer
than I would have thought. I thanked the clerk, left, and returned to West Philadelphia. I had hardly begun and had run
into my first complication, and would therefore be forced to
add an additional and potentially dangerous step. My next
stop was the Dead House.

I entered through the Blockley entrance, hoping that this
would not be one of the rare days that the Professor was
performing an impromptu autopsy. I had never spoken to
Cadaverous Charlie except to pass an occasional comment on
his duties. I tried the handle on the heavy door, found it un-
locked, and entered. The dissecting room was empty, but I
heard a gravelish sound emanating from the morgue. When I
peered in, Charlie was changing the ice, muttering as he
transferred shovelfuls from a large bucket in the middle of the
floor into the chests that held the cadavers. Shoveling ice was

an extremely arduous activity and I realized that, despite his bony frame, Charlie must have been quite strong. He was from some region in western Germany—Alsace, I believe the Professor had said—and he seemed to be surviving the chore by swearing in a mixture of German, French, and English. Charlie had doubtless heard someone knock and move about, but remained at his task with his back toward me.

I cleared my throat, but he continued to refuse to acknowledge my presence. "Excuse me . . . Charlie . . . could we speak for a moment?" I uttered finally.

Charlie deposited another shovelful of ice into one of the chests, which held the corpse of an enormously corpulent man of about thirty, and then paused, as if deciding whether to grace me with an answer. After a moment, he straightened up, leaned the shovel against the wall, and turned. He was covered in perspiration. It glistened off his extremely flat and fleshy nose, giving him the appearance of a giant exotic marsupial.

"I would like to ask you a question or two," I began affably.

Charlie stared back at me.

"About what is done with the cadavers after dissection . . ."

Still, not a word in return.

"I would be happy to pay for the information."

Charlie nodded slowly, as if I had uttered a magical phrase, and then wiped his hands on his apron. "How much?" he asked.

"Fifty cents?" I offered. The price of a steak dinner should seem a bounty to a man of Charlie's rank.

"Fi' dollars," he countered instantly, holding up the requisite number of fingers in case I had missed the message. I had forgotten that taking bribes was Charlie's *métier*. For a man who toiled at such a menial task, given his income from the Professor, Reverend Squires, and goodness knew who else, he was likely substantially wealthier than I.

I dug through my pockets. I had some money with me but not nearly enough to satisfy Charlie's rapacious tastes.

"I can offer you one dollar," I said, holding out my hand.

Charlie sniffed, but allowed me to drop the coins into his palm. "Vot you vanna know?" he asked.

"I was just wondering what happens to the cadavers after we finish our work here."

"Dey get buried. Sometime cremated."

"Why, yes," I agreed quickly. "I know that they are buried... or cremated...but who handles the arrangements?"

"Vhy you vanna know dat?"

Why indeed? "It occurred to me that the poor are not always properly interred and it has weighed on my conscience."

Charlie stared at me as though he were confronting an inmate from the lunatic ward. "Dey get buried fine," he said.

"By whom?" I pressed.

"De city sometime."

"And other times?"

Charlie began to shift from one foot to another and I realized that I had actually unearthed a clue. I felt quite triumphant. "Well," I pressed. "I did not pay you for nothing."

The pecuniary argument was persuasive.

"Sometime de League bury dem," he said.

"Reverend Squires' League?" I asked. "The same people who try to keep us from conducting autopsies?"

"Yeah," Charlie replied. "How many leagues dere are?"

"Does Formad decide who buries whom?"

"Formad?" sneered Charlie. "Vat he know?"

I had a revelation. "He pays you, does he not? Reverend Squires? To allow him to take the cadavers for burial?" Charlie did not reply, which was reply enough. This explained why the cadavers had been removed so quickly after we autopsied them. Charlie, in effect, had sold the bodies to Reverend Squires. "I think, Charlie, that under the circumstances, it would not be a good idea for either of us to mention this conversation. Do you agree?"

Charlie most certainly did.

I still needed one last bit of confirmation.

"Does anyone on the medical staff ever urge you to bury the bodies quickly?"

"Vot you mean? Like Formad?"

"Other than Formad."

"Ve always get rid of ze bodies quick."

I considered pressing the matter further, trying to bring it around to the body that I suspected was Rebecca Lachtmann's and whether it had been the Professor or Reverend Squires who had given Charlie special instructions, but decided against it. Arousing Charlie's curiosity, I was certain, would result in even more money changing hands, more secrets exposed. If the Professor learned that I had continued involving myself in these affairs, I was finished. If it had been Reverend Squires, I would have to find out from him independently; if not, there was no point in alerting Charlie to my motives.

The problem of how to proceed, however, was not so easily disposed of. I knew at once that I could not hope to obtain information from the head of the Philadelphia League Against Human Vivisection by revealing that I was a physician. I was going to need assistance and there was only one person to whom I might turn.

This time, when I arrived at Mount Vernon Street, I did not catch a glimpse of the man with the mustache. "Why, hello, Dr. Carroll," Susan Eakins said as she opened her door, as if I had just returned from an extended journey, "how lovely to see you again." She did not, however, move to invite me in.

"Hello, Mrs. Eakins—" I began.

"Susan," she corrected.

"Susan." I cleared my throat softly. "I wonder if I might have a very brief word with your husband?"

She shook her head with a sigh. "I'm so sorry, Dr. Carroll, but Thomas can never be disturbed while he is working."

"I understand that this is an unconscionable intrusion," I persisted, "but it is quite urgent."

She considered this for a moment. Then she nodded. "I'll let him know you are here."

A few moments later, Eakins came down the stairs. He looked like a madman, hair mussed, wild-eyed and paint-stained. I understood why it was unwise to disturb him. He ushered me into the small parlor.

"I need your assistance," I said.

I told Eakins of my conversation with Cadaverous Charlie. He reached up with paint-spattered fingers and tugged on his earlobe. "I agree that our next step is to interview this Reverend Squires. What role did you have in mind for me?"

I explained why I could not see Reverend Squires myself. "Even if he did not discover that I worked with Dr. Osler, I am sure that he would never confide in a medical man."

"And you think it more likely that he would confide in me?" asked Eakins. "I'm sorry, Carroll, but I must tell you that you have not thought this through. If this Reverend Squires is as you describe him, he will not be a party to any conspiracy, regardless of who seeks to engage him. It seems clear to me that he must be made to reveal information without being aware he is doing so, or at the very least, unaware of what we are actually attempting to learn."

"I don't see how we can cause him to do that," I confessed.

Eakins thought for a moment. "He must *want* to give information rather than be coerced. He must think he is speaking with someone who can be of assistance to him."

"Are you going to suggest that you wish to paint him?" I asked.

Eakins shook his head. "No, no. That's not at all what I mean. We wish him to reveal his activities, not sit for a portrait. . . . Wait!" he exclaimed, then smiled slowly, looking quite feline. "Of course. You must go as another," Eakins said.

"As another? Misrepresent myself?"

"As you said, he will not confide in a physician."

"Impossible. He would see right through me. This is your scheme; you should execute it."

Eakins shook his head. "I'm sorry to inform you, Dr. Carroll, but I am sufficiently well known that I can hardly go anywhere in this city as anyone but myself. Even in that guise, I am often unwelcome. No. I'm afraid it will have to be you."

"I expect you have a firm idea of who that alter ego should be."

"A very firm idea," said Eakins.

I listened as Eakins told me. "I'll be back," I said.

One hour later, I pulled up in a hansom at the Germantown Mission on Wayne Avenue, a wide, tree-lined road just off Fairmount Park. The two-story building with the gold cupola at which the carriage stopped was part of a larger complex that seemed to sprawl across the street on either side. The Germantown Mission, in addition to its ecclesiastical activities, housed an orphanage and a soup kitchen, and provided a number of other services for the poor.

I informed the young man who answered the door that I had come to see Reverend Squires. After a moment in the vestibule, I heard footsteps and soon the Reverend himself made his appearance.

I had formed a picture in my mind's eye of a tall, glowering fanatic who intimidated society matrons into opening their pocketbooks, but Reverend Squires was instead short and plump with a florid countenance and what seemed to be indefatigable good cheer. He bounced across the floor to greet me. I was heartened. A man more susceptible to flattery would be difficult to imagine.

"Good afternoon, Reverend," I said. "I'm so lucky to find you in, as I have traveled overnight to see you."

"Indeed," replied the Reverend. "And where did your journey begin?"

"New York," I said, stepping forward and extending my hand. "Allow me to introduce myself. My name is Galen Harvey and I work for the *New York Sun*."

Reverend Squires shook my hand with appropriate awe. Eakins had judged our man well. "The *New York Sun*? And you wish to speak with me?"

"Quite so," I said. "Word of your good work has spread, Reverend Squires, and the *Sun* believes that the citizens of New York should have the full story." I sounded very much like a reporter, I decided.

The Reverend apparently agreed. "Well, well," he said, hardly able to contain his elation. "I would be happy to discuss any of our work here. Is there some specific aspect of our efforts in which you are most interested?"

"Oh, yes," I said, with a deferential nod. "We feel that your labors on behalf of the poor in obtaining a decent burial are remarkable and noteworthy. In fact, it has been commented that they are unsurpassed. After all, these poor wretches should at least be entitled to their final dignity."

"Yes, yes." Reverend Squires nodded, almost dancing before me. "That is so true, Mr. Harvey. They are so often abused in life, why should they also be abused in death?"

"Quite so. And I understand that even after death, paupers are often the subject of hideous medical practices."

"Yes, yes," the Reverend said once again, his face now as red as a cherry. "The wretches are butchered, cut up, their insides ripped out and then shoved back in so that they may be stitched up again like a sack of grain." He leaned forward and lowered his voice. "Sometimes they don't even get their own parts back."

"Really?" I said. "I must report that."

Reverend Squires knit his brows. "You do not seem to be writing what I am saying, Mr. Harvey."

"It is true, Reverend." I nodded, trying to form a response, cursing myself for the sin of arrogance. "I have trained my memory to record my interviews. This allows me to give full attention to those with whom I speak."

Reverend Squires mused on this for a moment. I was fortunate that the man before me so desperately wanted to believe that the *New York Sun* sought to report on his crusading activities. "Very clever of you, Mr. Harvey," he admitted finally. "You must be quite important at the *Sun*," he added hopefully.

"Alas, Reverend Squires, I have not yet the experience to be important, but with essential stories such as this one, I hope to become so."

"I wish you the best in that regard," he said.

"Thank you. I understand that you have created an official organization to support your efforts," I went on.

"Yes, yes," he replied. "The Philadelphia League Against Human Vivisection. We are trying to end the un-Godly practice of dissecting human beings. We have great support, particularly among those of means, which is gratifying since the wealthy never need concern themselves with such indignities, only the poor."

"That is highly commendable, Reverend Squires," I agreed. "It must be a great relief to have an abundance of funds at your disposal."

"Oh, never an abundance, Mr. Harvey," the Reverend assured me. "Never an abundance. There is so much work to do, so many souls to care for, that our funds are disbursed almost as they arrive. In fact, I am scheduled to speak at a gathering tomorrow evening at the home of one of Philadelphia's leading citizens who has volunteered to become a major benefactor. Do you know of Elias Schoonmaker?"

I assured the Reverend I did not. Dinner at the Benedicts' had apparently gone even worse than the Professor and I had imagined.

"You should meet Mrs. Schoonmaker. She is an extremely distinguished woman. Did you intend to remain in Philadelphia overnight?"

"Alas, no. I must return directly to New York."

"A pity," he said. "I was hoping you might witness for yourself the outpouring of support for our cause."

"I'm sure that everyone in the city applauds your efforts."

"Oh, no," he exclaimed with a wag of his finger. "Not everyone. There are those in the medical profession who believe that it is perfectly acceptable to go against Scripture simply to satisfy morbid curiosity." His features puckered. "The worst is this Canadian . . . man named Osler. . . ." He pronounced it *Ah-sler* instead of *Oh-sler*. "This Osler dared come to see me, to try to convince me that carving up the dead was part of the advancement of science." His jaws began to work back and forth at the memory of it. "Blasphemy," he muttered.

"Quite so," I replied. "I would like to return to your efforts to serve those who have died without funds for burial. Does your League pay for those burials as well?"

A cloud passed over the Reverend's plump face. "It is the city's responsibility to provide services for the indigent," he said. "Private citizens cannot simply bury who they wish."

I smiled, with what I hoped was a conspiratorial glint. "Nonetheless, Reverend Squires, I have heard that you have sometimes taken it upon yourself to provide a more dignified service than that offered by the city."

"Where did you hear that?" he demanded, looking far less jolly than a moment before.

"I would not be much of a reporter if I could not unearth a story. Especially of a man who does God's work with such zeal. I would, of course, not include any details that might prove embarrassing to you in any article we publish, but the *Sun* would be that much more interested in a man who takes risks for his convictions."

Reverend Squires was eager to demonstrate that he was indeed such a man. "Of course, we provide burials," he said. "It is a far more humane alternative than letting the poor be dumped in a hole in the ground."

"I could not agree more strongly," I said. "But it must stretch your resources to provide services for so many."

"It is one of our most pressing expenses. You would be

surprised, Mr. Harvey, at everything that is involved. One must obtain the space at the cemetery—we use St. Barnabas—hire men to prepare the site, obtain suitable transport. . . ."

And bribe Charlie to keep his mouth shut, I thought, but instead I asked, "But how can you possibly keep track of everyone?" I asked. "The task is so laborious."

"That is true, Mr. Harvey," the Reverend replied. "But it is imperative that we know where each of these unfortunates has been laid to rest in the event a friend or loved one surfaces."

"But are not many of those for whom you perform this service anonymous? How then . . ."

The Reverend smiled broadly. "An excellent question, Mr. Harvey. An excellent question." And one to which I hoped he had an excellent answer. "Come," the Reverend continued, "let me show you."

Reverend Squires led me through the rectory to an office in which two young women were busily working on open ledgers. "We keep scrupulous accounts of everything we do here," he said, walking to a shelf and removing an oversized journal. He hefted the book to the table and swung it open. "These are the records of this month's interments," he told me. "As you can see, every soul for whom we are accountable is identified, if not by name, then by physical characteristics, as is the exact location where the poor unfortunate has been laid to rest."

"This is most impressive, Reverend." I turned and smiled at him. "So, then," I continued, running my fingers down the page. "If for example, you wished to access the burial records for, say, Thursday of last week . . ."

"That would be here," the Reverend replied proudly.

"And Wednesday before that?" I asked, so as not to appear interested in one particular day.

"That would be here."

I had already noticed the listings I wanted—three of the

five were there—but did not ask about them specifically. Instead, I committed the location of the grave to memory— hoping that my recall was as good as I had boasted—and pro- fusely congratulated him on his record-keeping until he had closed and replaced the ledger.

Reverend Squires wanted to show me the rest of the mis- sion, but I told him that I must return home to ensure that the story be submitted to the *Sun* as soon as possible. He in- quired as to when I thought it would appear, but I told him that a mere reporter could not make that decision. As he es- corted me to my carriage, he was quite insistent that any- thing, anything I might need to embellish my story, I need do nothing but ask.

Repeating the location of the grave site in my head, I thanked him and assured him that he had given me all that I needed.

By the time I had returned to Eakins' home, it was already mid-afternoon. Over tea, as I told him of my adventure, I could not suppress the exhilaration I felt in having executed the masquerade with such deftness.

"Have you alerted the authorities?"

"No," I said. "I had a rather different course of action in mind."

When I told him the details of my scheme, Eakins cocked his head and barked out a single laugh. "You are mad," he said simply. "What if we should be found out?"

"We must take every precaution not to be found out," I replied.

"Why would you of all people take such a risk?" he asked. "You are not personally involved, and have little to gain but quite a bit to lose."

It would be pointless to reply that I wished to exude more intelligence, strength, and resolve than he, so I merely said, "I wish to help Abigail. Don't you?"

"Yes, of course I do," muttered Eakins, "but I have been

embroiled in scandal enough. I don't wish to add a prison stay to the list."

"Nor do I," I said. "But look at it this way. If we are caught and you are incarcerated, the price of your paintings will increase precipitously."

"That's idiotic, Carroll," Eakins snapped, but he actually seemed to be mulling it over.

"There is no other way, Eakins," I argued. "As you noted, neither of us is immune to Jonas Lachtmann's wrath nor, I daresay, to that of the police. We must know the circumstances of his daughter's continued disappearance before they do. If she is alive, the last thing we want is to appear to be involved in a conspiracy, and if she is not, we must be prepared to present them with a full explanation lest we be it." I shrugged and added, "And just think . . . you will get to experience realism and truth in a way you likely never imagined."

"Allow me to withhold my gratitude," he said. "Suppose I refuse to go along with you?"

"You won't refuse," I informed him calmly.

"And why in heaven's name not?"

"Because Abigail will lose respect for you. And besides, you're insatiably curious."

"Perhaps," he allowed. "But tell me, Carroll, can you be certain you could identify the body as being Rebecca's—or not—if you saw it?"

"I cannot be certain, unless there was some physical characteristic that would survive two weeks' interment."

Eakins thought for a moment. "She had a mild case of rickets as a child," he said. "I am told that causes bone distortion. Could you identify it?"

"Without question," I replied. "Even if there is no bowing of the arms and legs, there will be bony spurs on the ribs. I do feel that I should warn you . . . it will not be like sitting in on an operation."

After we made our plans, I left the Eakins home and

returned to the center of the city. I purchased the only instrument I would require, an anatomist's scalpel, from a medical supply emporium on Broad Street, and then repaired to Mrs. Mooney's to get some sleep before our agreed-upon midnight rendezvous.

CHAPTER 21

I CREPT DOWNSTAIRS AT THE appointed hour and, in case she should awaken, left Mrs. Mooney a note explaining that my absence was due to a medical emergency.

Eakins was outside in a carriage; we immediately set out. Neither of us had experience in nocturnal intrigues, so we agreed to err on the side of caution and both of us were as vigilant as possible during the ride to South Philadelphia. Eakins made a number of turns and circles in order to detect anyone who might have been following, but we seemed to be alone on our route. Rather than proceed all the way to St. Barnabas, Eakins stopped about a half-mile away. He tied up his carriage in a quiet part of town where it was unlikely to attract attention, even at such a late hour.

We took great care on our walk to the cemetery, secreting two short shovels under our overcoats. Eakins also carried a hooded lantern, which was kept shut, emitting virtually no light. We glanced over our shoulders frequently and occasionally stopped abruptly to listen for other footsteps. Except for the distant barking of dogs and a lone owl, we heard nothing. It was dreamlike, prowling down the quiet streets in long coats on a cool, dark night, the moon and stars largely obscured by an overhang of low clouds. For his part, Eakins seemed to observe the night as a panoply of muted color, a study in composition and design.

We arrived at the back fence of St. Barnabas in about fifteen minutes, and once more waited in silence to ensure that we had no unseen companions. It was then that my heart began to race and my hands grew moist. Even in the half-light, I could see the painter had been affected similarly.

The fence was low and easy to scale, and we were over in a matter of seconds. Once we entered the cemetery grounds, we had journeyed to the far side of the law. If apprehended, we had agreed that our only defense was to admit exactly why we were there, of our suspicions of foul play in the death of Rebecca Lachtmann, and a desire to determine if those suspicions had any basis before leveling accusations. That explanation might not totally spare us the wrath of the authorities, but might mitigate against the most serious of charges. We fervently hoped, of course, that no such account would be necessary.

With April soon upon us, the ground had lost the hardness of the winter frost and we made our way silently through the cemetery, navigating carefully through the rows and rows of graves. It was a simple matter once I had noted the designations of two or three of the rows to move toward the location where the five cadavers in question had been interred.

The section that St. Barnabas had allocated for Reverend Squires' charges was an uncared-for area at the far end of the cemetery. The rows of shabby graves were interspersed with large trees and would most certainly be avoided by anyone who did not have specific cause to be there. I wondered how much worse Potter's Field could have been than this grim and neglected place.

Although the silence was, in its own way, as unnerving as sound, we were both relieved that we were so unlikely to be discovered while completing our task. I counted eight graves up from the marker at the end of the proper row to a recently filled mound of earth marked with a simple cross. Without a word passing between us, Eakins and I threw off our coats, grabbed our shovels, and began to dig.

Immediately under the surface, the soil was rocky and surprisingly difficult to move for being filled in so recently. I was unused to such labor and tired quickly. Eakins, however, despite his slight frame had impressive reserves of strength, much as Charlie had shown shoveling the ice. I began to wonder if common assumptions of size and musculature might not be completely false.

We had gotten down about eighteen inches when my shoulders began to ache. Fortunately, just a few inches later, Eakins' shovel hit the flat wooden top of the pine coffin. Paupers' graves, even when subsidized by Reverend Squires, were not deep. About three minutes later, we had shoveled off the remaining earth and cleared the top of the lid. Eakins' shallow breathing was the only sound I heard.

I wondered in what state the body would appear, how much decomposition would have occurred, even in cool weather. Other than identifying the body, would I be able to learn anything at all? A feeling of horrible ghoulishness passed through me that I was eager to lift off the lid. I reached down, took a deep breath, and used the end of the shovel to pry it up.

Eakins gasped. "My God, what is that?" he exclaimed although his voice barely rose above a whisper.

Inside the coffin, rather than the remains of a slender, light-haired young woman, there lay a large, dark, shriveled object. The stench was overpowering and immense insects were everywhere. A moment later, a rat scurried from under the body out a hole it had gnawed in the coffin's soft pine. Eakins turned away to keep from retching. As I had predicted, witnessing surgery had not prepared him for this. I hastily closed the top.

"What is that?" he repeated, his voice wavering.

"It is a Negro who died of alcohol poisoning," I replied. "We autopsied him the same day as I saw the girl."

"Then where is she?" he asked, averting his eyes from the coffin as if it contained a spirit.

"Perhaps I counted wrong." I lifted myself out of the hole, and checked the row again. Holding the lantern closer to the ground, I saw that I had missed a grave and therefore we had dug one too far. When I told Eakins of my error, he could barely restrain his fury, but there was little time for recrimination. We fixed the top of the Negro's casket, filled in the hole, and dug another, one site over. By this time, my shoulders were quivering with fatigue and my palms burned.

When I pried open the top of this second coffin, we faced another decomposing corpse, this time of a young girl with fair hair, wrapped in a brown shroud. The skin on her face had shrunken taut. Vermin had been at the eyes. As I moved the thin fabric aside, I heard Eakins emit a series of soft sobs. With one quick cut of the scalpel, I cut through her paper-dry skin, down to the ribs, and exposed the telltale nodules. There could be no doubt now: We had found Rebecca Lachtmann.

But I was not yet finished. I barked at Eakins to hold the light over her abdomen. In the slanted light from the lantern he looked as ashen as a cadaver himself.

My main objective was to determine if an abortion had been performed or begun, and to that end my first task was to determine if any fetal evidence remained in the uterus. From there, I was hoping to discover some indication as to the cause of death, but there was a quite severe limit to the information I might hope to extract from Rebecca Lachtmann's corpse. Drug residue was undetectable and, in any case, it is unlikely that anesthetic would have been used in such a procedure. Ordinarily, the most likely cause of death from abortion would have been internal bleeding—all but impossible to detect, particularly in a cadaver at this stage of decomposition. In this case, however, I suspected another immediate cause of death if the operation had been botched.

I made a vertical cut through the desiccated skin of the girl's abdomen from breastbone to pubis, then transverse cuts on top and bottom. The skin peeled back easily. The intestines and uterus were almost gone, but what was left was sufficient to tell me what I needed to know.

I looked up at Eakins. He was struggling to hold the lantern steady, a look of frozen horror on his face.

"Don't worry," I said. "We'll be on our way in moments. Our time wasn't wasted. I found what I came for."

"Thank God for that anyway," he replied in a raspy whisper.

"And when you fine gentlemen tell me, we'll all know," said a voice from the shadows.

Eakins and I lifted our heads. A man in a bowler hat was moving forward toward the grave site. He sported a handlebar mustache and had a revolver leveled directly at us.

CHAPTER 22

Jonas Lachtmann lived on DeLancey Place, a few streets south of Rittenhouse Square. His town house was not as large or opulent as Hiram Benedict's but, from the brief glance we had on our way in, there was no mistaking his wealth or position. The Lachtmanns' taste was more modern than the Benedicts', and Eakins, despite our predicament, could not hide his contempt when he noted the paintings on the walls.

"Impressionists," he sniffed. "What rot! In ten years all of their paintings will be in the trash bin."

Given what I had heard about Jonas Lachtmann, I was less inclined to discuss art than was Eakins, and marched silently through the house, the mustachioed man walking just behind us. We were directed to an open door, which led to a study in which Lachtmann himself stood rigidly before a set of long, midnight blue draperies at the far end. The room was illuminated only from two low-set wall sconces. The light cast elongating shadows over Lachtmann's eyes, and the effect was unsettling, almost Satanic. We might easily be standing in the way station to Hell.

Lachtmann stared at us through unblinking eyes, although he seemed to quiver as he struggled to maintain control. I could not be sure from the stolidity whether fury or grief was the emotion he was most forcefully suppressing at that moment.

Even the man with the gun seemed unnerved. He hesitated

before padding softly across the room to whisper a few words in Lachtmann's ear. Lachtmann nodded perfunctorily, then took one step forward, extending his hand toward two armchairs. His hand moved slowly but did not waver. "Come in, gentlemen." He pronounced each syllable with studied civility. "Please sit." He perused our dirt-covered clothes. "I see that I will have to have this room cleaned in the morning. Now, where have you two been rummaging about?"

Neither Eakins nor I responded but rather took seats as ordered.

"Ah, yes," Lachtmann went on, the words studied, his tone almost artificial. "Now I remember. St. Barnabas Cemetery, wasn't it?" He pressed his lips together and forced himself to continue. "Brandy?" he asked, gesturing toward a decanter and two snifters on a side table. "Keuhn," he said to our escort, without waiting for an answer, "would you please pour for these gentlemen?" Lachtmann cocked a thumb in the man's direction. "Keuhn is from the Pinkerton Detective Agency. They offer a remarkable variety of services. They pour brandy, they track the scum who defile other men's daughters, and they have even been known to use physical force when asked by their employers. Isn't that right, Keuhn?"

Keuhn, who had finished pouring the brandies and was handing them to Eakins and myself, nodded. His hands were large, with thick knuckles. "Whatever you say, Mr. Lachtmann." He had a slight western twang to his speech that could have come from Ohio.

"Keuhn is correct," said Lachtmann, once more directing his comments to us. He was breathing deeply between sentences, gathering himself like a man preparing to undergo a surgical procedure in the days before anesthesia. "It is whatever I say, and at this moment, I am thinking of saying something quite severe."

I had never in my life been so terrified, but I could not afford to let him speak unchallenged. I wanted to brace myself with a sip of the brandy, but I knew that my hand would shake if I lifted the glass. I forced out the words. "That would be a mistake, Mr. Lachtmann. Whether you choose to believe me or not, I am very, very sorry that my suspicions turned out to be correct."

Lachtmann did not interrupt, waiting for me to condemn myself. I went on. "I know how much you loved your daughter, but I can assure you that Eakins and I have had precisely the same aims in this matter as have you. If you do not listen to what we have to say, you will likely never find out who was responsible for what happened to her."

"He was responsible," Lachtmann hissed, leveling a manicured index finger at Eakins. His eyes had gone wide, his face red, and his hand had moved so fast that it was a blur. Eakins cringed and pushed himself backward, as if he were determined to disappear into the chair back. Eakins might exude animal energy in the studio, but he was no match for the enraged creature that now faced him.

"Mr. Lachtmann, you must listen!" I exclaimed. The man needed desperately to lash out and unless I could provide him a reason to do otherwise, there was little to persuade him that Eakins and I would not be suitable candidates for his wrath. If I could not convince him that Eakins was blameless—whether true, untrue, or half true—I was certain neither of us would leave here alive. "Eakins was not responsible for any of Rebecca's misfortunes. He has been working desperately to try to find her and render assistance. Setting upon him or me will get you no closer to the revenge you seek. You will merely have the satisfaction of watching pain inflicted on two men who were trying only to help."

"You are denying that he despoiled my daughter?" Lachtmann snapped, still refusing to speak Eakins' name. The intensity of the man, the homicidal ferocity, was physically oppressive. It robbed me of breath. But, at least he was now addressing himself to me and not my companion.

"Not only am I denying that Eakins was the father of

Rebecca's child, I am also telling you that he had nothing whatever to do with her death. In fact, he cajoled me into helping because he was so worried about her. It was only because of his overriding concern—and that of Miss Benedict—that I agreed to become involved in Rebecca's disappearance. It was, as it turns out, fortuitous that they asked me, because I have discovered a great deal."

"And what exactly have you discovered?" I had stopped him, momentarily at least.

"I will be happy to tell you all I know," I said, "if you will answer one question for me first. Keuhn here has been following Eakins for days, possibly weeks. Has he come up with one scintilla of evidence that Eakins has been anything but a friend to your daughter?"

Lachtmann refused to respond directly to my question. Instead, he said, "Go ahead, Dr. Carroll. Tell me your story."

I favored Lachtmann with much the same version as I had given to Eakins and Abigail at dinner, with one extra detail. If Turk was the only culprit in his daughter's death and he was himself dead, Lachtmann had no incentive to let Eakins and me continue on the loose. He would either turn the Pinkerton man on us, or alert the authorities as to where we had been found. Even if I did not land in prison, Johns Hopkins was unlikely to employ a physician who had been apprehended as a grave robber. Lachtmann had to have reason to let us go, so I added that I believed Turk had an accomplice, someone who may have performed the actual operation from which his daughter died.

"It was only to spare Miss Benedict . . . and by association, you," I concluded, "that we undertook something as harebrained as digging up the coffin ourselves instead of going to the authorities. We decided that if the police became involved prematurely, Turk's associate would be alerted and have the opportunity to cover his tracks." I finally felt sufficiently in control to down some brandy. "Mr. Lachtmann, do I seem to you fool enough to risk my career and my freedom on such an act without good cause?" It would be quite an irony if it was only the height of my own stupidity that saved me.

Again, Lachtmann ignored my question. "Do you have any idea who this accomplice might be?" he asked instead, going to the heart of the matter.

"I'm not sure," I replied, "but I think I'm close to finding out."

Lachtmann eyed me for a moment. I felt like a field mouse being perused by a hawk. "You had better," he said.

There was a knock on the door and Lachtmann bade whoever was there to come in. It was the other Pinkerton agent, Keuhn's associate, the man I had noticed the day that Abigail and I had visited Eakins on Mount Vernon Street. In hushed, respectful tones, the man told Lachtmann that the arrangements for both matters had been completed.

Lachtmann nodded, wrote some instructions on a piece of paper, handed them to the man, then waited for him to leave. When the door had closed, Lachtmann's eyes remained fixed on it, as if there were a vision in the oak that only he could see.

"I have had my daughter removed from that place," he said in a strangled voice, as if the sound had passed through liquid. "My child will get a proper burial. I suppose I can at least be grateful to you for making that possible. As far as the newspapers are concerned, she will be said to have died in Italy and returned here for interment."

I risked speaking once more. "I am terribly sorry, Mr. Lachtmann. Please believe that it pained me to find her." I could see that Eakins wanted to offer his sympathies as well, but was still too frightened of Lachtmann to speak. "I will do anything I can to help you find the person responsible."

Lachtmann considered my offer. The self-control of the man was staggering. "All right, Dr. Carroll," he said softly, "I may allow you to do that. Tell me first what you learned from your *examination*." He could not suppress a burr of sarcasm as he spoke the last word.

I told Lachtmann what I discovered in the graveyard, that his daughter had died from a perforated bowel. The bowel had yet to decompose and evidence of the puncture was clear. I neglected to tell Lachtmann how agonizing it would have been, and that, ordinarily, it would have taken the victim of such a condition days to die. Given the bruising on her upper left arm that I had observed in the Dead House, however, I deduced that, to stifle her screams, whoever was at the table had held Rebecca Lachtmann down and then suffocated her and disposed of the body from Wharf Lane. Although there was no way to determine suffocation as the immediate cause of death from the state of the corpse, it was the only explanation that fit all that I had observed.

"So who did this?" Lachtmann asked, his anger stoked once more at hearing the cause of his daughter's death.

"Abortion is not a simple procedure—it takes a decent amount of skill—but neither is it complex. The location at which it was done would have added a level of uncertainty but, if forced to surmise, I would have to say that whoever performed the abortion was not a skilled surgeon."

"Was this Turk a skilled surgeon?" he asked.

"No. But as I said, I don't believe that Turk performed the actual procedure. He was far too canny for that. It was one thing to perform abortions on denizens of the waterfront, where any mistake could be easily covered up, and quite another to risk exposure with a member of a prominent family."

Lachtmann scowled and turned away. He faced the drapes for some moments before turning back. "All right, Dr. Carroll, you may have bought yourself some time. If what you say is true . . . if . . . then you are probably more capable of uncovering this accomplice than are the police. You understand, of course, that in order to have my daughter buried properly, I will have to inform the authorities that I have given instructions to move her and that, in turn, will bring at least some of the circumstances to their attention. I will have to trust in the discretion of the police to keep the full story from public consumption."

"Of course," I said soberly, masking my elation at the reprieve. "But I also understand that, given the presence of the Pinkerton Detective Agency, you will not have to explain to them how you came by your knowledge. They will simply assume that the Pinkertons found out by means of their own."

"Exactly," Lachtmann agreed. His grief remained palpable but, man of action that he was, he had shifted his attention to practicalities. "And, for the time being, I may do just that. If, as you say, you are both innocents...even him..." Lachtmann glowered at the petrified painter. "If events are as you say, Dr. Carroll...and we shall find that out in a moment...if that is so, I have no wish to destroy your career... although I suggest you take better care in your associations. More to the point, if there is someone at large who is responsible, I have no wish to waste my vengeance on you...I am not an animal, Doctor, despite what you may have heard from others...on the condition, of course, that I actually succeed—with your help—in locating this mysterious accomplice to whom you referred."

"That seems more than generous," I said. "I am very grateful for your trust."

"*Trust?*" he snapped. "Please don't mistake me, Doctor. I don't *trust* you in the least. If I find that you have been less than truthful or less than candid...I'll crush you." He turned to Keuhn. "Bring her in," he said.

Keuhn opened the door and nodded to someone in the hall. A moment later, the second Pinkerton man entered. At his side was a petrified young girl. She appeared to be no more than eighteen, quite pretty, with long blond hair.

"Lucy!" exclaimed Eakins, his terror renewed. It was the first word he had uttered since we were brought in.

"Indeed," said Lachtmann. "Dr. Carroll, meet Lucy

Arkwright, Rebecca's maid, just returned from Italy, although not by choice."

The girl's gaze dropped to the carpet. Her hands were clasped together in front of her and she was shaking visibly.

"Lucy," Lachtmann went on, "decided that, with her purse filled with my money and a young Italian art student fawning over what he believed was an American heiress, there was no need to continue to follow instructions and remain inconspicuous. The two of them were leading quite a merry—and public—existence. She was, as a result, observed in Rome by an acquaintance of mine. He cabled to ask me if I knew that a young woman was living the high life, passing herself off as my daughter. Keuhn's associates had little trouble finding her. Now she is back, although her return voyage was likely not as pleasant as the outbound. Am I right, Lucy?"

"I'm sorry, Mr. Lachtmann," the girl moaned. "I was just trying to help Miss Rebecca..." Her speech had acquired some refinement from exposure to better society, but betrayed lower-class Scotch-Irish origins.

"Of course, Lucy," Lachtmann said soothingly, "and that is just what you are going to do now. You are going to help her by speaking the truth."

"Yes, sir."

"First, did my daughter tell you why she wanted you to impersonate her in Europe?"

"Yes, sir. She said she didn't want you... anyone to know she wasn't going to have the baby."

"She told you everything, didn't she?"

"Yes, sir. Me and Miss Rebecca was quite close."

I anticipated what was coming and ventured a peek at Eakins. The painter was sitting rock still, afraid to breathe. I was frozen as well. The wrong answer to the next questions and we were dead men.

"So, Lucy," Lachtmann went on, "do you know who the father was?"

"Yes, sir."

"Was it *him*?" Lachtmann once more leveled a finger at Eakins. Eakins gasped at her, his eyes wide, like a rabbit looking down the barrel of a shotgun.

The girl shook her head. "No, sir. Weren't Mr. Eakins."

Eakins exhaled audibly as Lachtmann stood stunned. "Are you sure?"

"Yes, sir. Quite sure."

"Who, then?" he demanded.

Lucy's lips barely moved as she whispered, "Mr. Albert."

"Albert? Albert *Benedict*?" Lachtmann had been caught totally unprepared. As had I. Smug, arrogant Albert Benedict. Abigail's brother. What a cruel, ghastly irony.

As Lachtmann absorbed this stunning reality, he glanced at Eakins. He had expected to be able to condemn the painter and be done with him right here in his study. "Are you certain?" he snapped at the terrfied maid.

"Yes, sir," Lucy replied, quaking. "Miss Rebecca told me." She glanced at the door and seemed for just a second to be considering making a run for it. "Mr. Eakins here was just trying to help," she added.

Lachtmann remained incredulous. "My daughter and Albert Benedict?" he repeated.

"Wasn't her doing, sir," she said, so afraid now that her teeth chattered. "He . . . he forced her."

At that last, horrible revelation, I expected Lachtmann's rage to explode, but instead he became frighteningly calm. His movements slowed and he spoke to Lucy softly, as he would a small child or pet. I was no Weir Mitchell, but I had sufficient experience with nervous disorders to know that he was more dangerous in this state than before.

"Did Albert ever know about the child?" he asked her.

"Oh, yes, sir. But he told Miss Rebecca he couldn't have nothing to do with her no more. That no one could find out. I think he was worried more about his father than his wife."

"Did his sister know?"

Lucy shook her head. "No, sir. Only the three of us—Miss

Rebecca, Mr. Albert, and me. She couldn't have anyone else know. She was so ashamed."

Lachtmann took a moment, digesting the information. "All right, Lucy. You can go now."

After the girl was gone, Lachtmann looked to Eakins, then to me, then back to Eakins. "It seems as though I may have misjudged you . . . may have. In any case, may I suggest that after you leave here, I never have occasion to set eyes on you again."

Eakins said nothing, but was doubtless thrilled to consent.

"As for you, Doctor," Lachtmann said, "our business is not yet done. Your offer to help me find the butcher who killed my daughter still stands. Whoever this mysterious accomplice is, I expect you to help me find him in every way you can."

"I said I would," I replied.

"If you don't," Lachtmann went on, still speaking as matter-of-factly as if we were at luncheon, "I will have an additional chore for Keuhn. You understand my meaning, do you not?"

I had told my tale and now, it seemed, I would be forced to make it true.

"One more thing," Lachtmann said. "*Nothing* you have heard here leaves this room."

With that, Eakins and I were dismissed. Keuhn led us to the door, leering in the way bullies have in the presence of an intimidated foe. As he opened the door to let us out, he said, "Be seeing you again, Doc, I'm sure."

Eakins waited until we had reached the end of the street before he breathed. "Thank God." Then he exclaimed, "Albert Benedict! The worm!" He mused for a moment. "If it were anyone else, I wouldn't give two bits for his life, but a Benedict . . ."

"I wouldn't give two bits for his life in any case," I said.

"Perhaps," Eakins agreed. "If there is any justice."

"Someone must tell Abigail," I said. "She must be fore-warned."

"It's three A.M., Carroll. I don't think it would be wise to go pounding on her door now."

"I'll go in the morning," I said.

"Better wait until the old man has left for the bank."

After I agreed, Eakins asked, "All that palaver about an accomplice. Another bluff or was it true?"

"I'm not positive," I replied, "but, yes, I think it's true."

I was, in fact, reasonably certain that Turk would never have risked performing Rebecca Lachtmann's abortion personally. While abortion, as I had said to Lachtmann, was uncomplicated—essentially a progressive dilation of the cervix with a series of sounds, each one bigger than the last until the opening of the cervix is a centimeter or slightly larger, allowing for the insertion of a curette to scrape out the lining of the uterus—there was some delicacy required and accidents were common. Still, the perforation I had seen in Rebecca Lachtmann could only have been produced by a novice or an incompetent—or by an extremely skilled surgeon working while under the influence of diacetylmorphine. Perhaps that was the "deal gone bad" to which Haggens had referred when I asked him about the argument in The Fatted Calf.

"And do you really know who it is?"

"Perhaps."

"Can you tell me?"

"No," I said.

"Just as well," Eakins said. He turned up the street without saying good-bye. His animal intensity was gone, replaced by the slouch of a prematurely old man. He had survived all manner of attacks on his work and his person, but I was not sure he would survive this. He turned the corner and disappeared. I would never see him again.

December 22, 1888

S HE WAS BETTER NOW. SHE *still shivered,* *but the blanket and the fire had finally warmed her.* *When she had first stumbled into her bedroom, she* had been so terribly cold and weak, and the raw ache would not cease. She had tried to undo her dress, but her hands trembled so. It was only then that she realized she was bleeding. She knew not to cry out, but she must have whimpered, because suddenly her maid was there.

Lucy had taken off her torn dress and soiled undergarments and fetched one of her own dressing gowns, so that there would be no evidence for her parents to discover. It was Lucy who had covered the chaise in old towels, and then wrapped another one around her, assuring her the bleeding would soon stop on its own. Then, she might finally get into bed. It was Lucy who had built up the fire and then crept to the kitchen to prepare a glass of warm milk laced with brandy. And, most of all, it was Lucy who had held her in her arms as she sobbed noiselessly, listening as the entire horrible tale came pouring out.

It had all been just as she had imagined, a perfect evening. He had been so attentive, so charming, so vulnerable in his need for her. First, there had been the walk in the garden in the clear frosty night, she wrapped in his coat. So many stars in the sky. He had taken her hand. Then, to talk, to confide, he led her back into the house, and up the back stairs into one of the spare bedrooms.

But there had been no talk, no confiding—only struggle, pain, and humiliation. When she had begged him to stop, he laughed, and then growled at her in breath sweet with wine that he knew she had done it before.

CHAPTER 23

I WAS UNSURE OF WHEN a bank president departed for work, so I waited until ten A.M. to arrive at the Benedict home. I apparently had not waited long enough, however, because when the door opened, it was Hiram Benedict himself who stood in the vestibule. Alone, he appeared even more outsized, looming over me like a grizzly.

"Dr. Carroll," he said evenly, "I have been expecting you. Jonas Lachtmann got in touch with me early this morning."

Jonas Lachtmann? What would Jonas Lachtmann have told him? Certainly nothing of his daughter and Albert. Was it about me? Did he know about St. Barnabas? Had he told Abigail? I could only find out from her.

"I am very sorry about Rebecca," I replied. "I thought Abigail should be told as soon as possible."

"Abigail has been told," Benedict said.

"How is she? May I see her?"

"She is distraught. As I am sure you would have expected. And no, you may not see her."

"Mr. Benedict," I said, "I am all too aware that you do not think me a suitable match for your daughter, but we have feelings for each other. I do not think it fair or in Abigail's interests for you to deny me the right to see her."

"I don't think you fully understand, Dr. Carroll. *I* am not denying you access—*she* is denying you access."

It was not possible. "Did she say why?"

"She did not need to."

"I would feel more comfortable if I might hear these sentiments directly from her," I insisted.

"Your comfort is not my concern. And now, I must bid you good day. Rebecca Lachtmann's funeral is this afternoon and I have a number of matters that must be addressed before then." I wondered if Albert would be going to the funeral as well. "By the way," he added, "I would strongly advise against your trying to attend."

A moment later, I found myself standing in the street, the Benedicts' door closed behind me. It had shut with a resonant bang that had a finality about it—I was not being dismissed from a home, but from a way of life.

I needed to see Abigail, to explain, to have her tell me that she would not stand for such blatant disregard for her feelings. She would demand that her father relent. I would see her that evening, after Rebecca's funeral. Perhaps I would arrive and insist on paying my condolences, or perhaps I would simply wait outside in the street until she appeared. I was not sure how, but I would find a way.

I had scant time to dwell on the issue, however, and as I left for my next stop, the cable office, I saw that the morning had yielded a second unpleasant surprise. I had apparently inherited Keuhn. The Pinkerton man was waiting across the street, at the edge of Rittenhouse Square, making little effort at concealment. His presence was so obvious that it was clearly less to discern my movements than to remind me that Jonas Lachtmann was always close, holding me to my promise of identifying Turk's accomplice.

As I went to check on my inquiry at the cable company, Keuhn stood directly across the street from the front door. The eager young man was not working that morning and I was left to deal with a more typical clerical type—mid-thirties, bored, and surly. But my reply had indeed arrived. As I thanked the clerk and paid for the wire, a woman walked in and, in a heavy accent, greeted Mr. Schultz.

"Schultz?" I asked. "Does either of you speak German?"

The woman did. I showed her the cable, which was quite brief, and asked if she could translate.

"*Ja*," she said. "Maybe." She looked over it a few moments. "It say they not doing any... uh..." She was hung up on one word. "Tries?"

"Experiments?" I asked.

"*Ja*," the woman replied. "Must be... speriments. They not doing any speriments on anything like you say."

"Thank you," I said.

When I emerged and took the streetcar to the hospital, Keuhn jumped on at the last minute. He dallied in the lobby as I made my way to the changing room, and he was down the corridor when I emerged five minutes later. Any time I chose, I could go through the laboratory and use the service stairs, from which I might walk out the back of the hospital and leave West Philadelphia by way of the Blockley. Attempting to shake Keuhn off, however, would be tantamount to admitting to Lachtmann that I had something further to hide. For the moment, it seemed, I was stuck with the Pinkerton man as a companion.

As I walked down the corridor in his direction, he smiled and backed around the corner. I was wondering if he would be in sight when I got to the turn, so I was fully unprepared to run face-to-face into the Professor. When he saw that it was I, he frowned in a manner that would ordinarily be reserved for a student who had misdiagnosed an encephalitic tumor.

"I've been looking for you," he said tersely. "I want you to call on me this evening at my lodgings. Seven o'clock."

He could not have chosen a worse possible night. It was imperative that I see Abigail as soon as possible. "I'm sorry, Dr. Osler," I said, "but I've got a very important engagement this evening."

"Cancel it," he snarled and stalked away. I was left standing in the corridor, my hands hanging at my sides, Keuhn at one end, the Professor marching off down the other. Lachtmann had not kept his word. The truth was out and I was done for.

The Professor's rooms were on Twelfth Street, north of downtown, two floors of a fashionable town house in a better section of the city, but removed from Millionaire's Row. Like every other aspect of the Professor's fortunes, his living standards were soon to be vastly enhanced. I had learned during our weekend that Gilman had arranged for him to reside in a large, extremely well-appointed town house in Baltimore.

I arrived precisely on time. Widows were the servants of choice for bachelors and, like my arrangement with Mrs. Mooney, the Professor engaged Mrs. Barlow to cook his meals and tend to his domestic needs. She opened the door and smiled when she saw me. Mrs. Barlow was an open-faced woman with six grown children. She was almost shapeless, but utterly unflappable, as if there were not a single of life's crises or calamities that she had not witnessed or was without a plan to manage. With total aplomb, she removed vials filled with tissue samples that the Professor had deposited absentmindedly in his coat, or answered the front door for four A.M. emergencies as if she had been awake for hours. I had been a guest here often and Mrs. Barlow had taken to doting on me, attentions that I accepted with a combination of embarrassment and gratitude.

"Come on in, Doctor," she said in a soft brogue. "The Professor is waiting in the drawing room. You know the way." Mrs. Barlow was the only person I knew other than myself who referred to Dr. Osler as "the Professor."

She turned for the kitchen, leaving me to make my own way. As I trudged toward the drawing room, I heard a soft hum of voices. Who had the Professor invited to share the occasion of my dismissal? Was it Gilman himself, or Billings, or even Welch, up from Baltimore to make things official? I turned into the room and saw that it was none of those men.

It was Halsted.

He rose as I entered, dressed as before in a perfectly cut dark suit, with a brilliantly white shirt and collar, pearl cuff links, and dark cravat. A silver-framed *pince-nez* rested on the bridge of his nose.

He offered his hand, and I realized that, at Hopkins, I had failed to notice the lines around his eyes and tinge to the skin. I had learned during the visit to Hopkins that Halsted was only thirty-seven, three years younger than the Professor, but he appeared at least ten years older. The cause of the disparity between appearance and reality was not difficult to deduce.

We shook hands, Halsted with that same strong and confident grip, and he said, "Thank you for coming, Dr. Carroll. I was hoping to have the opportunity of speaking with you. The last occasion was hardly conducive." There was still a rigidity to the man, which in Baltimore I had attributed to coldness, but which now seemed to stem more from a need for self-control.

I told Dr. Halsted stiffly that I was pleased to see him again as well, trying once more to read something in his eyes.

The Professor stepped forward and placed his hand upon my shoulder, an odd show of amity after his icy behavior in the hospital. It left me completely unsure of my ground. Might I be reprieved after all, or simply slaughtered more amiably?

"I thought, Ephraim," he said, "that you should meet the man whose life you are about to destroy."

"But I was not . . . never . . ." I stammered.

"Oh, come now, Ephraim," said the Professor. "You are not the only person capable of building a theory from incongruent bits of data. We are physicians, after all. We use logical extension every day in moving from symptom to diagnosis. It was not all that difficult to work backward from your activities to the motivation that prompted them. Quite evidently, your theory, which you were attempting to prove by surreptitious visits to the medical library, dens of iniquity and, finally, a cemetery—Oh, yes, we are aware of that—was that Dr. Halsted was complicit in the death of Rebecca Lachtmann and quite possibly responsible for Turk's murder." He smiled. "You were also trying to figure out whether I was involved too, eh?"

"No, Dr. Osler," I protested, feeling my shirt stick to my back despite the chill in the room. "I was not trying to prove a theory . . . only to find out if it was true. And I prayed every minute that it was not."

"It was not," said Halsted, with finality. The eyes behind the thick lenses never wavered.

"The poor girl was finally given a proper interment today," said the Professor. "It was in the afternoon papers. It was a private affair. I don't know how the family is going to be able to maintain that she died abroad, though, if they expect to eventually bring someone to trial for her murder."

I did not comment, although I believed Jonas Lachtmann had little intention of putting his faith in the judicial system.

"In any event, Ephraim," the Professor went on, "I am afraid you have evaluated the symptoms and come to a faulty diagnosis, but given the circumstances, neither I nor Halsted here can take you too much to task. In fact, in any other context, your behavior would have been quite praiseworthy. You showed yourself to be a dogged and clever investigator and your conclusions were actually quite reasonable. We can only hope that you will continue to bring similar zeal to your duties as a physician."

"Dr. Carroll," Halsted said evenly, "I had nothing at all to do with Rebecca Lachtmann's death and certainly nothing to do with poisoning George Turk, although I will say in candor that I am not the least bit sorry that he is dead." The dispassion of Halsted's delivery made the denial itself more persuasive. "The man was evil, a parasite. He preyed on the misfortune of others to line his pockets. I have heard tell that Turk's activities may be excused because of the deprivations he experienced when he was a youth, but I can think of no justification for performing abortions or selling morphia to those who could not live without it."

"Activities, by the way, Ephraim," added the Professor, "of which I knew nothing until just before his death."

"As a result of all this innuendo and confusion, Dr. Carroll," Halsted went on, "Dr. Osler thought that you should hear the truth from us... from me... particularly since we will be working together."

Working together? For a moment, I doubted my hearing. "Thank you, Dr. Halsted," I said. "I would like that very much. I am mortified at having misjudged you."

Halsted nodded perfunctorily, but his expression did not change. Still, he seemed much more to fear the rejection of others than to be rejecting others himself.

"Let's sit and have some wine," said the Professor, "and afterward, if you still wish to remain in our company, Ephraim, Mrs. Barlow can make us some dinner."

I took a seat as the Professor poured two glasses of claret, one for me and the other for himself. I had arrived expecting to be eviscerated and instead I was apparently being... courted. I glanced to where Halsted was seated and saw a cup of tea on the side table next to his chair. After each of us took a sip of our respective beverages, Halsted replaced his cup on in its saucer and began.

"Let us first dispense with the obvious. My addiction to drugs is not to be denied, either in the past or, unfortunately, in the present. It is why, to answer your unspoken query, I do not take alcohol. I have learned that it is far too easy to substitute one dependency for another. But before you judge me, Doctor, allow me to enlighten you as to the genesis and history of my condition."

I had heard of Halsted's coca experiments before, but never from the man himself.

"As I believe you know," he began, "I came late to medicine, during my final year at Yale. I had been an uninspired student before but medicine fascinated me such that I graduated first in my class from the College of Physicians and Surgeons in New York City." Even reciting the story of his own life, Halsted seemed personally removed, as if he were listing a set of symptoms. "I was accepted on the staff of Bellevue Hospital and my interest turned from general medicine to surgery. Although Lister's advocacy of asepsis had converted a small percentage of the staff, most of the surgeons continued to perform operations under filthy conditions, wearing street clothes and handling instruments with unwashed hands. One or two even smoked cigars as they cut.

"I was convinced that hygienic surgery would vastly reduce infection, and I became somewhat fanatical on the subject. Many of my colleagues grew more than a bit annoyed, being lectured to by someone no older than you are now, Dr. Carroll, but subsequent events have more than justified my behavior. Still, I was forced to move on to New York Hospital, which had a more enlightened view of scientific advance, and, I daresay, I began to build a sterling reputation as a surgeon and a researcher." Halsted's tone still did not waver, and there was not the slightest degree of braggadocio in his words.

"It was at New York Hospital that I met Welch. He was just my age, a brilliant pathologist, and was, at the time, teaching the first pathology course in the United States. He had converted an old morgue near the East River into a laboratory. We each saw instantly that surgery and pathology formed a symbiosis and we became both professionally inseparable and intimate friends. It is to that friendship that I owe my professional survival and quite possibly my life.

"As was customary, I left New York for two years to study in Europe. I wanted in particular to observe Billroth, who, with apologies to Gross, was certainly the finest surgeon in the world. While there, I observed the most extraordinary phenomenon, not from Billroth, but from one of his students.

Mikulicz, the Pole, had taken to employing clamps to stanch the flow of blood whilst he operated on the large bowel, thus improving his view of the affected region. I realized immediately that not only would clamping render the tissues in the open area more visible, but that it would prevent surgical shock. That, in turn, would not only save lives in and of itself, but would also allow the surgeon to proceed at a more thorough, less frenetic pace. When I returned, I employed both clamping and asepsis, and achieved astounding results."

"You must understand, Ephraim," interjected the Professor, as Halsted took a sip of tea, "that the innovations Dr. Halsted employed at first made him an object of ridicule. He was, after all, only twenty-eight years old. Soon, however, the results inspired many to copy his methods while arousing the enmity and jealousy of others."

Having seen Burleigh operate, I did not need to be persuaded of that.

Halsted waited until he was certain that the Professor had finished before speaking again. "By 1884, I was at the peak of my profession. I had perfected radical mastectomy, a technique that bears my name and has saved the lives of hundreds of women. I also developed techniques for emergency transfusion and saline infusion as a treatment for shock. I was teaching anatomy to private students, was an attending physician at four hospitals, and was engaged to perform surgery for private patients who paid up to ten thousand dollars for my services."

Ten thousand dollars? I almost asked Halsted to stop to confirm that stupendous figure, but he was continuing as if he had said "ten dollars."

"I was also, although it is difficult to comprehend now, considered one of the leading *bon vivants* in New York, accepted and valued in the highest society. Then, Dr. Carroll, I read an article that changed my life. Karl Koller, a German ophthalmologist, had introduced a solution of cocaine, an alkaloid of *Erythroxylum coca*, to his own eye, and then pricked it with pins but felt no pain. He had successfully anesthetized the cornea and conjunctiva. Koller, like Mikulicz, saw only the narrow applications of his finding, but I knew at once that he had discovered that cocaine could block individual nerves. It was potentially one of the most important discoveries of the century. As you know, at the time, surgeons had to choose between chloroform and ether. Ether was safe, but unreliable. Anesthetized patients had been known to get up off the operating table and walk away. Chloroform was more reliable, but extremely hazardous. Cocaine seemed to hold promise of both safety and reliability and so I felt I needed to test it at once. I recruited a like-minded colleague at Roosevelt Hospital and we injected ourselves with a solution of the drug.

"Before I continue, it is important to point out that Hall and I were correct. Nerve blocking was possible and cocaine was a correct agent to achieve the result. But, as you know, there were other results as well. I continued my experiments and within months, I had become addicted.

"I hope for the sake of your soul, Dr. Carroll, that you never have to cope with addiction. It is not, as portrayed in dime novels, a fall from Grace brought on by weak character or a plunge into sin—it is a far more insidious phenomenon that comes on gradually, soundlessly, invisibly. The poor wretch who is afflicted is the last to know and, by the time he does know, the vise has clamped shut and he is doomed.

"We all pass through adolescence, believing that we are in control of our destinies, that life is an exercise in free will. If one's will is sufficiently strong, there are virtually no obstacles that cannot be overcome." A wry smile passed across his face. "I know I believed so.

"At Yale, I became a superb athlete despite a lack of stature. Although I received what might best be described as mediocre grades, after I purchased a copy of *Gray's Anatomy* in my senior year and decided to become a physician, once again, by dedicating myself to the goal, I made it so. My career was testament to the power of will and the drive to succeed. And success fathered success. What's more, my achievements were not simply such that they brought me personal wealth or fame—I was saving lives, many lives. If there was a formula as to how one should lead one's life, I had found it, or so it seemed.

"Imagine then, Dr. Carroll, if you will, the shock when I realized that not only had I fallen into the grip of a hideous drug, but that I was unable, regardless of effort or will, to rid myself of it. That was a far more painful realization than finding myself in the throes of addiction itself.

"The realization did not come immediately. Quite the contrary. At first, I decided that I would overwhelm cocaine as I had overwhelmed every other obstacle. I took a leave from my practice and entered a convalescent clinic in Providence, where I remained for a year. For my first months, although it was torture to abstain, I sustained myself with the knowledge that I was asserting my will over a demon, that I was persevering through to victory. But slowly I wore down. Eventually, I was helpless to resist. I began to make arrangements with members of the staff, the very people who were charged with ensuring that the facility remained untainted, to purchase and smuggle the drug to me. It was a costly proposition, but I would have paid anything.

"Upon my departure from Providence, I was pronounced cured, my secret safe. Still, when I returned to New York, my friends and associates abandoned me. For many, the opportunity to sneer at the fallen Halsted was simply too great a temptation to resist. Except for Welch. Welch remained as intimate as before and was also the only one who at first guessed that I was still in the grip of the drug. My demeanor had been so altered, however, that it was not long before tongues began to cluck. When Welch went on to Baltimore, I was left completely alone, a pariah.

"But my salvation was at hand. Welch persuaded Gilman and Billings to take me on. My gratitude was boundless and I was determined to justify his trust by ridding myself of my addiction once and for all.

"I decided that if I could not resist the drug, I would put myself where there were no drugs to be had. I booked passage on a ship bound for South America, and, lest I lose control completely, took with me a minimal amount of cocaine. Within two days of sailing, I had used my entire supply. I stayed in my cabin, refusing to come out, even for meals. The agony became so great that I was emitting loud moans, more animal than human. On more than one occasion, the steward knocked on my door and asked if I needed the services of a physician . . . quite humorous, don't you think?

"Finally, I could endure it no longer. I burst from my cabin in the middle of the night, tore through the ship, and smashed my way into the captain's cabin, with the aim of availing myself of whatever narcotics were in the medicine chest. I overpowered the captain and was subdued only when he raised the alarm and four sailors came to his assistance. By that time, the captain had grabbed his pistol and it was only because I was so obviously mad that I was not shot. I eventually managed to explain my situation, how I had come to be the way I was, and the captain, a decent and sympathetic man, did not have me arrested when we reached port. He even supplied me with small amounts of morphia on the return voyage to keep my situation manageable."

"On Dr. Halsted's request," said the Professor, "the captain had cabled Welch in Baltimore. Welch came immediately and, as a result, the affair was not made public, not even to the Hopkins administration. I am counting on your discretion, Ephraim, to see that it remains that way."

"I will not repeat what I have been told in confidence," I said.

"I have no doubt of your honor," the Professor replied. The remark stung like nettles.

"Welch took me to Baltimore," Halsted went on, "and into

his home. He watched over me as one would tend a sick child.
I told him of the success that the ship captain had substituting small quantities of morphia for cocaine, and Welch
thought that an excellent idea. His hypothesis was that if cocaine addiction was the more powerful, it was vital to put an
end to it by any means possible. That hypothesis proved correct. By injecting small amounts of morphia, I was able to rid
myself of cocaine. It was my most blissful and productive period in five years. And, although I found that I had to slightly
increase the frequency of my morphia injections over time,
the effects of that drug were far less deleterious than of the
other. Moreover, Welch was able to quietly spread word that
Halsted was cured.

"Everything seemed to be going smoothly until six months
ago, when I had occasion to come to Philadelphia to consult
with a private patient. This patient, quite well-to-do, had a testicular tumor and was too embarrassed to come to Baltimore.
He had set up a surgical facility at his country home and
asked me to remove the growth there. His personal physician
would assist and three private nurses would tend to him during his recuperation.

"More to the point, however, this man had also used morphia, but was of course unaware that we had that in common.
He had been attempting to cure himself for years, although
his wealth enabled him to remain a user with no one the
wiser. Whilst we spoke, he told me of a new and miraculous
substance, whose origins and composition were unknown,
which had allowed him to break his dependency. It was only
available, he said, through underworld channels and was extremely costly, but well worth it to anyone of means who
found himself in a similar state.

"As you might imagine, Dr. Carroll, I was buoyed by this
news, but unable to request specifics from my patient without revealing my own dependency. I immediately made inquiries in the lesser areas of the city, however—one learns by

necessity how to do such things—and was soon rewarded with the information that someone known as 'George' was the source of this new drug."

"And 'George,' of course, was Turk," I said.

"Of course." Halsted was so terse in his confirmation that I felt a fool for my comment. "I arranged a rendezvous at which I purchased a small quantity of the drug. I had no idea that this mysterious 'George' was a doctor, just as Dr. Osler had no idea that he was a drug supplier. To my view, while obviously a more educated and polished sort than one usually encounters in such places, I assumed that he was simply a man who had been raised in wealth and descended into iniquity. I am, as you know, familiar with the breed."

"Nonsense," said the Professor. "You have never and will never descend into iniquity."

Halsted ignored the comment. "Before injecting myself, I performed an analysis of the powder with Frohde's reagent, as I am sure you have, and then checked the literature. When I came across Wright's experiment, I knew precisely with what I was dealing. Only then did I inject the drug and, once I did, it became clear that my patient was correct. Diacetylmorphine did most definitely quell the need for the more pedestrian form of the drug.

"I decided to be clever. Not wishing to be dependent on a denizen of the underworld, I attempted to replicate Wright's experiment. I would synthesize diacetylmorphine myself. Wright must have been lucky, though, because my attempts were not successful. As far as I can determine, acetylizing morphine renders it fat-soluble and therefore more efficacious, but my efforts produced no such result. Assuming that Turk was also not producing the drug himself, my next step was to attempt to discover where he was acquiring his supply of diacetylmorphine, but I failed here as well. I wonder, Dr. Carroll, if you have had more success?"

"Actually," I said, feeling quite proud of myself, "I have." I began to recount my correspondence with the Bayer

Company, but then stopped, knowing that I could have no honest reason to suspect that a German dye maker was synthesizing diacetylmorphine. But it was too late.

"The Bayer Company?" asked the Professor. "Wherever did you get hold of that?"

I was trying to think of a creditable lie, but Halsted made it unnecessary. Rather than pursue the Professor's query, he began to tug lightly on his beard.

"Aniline dyes," he mused. "Very interesting."

"I don't understand," I said. "Why would a dye maker be involved with such a substance?"

"You should have read further, Ephraim," said the Professor. "There has been growing awareness in Germany of a parallel between aniline dyes and synthesized medicines. As you may know, mauve, the first synthesized coal tar dye, was discovered quite by accident in 1856, while the Englishman, Perkin, was attempting to synthesize quinine. Three years ago, the most effective antipyretic we have was discovered by two German interns who used a mislabeled jar of naphthalene while experimenting on treatments of intestinal parasites. The substance, which reduced fevers, but did nothing to the parasites, turned out not to be naphthalene, but acetanilide, a commonly used aniline dye intermediate made by the Kalle Company. Kalle had no previous experience in pharmaceuticals, but immediately sought a patent, and so we now have Antifebrin. Bayer, another dye works and one of Kalle's competitors, then also began experimenting heavily in medicines. Two years ago, they thought they had stumbled on a pain reliever, which they called phenacetin, but it was found to cause kidney failure. Diacetylmorphine is obviously one of the substances with which they are currently working."

"But they responded to my cable denying any such work."

"That is hardly surprising, Doctor," said Halsted. "There are millions to be made in pharmaceuticals. We are dealing with easily synthesized substances here. The trick is to find one that works before your competitors. If diacetylmorphine is seen to have medicinal properties, whoever acquires the patent will accrue all the profits. Bayer would never chance alerting any potential challenger to its researches."

"Then how did Turk get it?"

"Drugs are like a leaky roof, Ephraim," said the Professor. "Water always finds the hole. In this case, someone at Bayer must have been stealing a supply of the drug and either he or a confederate had the foresight to ship it to America, where demand is always high and German authorities would have no power."

I turned my attention back to Halsted. "But isn't diacetyl-morphine addicting in its own right?"

"The evidence is not clear," replied Halsted. "I am able to maintain equilibrium on a substantially more modest dose than of morphia, so it is quite possible that it can be used safely for clinical purposes. Addiction tends to be progressive, however, so there is no telling what the future holds."

"We are dealing with that issue in Dr. Halsted's case," said the Professor, "as you will see." I thought we would move on from there, but the Professor had not forgotten. "So, Ephraim, how did you come up with the Bayer Company?"

I had no choice at that point than to admit that I had not simply found a key and turned it over to the police, but had visited the den on Wharf Lane before the police. I told them of the discovery of the hidden compartment and finding the drugs and the weapons inside. I did not mention the journal. I wanted to decipher the entries before I divulged its existence to anyone.

They both listened, rapt. When I was done, the Professor sighed and shook his head. "Ephraim," he said. "We have underestimated you. You've been cleverer than we supposed—and a good deal more reckless. You must have had the devil of a time of it, juggling the police, Miss Benedict, Jonas Lachtmann, and us."

"It has been something of a strain," I admitted, but I was

also feeling more than a little self-important at having impressed Halsted and the Professor with my sleuthing.

"Well, Ephraim, I think you can relax now. Perhaps we should allow Dr. Halsted to finish."

Halsted nodded and took another sip of tea. He was methodical in his movements, almost practiced, as if he had taught himself to think through even the simplest action before actually performing it. "During one of my visits to Turk," he went on, "he informed me that he knew that I was a surgeon of some repute. At the time, I could not imagine how he had come on such knowledge. I was making only occasional visits to Philadelphia and had in no way identified myself. Now, of course, it is clear from whence this bit of knowledge emanated.

"As a price for his silence—and an uninterrupted supply of the drug—Turk demanded that I perform certain services for him. When I asked what services he had in mind, he told me that, from time to time, young ladies in trouble came to him for assistance. His meaning was instantly clear. I told him he was insane if he expected me to perform abortions. He merely shrugged and said that there had been no harm in trying.

"When I returned to Baltimore with the supply that Turk had then sold me, I discovered that it was not diacetylmorphine at all, but simple morphia. I confess to say that I panicked. The prospect of a return to morphia addiction was terrifying. I surreptitiously returned to Philadelphia to confront him. I had a difficult moment when I ran into Weir Mitchell on the street, but I told him that I had come to town to perform surgery.

"I found out where Turk lived...a tortuous process, as I am told you know as well...and surprised him at his home. He told me that I could have the new drug anytime I wanted—all I needed to do was to help him out. I refused.

"I went back to Baltimore, but became increasingly

desperate. I returned to Philadelphia yet again and accosted Turk at that waterfront saloon he frequented."

"The Fatted Calf?" I asked.

"Yes. That was the place." Halsted removed his *pince-nez* and polished the lenses with a handkerchief that he removed from his vest pocket, slowly, his fingers moving at constant speed like a metronome. When he was done, he checked the result, then replaced it on the bridge of his nose. "By that time, Welch had begun to suspect that my situation had deteriorated and that it had something to do with my frequent trips to Philadelphia. He made Dr. Osler aware of the situation. Together they resolved to once more render me assistance beyond that which anyone has a right to expect.

"I was beside myself by the time I arrived at the bar. I had come to see Turk as the embodiment of evil, a fiend withholding a lifesaving drug from a desperately ill unfortunate. I burst in and accosted him. Turk responded by threatening to expose me to the world. 'The great Halsted on drugs again,' was I think how he put it. At just that moment, Dr. Osler arrived. Unbeknownst to me, Welch had been observing me and cabled Dr. Osler that I was on the train. Dr. Osler followed me from the station to the bar, and then took me back to the station and returned me to Baltimore."

"Even then," the Professor said, "I never knew that it was Turk whom Halsted had come to see. I waited at the door whilst someone else went across the room to fetch him. When we left, Halsted merely said that the man was a monster. He did not identify him by name."

"Thus, when you saw me arguing with Turk at The Fatted Calf," Halsted went on, "it was natural to assume that I knew him as a physician or even a fellow conspirator, instead of merely as a drug supplier. In that, Dr. Carroll, you were mistaken."

"How did you know that I saw you at The Fatted Calf?" I asked, astonished.

"I knew you had been with Turk that evening," said the Professor. "The extrapolation was not unreasonable."

At that point, Halsted placed his hands in his lap. He had finished. For some moments, no one spoke as I tried to digest all of what he had said. He had accounted for every incident, every open question. Each conclusion that I had drawn could be accounted for by this alternate construction of the facts. Halsted's version amounted to a set of coincidences, certainly, but no more so than mine.

But the more powerful impression was of Halsted, the man. The Professor had been correct. Greatness fairly flew off him. I thought of the passion with which Dr. Osler had spoke of the noble, doomed Servetus and understood why he would go to such enormous lengths to protect the man before me. For the Professor, Halsted, like Servetus, had every element of the protagonist of a Greek tragedy: accomplished, courageous, indomitable, but ultimately struck down by circumstance and coincidence. For Servetus, there had been no pulling back from tragedy, while here, Welch and the Professor—and quite possibly I—might succeed in carving a very different end to the story.

"So, Ephraim," Dr. Osler said, "now that you have heard the truth, perhaps you will enlighten us as to your theory of the events? It seems apparent that you believe that Dr. Halsted bungled Rebecca Lachtmann's abortion and, to cover it up, he poisoned Turk."

"Yes," I was forced to admit, "that is what I thought."

"In your version, was I complicit in these crimes? Or simply aware of them and covering up?"

"The latter," I confessed weakly.

"Very well," the Professor said. "Not an unreasonable conclusion, as I said. But how did you account for a surgeon of Dr. Halsted's talents perforating the bowel during a routine procedure, even granting that the environment was challenging?"

"I assumed that the drug had rendered his hand unsteady."

"I'm afraid that won't do at all, Dr. Carroll," said Halsted. "I've performed hundreds, if not thousands, of operations under the influence of drugs and have never...not once... botched any of them."

"That is what I wanted to tell you, once again trusting in your confidence," interjected the Professor. "Dr. Halsted is too valuable to society—too many lives are at stake—for us to take a risk on his incapacitation. Dr. Halsted's efforts to shake free of drug addiction have been Herculean and, one day, might well have resulted in a freedom from dependence. For the time being, however, Welch and I have convinced Dr. Halsted that, rather than continue to compromise both his health and his abilities, he should instead maintain himself on morphia. He can do so at minimal levels, which will allow him to continue to work."

"Is it possible to attain such an equilibrium?" I asked, skeptical.

"Most definitely," avowed Halsted. "Once I had freed myself from a need to eliminate morphia entirely, I found that I could control the cravings with judicious administration. Would that I had done so before I encountered Turk."

I had a final question. "Dr. Osler, why did you refuse to autopsy Rebecca Lachtmann if you had no idea who she was or how she died?"

The Professor's expression grew serious, almost sad. "In that, Ephraim, Turk was correct. While in Montréal, I fell in love with a young woman named Elise Légér. She was a remarkable beauty, but her father was a clergyman who disapproved of my profession, or at least the manner in which I conducted it. He refused to give his consent to my proposal of marriage. Elise and I were heartbroken. We even discussed elopement. In the end, however, she simply could not disobey her father and we never saw each other again. But she is in my thoughts often."

The Professor's eyes drifted away, into his youth. "When I swung open the cover of the ice chest, the resemblance was remarkable. It was as if I were staring at Elise. I knew after a few seconds that it could not have been, of course. I had not seen her in over fifteen years, and she would by now be thirty-five, far older than the woman we saw. But it was quite a shock all the same. It is not every day that one sees a ghost of one's past, eh?

"It seems," he went on, "that this was another occasion where you took a set of symptoms and extrapolated into a reasonable diagnosis that turned out to be incorrect. Turk reacted because he *knew* it was Rebecca Lachtmann, and it must have given him quite a fright to believe that I was reacting for the same reason. So, knowing that I often confided in you, he asked you to join him for the evening, gave you too much to drink, and then, I am sure, tried to persuade you to divulge anything that I might have said that would have put him at risk."

"Yes, he did try to get me to talk about you," I admitted. "This all seems plausible, certainly, but then who poisoned him?"

"We may never know. I am sure Turk had any number of enemies."

"Despite what you seem to think, Doctor," interjected Halsted, "it does not take a scientist or a physician to administer arsenic in an appropriate quantity to replicate cholera. Poisoning has been a time-honored means of murder for centuries, and there are countless cases in which poison was confused for some other malady. In its storied history, arsenic was often referred to as 'inheritance powder' because of the facility with which an heir might dispatch an unwanted legator."

"You are a fine scientific practitioner, Ephraim," the Professor told me. "Your method, tenacity, and use of logic, as this episode has demonstrated, are all first-rate. But there is more to science than logic. You need instinct and, yes, even heart. You will develop these qualities, I am sure, but you should always bear in mind how, in these events, pure method not only led you astray, but came perilously closer to causing the ruination of an innocent man."

There was nothing to do at that point but agree and ask Dr. Halsted's forgiveness. He was quite magnanimous in granting it. Dr. Osler then asked if I could still feel comfortable in having him and Dr. Halsted as colleagues. Of course I was comfortable—I was a man reprieved. A little less than twenty-four hours earlier, I had sat in Jonas Lachtmann's study with my freedom and even my life left to the financier's whim, and now I would leave for Johns Hopkins in three days to take up a position of responsibility and respect.

As promised, Mrs. Barlow had prepared dinner. For the next ninety minutes, I sat and discussed the future of medicine, with two of the greatest men in the field. They treated me thoroughly as an equal. It was perhaps the happiest hour and a half of my life.

As soon as I was out of Dr. Osler's door, however, I was reminded that I had not quite fully emerged from the shadow of Rebecca Lachtmann's death. Waiting outside, a reminder of my promise to deliver up a murderer to Jonas Lachtmann, was Keuhn.

CHAPTER 24

THREE DAYS. I TRIED TO convince myself that once I left for Baltimore, the threat from Lachtmann would recede, that the man's power somehow ended at the city limits. But distance would only prolong my separation from Abigail. I must see her, help her to defy her father, and come with me to start a new life in a new city. What impact her brother's despicable behavior would have, if she or her father even knew of it, was not clear, but I was certain that she and I could surmount any obstacle. I wanted to rush once more to the Benedict home, but the appearance of desperation was not the answer. I must seem calm and in control of events if I was to expect her to place her trust in me.

Upon my arrival at the hospital the next morning, Keuhn once again an obvious presence at a respectful distance, I went straight for the administrative offices and, after complimenting her on her dress, I asked Miss Prendergast to please allow me to use the telephone. She cocked her head disapprovingly and noted that the telephone, one of only three in the entire hospital, was restricted to official use and emergencies.

"But this is an emergency, Miss Prendergast." I sighed. "A sort of emergency, anyway."

Miss Prendergast pursed her lips and looked out at me over the tops of her glasses. "An emergency of the heart?" she asked with a knowing smile. Miss Prendergast was a rail-thin spinster of forty with muddy brown hair who, it was rumored, had rejected the one man who had proposed marriage on the grounds that a better proposal was in the offing, but no other proposal ever came. Now, her only opportunity for passion was in observing the passion of strangers.

I confessed that, yes, I did wish to telephone a young lady. When I told her which young lady so that she could place the call with the exchange, she fluttered with excitement. To a woman of Miss Prendergast's romantic bent, a young, rich, and beautiful woman such as Abigail Benedict was an object of both fascination and self-satisfying contempt. "Why, Dr. Carroll," she said with schoolmarm disapproval, "you do fly close to the sun. You'd best be careful if you intend to go traipsing with *that* set." She allowed her judgments to lie in abeyance at the prospect of overhearing my conversation, however.

To Miss Prendergast's disappointment, and mine, the Benedict servant who answered claimed that Abigail was not yet awake, so I was forced to leave word that I would call on her that evening, and hope the message would not be intercepted. I thanked Miss Prendergast for her kindness, swearing her to secrecy about our little conspiracy, and then left the office.

As I stepped outside, Simpson came running up to me. "Ephraim," she said with atypical agitation, "we've been looking all over the hospital for you. Dr. Osler needs you in his office immediately."

I hurried with her down the hall and then up the stairs. When we arrived at the Professor's office, the door was closed, an unusual occurrence in itself, and there was a uniformed policeman outside. Reflexively, I glanced down the hall before entering, expecting my Pinkerton doppelganger to be in sight, but Keuhn was not there.

As I opened the door, I saw Sergeant Borst in the center of the room, rocking forward and back on the balls of his feet, his hands clasped behind him, a thin smile stretched across his face. Seated next to the Professor's desk, looking ashen and forlorn, was Farnshaw.

The Professor gazed up somberly as we entered the room and motioned me to close the door behind us. I could tell instantly that he was making a huge effort at self-control.

"Sergeant Borst has come to arrest Farnshaw," he said. His voice wavered in anger.

"What? Farnshaw? For what?"

Borst was enjoying himself far too much to allow the Professor to steal the initiative. "Complicity in murder."

"Murder?" I exclaimed. "Farnshaw? Absurd. Who is he supposed to have murdered?"

"George Turk. Death by arsenic poisoning."

"Farnshaw kill Turk? That's absurd." I might have laughed had the circumstances not been so obviously dire.

"That's what we told him," Simpson said.

"Absurd, is it?" Borst replied, not the least bit put out. "Not nearly as absurd as a bunch of doctors trying to cover for one of their own. That is what you people do, isn't it?"

"We people do nothing of the sort," muttered the Professor. "It is you people who want to make an arrest without caring very much about whether the person is guilty or innocent."

"Is that so?" exulted Borst.

"Farnshaw?" I repeated. "You can't be serious. Farnshaw is...as...as likely a culprit as President Harrison," I stuttered, unable to find words to question such idiocy. "You can't possibly have any evidence."

"That's what I told him," murmured Farnshaw from the chair. It was the first he had opened his mouth since I'd walked in.

"No evidence, huh?" said Borst.

"Must you keep speaking in the interrogative?" snapped the Professor.

"The interrogative?" Borst replied. "Bet you think I don't

know what that means. Well, I do. And I'll tell you something else I know. I know that we've got plenty of proof—evidence. Your friend Farnshaw here was the one who messed up Rebecca Lachtmann's abortion...although in respect to the family, we ain't made that part public, but you all know all about it, don't you? Then, to cover his crime, he fed the arsenic to Turk."

"I've never performed an operation in my life," bleated Farnshaw. "I'm no surgeon."

"So the results would say," Borst retorted.

"Wait a minute, Sergeant," I said. "Where could you possibly have gotten the idea that Farnshaw was involved with Turk?"

"Actually, Dr. Carroll," the policeman replied, favoring me with an especially broad grin, "we got it from you."

"From *me*?" I shook my head violently. "I never..."

"It's funny...sometimes you don't find something that's right under your nose until you look for it. We weren't thinking about an accomplice until you told Mr. Lachtmann about one. Once we started to look for an accomplice, we worked backward from what we had and from there, it was pretty easy to figure out it was George Farnshaw."

I felt the Professor's eyes on me. Simpson's and Farnshaw's as well. What could I say? That I had deliberately misled Lachtmann? That I had since spoken with poor, pathetic Halsted and realized that he was innocent? Borst would never believe me. He would pursue Halsted regardless, on the chance that he might uncover enough to arrest a prominent physician.

"Whether there was an accomplice or not," I said, doing my best to make the notion sound ludicrous, "it most certainly was not Farnshaw."

"Who, then?" asked Borst.

"How should I know?"

"You told Mr. Lachtmann that you knew. Want us to go back and tell him that you lied to him? He won't like that.

'Specially the way his daughter was found. An' notice..."
Borst wagged a finger at me. "I ain't asking you about that,
though I might."

"I said I may know," I protested.

"Well," Borst went on, "don't matter now if you do or you
don't. We know. Want me to tell you how we know? Dr.
Carroll was a real big help here, too. First, he was not only
kind enough to find where Turk lived, saving us lots of leg-
work, but also to be there when he died. I'd lay you ten to one
that if Turk had croaked with just that old lady in the room,
nobody'd ever have seen the body again. Then, he did us an
even bigger favor by figuring out that Turk died of arsenic poisoning and not cholera. The other doc here"—Borst turned to
me and crooked a thumb at the Professor—"told me that it
was you who checked his hair when he was cutting him up.
Very clever. Of course it means that you suspected foul play in
the first place, but we'll leave that go for now. Then, you did
us the biggest favor when you missed the money in the floorboards after you searched his rooms—"

I began to protest, but Borst waved me off. "C'mon, Doc.
We ain't so dumb that we can't tell when somebody's been
through somebody else's things. Missing the money was the
biggest favor, 'cause along with the money—I must have forgot to tell you—was a journal. Seems your friend Turk kept a
record of his dealings. Not all that unusual, actually."

A journal? What journal? I had the journal. I had found it
at Wharf Lane.

"Now, we couldn't get much from the journal at first—
Turk had used letters instead of words—so we put it aside in
case it came in handy later. That was about where things
stood, when the doc told Mr. Lachtmann about the accomplice. As soon as Mr. Lachtmann told us, we went back to
Haggens' place. Once we know what we're looking for, we
know how to get information out of folks. We found out that
there was another George that Turk was friendly with. We
also found out that after Turk had a couple of accidents with

some young ladies he came up with someone else to do the actual dirty work, or at least that's what he told potential customers. Even women in desperation ain't gonna just lie there and die. There was even one girl who told us that Turk told her that if she ever needed fixing up, George was just the guy to do it. That sent us back to the journal 'cause there seemed to be money moving between Turk and a 'GF.' We had figured it was money coming in—payment for goods, so to speak—but after we heard what we did, we figured maybe it was money going out—services rendered kinda thing. Once we had that, it wasn't too hard to figure out who 'GF' was."

"That doesn't mean anything," I protested. "Just because Turk wrote something in a book, it doesn't mean it happened."

"Oh, yeah, Doc. Sure. Turk takes the trouble to write all these letters and numbers in a book and hides it where's he figures no one's gonna find it, but it don't mean nothing? If that makes sense to you, all I can say is I hope I never get sick."

Borst reached down and took Farnshaw by the arm. "Well, if there's nothing else, me and Dr. Farnshaw will be going." The three of us were forced to watch helplessly as Borst led our young colleague out the door. Before he left, he turned back. "Been a pleasure chatting with you."

We remained in the office, stupefied. Simpson and the Professor were merely overwhelmed by the episode itself. I had other questions to consider. *Two* journals—I had to decide which was real or, in fact, if either of them was real. Turk might well have created a spurious document implicating Farnshaw to barter with in case the police uncovered his activities. The more information to be traded, the better the deal. It was certainly preferable to be able to bargain with the police for the name of the person performing the actual abortions than to be forced to face the entire charge alone. It would explain why Turk took Farnshaw out that evening—to let his face be seen and get it around that this was the other "George." And now, I realized bitterly, he may well have had the same plans for me. In that case, there might easily have been a different journal under the floorboards, with the initials "EC."

"Someone should go with him," Simpson said, looking searchingly at me.

"I'll go," I replied.

I expected the Professor to agree immediately but, instead, he seemed to hesitate at the prospect. "I'm not sure," he mused. "It might make Borst even more vindictive."

"More than he is already?" I asked.

"One of us must be there, Dr. Osler," Simpson pressed. "I would go myself..."

"No," the Professor agreed finally, "Carroll is right. And they'd never let a woman near a jail. Yes, Carroll, by all means go. Let us know if there is anything at all you need. I'll get word to Farnshaw's family in Boston."

Keuhn was down the hall when I left the office, but I ignored him as I raced through the halls and down the stairs, trying to overtake Borst before he left with Farnshaw. I caught up with them just inside the front door.

"I'd like to go with you," I said.

Borst seemed pleased. "Of course, Doctor. Nothing is too good for our medical community. We have a private carriage. You can join your friend in the seat of honor. It's only too bad that I can't take you the whole way."

"Yes, Sergeant," I replied. "Since you obviously don't care who you arrest, I'm sure you are heartbroken."

Borst wheeled and stood face-to-face with me before I knew it. "Look, Doc. You and your boss have lots of fun making me out to be stupid. You put that little 'doctor' in front of your names and you think that gives you the right to kill people without nobody being able to do nothing about it. But I'll tell you how stupid I am. I know that you, or him, or both of you, know a lot more about all of this than you're telling. Fine. But now I've got enough to lock your little chum up in Eastern State Penitentiary for the rest of his life—if he ain't hanged. You or your boss decide to give me someone who fits better, and your pal will be out before you can spit. If not, he goes for it. That's how stupid *I* am. Now, if you want to ride, get in the back of the wagon. It'll give you an idea what it's gonna be like for him."

The "wagon" was a two-horse, closed box with one tiny barred window on either wall, not tall enough to allow one to stand. There was a bench along each side built to accommodate three or four people. Farnshaw was alone, seated on the right side and I got in and shuffled, hunched over, to a seat across from him. He looked up for a moment, surprised and grateful, and then dropped his gaze to the floor. As soon as I had entered the compartment, the door slammed shut and I could hear the sound of a key turning a padlock. That click was the most terrifying sound that I had ever heard. I wanted to stand up and scream to whoever could hear me to "Let me out!" but Farnshaw was frightened enough. Moreover, I would be getting out in short order, while Farnshaw would be forced to go from here to an incarceration far more horrible.

The wagon began to move, but all we could determine was that we were bouncing along the cobblestone streets. We knew when we made a turn because the sunlight coming through the bars shifted its angle. Farnshaw continued to sit mutely, staring at the floor, and I expected him at any moment to vomit, but he didn't. Finally, he looked up.

"I'm completely innocent, Carroll. I swear. I had no involvement in any of this."

"I know," I replied. "Don't lose hope. We'll prove you innocent." I tried to sound casually confident, but now, with Halsted no longer in my calculations, I had no idea how I was going to achieve that end. Lachtmann had caught me by surprise by enlisting the police when I had been convinced that he would handle the entire affair privately. Of course, without the police, he never would have landed Farnshaw, as dubious a catch as it was.

"I need to know, Farnshaw. Did Turk say anything at all that night you were out with him . . . or any other time . . . that might help us in our inquiries? Anything about his activities, who paid him, whether he really had an accomplice . . . anything?"

He shook his head miserably. "No. I had no idea, Carroll. I was as stunned as anyone when Turk's true nature was revealed. It was as I told you. Turk seemed most amiable, introducing me to everyone—including a number of ladies who I suspected were not of strict virtue. But there was nothing else. I'm certain."

Turk had chosen the perfect lamb.

Farnshaw and I sat in silence, bumping along in an indeterminate direction in semidarkness. Street noises penetrated the gloom, emphasizing that, on the other side of the walls, people were moving about, engaged in their daily routines. And they were free. There seemed little else I could say. I could only hope that my presence provided some comfort.

After what seemed hours, but was likely not more than twenty or thirty minutes, the wagon stopped. There was a clamor outside and soon I heard a key rattling in the padlock on the door. When the door itself swung open, I was nearly blinded by the profusion of light that flooded into the wagon. A policeman ordered us out. He grabbed each of us roughly by the upper arm. Once we were standing on the pavement, the policeman ignored me, but retained his grip on Farnshaw.

We were in front of the Fifth Street station house, although it took a few moments in the glare to determine that it was the same building I had visited the night I had left the Wharf Lane key for Borst. Farnshaw moved in misery toward the building. As I followed, Borst was at my shoulder.

"Enjoy the trip?"

I didn't wish to make matters worse for poor Farnshaw, but the blatant sadism of the man finally overwhelmed me. "You are a bastard," I growled, looking him in the eye.

Instead of taking umbrage, Borst merely smiled. "I am that, Doc. I am that. But just remember: Any time you wish to help your friend in there, all you have to do is to distract my interest. A little truth should do the trick."

"And what if there is no truth to tell?" I retorted. "Have you thought of that? I know you think that I have the secrets of the crime at my fingertips, but what if you are wrong?"

The policeman shrugged. "Then, if you don't know nothing else, I'll just have to figure that I got the right guy."

"Even if you send the wrong man to the gallows?"

"Won't be the first time," the sergeant said placidly. "Now, Doc. Want to come inside?"

But I wasn't finished yet. "Jonas Lachtmann put you up to this, didn't he? He called you to that fancy home of his to tell you that he had found the body of his daughter and that he knew that Turk had an accomplice in her murder and that you had better make an arrest quickly. I notice that Farnshaw has not been arrested for performing abortions, just for poisoning Turk. The part about Miss Lachtmann will be kept out of all this, won't it? How did he convince you? Threats? Or did he take a more friendly approach?"

Borst never stopped smiling, but he spoke to me through clenched teeth. "Next time you say anything like that, your friend Farnshaw's gonna have company. Nobody tells me what to do, not Jonas Lachtmann or anyone else. The reason his daughter's being kept out of this is 'cause of respect to a grieving family. I'd do that for anybody. Now you wanna come inside or not?"

I did, of course, so I said no more and let Borst lead me into the station. The ferocity of his denial, however, convinced me that I was correct: Jonas Lachtmann had pressed him for an arrest and so he had made one. It also meant that it would be that much more difficult to force him to admit that he had made a mistake—assuming that I could succeed at all in mustering the evidence with which to confront him.

The tumult inside surrounding the big arrest had begun. Borst was obviously quite popular with his fellows, many coming up and clapping him on the back, congratulating him on such an impressive display of police work. More than once, I heard the word "promotion." A few of the policemen cast curious glances at me, but most were too busy eyeing the arehcriminal Farnshaw to care much about another civilian in their presence. As to Farnshaw, he was forced to stand before a high desk, while a thick-necked police sergeant with waxed hair asked him questions and laboriously recorded the answers.

Soon, a young man—even younger than Farnshaw—sidled up to me. He wore a cheap checked suit and a low derby set just over his eyebrows, and his face was hairless. Had I encountered him on the street, I'd have feared he was a pickpocket. "Hi, Doc," he said.

"Do I know you?"

"No. But I know you. You work with Farnshaw, right?"

"I thought you said you knew me," I replied.

"Not personally, Doc." The young man lifted his hat a few inches off his head. "Ben Taylor. Police reporter for *The Inquirer*."

A reporter! If this was how a genuine reporter appeared, my impersonation at the Germantown Mission was indeed lacking. I had been fortunate then that Reverend Squires was such a willing and enthusiastic subject.

When I did not further the conversation, young Taylor did. "I'm told you know more than a bit about this. How's about you give me an exclusive?"

"Whoever told you that was mistaken," I replied, wondering if it had been Borst himself. "All I can say is there is no man on earth less likely to have committed these crimes—this crime—than George Farnshaw."

"That's not what I hear," Taylor said. It occurred to

me that he was employing the same technique as I had with Reverend Squires—pretending to knowledge to entice the other party to give information.

"You hear wrong," I said tersely.

"Well, he's in for it, in any case," Taylor said.

"What do you mean?"

The youngster eyed me as if I were mentally deficient. "You joking? A doc accused of poisoning another doc? The whole city'll turn out for the hanging." He glanced about, then said, "Unless there's more to it. Cops talk to cops, you know. You can hear a lot in a police station. Nobody's coming out and saying it, but there's some mumbling about rich birds and strange goings-on down at the docks."

"I'm sure you are mistaken," I said. "About everything."

I saw that Farnshaw was being marched back outside toward the wagon, despondent in a sea of happy, raucous police and hangers-on. Without excusing myself from the reporter, who deserved no such courtesy, I hustled forward. But Borst stepped between us before I could reach Farnshaw.

"End of the line, Doc. He's official now. It's off to Moko."

"Moko?"

"Moyamensing Prison, Doc. That's where we take prisoners to wait for trial."

"Come on, Borst," I said. "Couldn't you let me ride with him?"

Borst considered this. "Well, it's against the rules and we know what a bastard I am, but sure. Why not? I don't figure you're gonna try and slip him a pistol on the way." He smiled. "Maybe when we get to Moko, they'll think there's supposed to be two for the lockup."

"Yes. Perhaps. Thank you, Borst."

"Don't thank me. The more you see, the more likely you are to tell me the truth, Doc."

The trip to Moyamensing Prison, where Tenth and Reed Streets were intersected by Passyunk Avenue, was not a long one. I noted that the jail was not far from Mary Simpson's home and the Croskey Street Settlement. Once again, Farnshaw and I didn't speak during the ride. When we emerged, hunched and blinking in the sunlight, we saw before us what appeared to be a medieval fortress, more suited to repelling an attack by chain-mailed knights than housing felons. The building, in three sections of tan limestone, was set back sufficiently from the avenue to accommodate a moat. Its center section was three stories high, crowned with a huge battlement tower, and the top floor was ringed with a cornice. The two wings each featured a battle turret on the end. I was told that the wing on the right was the county jail, housing petty criminals of all stripes. The wing on the left would be Farnshaw's temporary home, a holding facility for those awaiting trial. A twenty-foot-high stone wall extended out from either end turret, the full length of the street.

The wagon had pulled up to the door in the center wing, which was part prison, part residence for the county sheriff, and part administration area. Once more, Farnshaw was led roughly from the wagon. Inside, the Moko was grim and forbidding. A uniformed prison attendant, exuding a mixture of boredom and cruelty, asked Farnshaw a number of questions, to which he did not seem to care if he got answers. He then perfunctorily nodded to another uniformed man, obviously a jailer, to come and take the prisoner away.

That was when Farnshaw lost control. He spun around. "Carroll!" he yelled. "Don't let them take me! I'm innocent. Oh, God!"

I ran to him, but two other prison attendants jumped in and held me back. Guards began to drag Farnshaw off. His face was wan and strangled, the most pathetic sight I have ever seen.

"I'll help you," I yelled to him. "I promise!" I doubted he heard the words as he was half-dragged through the door and off to be placed in a cage.

I felt perilously close to tears as I pushed my way outside, determined to keep my promise to poor Farnshaw, but still unsure how. I was not even certain how to get back to the center of the city. Before I could decide on any course of action, however, I was intercepted by Keuhn.

"I got a message for you," the Pinkerton man said softly. "Mr. Lachtmann says that you two are square. He thanks you for your help. He wants me to tell you that he don't want no more of it."

"I don't take orders from Jonas Lachtmann," I replied.

"You do now," Keuhn said, and walked off.

CHAPTER 25

IT TOOK THREE STREETCARS FOR me to make my way
back to the hospital. I needed to tell the Professor what had
transpired. If I thought that Keuhn had ceased to dog my
footsteps, I was mistaken. When I arrived, the Pinkerton man
was already inside the front door, waiting for me.

I started for the stairs to the Professor's office, but
abruptly changed my mind. Instead, I went to the women's
ward. There I found Simpson, at the bedside of an elderly patient with wispy white hair done in a single thin braid, her
veins showing blue through almost translucent skin. Just
from the rale of breath I heard as I neared her bed, I knew
that the woman would not last out the day.

"Do you have a moment?" I asked Simpson softly.

"Now, Polly, you rest and I'll be back soon." Simpson nodded at me, then waited, but Polly gave no sign that she had
heard.

We moved away from the dying woman's bedside and I recounted the ghastly tale of Farnshaw's incarceration. Simpson
listened, tight-lipped. "We must try and help him," she said
resolutely.

"I agree," I said, "but I'm not sure how to go about it."

"I have some thoughts," she said, "but I need information
before we can proceed."

"Anything. I appreciate any assistance you can provide.
Lord knows, I don't deserve it."

"Perhaps not," she said. "But Farnshaw does." Then she

added, "But from this moment on, Ephraim, we must be honest with each other."

I agreed gratefully, but not without embarrassment. I had never specifically lied to Simpson. But nor had I ever told her the complete truth. Perhaps that was the most insidious brand of lie of all.

"Let us begin with this notion of an accomplice," she said. "Perhaps we can work our way backward from there and find something with which to prove Farnshaw's innocence."

In the doctors' lounge, I beckoned her to the same chairs in the corner at which we had had tea. I recounted the events, omitting nothing, not my discovery of Turk's journal, not my visit to St. Barnabas, not the previous evening's dinner with Halsted and its shattering revelations. She listened attentively, digesting all I had to say. Only when I told her of my romance with Abigail Benedict did even the slightest tightness pass over her face, but it vanished as quickly as it had appeared.

When I had finished, she asked, "You are certain that Dr. Osler and Dr. Halsted were involved only by coincidence? We've been taught by Dr. Osler himself to distrust coincidence."

"I agree," I said, "although, after sitting with Halsted, it seems persuasive enough in this case."

"Our first step, then, it seems to me, is to try to make sense of Turk's journal. The one you discovered."

"*Our* first step?"

"Together, we can make faster progress, Ephraim. You said you have the materials on cryptography from the library at your rooms? I'll meet you there this evening, after rounds."

"At my rooms?"

"Why not? We can sit in the parlor. I'll keep both feet on the floor, just like in billiards."

I felt myself smile—after this day's events, I would not have thought it possible. "Very well. I have an errand to run first, but I will meet you at eight."

We made to get up but Simpson placed her hand on my arm to stop me. "We agreed to be honest with each other, did we not?"

I assured her that I remembered.

"Good." She smiled. It was the warmest I had ever seen her look, and for a moment she appeared . . . pretty.

After checking through most of the hospital, I finally ran down the Professor in the pathology lab. He was alone in the room, so I spilled out my tale of the abominable conditions under which Farnshaw was being held.

"We must delay our departure to Baltimore," I urged. "We must stay here and help."

"I'm not sure that will be possible," the Professor replied. He was busying himself with papers on his desk, straightening and tidying. His movements seemed stiff and forced. "Gilman is expecting us and arrangements have been made. Besides, I was successful in contacting Farnshaw's parents in Boston. They will be here tonight. They are quite well-to-do, as you know, and I am sure they will do what is necessary to secure his release. I cannot see how our remaining in Philadelphia will achieve anything but add to the chaos."

"But, Dr. Osler, we know so much more about this than they do. Surely a few days won't matter, especially in such a just cause? Gilman could not object to our taking some time to prove that our colleague—our friend—has been falsely accused."

The Professor stopped tidying. He tugged at the end of his mustache in silence, then sighed. "Ephraim, what if the accusation is not false?"

"Impossible!" I exclaimed.

"You were too quick to declare Halsted guilty. Is it possible that you are now being too quick to declare Farnshaw innocent?"

"Halsted was a different case entirely," I retorted.

"Was he, now?" the Professor said. "The two cases seem remarkably similar to me. In the first, you leapt to a conclusion supported by little but the scandalous past and abrasive personality of one man. Now, in the second, you seem to be likewise jumping to a conclusion supported by little but the youth and pleasing personality of another."

"Perhaps," I conceded, "but a man is innocent until proven guilty."

"And Borst seems to be well on his way to proving it." The Professor shook his head. "No, Ephraim, we were betrayed by Turk and I do not intend to let it happen a second time. We will do all we can for Farnshaw while we're here, but we leave as planned."

I was stunned. I had never anticipated the Professor to be so embittered or so heartless. The wound that Turk had left must have been deeper than I realized. I too felt betrayed by Turk, but I had no intention of allowing Farnshaw to suffer for the sins of another—or my own.

"I cannot pretend to agree, Dr. Osler," I insisted, "but I do, of course, respect your judgment and will accede to your wishes."

The Professor placed his hand on my shoulder. "And I respect your loyalty and your honor, Ephraim. More than you know. If I thought we could help Farnshaw, I would move mountains to do so. But even you must see that, at every juncture, your involvement has made matters worse, not better. You have uncovered more evidence in this affair than has Borst. Without you, Halsted's secret would have been safe, Farnshaw would be free, and no one would be the worse for it.

"Every time you tried to loosen the knot, you succeeded only in making it tighter. It is only by good fortune that you pulled back before it strangled Halsted. Now you want to attempt the same thing with Farnshaw. I say no. I say let his parents hire the best lawyer in the city, or their own private detectives, or whatever the rich do when one of their own is in trouble. If Farnshaw is innocent, professionals are much more likely to prove him so than a well-meaning but clumsy amateur.

"Ephraim," he intoned at last, "come to Baltimore and be a doctor. That is where your brilliance lies."

There was little to say. I agreed to do as he asked, and left.

I did, however, have two more days.

I arrived at the Benedict home just before five. It was earlier than I had said, but circumstances had altered my schedule. Standing at the front door, I felt the familiar tightness in my stomach that always preceded seeing Abigail. As I had neared her home, I became conscious how terribly I missed her. How desperately I craved the solace of her embrace. Doubts as to her feelings for me, or even of her truthfulness, no longer mattered. I wanted her to be with me always, loving me the way I loved her.

I heard the latch disengage from the inside. How different this sound from that of the padlock on the police wagon. When the door opened, I found myself face-to-face with the Benedicts' emaciated butler.

"I'm sorry, Dr. Carroll," he said in a servant's monotone, "I've instructions not to admit you."

"Instructions from whom?"

The butler did not answer, but began to close the door. Purely by reflex, my right arm shot out and pushed the door back open. The butler looked astonished. In his world, someone forcing their way into a house was as unique a phenomenon as witnessing an active volcano.

"You must leave," he gasped. "If not, I will call—"

"You'll do nothing of the sort," I growled. "You will fetch Miss Benedict and you will do it now."

The butler's head began to swivel back and forth as if on a spring. "I cannot..."

"It's all right, Martin," an unexpected voice said from up the stairs. "Let Dr. Carroll in."

"Abigail!" She stood at the head of the stairs in a black silk gown.

"Hello, Ephraim," she said in tones as mournful as her

garb. She descended the stairs like a magnificent butterfly, seeming to waft rather than walk and, when she reached the bottom, took my hand, but did not kiss me.

Without speaking further, she led me through the house to the sitting room, the same one in which she had showed me the portrait of Rebecca Lachtmann. Not only had that painting been removed, but so had Eakins' depiction of the rowers. Two smaller, nondescript still-lifes now hung in their place, leaving a dark halo on the buff wallpaper around each, as if the Benedicts had wished to provide a reminder of the disgrace that had sparked the change. Abigail bade me to take a chair, but I could not sit.

"Abigail," I began, "they tried to keep me from you. I know that you would never—"

She put up her hand. Her movements were graceful, deliberate. "Ephraim," she said softly, "in one hour I am leaving for New York with my parents and Albert and Margaret. From there, we are sailing for Europe."

"Europe?" I echoed, stunned. "How long will you be gone? How can I reach you?"

"Father has planned an extensive tour of the Continent. There is no date for our return. And he has insisted that our itinerary remain secret."

"But what about us?"

Abigail did not drop her gaze or alter her expression. "I treasure our time together, Ephraim. Truly I do. I have deep feelings for you. But circumstances have overtaken both of us. I cannot bear to remain here with the memory of the horrible fate that befell my friend so fresh in my mind. I ache terribly. I need time and distance so that my soul may heal."

My throat had gone completely dry and I felt my heart tripping against my ribs. "What about my soul?" I whispered.

"I'm sorry, Ephraim."

"I thought you loved me."

"I said I have feelings for you. I never once said I loved

you. I have never loved any man. I'm not convinced that I ever will."

"But the night in the studio . . . the portrait . . ."

"Lovemaking is not the same thing as love, Ephraim."

"It was to me."

Abigail sighed. "It isn't my fault, Ephraim, that you made me into something I'm not."

I felt desperation, as does a patient who has been just told that he is terminally ill. How many times had I watched one of them grapple with this news? There must be something to say, something to do, each thinks, something that will alter the diagnosis, something to inject a glimmer of hope. I wanted to beg her, accuse her, charm her, plead with her, berate her for enticing me to fall in love with her and then abandoning me. Before I could do any of that, however, she spoke once more.

"When you came by yesterday morning, I was too aggrieved to see you and, to be honest, extremely distressed that you ignored my wishes. How could you possibly have made that grisly visit to the cemetery?"

"You begged me to help." I heard the shrillness in my protest. "To find out the truth about Rebecca. If I had not gone . . . done what I did . . . you never would have known."

Her face was beautiful, implacable. "I know now that sometimes it may be better to have a terrible truth withheld. I will never be able to look at you again without being reminded of poor Rebecca's coffin being dug up and opened in the dead of night."

"Perhaps after some time away . . ." I mumbled.

"Quite some time, I'm afraid. Simply put, Ephraim, I do not expect to return anytime in the near future, so it would be pointless to pretend there is any potential for us. You are an exceptional man and I have complete confidence that you will find the love and fulfillment you seek with another. Although I have no right to make such a request, I ask for your indulgence and understanding. I hope that one day you will be able to think of me with fondness rather than rancor."

A stunning emptiness came over me, as if I had been hollowed out, followed by a horrible pain—searing, tearing through me. Never to see her again, never to touch her, hear her voice. The helplessness, the sense of loss, was crushing. This was, surely, a death, how Halsted must have felt when he realized that his destiny had been totally wrested from his control.

"Then there is nothing..."

"I'm sorry," she said, but looking on her face, so placid, so utterly unaffected, I knew at once that she had been regretful before, that I was not the first man to sit across from her with dashed hopes and smashed dreams. I was surely not the only man who found her to be the most alluring woman he'd ever met, not the first to fall in love with her. Eakins, I now knew, was in love with her, too. Every man she met, I expected, was prone to the same fate.

While she loved none of them in return.

Then, suddenly, as with Monique, I saw Abigail for the person she was. Beauty without soul. All her passion went on her canvases. There was none in the person herself. It was she who was truly hollowed out.

There was nothing more to be said. I stood to leave.

"There is something I'd like you to have, if you want it," she said.

"What is that?"

"The portrait. I've had it wrapped for you. If you don't want it, I'm going to have it destroyed. I've already done that with Rebecca's painting. I want no reminders."

"I'll take it," I said.

Abigail rang and instructed Martin to bring the package. He soon returned with a parcel wrapped in cloth and tied with string.

She stood and faced me. "Good-bye, Ephraim."

I couldn't speak the word. I mutely took up the package and walked past her out of the room. As I passed into the vestibule, Albert was standing at the top of the stairs. I stopped and our eyes met. I considered confronting him for his perfidy, but I realized that he felt no more responsibility for Rebecca Lachtmann than the butcher surgeon Burleigh had felt for Mr. Whitbread. For a moment, we stared at one another and then, without the hypocrisy of false pleasantries, I left the Benedict home for the final time.

When I arrived home and placed the painting in the hall, Mrs. Mooney asked what it was. When I told her, she fetched a knife and, without uttering a word, cut the string binding the cloth. When the painting was unwrapped, she leaned it against the wall and stood back to examine it. She placed her right index finger to her lower lip and cocked her head back and forth, never taking her eyes from the canvas. Finally, she emitted a long breath, slowly shook her head, and retired to prepare me a light supper.

As I examined the portrait for myself, I also was not as taken with it as I had been earlier. What had appeared strong and indomitable in Abigail's studio seemed now to be only mean and self-absorbed. I looked carefully to see if Abigail had altered the painting in any way, but there was no evidence of change. Perhaps it was I who had changed.

Simpson arrived precisely on time. She was wearing a maroon dress, once again plain but not unfashionable. She stood at the threshold for a moment before entering. She was not alone.

"Samuel," she said, looking down at a boy of about eight standing next to her, "please say hello to Dr. Carroll."

The boy stepped forward and extended his hand. He had a mop of soft brown hair under a small cap and was dressed in knickers and a wool jacket. "Pleased to meet you, sir," he said.

Simpson stood across from me with hope and challenge. "Ephraim, I would like you to meet my son."

"Samuel," I said with a smile, suppressing my astonishment. "This is indeed a pleasure. I've wanted to meet the son of such a fine doctor as your mother."

"You knew about me then, sir?" asked the boy. "I'm supposed to be a secret from the other doctors...except Dr. Osler, that is."

"I didn't know," I said, with a glance at his mother. "But I should have suspected."

Samuel smiled. He was a fine-looking lad with an open and intelligent face. "Mother says that you're very smart... and a good detective."

"Did she? Well, I'm not sure she's correct, but I'm terribly flattered."

Mrs. Mooney had appeared at my side, as beamingly maternal as if one of her own grandchildren had appeared. "Why don't I take Samuel in the kitchen so that you two can work?"

After they had departed, Simpson said, "We agreed to be honest with each other." Before I could reply, she saw the portrait leaning against the wall. "Did she do that?"

I replied that, yes, Abigail Benedict had painted it.

"Doesn't look like you," Simpson remarked.

"It's not supposed to," I answered. "It isn't supposed to be realistic."

"No," said Simpson. "I mean that it *isn't* you. It's somebody else with your features."

I found myself relieved and pleased that Simpson had seen it so.

"Well, Ephraim," she said abruptly, "let's get to work."

"Before we begin," I said, "please tell me about Samuel."

"I'm sure you can guess most of it," she began self-consciously, but also with relief. "I was born near Pittsburgh..."

"I thought you were native to Philadelphia."

"No. I moved here just after Samuel was born. I became pregnant at sixteen by a man who claimed to love me but who then abandoned me when he discovered my condition. My father and mother railed at me, called me godless, and insisted I either publicly confess my sins to their congregation and then give up the baby, or leave their home. I chose the latter.

"You know all too well what choices are available to a woman who finds herself in my situation. I, however, decided to create an option of my own. I moved to Philadelphia and cajoled a 'home for fallen women' to take me in—that's what Croskey was at the time. While the women who lived there watched my baby, I worked at whatever employment I could find. I studied at night. I eventually registered at the university. I completed my studies about the time Dr. Osler arrived. He had a reputation for progressive thought, so I sought him out and asked him to allow me to study medicine under his auspices. He agreed without hesitation. What I am today is the result."

"So it was you who created the settlement house?"

"I and a number of others."

"Samuel is a fine boy, as I am sure you know," I said. "You should be immensely proud. But why bring him here tonight?"

"Living a lie is fatiguing," she replied simply. "I wish to stop." She eyed me carefully, wary of any false gesture or response. "But we should get to work now."

"Wait," I said. "There is something I want . . . need . . . to tell you. I need you to know about my father . . ."

For twenty minutes, I told Simpson of my past with relief but not trepidation, while she listened with sympathy but not judgment. When I was done, she smiled shyly, thanked me for my trust, and then said simply, "Now let's find something to save poor Farnshaw."

I was buoyed. With her help, I felt, for the first time, that I might find my way through the thicket.

Since I had already been through the materials, at least cursorily, I examined the journal while Simpson familiarized herself with some of the more common techniques of encryption. Even when we engaged in individual tasks, we worked together, as if at the autopsy table, two students of science applying logic and method to unravel an enigma.

"If Turk employed an exotic cipher, I'm not all at sure we can penetrate it," she concluded, "but if not, since we are able to form a solid hypothesis as to the subject matter that he wished to hide, we may be able to work backward to set us on the road to a solution."

I agreed. Inference would be vital in forming working hypotheses. We began with a page of the journal containing a number of entries. For the next hours, we tried substitutions, transpositions, the Caesar cipher, transliteral cipher, and polyalphabetic ciphers. We performed elementary frequency analysis, and tried some obvious keys for the Vigenère code. Once or twice, we seemed to be on the verge of a breakthrough, only to have our edifice crumble and collapse. At one point, Mrs. Mooney poked her head into the room to report that Samuel was asleep in her spare room.

By midnight I was deeply fatigued of the effort, despite Mrs. Mooney's indulgence with a large pot of coffee, but Simpson seemed unruffled. Finally, however, she put down the book.

"Ephraim," she said. "I do believe we may be wasting our time."

"Is it unbreakable, then?" I asked.

"I'm not sure, but it certainly seems so to us. Not every puzzle can be solved."

"But if this book holds the secret of Farnshaw's innocence..."

"I'm as frustrated as you, Ephraim, be we cannot simply divine a solution. I'm beginning to suspect another possibility, however. Have you considered that this journal may be nothing more than an elaborate hoax?"

"A hoax? I had suspected that myself with the journal Borst unearthed, but there is no such obvious direction here. If it were not to implicate another, why would Turk go to all that trouble just to create a specious clue?"

"I'm starting to know Turk," she said. "He might well have

done it for the very purpose of setting a couple of fools like us to frustration.

"We have been examining this book as if it were a heart or a liver. Cut it open and its secrets will be revealed. But this is not the Dead House. The character of the person is as important as the artifact. I have come to see that, despite all his pretensions to wealth, Turk did not do all of this just for the money. Turk needed to *get even*. He needed to *get away with it*, to laugh at everyone who he thought had laughed at him his whole life . . . motivation each of us can understand, I warrant. Perhaps Turk did not blackmail Dr. Halsted, but he would have. Gleefully. Halsted was rich, from a good family. He went to Yale. Turk would have done anything to bring him down, to prove that he was the smarter man, that it was only accident of birth that had prevented him from attaining similar heights. All of those silly precautions—hiding where he lived, that room on Wharf Lane—everything had to be so *complicated*. Leaving a key in a *book*. How silly. The best place to hide a key was with his other keys.

"Don't you see, Ephraim? There were no real practical advantages to his intrigues . . . he left plenty of hints that anyone interested could follow . . . he wanted things complicated because he had decided complicated meant clever. I can just see him, hunched over his desk at night, chortling to himself as he created his fakes. 'Let them try and figure *this* out,' he would have thought. He was *so* desperate to show everyone how smart he was. Well, he wasn't smarter than you and he definitely wasn't smarter than whoever killed him."

"Yes," I agreed, "I believe you're correct about the man. But to sit down and pen a meaningless journal and then hide it? That surely is too much trouble to go to."

"Approach the question from the other end. Ask yourself, why would he keep a journal? He would have known it could sink him. For money? How was a journal possibly going to make him money? Anyone Turk was blackmailing was not going to be more likely to pay just because Turk had written his name in cipher in a book."

"Why hide it, then?"

"Maybe he had plans to use it as a red herring in one of his schemes. Who knows? Maybe he simply did it for fun, telling himself that one day he would use it to have the inferior minds with whom he matched wits—like us—chase their own tails."

"But what about the journal in his rooms? The one Borst uncovered?"

"That was different. That one had an obvious purpose. You were correct. If he ever needed to bargain with the police or anyone else, he could point to the journal and use it as proof that it was not he who had done the deed. Then he could trade the identity of 'GF' for a better deal."

"So it is your contention that both books were fraudulent."

"Everything about Turk was fraudulent. He told you so himself. Didn't he say that he was a creation only of himself? You could not have known at the time just how true that was."

I should have known precisely, of course, being of similar creation myself, but I had missed the significance. "But how does this help Farnshaw?"

"It helps a great deal," she replied. "Don't you remember what Dr. Osler said to Turk, after we autopsied the carpenter who had died of hypertrophy? 'We have chronicled a case that does not correspond to accepted data. It is an enigma therefore open to the first who deciphers it.' The journals are just such an enigma.

"Think for a moment about Borst's case against Farnshaw. It rests on the assumption that the journal with 'GF' is genuine. But the existence of this second journal casts doubt on the legitimacy of the first. If it is authentic and eventually deciphered, it will likely contain the names of Turk's true associates and prove Farnshaw's innocence. In the more likely case that it is not deciphered, it will be dismissed as a hoax. If that comes to pass, it becomes difficult to assert that the 'GF' journal is not a hoax as well."

"We must get it into the right hands, then," I said. "I don't trust giving it to Borst."

"No. If Borst is under Lachtmann's sway, I am confident the journal would vanish before anyone could be made aware of its existence. What about Dr. Osler?"

"Of course," I agreed but, although I felt a sharp pang of guilt, I was not sure.

Simpson noted my ambivalence. "Yes," she agreed, "that is the conundrum. We cannot underestimate how well it suits everyone to have Farnshaw accused of this crime. No one will want him to *be* innocent, let alone be *proved* innocent. If Farnshaw is guilty, Lachtmann will have his revenge, the Pinkertons will have a success, the newspapers will have a juicy scandal, and the policeman who arrested him will have a triumph. Even Dr. Osler benefits—he can continue his career with neither scandal nor professional acrimony dogging his footsteps. I think it is important that we understand that in pursuing this matter, we do so against the interests of everyone involved, even those we admire and respect."

"Does it not disturb you to include Dr. Osler?"

"Of course. You are disturbed as well. But it is his own doing, really. It was he who trained us to be scientists, to follow the evidence wherever it might lead, no matter the consequence. I fully expect that he will be found to have no part in this, but we must account for every hypothesis. We cannot allow Farnshaw to hang for crimes in which he had no part. I think we must hold on to the journal and wait for the proper moment."

I agreed, and she stood and emitted a deep sigh. "That's all we can do for tonight."

"Thanks to you, we have made some significant progress."

"I'm sorry for the circumstances," she told me, "but it has been a pleasure working with you."

"Yes," I agreed, getting out of my chair. "I have enjoyed working with you as well."

"I suppose I had better be going," she said.

"You must stay here," I replied. "It's too late for you to be out alone with Samuel. It will be difficult to locate a hansom at this hour. Please stay in the spare room with your son. Mrs. Mooney will be delighted."

Simpson smiled. "All right. Thank you, Ephraim."

As I expected, Mrs. Mooney, who had waited up, was eager for a guest. As she went upstairs to prepare the room, Mary and I were left alone in the parlor. We turned and faced each other. For a few seconds, neither of us moved. Then the moment passed.

"Good night, Mary," I said. "And thank you."

"Good night, Ephraim." She remained for another second, and then followed Mrs. Mooney upstairs.

I awoke at six the next morning, but when I came downstairs for breakfast, I learned that Mary and Samuel had already gone.

CHAPTER 26

As soon as I entered the main wing of Moyamensing Prison three hours later, I spied an unsmiling, well-dressed couple in their forties sitting on a bench. The man appeared determined, the woman distressed. The resemblance was unmistakable.

"Are you George's parents?" I asked them. "I'm Ephraim Carroll. I work with George at the hospital."

The man was of my height, with glasses and a gray-flecked beard, dressed in a dark blue suit and top hat. "Dr. Carroll, I'm Mortimer Farnshaw. George has told us about you. We are greatly in your debt for your kindness to our son. May I present my wife, Thelma?" Despite the environment, he spoke with the absolute propriety that good breeding instills. We might have been meeting at a charity banquet.

I nodded to Mrs. Farnshaw, an attractive woman with rust-colored hair who seemed to be trying to blot out both where she was and the circumstances under which she'd been brought here.

"Have you seen George?" I asked, directing my question to Mr. Farnshaw.

He nodded. "It was extremely disturbing."

A ferretlike man appeared at the elder Farnshaw's side and excused himself for the interruption. He whispered something in Farnshaw's ear, which elicited a quick nod in reply.

"Dr. Carroll," said Farnshaw, "may I present Mr. Franklin.

Mr. Franklin is the attorney I have engaged to put this atrocious episode right."

The lawyer shook my hand. "Benjamin Franklin," he said, "at your service." He waited for the name to register, a regular party trick, it seemed, and then said, "No relation, but it certainly doesn't hurt in this city to evoke my namesake."

"Mr. Franklin was recommended by an associate. He assures me that he will have George out of here in a matter of days," Farnshaw informed me.

"Without question," the lawyer agreed. "Just a matter of approaching the right people in the right way." Then he actually winked.

"Excellent," I replied. Franklin's casual optimism confirmed my first impression. No matter who he was named for, he must have been aware that it would not be at all simple to free Farnshaw. The Farnshaws' money might talk in Boston, but it was the Lachtmann money that spoke here, and Jonas Lachtmann was every bit as anxious to keep Farnshaw behind bars in Moko as Mortimer Farnshaw was to get him out.

If I had been favorably impressed with Franklin, he would have been the perfect repository for the journal. Who better than a well-connected lawyer to make the right use of it? As it was, however, Franklin struck me as unctuous and potentially unreliable, so I decided to keep the matter to myself for the present.

While Franklin excused himself to "see about some things," I spoke with Mr. Farnshaw, telling him what a fine physician his son was and how, when this was over, George would claim a place at the very top of his profession. Mr. Farnshaw listened gratefully but, no fool, understood full well his son's limitations.

When decency had been satisfied, I asked, "Might I see George now, do you think?"

"He would like that a great deal," his father replied. "I think one makes arrangements at the desk."

It was, I was surprised to learn, remarkably easy to visit a prisoner who had not yet been brought up for trial. One could visit in a cell or have the prisoner brought to a common area. I chose the latter, assuming that the more time Farnshaw spent outside his cell, the happier he would be. Within ten minutes after making my request at the desk and following directions to the common area, Farnshaw was brought out.

I was appalled. My young colleague seemed to have aged ten years in one night. He smiled dispiritedly when he saw me. "Hello, Carroll. Nice of you to come by."

"It's my pleasure," I replied, trying to exude confidence. "I spoke to your father. He has retained a fine lawyer and you will soon be out of here."

Farnshaw nodded slowly. "Yes. A couple of fellows inside said that Franklin was just the man to have if one didn't care about niceties of the law." His eyes darted this way and that to see if we were being overheard. "Carroll," he said, terror in his voice, "I didn't tell my parents, they're so worried already, but you've got to see that I get out of here right away. I've already had my watch taken and they said they were going to kill me."

"Who said they would kill you, Farnshaw?"

"Everyone. The guards said the prisoners will kill me and the prisoners said the guards will kill me."

"They're just trying to frighten you, that's all," I said soothingly. Borst knew the man was probably innocent, and I hoped he was decent enough to have given instructions that his well-being be assured. Then, too, his promotion would not come to much if the innocent scion of a prominent Boston family was murdered as a result of his erroneous arrest. "You're not one of them and they're making sport of you," I went on. "No one would dare harm someone whose family could raise a public howl."

"Do you really think so?" Hope flared briefly in Farnshaw's eyes.

"Of course. In a day or two, you will be out and you and I will go to celebrate. I know just the place where we can each get a first-rate porterhouse."

"That would be nice. But they did not seem to be speaking in jest. Someone really is going to murder me."

"Farnshaw," I said sharply, "you must keep up your spirits. You will be free in a matter of days. Your father will move heaven and earth for you; Franklin, as you said, is adept at this sort of thing, and I am not without resources as well. I know Turk's haunts. I will not rest until I have found evidence to prove you innocent."

"Thank you, Carroll," he replied, his eyes still darting about as if the room itself could be his executioner. "That's very decent of you."

"Not a bit of it," I replied. "It is a pleasure to be able to help."

Some are more fit to tolerate such circumstances than others and, while I could not be certain how I would fare, it was hard to imagine someone less equipped to cope than Farnshaw. It really was imperative to free him, if not for his physical well-being, then for his sanity.

Farnshaw reached across and grabbed my wrist in a claw-like grip much like that of Turk just before he died. "I'm afraid, Carroll."

"Anyone would be," I said, although the words, I knew, would have no meaning.

I left Farnshaw minutes later. He urged me to stay so that he would not have to go back to his cell, but I could not dally at Moko if I hoped to find evidence to free him. I could feel how close I was to success. While the journal, if Simpson was correct, would provide ballast for an alternative version of the events, it was unlikely to be enough to turn the tide by itself. Any other bit of information that I could unearth, however, might be sufficient, when added to the journal, to force even Borst to admit he had acted without sufficient cause.

I spent the day going over the events, reviewing everything

that had transpired, looking for weak spots in Borst's case. The most damning evidence, other than the written record, was Turk's announcement at The Fatted Calf that "George" was his associate. If Simpson was correct and Turk had a constant need to demonstrate how clever he was, might he have boasted to an intimate down there of his scheme to create a scapegoat?

I arrived at about ten that night. As I dismounted my carriage, Keuhn jumped from his and accosted me. For the past two days, he had contented himself to be a shadow, but that was apparently at an end. "Mr. Lachtmann isn't happy with you, Doc. He thinks that you ain't been taking him seriously about butting out."

"Why? Because I went to see Farnshaw?"

"Don't play us for fools, Doc. It's unhealthy." Keuhn grinned at his joke.

"Has it occurred to Mr. Lachtmann that perhaps the wrong man is in custody and that I am doing him a favor? If I obtain the release of an innocent man, we might find the one who is guilty," I said in reply.

"It's occurred to Mr. Lachtmann that you're trying to get someone off who's guilty because he's a friend and a 'fellow doctor.' It also occurred to him that you only admitted the part about the accomplice because you was scared, but once you was out of the room, you wanted to take it back, so now you're trying to undo what you did. But, you know, Doc, it doesn't matter what occurred to Mr. Lachtmann. It only matters that you do what he says. This, as they say, is your last warning."

"Thank you, Keuhn," I replied. "I understand you completely. Now, would you please step out of my way? I have no intention of going through life with you telling me where I may or may not go."

I stepped around him and walked through the door, greeting Mike only perfunctorily. The giant actually seemed hurt that I did not acknowledge him more cordially. Once inside, I headed for the bar. The bartender made to greet me but, when I stood stone-faced, knew to pretend to ignorance. I ordered what passed for a whiskey, and then waited until Keuhn decided that the interval was sufficiently discreet to make his appearance.

Less than two minutes later, he sidled up to the bar himself. Glancing at the shot glass in front of me, he ordered a whiskey as well. As the rules of our little theater dictated, he never acknowledged my presence in public. Keuhn downed his shot and asked for another. He seemed not the least surprised at the quality of the whiskey. I, on the other hand, merely dallied for an additional moment or two, and then strolled across the room, taking care to leave my hat on the bar next to my glass. I knocked on the door of the office and announced myself. A moment later, I was asked to enter.

As I did, Haggens was just closing a drawer of his desk, looking like a guilty schoolboy. The smell of the real stuff permeated the room.

"I told you . . ." I began.

"Yeah, Doc, I know," he replied. "It was my first one of the day."

"I'm sure. Haggens," I went on, "I need information."

Haggens cocked his head like a spaniel. "Information? You paying?"

"No," I said.

Haggens chewed this over. "Well, since I ain't got your bill yet for listening to my heart, I guess I could give you some free information. You got a medical problem?" he joked.

"Thank you, no." I asked whether Turk had ever bragged about setting up a sucker to hand to the police in case he was caught. Haggens listened carefully, and I think he would have told me had he known, but apparently Turk had said nothing to him.

"By the way," I said. "There's a man at the bar. He's from the Pinkerton Detective Agency. He's been following me."

"You got the Pinkertons on you? That's not good. They can be as fatal as endo... what was it?"

"Endocarditis. I'm afraid his presence has something to do with you as well, Haggens."

Haggens emitted an exaggerated sigh. "What could that be? Me and the Pinkertons have always had kind of an understanding—we stay out of each other's way. Kinda like you and me was supposed to do before it came to you that you like it here."

"It's true, Haggens. You have turned me into a Fatted Calf devotee." I went on to relate the circumstances of the agency's engagement by Jonas Lachtmann and Lachtmann's obsession with avenging his daughter.

"I heard they pinched someone for that already. That other doc."

"I fear that Lachtmann is not satisfied with Farnshaw. He intends to pressure me into revealing the identity of everyone involved, even peripherally."

"Per...ipherally? That me, Doc?"

"I'm afraid so."

"What about our bargain?"

"Haggens, I will do everything I can to keep our bargain—you know the affection in which I hold you—but if you are threatening me with death if I reveal your name and the Pinkertons are posing the very same threat if I don't, it is hard to say what will eventually happen."

Haggens scowled at me for a moment, then clapped his hands to his knees and emitted a bark of a laugh. "Ah! I see! Okay, I get it. Sorry for taking so long. That miteral... what is it?"

"Mitral stenosis."

"Right. Miteral stenosis. Must be rotting my brain. But I got it now." Haggens pushed himself to his feet. "It's been a slow night anyway." He snickered. "You just wait right here, Doc." Haggens left the office for a few moments and, when he returned, left the door open so that we could both see the room. Keuhn was leaning sideways against the rail with one elbow on the bar, a refilled whiskey glass in front of him. He seemed to be idly taking in the scene, but I knew he was watching me.

Through the haze, Mike appeared. For a man of his immensity, he moved with great fluidity, seeming to glide rather than walk. He went to the bar, stood next to Keuhn, and said something softly. Keuhn's hand quickly went to his vest. He was fast but Mike was faster.

Since the dawn of time, man has dreamt of flight. Keuhn achieved it. Mike's right hand appeared to travel less than six inches, but the force of one blow was sufficient to literally lift Keuhn off his feet and send him backward through air. I actually saw the bottom of his shoes. He landed on a table that broke apart with a splintering crack, sending a combination of wood, two customers, and the Pinkerton man crashing to the floor. Keuhn lay stunned for a moment but, tough as he was, his hand again went for his vest. Mike was again too quick for him. In one step, Mike had reached where Keuhn was lying and, with one short kick of his left foot, sent the derringer that Keuhn had drawn skittering across the floor.

Keuhn was still not beaten. Although I could not see from whence it came, at once he had a knife in his hand and was lunging for Mike's legs. Mike sidestepped with amazing agility and, as soon as his feet were on the ground, kicked once again, this time his heavy shoe catching the Pinkerton agent square on the jaw. Keuhn rocked backward, teetered for a second or two, then fell flat, and out.

Haggens waited until Keuhn was motionless and then heaved a sigh. "That's four tables this month," he muttered. "I wish Mike could learn to be more careful." Then he motioned for me to go with him to where Keuhn was struggling to blink himself back into sensibility.

Haggens fetched a shot of brandy which, if it was anything like the champagne, was more likely to kill Keuhn than bring him around. I gave him water instead. Haggens leaned down and spoke to him.

"Look, pally," he said, exuding the same casual menace with which he had first greeted me, "I've dealt with you folks before. I don't eat your soup and you don't eat mine. You can tell your boss or whoever hired you that you've got all you're gonna get. And as for the doc, here . . . well, he's a friend of mine, savvy?" Haggens then spoke to the bartender, and within five minutes a couple of ruffians had showed up to carry Keuhn out.

"Will it work?" I asked, when the Pinkerton man had been carted off. "Will they really leave me . . . us . . . leave us alone?"

"Oh, yeah," Haggens replied, as if I had just asked him if the sun would come up in the morning. "Can't keep a reputation for muscle if you get out-muscled. They'll leave you be for now, until you leave town anyways. But they're gonna remember you . . . if you run afoul of them again, watch out. But for now . . . well, I recommend that you just try to avoid nervous stress."

"Very funny," I muttered. I walked to the bar to where Mike had downed a series of whiskies to no visible effect. "Thank you, Mike. That was most impressive."

The giant smiled. It was the first time I had ever seen him do so and I noticed that he was missing more than a few teeth. "Glad to oblige . . . Doc." He drank two more shots in quick succession. "Well," he said, "back to work," and ambled toward the front door, as if he had come inside to use the toilet instead of to bludgeon a thug into submission. I wondered if I appeared so nonchalant after an autopsy.

"Got a few minutes for an old friend?" It was Haggens, who had followed me to the bar.

"What old friend is that?"

"Follow me." Haggens led me to a section of the room that, at least by comparison, was relatively tranquil. He walked over to a table for two, and waved his arm with a flourish at one of the occupants.

"I think you two know each other," he said.

"Hi, Ephie."

"Hello, Monique."

She shook her head. "Got tired of Monique. I'm Collette these days."

"Then hello, Collette." I bowed. "And who is your friend?"

"She's Danielle," she said with a laugh, gesturing to the woman next to her. Danielle was flaxen-haired and thin, with the hardened look that was *de rigueur* at Bonhomme's Paris Revue. I remembered her as the woman in the dressing room who had made no effort to cover her breasts.

"Am I allowed to just call you Brigid?" I asked "Collette," remembering that Borst had told me that Brigid O'Leary was her real name.

"Well," she replied, "seeing how you're almost family..."

"And your friend?"

"Danielle," she said coldly. "You're not family with me."

"Aren't you dancing tonight?" I asked Brigid.

"Nah," she replied. "Needed to be off my feet for a bit." I let that pass. "Took a night off."

"Very well," I said. "May I join you?" Brigid might not have looked as good as the first time I saw her, but nor did she look as bad as the second.

"Of course, Ephie. You can always join us."

As I pulled up a chair, a bottle of presumptive champagne arrived at the table. "On the house," grunted the waitress who brought it.

Danielle showed more interest. "You could be family, though," she said.

"Back off," Brigid growled. "If he'd be anybody's he'd be mine, but Ephie don't go in for the likes of us. He prefers so-ci-e-ty types."

"Where did you hear that?"

"Word gets around," she replied. "But why talk about such things now? Let's drink."

The champagne had not improved with age, nor had

Brigid's life. Recent events had brought her some unwanted attention from Sergeant Borst, while the attention she would have wanted, that of well-to-do males, seemed as elusive as ever. Danielle recounted similar tales of life's cruelties. It was odd to be sitting with these two downtrodden women, little more than prostitutes, and feel quite relaxed and at home. I was ashamed for having judged Brigid without charity.

Haggens' bigheartedness did not extend beyond the bottle at the table, but I called the waitress over and asked for a second on my tab, which brightened her considerably.

Soon, I turned the conversation to Turk. Perhaps he had preferred to boast to women. "I kinda miss ol' Georgie," Brigid said. "He was a mean cuss when you crossed him, but he was good for a laugh and he sure did know how to spend money."

"Sterling traits to be sure," I agreed.

"It's a lot easier to spend money when yer making barrels of it," grunted Danielle.

"Yeah," Brigid agreed. "He was kinda our Carnegie."

I laughed. Turk as a captain of industry—or robber baron—made a more persuasive picture than they knew. I then asked, as I had with Haggens, if they were familiar with Farnshaw, the other George.

"Sure," said Danielle. "Don't you think I read the papers? He's the one slipped the arsenic to Georgie. He was kinda cute. Was in here about two months ago."

It seemed, however, that, like Haggens, Brigid had seen Farnshaw but the one time. "Danielle would know better though," said Brigid. "She and Georgie was tight." She smiled. "Really tight, if you get my meaning."

"So, you would know if he had...uh...associates in his business?" I asked her.

"Not personally. The one time I needed services, Georgie did it himself," she answered. "I was lucky."

"Lucky?"

"Yeah. Georgie wasn't real good at it. Word was getting around that maybe he wasn't worth the risk. A little bit after that, he got someone else to do the work. He was the one took the money, though."

"You mean the other Georgie? He did the work? That's what the police say anyway."

"Maybe," said Danielle. "But I always figured it was the old guy."

"Old guy?" I asked. I felt a reflex to start, but tried to cover it by taking a sip from my glass. "What did he look like?"

"Little fella. Dressed like a millionaire. I ain't never seen a collar so white."

"Did he have glasses?" I asked.

"Yeah. The ones without the hooks for your ears. Why? D'you know him?"

"I'm not sure," I said. "I might. He was clean-shaven, am I correct?"

"Nah," Danielle replied. "This musta been a different millionaire. He had a mustache and beard both. Took real good care of them, too."

"That couldn't have been who I was thinking of," I said, playing with the stem of my glass and praying that I was giving nothing away.

"They had a tiff one night," said Danielle. "Georgie and the old gent. Musta been something big. Georgie got scary, the way he got all quiet when he was really hot. I think even Haggens backed off him then."

"That says something," I agreed.

"It does, mister." Danielle nodded. "I can tell you. But Georgie . . . he could really make you quake."

"What was the fight about?" I asked casually.

"Georgie had something on the old guy . . . I couldn't hear exactly what . . . but it had something to do with some young bird. I think Georgie wanted money to keep his mouth shut, but the old guy didn't wanna come across. So Georgie got real quiet, leaned over and said something, too soft to make out, and the old gent went as white as his collar. A few minutes later, he agreed to do what Georgie wanted."

"That's funny," said Brigid. "The night I was here with Ephie, Georgie had some big set-to with a geezer looked just like that. Remember?"

"Sorry. I don't remember anything about that night...except you, of course."

She laughed, a real laugh, like a girl. For a moment, she looked quite sweet and innocent. "Ah, g'wan."

"Oh, wait a minute," I said, clapping a hand to my forehead. "Now I remember. Haggens had come over and told Turk someone wanted to see him. It was the, uh, geezer." I considered this revelation for a moment. "But from what I saw, he hardly looked afraid of Turk."

"He was scared that night, I'll tell you," said Danielle. "After the old boy left, Georgie was pig-in-clover happy. He said, 'Just goes to prove, Annalise'—I was goin' by Annalise then—'you can always find some way to get anyone to do anything. Even big, important snobs.' I asked what he meant, but he just laughed. 'Sometimes you give 'em what they want, and sometimes you take it away.' I never did figure out what he meant."

But I knew. What a fool I'd been!

"I've got to go," I said to them both. "I'm sorry." I left five dollars on the table and headed for the door.

CHAPTER 27

THE ENTIRE WAY TO TWELFTH Street, I yelled at the driver to go faster. Every moment I wasted was another moment that Farnshaw had to remain in that filthy jail.

I had never felt such a raging anger. Halsted had sat there, never flinching, never changing expression, feeding me one half-truth after another. Except when he fed me total lies, of course.

Wrong diagnosis? Ha! It had been Halsted all the time. He had butchered Rebecca Lachtmann, not because Turk had given him drugs, but because he had *withheld* them. An unaccountable gaffe by Turk, but I supposed he had simply assumed that Halsted would never have bungled an operation, no matter how much in need. Or perhaps he merely wanted to watch Halsted cringe and sweat his way through an ordinarily simple procedure, forced to ply his skill without his morphia crutch.

What must they have thought, after Halsted had perforated that poor girl's bowel? The great Halsted confronted with a screaming, hemorrhaging woman on a filthy table in an ill-lit room by the docks? From his hand! And Turk standing by, knowing that a daughter of the city's elite was dying in agony in his den. Would it have been Turk or Halsted who moved first to stifle the screams? Turk, most likely. Halsted probably would have gaped, disbelieving, that such a thing could have happened, that his hand could have betrayed him.

But Turk would have taken action, swift and determined action, the only action possible to avoid prison. He would have held the poor, screaming girl down by pinning her left arm just below the shoulder, grabbed for whatever was at hand, one of the unused sheets perhaps, and jammed it over her face. What would Halsted have done then? Would he have fought Turk and tried to save the wretched victim on the table? Or taken a step back and waited as Turk snuffed out her life?

After Rebecca's screams had been permanently silenced, Turk would then have made arrangements to dispose of the body—Monique had said that there had been accidents before. Surely, any number of society's dregs would be more than happy to earn a few coins by burying a body in the woods or an open field, or tossing a weighted body into the harbor. But dregs are what they are. Instead of doing what he was told, whatever hooligan Turk hired must have simply pocketed the money and dumped Rebecca Lachtmann in the streets. She had been found by a passerby, who sought out the police, and thus the body had eventually made its way to the Dead House. No wonder Turk was astonished when the ice chest was opened. He must have felt haunted. And then he needed to find out what had accounted for the similar reaction by the Professor—that was where I had come in. Little did Turk suspect that I would be seeking the same information from him.

Halsted had certainly poisoned Turk. Whether he had done so to cover up the first crime or simply out of hatred was moot. Halsted had committed two murders. Even then, I might have been able to forgive him—after all, he had been blackmailed into perpetrating a heinous deed and then dealt just desserts to the blackmailer—if not for Farnshaw. Farnshaw had been arrested for Halsted's crimes. It was appalling and indefensible that the man refused to come forward, knowing that an innocent languished in a prison cell in his place.

Then there was the Professor. Was one doctor covering up for another, as Borst had surmised, or had the Professor been duped as well? I would soon know.

Borst's hypothesis, despite my contempt for him, was a good deal closer to the truth than mine had been. He could not have guessed at Halsted's identity, but other than that, he had deduced the facts of the case almost precisely. He knew that there were gaps in his formulation and was using Farnshaw as a lever to fill them in. I intended to make that ploy unnecessary. Farnshaw would be out of prison before noon tomorrow.

When I arrived at the Professor's house, the lights were on—he often worked long into the night. I pounded on the door and needed wait only a minute or two for the unflappable Mrs. Barlow. Without waiting for her to ask what was wrong, I burst through, demanding to see the Professor immediately. Before she could move to fetch him, Dr. Osler appeared in the doorway. Except for the lack of a coat, he was fully dressed.

"Hello, Ephraim," he said, looking me up and down. He could not have failed to notice my distress, but behaved as if the circumstances were completely normal. "What brings you out at such an hour? It is fortunate that I was working on my textbook or you would have found me retired."

"Dr. Osler," I cried, before he could extend the conversation, "Farnshaw is innocent! We must get him out of jail immediately."

The Professor nodded slowly, matching my urgency with dispassion. "Ephraim, I thought we were done with this. I feel for Farnshaw as well, but I'm certain that this affair will resolve itself best without our interference."

"But you don't understand, Dr. Osler! Farnshaw is innocent! I have proof."

The Professor considered this. "All right, Ephraim, come into the study. Let me hear your proof."

We walked through the door into the room in which

Halsted had sat just days before. The Professor beckoned me to a chair and then sat down himself. He was not going to be rushed.

I took a breath, tried to calm myself, and related, in as scientific a tone as I could muster, what I had heard from Monique. I then reminded the Professor of what Halsted had told us earlier and how the two stories must be inconsistent. "Dr. Osler," I said in conclusion, "Dr. Halsted lied. He did perform an abortion on Rebecca Lachtmann. The abortion went bad because Turk withheld drugs, not because Dr. Halsted had taken them. After Halsted perforated her bowel, Turk suffocated her on the table, and then made arrangements to dispose of the body. Dr. Halsted almost certainly then poisoned Turk to cover the crime."

"Your evidence would be persuasive," the Professor said, "if not for the fact that the fulcrum for this entire theory is the word of a prostitute."

"The woman's profession would surely work against her veracity," I rejoined, "save for the fact that she has no motive whatever to be untruthful, whereas Dr. Halsted has every motive."

"Who can tell what motives these people have?" the Professor retorted. "Frankly, Ephraim, it is difficult for me to think of this as in any way constituting 'proof.' You have made a grievous mistake in accusing Dr. Halsted once. It is only because you are young and passionate that he was willing to overlook the insult. I would, if I were you, be extremely hesitant in making the same mistake again."

"Dr. Osler," I began, "does it seem credible to you that Farnshaw would become involved in something so disgusting? There was no reason for him to do so. He certainly was not in need of funds."

"True. But even if Farnshaw is innocent, that in no way means that Halsted is guilty."

"But if Farnshaw is innocent, how can we let him sit in jail?"

The Professor shook his head. "We have no way of knowing whether Farnshaw is innocent or guilty. All we know is that a seemingly likeable young man from a very good family has gotten himself involved with some highly disreputable associates. Before we burst into a police station, telling Sergeant Borst his business—behavior, if on the other shoe, we would find quite offensive—I think we must have more to go on than the word of a prostitute. . . ."

I was about to interrupt, to tell him about the other journal, when the Professor put up his hand. "But I'll tell you what, Ephraim. I'll sleep on it. It is far too late to accomplish anything tonight in any case. Come here first thing in the morning. We can resolve this then. That is fair, surely."

The Professor sat across from me, thoughtful and reasoned. What he proposed was indeed fair and, as it was unlikely that anything could be achieved before morning, also made complete sense. We should, after all the bungles and false conclusions, move carefully. Yes, it was all very reasonable, except for one small fact.

At that moment, I knew—knew beyond any doubt—that the Professor was lying. He had been lying from the beginning. There had been no Elise Léger, or if there had been, she bore no physical resemblance to Rebecca Lachtmann. He needed the fabrication to cover his recognition of Rebecca Lachtmann, and he could only have known of Rebecca's fate from one source.

I rose stiffly and agreed to follow the course he had suggested. Evidently, however, I did not lie as well as he did. He fixed his eyes upon me in a manner that I had never seen before—not even as he watched Burleigh murder a patient in the operating theater.

"Don't do it, Ephraim. Halsted is too important. Thousands of lives—literally thousands—are at stake. It doesn't matter what he's done. It matters only what he will do. He will alleviate suffering on a scale comparable to few men in history. If you cut short his life, it will be a crime against the human race."

"You talk of thousands of lives, Dr. Osler. What of the one? What of Farnshaw, who will hang although innocent?"

"Farnshaw will not hang," he said. "We will get him out of prison, I assure you. It will be only a few days . . . but in the meantime, we must not sacrifice Halsted."

"Then you know Farnshaw is innocent?"

"I know he is innocent of the deaths of Turk and Rebecca Lachtmann. I assume he is innocent of other wrongdoing."

"How do you know?" Although I had heard the words, I could not yet grasp that the man on whom I had modeled my life had just admitted to being an accessory in two deaths.

"Halsted told me." He tried to speak evenly, without passion, as if he were dictating statistics in the Dead House, but his voice quavered. "As you have learned, Turk had found that doling out drugs to his victims in the proper quantities could render them helpless when the drug was withheld. Turk was frightened of performing an abortion on someone of Rebecca Lachtmann's social standing, lest something go amiss . . . quite an irony, as things turned out. He told Halsted only that the patient was from a prominent family and then forced him to agree to perform the odious chore. Halsted begged Turk to supply him with some of the drug before he operated, but Turk, fearing that once in control, Halsted would change his mind, refused.

"You have guessed accurately what transpired. Halsted's hand was shaking from drug deprivation. One of the surgical sounds slipped and perforated the poor girl's bowel. When she began to scream, Halsted tried to save her, but Turk pushed him aside. He suffocated her lest the noise be heard on the street below. After she was dead, Turk gave Halsted a supply of diacetylmorphine to keep him quiet.

"Halsted came straight to me after the abortion, distraught. I was the only person in Philadelphia he could trust.

He told me that a hoodlum had forced him to perform an abortion and the girl had died. He described her, but assured me that he never learned her name. His first instinct was to go to the police, but he was afraid. It's a lot to ask for a man to turn himself in for murder. I told him not to say anything but instead to return to Baltimore. After all, the poor girl could not be brought back to life and it was hardly Halsted's negligence that had caused her death. I was sorry for the family and that the girl, whoever she was, would not receive a proper burial, but there seemed little alternative since I assumed the body had been disposed of in a location where it would never be found.

"Then, of course, a woman who precisely matched the description Halsted had given me turned up in the Dead House. I knew instantly. I had met Miss Lachtmann once at a charity function and put a name to the face. Turk knew the wind might be up when he noted my reaction. Then, that night, Halsted took care of matters on his own, although I daresay he would never have done so without Turk's initiative."

"I don't understand."

"Turk contacted Halsted after his return to Baltimore and demanded that he continue to travel here and perform abortions. I tell you, Ephraim, it made no sense. The last thing Turk should have wanted was Halsted in Philadelphia, where at any time he could bring both of them down. It almost seemed that Turk bore Halsted a personal grudge so deep that it eroded his judgment. I asked Halsted later if he had wronged Turk in some way, but there was nothing."

Mary had been correct, then.

"Halsted did come to Philadelphia, but only to confront Turk. During the altercation Halsted insisted that they speak at his hotel afterward. After Turk took you home, he went to meet Halsted. Halsted pretended to reluctantly agree to Turk's demands. As you have seen, Halsted does not take alcohol, so Turk was not suspicious when he was the only one drinking the port. When Turk began to feel ill, Halsted got a carriage to take him home."

"Yes," I said. "Turk's landlady said that he had gotten home at three, although he had dropped me off at one."

"By the time he realized that it was not simply a reaction to bad liquor," the Professor continued, "there was no saving him. He must have thought that if he went to any hospital, I would learn of it and do him in, you see. If the police had been better at their jobs, they might well have filled in the sequence of events and traced Turk to Halsted's hotel, but they never noticed the two-hour discrepancy."

"And what of the family, once you knew Rebecca Lachtmann's true identity?"

The Professor heaved a sigh. "We would have gotten word to them somehow. I learned at the Benedicts' dinner, as did you, that her parents believed she was in Italy and, from their manner, it seemed certain that they had not yet learned the truth. Before they were contacted, I wanted to find out where she had been buried, but there seemed to be no record. Once you found out why, and Lachtmann had his daughter's body, there seemed to be nothing further to do—until Farnshaw's arrest."

"Why didn't you tell me any of this?" I asked. "Hadn't I earned your trust?"

"These were not my secrets to reveal. You heard Halsted's history. He is like a terrified child in many ways. It was all I could do to persuade him to sit with you the other evening. But I can tell you this: Halsted will not let Farnshaw be punished for either crime. He has even written out a confession to be used if all else fails."

"Where is the confession?"

"He has it, but has sworn to make it public if the need arises. So surely, Ephraim, surely you can see that a few days in jail is not such a steep price if it will save Halsted? He must continue to work."

"It is a small price for us, Dr. Osler. We are not in prison. You did not see Farnshaw."

"No, that is true."

"How are you intending to bring about Farnshaw's release?"

"Pressure will be brought to bear," the Professor insisted. "Farnshaw's parents have pledged any monies necessary. And my friends are not without influence."

"What about Lachtmann?" I asked. "Won't he use his money and influence to elicit the opposite end?"

"He will try, but he will fail."

There was little more to be said. I rose and thanked the Professor for his time. Then, replacing my hat, I turned and said, "Good-bye, Dr. Osler."

Again he pleaded with me to consider my actions carefully, but I was already at the door. Within seconds, I was back in the carriage and on my way to Borst's precinct house. He would not be in, of course, but for a matter of this urgency, he could be fetched from home. He wouldn't even mind. Halsted was a far bigger fish than Farnshaw.

"I wish to have Sergeant Borst fetched from home," I said firmly to the grizzled officer at the desk. "I have urgent news."

The old policeman eyed me. "No need. Borst's here. In the back. First door on the left up that corridor."

Sergeant Borst appeared decidedly morose as I entered the room, which I assumed was his standard posture while working in the middle of the night. He was, understandably surprised to see me. But there was something else. "How'd you find out so fast?" he asked. "I just heard myself."

"Find out what?"

"George Farnshaw is dead. Knifed in his cell. No more than an hour ago."

"That isn't possible!" I yelled. "Are you sure?"

Borst leapt back, to keep me at a distance. "Of course I'm sure."

All the energy went out of me and I sank into a chair. "Oh, God," I moaned.

Borst came around and pulled up a chair next to me. "I never expected it to end like this," he said.

"But you knew he wasn't guilty."

"Didn't know. Thought it possible. You and your mates left me no choice, though."

"How did it happen? Farnshaw, I mean."

"Someone busted into his cell. Wasn't no accident."

"Lachtmann. Lachtmann paid to have him killed, just on the chance his parents could get him out."

"Likely, yeah. Never prove it, though. No one at Moko saw anything. Don't even know if it was a prisoner or a jailer."

"Poor Farnshaw." I felt tears come into my eyes, but forced them back. I would never show such emotion to this detestable man.

"So who *shoulda* been in that cell, Doc? I know you know." Borst's face held no smirk now, just anticipation, a plea for me to help him make this all come out right in the end, to ensure that at least the real murderer would be apprehended in exchange for Farnshaw's life. Justice to counterbalance injustice. I was to forget all that he had done: forget the torture that he had inflicted on an innocent; forget that he had allowed his loathing of my profession to rob him of human decency. I was supposed to give him Halsted so that he might feel justified in his odious methods, methods he had undoubtedly used in the past and would use again in the future. I was supposed to adhere to the letter of the law, not because it would help poor, pathetic Farnshaw or the wretched Rebecca, or even bring consolation to four grieving parents. I was supposed to do so because, as cruel, self-serving men like Borst always tell us, the letter of the law represents the greater good.

The greater good.

For some moments, I looked across at the policeman's stricken face, then finally said, "No, Borst. You've let him die for nothing. You see, I don't know whom you should have arrested instead of Farnshaw. I never did."

———— ❧ ————

PERHAPS IT WAS THE SNOW, *heavy and silent, coating the trees in the garden, transforming the branches into spectral fingers reaching for the sky. She stopped dressing, her new Paris gown laid out on her bed, the iridescent folds softly reflecting the light from the chandelier. She picked up the slim volume at her bedside, moved to the bay window, and read aloud just above a whisper,*

> One only passion unrevealed
> With maiden pride the maid concealed,
> Yet not less purely felt the flame;—
> O, need I tell that passion's name?

Like the Lady of the Lake, *all her life, she too had been waiting, waiting for that flame. The very beauty of the world outside her window, the expectation of the holiday fete tonight, the glow of the candles on the table, the elegance of the silver, the silken taste of the wine, and, most of all, the thrill of a* chance encounter, all bespoke the imminent realization of her desires. She had been to countless dinners, parties, and teas, of course. But tonight would be different.

She read the poem once more, took one last look out the window at the falling snow, then rose to ring for her maid to finish dressing. Never had the world seemed so rich with promise.

EPILOGUE

Seattle, Washington, July 3, 1933

The greater good. The one or the many. Should the life of one man be sacrificed to save thousands? Forty years later, will anyone care that an obscure young physician named George Farnshaw bled to death on a prison floor so that William Stewart Halsted might continue his brilliant work and in large measure invent modern surgery? Is one man's murder the price that the human race must pay in order to progress?

Moral philosophers, I am certain, could wax eloquently on this issue, but moral philosophers rarely speak from their own experience. For all but a handful, George Farnshaw vanished into history within weeks of his death, but I was among that handful.

On the occasion of my seventieth birthday, as I reflect on the astounding changes that have accrued to mankind, I can only note that George Farnshaw should have been witness to those changes, should have grown and aged and marveled as I did at the progress in all forms of human endeavor, some exhilarating, some terrifying.

The world of 1933 bears almost no resemblance to that of 1889. It might have been four centuries rather than four decades since Rebecca Lachtmann, George Turk, and George Farnshaw died, for indeed centuries of tradition have been thrown over.

As a result of the Great War, monarchy ended in much of Europe: thus, Czar Nicholas of Russia was supplanted by the Bolshevik Lenin and now Stalin; King Victor Emmanuel of Italy by the Fascist, Mussolini; and Kaiser Wilhelm of Germany by a series of leaders, the most recent being a demagogue named Adolf Hitler. Change, yes, but it remains to be seen whether the new governments will be an improvement over the old.

In our own nation, women—including my own wife, daughters, and granddaughters—vote. Americans may again drink alcohol, after a tumultuous decade of prohibition. Our new president, Franklin Roosevelt, survived polio but, more astoundingly, millions of Americans can listen to his voice as he speaks although they might be thousands of miles away. Radio, this new miracle of communication that sends electrical impulses through the very air we breathe, has made cable telegraphy seem ancient.

The West has been opened and, with the admission of Arizona twenty-one years ago, America now consists of an incredible forty-eight states. The great expanse of our nation has been rendered smaller, not simply by the profusion of railroads that now crisscross the landscape, but by travel through the air. Horse-drawn locomotion will soon disappear entirely as internal combustion vehicles come within the financial reach of all but the very poor.

Abigail once told me that art was changing the way men and women see their world, but in 1905, an obscure German physicist working in a patent office in Bern, Switzerland, created the same phenomenon in science. He postulated that we live in a world without absolutes, a theory scoffed at in popular circles, as had been Darwin's, until, in 1919, observations during a solar eclipse proved to the world that he was correct.

The Bayer Company thrived. In 1897, one of its chemists, Felix Hoffmann, applied the acetylizing process that Wright had used on morphine to salicylic acid, thus synthesizing acetylsalicylic acid, which Bayer marketed under the trade name "Aspirin." Aspirin had the analgesic, antipyretic, and anti-inflammatory qualities of the nonacetyl variety, but without the horrific side effects. Two weeks after he synthesized aspirin, the very same Felix Hoffmann finally succeeded in synthesizing an easily manufactured version of diacetylmorphine. The next year, 1898, the Bayer Company finally offered up a tacit admission of its experiments with the substance, when it sought patent protection for Hoffmann's process under the trade name "Heroin." Bayer then marketed Heroin, named for its miraculous and nonaddictive qualities, as a nonprescription pain reliever, cough remedy, harmless sedative, and cure for morphia addiction.

Heroin became the wonder drug of the early twentieth century. Bayer embarked on a worldwide sales campaign and soon, Heroin lozenges, tablets, elixirs, powders, and dietary supplements were all the rage, despite growing evidence among chemists that the substance was far more toxic than the morphia from which it was derived. Among its more popular applications was as a cough remedy for children. I was among the few doctors who opposed its use. I was scoffed at by my colleagues until, inevitably, its ravaging effects made themselves known and, in 1914, the United States Congress passed the Harrison Narcotics Tax Act to regulate opiates. Still, by 1920, there were 200,000 Heroin addicts in America. In 1924, the substance was banned entirely. Aspirin, Bayer's stepchild invention, replaced Heroin; it has become the single most successful drug in history.

As for me, after I left his rooms on that early April day in 1889, I never saw Dr. Osler again.

I agonized whether or not to send the journal to Farnshaw's parents with an explanatory note, so that they might pursue the matter and attempt to clear their son's name. But would it have been genuine consolation for them to know how close their son was to being freed before he was murdered? I thought not.

I had been taught to distrust coincidence, but sometimes people are correct only by chance. Although he had made the statement simply to stifle my inquiries, Dr. Osler had spoken the truth when he opined that from the moment the cover of the ice chest was opened in the Dead House and its contents revealed, every time I tried to help, I had made matters worse. I vowed to do so no longer. Or perhaps I simply wanted to be free of everything to do with my life in Philadelphia. Whatever the case, I destroyed Turk's journal and hoped that I had saved Farnshaw's poor parents further torment.

I waited until the following evening and then called on Mary Simpson at the Croskey Street Settlement House. I informed her of my decision to decline the appointment at Johns Hopkins and of my intention to leave Philadelphia. Although I had settled on no firm destination, I had resolved to finally heed Reverend Audette's advice and head West. I asked Mary to join me. I told her she was the finest woman I had ever known, and likely would ever know. I should be lucky and privileged if she would consent to be my wife. I promised to love her son as my own.

She refused.

"You don't love me, Ephraim. You are fond of me, I know, and I think that you would be kind and generous to Samuel. But I've struggled too arduously to accept a proposal from a man who would have chosen another. Also, my work here in Philadelphia is far too important to me."

My choice of Abigail over this exceptional woman was yet another of my mistakes that would have no remedy.

In the end, I put as much distance as I could between myself and Philadelphia, settling in the small but growing city of Seattle, Washington. Physicians were scarce and I was welcomed without question. There, I courted and married a lovely woman. She was not mercurial and intoxicating like Abigail Benedict, nor formidable and determined like Mary Simpson, but she is kind, gentle, and accepting of my faults. We have been married forty-one years, and have three sons, two daughters, eleven grandchildren, and, as of last year, a great-grandson. I will retire as a physician this year—my eyes and my hearing are not what they were—but the children's hospital I helped found, the most progressive institution of its kind in the West, I am proud to say, will continue here under the guidance of others.

With age, I have come increasingly to gaze at progress from afar. Air travel astounds me. While my scientist's mind can accept Bernoulli's principle in theory, I will never consent to sit inside a metal tube shooting through the clouds with nothing to keep it from hurtling to earth except forward motion. My son George, however, flies often, and my grandson Ephraim, all of sixteen, insists that he will be a pilot. I am more sanguine about earthbound conveyance and love my Nash.

I followed Dr. Osler's remarkable life almost to obsession. He took his position at Johns Hopkins and was so instrumental in altering the manner in which physicians viewed their work that his life could be considered the fulcrum upon which the science of medicine pivoted. During the next decade, he completed his textbook, *Principles and Practice of Medicine,* which is still the standard by which all similar works are judged. In 1892, Dr. Osler was named president of the American Pediatric Society. He has received honors and awards sufficient to fill a volume of their own.

In 1905, he left Johns Hopkins to accept the Regius Professorship of Medicine at Oxford University, the most prestigious medical appointment in the English-speaking world. At Oxford, although it seems impossible, his achievements were even greater than those in America. In 1911, he was knighted by the king, Edward VII.

Dr. Osler did indeed marry the widowed Mrs. Gross, and the couple had one son, Edward Revere. When young Lieutenant Osler was killed in Flanders in 1917, it broke the Professor's heart. He died a mere two years later. He did, in fact, order a postmortem on himself and his prediction of what would be found—thoracic empyema, pus in the right pleural cavity, a massive pleural infection—turned out to be exactly correct.

In addition to his professional achievements, Dr. Osler amassed one of the most astounding personal libraries in the world, over eight thousand volumes, the majority devoted to the history of science and medicine, including the most exhaustive collection of material on Servetus ever compiled. He spoke of Servetus often, even using him as the subject of his annual address to the Johns Hopkins student body, and he was among the benefactors of a monument that was erected in Annemasse, France, just across the border from Geneva, where Servetus had been burned at the stake.

William Stewart Halsted remained at Johns Hopkins for the rest of his life. Although always a brilliant surgeon and teacher, he was responsible for few surgical innovations after the early 1890s. Perhaps morphia had sapped his genius. Still, it is fair to say that every great surgeon of the first three decades of this century has walked in Halsted's footsteps. He married Caroline Hampton, the nurse who had been the inspiration for his invention of surgical gloves, and they lived something of a reclusive life together. Although there is no evidence in either direction, I suspect he remained addicted for the rest of his days. In one of medicine's great ironies, Halsted died in 1922 after complications from the same gallstone surgery that he had invented forty years earlier to cure his mother. Two of his former students performed the operation.

After Dr. Osler left for England in 1905, Mary Elizabeth Garrett, Hopkins' major benefactor, commissioned a group portrait of Osler, Halsted, Welch, and the gynecologist Howard Kelly, to be called "The Four Doctors." For this task, she engaged not Thomas Eakins, but the expatriate American John Singer Sargent. Only Dr. Osler lived in London, where Sargent's studio was located, so the other three crossed the

Atlantic to sit. During the process, Sargent found Halsted so unpleasant and overbearing that he was rumored to have painted his image so that it would fade over time.

Neither Abigail Benedict nor her brother ever returned to America. Albert died in a traffic accident, run down by a carriage in Zagreb in 1892. The driver was never apprehended. After her father's return to America later that year, Abigail lived in London for a time, then in Florence. In 1895, she married a French count twenty years her senior. The couple, childless, spent much of their time traveling about in Europe and Asia. When Abigail's husband died of esophageal cancer, Abigail retired to his ancestral home near Avignon, where she lived as a recluse until her own death last year. As far as I could learn, she never exhibited any paintings. I was saddened at her death, but more at what seemed to be a lonely and unfulfilled life.

Thomas Eakins remained at his home on Mount Vernon Street until he died there in 1916. Although the Pre-Raphaelites he despised slipped from public acclaim, Impressionists did not. Art continued to retreat from realism and, with the rise of abstractionists like Picasso, Eakins saw his reputation wane even further. After the Lachtmann affair, Eakins devoted himself almost entirely to portraiture. He could not hide his bitterness, however, and his subjects were almost always rendered in an unflattering light, often as much older than they were. In desperation, he even attempted to incorporate some of the modernists' techniques into his later paintings, but was nonetheless no more than a footnote in American art at his death. Susan Eakins still lives in Philadelphia, an indefatigable champion of her husband's work. Whatever Eakins' faults, I can only hope that one day his great talent will finally be appreciated by a nation that has spurned him.

Mary Simpson never married. The Croskey Street Settlement House thrived and became the model for similar institutions. During a speaking engagement in 1912, Mary was approached by a woman who claimed to admire her work greatly, and sought to create even more progressive enterprises for women. That woman's name was Margaret Sanger. I corresponded with Mary from time to time, and I hoped that we would always think of each other as friends. She died peacefully of congestive heart failure four years ago, surrounded by friends and admirers. I can only hope that when it is my time, I will be so fortunate.

Haggens, despite both his style of life and his heart condition, lived for another twenty years, although Mike was shot to death in front of The Fatted Calf not six months after I left Philadelphia. Sergeant Borst was indeed promoted, eventually to captain, and he was a mainstay of the Philadelphia police department until his retirement in 1915. As far as I know, he still lives in the city. Jonas Lachtmann returned to California, where he had gotten his start, just after the turn of the century. I was more than a bit anxious when I learned that we lived in such proximity, but Lachtmann was never the same man after 1889, and he preferred to ignore me than revisit the tragedy of his daughter's death.

I kept Abigail's portrait of me, not as a reminder of the man I wished to be, but rather of the sins of pride and arrogance that I wished never to repeat. I dedicated my life to atoning for my role in the death of George Farnshaw although, for quite a while, despite my wife's assurances, I felt that I never would. Then, ten years ago, at Christmas dinner, I looked around at my family, and walked into the study to read a testimonial from the grateful citizens of Seattle that I had mounted on the wall. I considered the sum of my life, went to the attic, fetched the portrait, and threw it into the fire.

My life would have been very different, I know, had I accepted the Professor's offer and accompanied him to Johns Hopkins. I would, as Dr. Osler predicted, have achieved wealth and fame; more importantly, I would have undoubtedly contributed, as he did, to the saving of thousands of lives. But among the many decisions of my life I might wish to rescind, that is one that I have never regretted. For in turning my back on the many, I believe that I saved myself.

AUTHOR'S NOTE

To ADDRESS THE MOST IMPORTANT point first: *The Anatomy of Deception* is a work of *fiction*. There is not a scintilla of historical evidence to suggest that William Halsted ever committed murder. Nor is there any indication that he ever performed an abortion, although, in the thousands upon thousands of surgeries he did perform, many of them private, it is not impossible that he terminated a pregnancy or two. As to his continued drug addiction, however, and thus his susceptibility to blackmail, extremely persuasive evidence does exist, and it emanated from the unlikeliest of sources.

For the last thirty years of Dr. Halsted's life, and for almost half a century after his death in 1922, it was assumed by the public, his students, virtually all of his colleagues, and certainly his patients that he overcame his drug dependency in the 1880s by sheer force of will. The three extant Halsted biographies, none of them scholarly (the last of which, provocatively titled *Cocaine, Cancer, and Courage*, was published in 1960), were written by friends, colleagues, or offspring of colleagues. Each extols the man for the indomitable will required to perform such a feat of self-control.

Then, in 1969, a manuscript Dr. Osler had written but instructed be kept sealed until fifty years after his death was finally opened. In this account, called *The Inner History of the Johns Hopkins Hospital*, Dr. Osler revealed that Dr. Halsted had remained a drug addict. The great surgeon continued to inject morphine—regularly and in large doses—during

Osler's entire career in Baltimore. (Osler left for Great Britain in 1905, but one can reasonably assume that after two decades of addiction, Halsted did not choose to go through withdrawal in his fifties.) Thus the many operations that Dr. Halsted performed—for which he indeed was sometimes paid more than $10,000—were completed while under the influence of opiates. According to the manuscript, only Osler himself knew of Halsted's ongoing drug use, although Michael Bliss, an Osler biographer, stated Welch possibly knew as well.

The failure to speak out about Halsted was not the only incident in which Dr. Osler turned a blind eye to the malfeasance of a fellow physician. He also remained silent after an incident in Montréal in which a patient died as a result of a colleague's obvious blunder. Dr. Osler reassured the other doctor that no one would remember the incident in six months.

The disclosure that, whether for altruistic motives or not, Dr. Osler would keep such secrets gave me the idea for this novel. From my research, I have no doubt that William Osler personally epitomized the very peak of medical ethics and was a man of exceptionally high moral fiber. Had he paid a price, I wondered, for ignoring the immoral acts of others in pursuit of the advancement of medicine and the betterment of mankind? Would he have reported Dr. Halsted to the police if Halsted had committed a crime under the influence of drugs?

The larger question, of course, is whether science must inevitably be willing to compromise ethics in order to achieve great and beneficial change. Medicine in 1889 was a science teetering on the edge of immense advances in curing disease and alleviating suffering. I believe we as a society are in a similar position today. Dr. Osler's dilemma could easily be our own.

From a narrative standpoint, I strove to portray the personalities of both men as they were. Osler was affable and well liked, while Halsted, after his addiction, became sarcastic and aloof. (Despite the rumors, Halsted's face in the Sargent portrait did not fade over time.)

I thought it crucial to get the science right, and thus all of the medical tradecraft depicted in *The Anatomy of Deception* is as historically accurate as I could make it, from the instruments used to the order of procedures. The autopsies conducted by Osler in the first chapter come from his own notes; the manner in which he examined patients in the ward and the discussion of a physician's four compass points also come from life.

For dramatic flow, I did take minor liberties with chronology. Rubber gloves, for example, while first fabricated in 1889, were evidently not used by a surgeon until 1890. William Osler often had tea at the home of Samuel W. Gross before Dr. Gross' illness, and thus was introduced to Grace Linzee Gross before she became a widow.

The art side of *The Anatomy of Deception* is also, I hope, substantially correct. Thomas Eakins did teach in Philadelphia, where he had a nervous breakdown, and was sent out West to recover by Weir Mitchell, who was at the time considered the preeminent authority on nervous diseases. Eakins remains one of the great controversial figures in American art, and he did pose frontally nude for his own photographs. His reputation plummeted with the rise of abstract art, but he was eventually rediscovered and is now considered one of the great painters in our history. His medical paintings and their impact are as described.

Once again, for smoothness, I made some changes. Eakins, for instance, did not convert the top floor of the house on Mount Vernon Street to a studio until after his father's death in 1899. From 1884 until that year, he worked out of a rented studio on Chestnut Street.

While Reverend Squires and the Philadelphia League Against Human Vivisection are fictional, there was great resistance to autopsy in 1889, and all the machinations necessary

to secure cadavers are as they were. The Blockley Dead
House was as described, and the attendant was an Alsatian
whom Osler nicknamed "Cadaverous Charlie," who had indeed been caught on more than one occasion drinking from
the specimen jars. There was an exhumation in which a corpse
was discovered to have three livers. Although Wilberforce
Burleigh is fictional, his surgical techniques are not. More
surgical patients died of shock and blood loss than of illness
in 1889. Cesarean section had a mortality rate of 80 percent.

The notes from Wright's experiment and the animal tests
afterward are taken from the journals, and all the details of
the development of heroin are accurate. While there is no
specific evidence of experiments at Bayer to acetylize morphine as early as 1889, the competition between the German
chemical companies to develop drugs from industrial products was as described.

ACKNOWLEDGMENTS

I HAD A GREAT DEAL of help in completing this book, both in the research and the writing. For the former, I wish to thank Dr. H. Wayne Carver, III, chief medical examiner for the State of Connecticut, who took great pains to educate me on the intricacies of autopsy and the history of opiates and cocaine. Carol Fletterick, also of the medical examiner's office, was consistently helpful and gracious in answering what must have been some pretty dumb questions.

Drs. Dennis Wasson and Greg Soloway both read the manuscript to ensure that I didn't make any egregious errors in the medical sections, and Dennis imparted some wonderful anecdotes about nineteenth-century surgery. Any errors that remain are certainly mine and not theirs.

I queried any number of others. Christine Crawford-Oppenheimer at the Culinary Institute of America provided some terrific old menus and background on social mores of the period. Robert Eskind at the Philadelphia Bureau of Prisons filled me in on police procedures for the newly arrested. Beth Bensman at the Presbyterian Historical Society was an excellent resource on Philadelphia history, as was her husband, Martin Levitt, librarian at the American Philosophical Society. Toby Appel, head librarian at the Harvey Cushing/John Hay Whitney Medical Library at Yale, unearthed some wonderful material, particularly Dr. Osler's autopsy notes. John Rees, curator of archives and modern manuscripts at the National Library of Medicine directed me to some fascinating sources, including the Tiemann & Co.'s 1880s catalog.

On the editorial side, this book could not have been written without the indefatigable and insightful attention of my agent, Jennifer Joel. I simply have never experienced or heard of an agent who took more care with a manuscript. I am also indebted to Jenn for directing my manuscript to my editor, Kate Miciak. Kate's vision for the book matched my own and she was patient, tireless, and thoroughly professional in nudging a sometimes reluctant author to continue to make the book better.

Finally, I want to thank my wife, Nancy, and my daughter, Emily. Each read the manuscript (in Nancy's case, more than once) and was helpful and wise in her suggestions. But mostly I want to thank them for their tolerance, understanding, forbearance ... and endurance. Living with me requires each of those traits and in some magnitude, and I am lucky to have them both.

ABOUT THE AUTHOR

LAWRENCE GOLDSTONE, with his wife Nancy, is the author of two critically acclaimed narrative histories of science. He has written for the *Boston Globe*, *Los Angeles Times*, *Chicago Tribune*, and *Miami Herald*. He lives in Westport, Connecticut.